PRAISE FOR *IT ENL*

"Once in a while a character comes along that gets under your skin and refuses to let go. This is the case with Brianna Labuskes's Clarke Sinclair—a cantankerous, rebellious, and somehow endearingly likable FBI agent with a troubled past. I was immediately pulled into Clarke's broken, shadow-filled world and her quest for justice and redemption. A stunning thriller, *It Ends With Her* is not to be missed."
>   —Heather Gudenkauf, *New York Times* bestselling author

"*It Ends With Her* is a gritty, riveting, roller-coaster ride of a book. Brianna Labuskes has created a layered, gripping story around a cast of characters that readers will cheer for. Her crisp prose and quick plot kept me reading with my heart in my throat. Highly recommended for fans of smart thrillers with captivating heroines."
>   —Nicole Baart, author of *Little Broken Things*

"An engrossing psychological thriller filled with twists and turns—I couldn't put it down! The characters were filled with emotional depth. An impressive debut!"
>   —Elizabeth Blackwell, author of *In the Shadow of Lakecrest*

GIRLS
OF
GLASS

ALSO BY BRIANNA LABUSKES

It Ends With Her

GIRLS OF GLASS

BRIANNA LABUSKES

THOMAS & MERCER

Text copyright © 2019 by Brianna Labuskes
All rights reserved.

Published by Thomas & Mercer, Seattle

www.apub.com

Amazon, the Amazon logo, and Thomas & Mercer are trademarks of Amazon.com, Inc., or its affiliates.

ISBN-13: 9781503959750 (hardcover)
ISBN-10: 1503959759 (hardcover)
ISBN-13: 9781503902282 (paperback)
ISBN-10: 1503902285 (paperback)

Cover design by Rex Bonomelli

Printed in the United States of America

First edition

*To Raegan and Gracie,
my shining girls made of stardust and lightning
and wind—
you are the very best of this world.*

PROLOGUE

August 5, 2018
Seven days after Ruby Burke's kidnapping

Charlotte Burke blinked, her lashes heavy so that they rested against her cheeks for a heartbeat longer than normal. Then her eyes snapped open.

When they did, all she saw was red. It was thick and ruby in color and tacky on her hands, on her arms, on her clothes.

The blood was on the carpet, too. If the fabric had been plush once, now it was drenched, the slash of color obscene against the whiteness.

Her brain struggled to catch up to what was happening, but she couldn't think. She blinked again, but nothing came into focus.

Except . . . except the weight against her thigh. A gun. Her fingers tightened around the grip, more instinct than deliberate thought.

The pieces began slotting themselves together. She looked around, wishing the fuzziness at the edge of her vision would dissolve.

The light that was pouring in through the curtain hinted at morning, but early morning, when the sun was just starting to rise. It cast shadows into the room.

She pressed a shaky palm to her sternum, and it was then that she noticed the gash on her arm. It was jagged, as if the skin had been sliced with broken glass. There wasn't any pain, though, despite the freshness of the wound.

Adrenaline.

It was pouring through her still. That had to be why her arm didn't hurt, why her thoughts were so slow, why her legs trembled with the effort to keep her upright.

Oblivion begged her to sink into darkness and forget everything that had just happened. But she needed to see; she needed to make sure.

Because there was a body. There had to be. There couldn't be this much blood and not be a body.

She dropped her chin to her chest, her eyes on the floor.

Charlotte noticed the hand first. It was outstretched, reaching for her even in its stillness. A sob caught in the back of her throat, full and wet and painful where it lodged.

The first tear slipped from the corner of her eye just as a door burst open somewhere down the hallway. She didn't move, didn't hide. Just stood there, the tips of her toes brushing against a thigh that had gone limp against the floor.

The cops crashed into the room, weapons drawn, faces tight. Their lips moved, but she didn't hear any of them. Only one voice cut through the white noise.

"Drop the gun." Detective Nakamura was loud, urgent.

Charlotte brought her elbow up to bury her eyes in the crook of her arm and shield herself from the brightness of the other officers' flashlights. There was movement, yelling, as if they thought she was about to shoot them.

"Drop the gun, Charlotte," Nakamura said again. Some of the panic had slid from his voice, but there was a sadness in it now.

This time the command traveled down her nerves to her fingertips, which obeyed. The metal clattered to the floor, and she put her hands in the air, palms out.

"There we go," he said.

Then there were hands on her, rough palms against her wrists, pulling her shoulders into odd angles.

"You have the right to remain silent. Anything you say can and will be used against you in a court of law. You have the right . . ."

CHAPTER ONE

ALICE

August 2, 2018
Four days after Ruby Burke's kidnapping

They were snapshots, those moments. Like Polaroids. The flash, the pop, the heartbeat between breaths as the white dissolved into a fully formed picture of a memory caught in ink.

For Detective Alice Garner, it was the last glimpse of pigtails; the push of a heavy woman drenched in Chanel No. 5, clutching a bedazzled sweater in her chubby arms; the unrelenting glare of fluorescent bulbs on tired eyes; the Christmas music that played at full volume despite the fact that it had been only early November. Every moment of that day her daughter disappeared was etched deep into her memory. Except the one that mattered.

For Charlotte Burke it would be different. Perhaps the smell of salt air would now be enough to send her body into dry heaves, like that perfume did for Alice. Or maybe it would be the sound of gulls that became fingernails clawing on the thin membrane of her eardrums. The roiling blue green of the ocean that drew out a thin sheen of sweat along her temples.

"Hey." Detective Joe Nakamura bumped into Alice's shoulder, but his attention wasn't on her. It was on the beach where the crowd was gathered. The techs and some uniforms were monitoring the scene, waiting on them to get there. "You okay?"

Coming from anyone else, the question would prod at the hackles that were always poised to rise along her back.

There was a script she was supposed to follow, lines she could read that would ensure the person who asked felt validated in their concern but not burdened by her emotions.

For Nakamura it didn't seem like the verbal tic it did for everyone else. They'd been partners for only six months since she'd moved to Florida, but she liked him. And she didn't like many people.

The older detective had come to St. Pete by way of South Central LA, and there were still ghosts in his eyes five years later. He didn't talk about them, and she appreciated that. She knew she had ghosts in her eyes as well.

Are you okay?

"Yeah," she finally murmured. Lying came too naturally these days.

Shitty Dollar Store aviators blocked his reaction, but she saw him slide her a look from the side. He didn't believe her. He shouldn't.

Still, he let it drop.

He took the last swallow of his coffee, then dumped the cup in the trash at the edge of the dunes. "Let's go."

The sun was just rising, cut in half by the sharp line of the horizon, turning the sky golden and pink against the green moss of the water. It was pretty. Far too pretty for what they were walking into.

Ruby Burke. For so many, for the countless millions across the country who had watched every move of the investigation unfold over the past four days, there'd been hope the St. Petersburg police would find little Ruby alive. Volunteers had flocked in to offer their services, searching wetlands and the long stretches of beach up and down both coasts of the miniature peninsula, each one hoping to be the person who returned with a bright-eyed girl in their arms. Each one hoping to soothe the nerves of the parents who desperately wanted this to be a case of an adventurous child who had wandered off. Otherwise, what stopped this from happening to their own girls?

Nothing, Alice wanted to tell them each time the media hounded her for an interview. Happy endings didn't exist.

"A jogger found her?" Alice asked, mostly just to talk. To fill the silence around them with something other than the wild tangle of thoughts running along the inner part of her skull. Her hands shook, and she jammed them into the pockets of her jeans.

The beach was up the coast from the city's public ones. The fact that it was waterfront property gave off the air of upper middle class or lower upper class, but the houses, with their gaudy colors and cutesy names painted across the fronts, screamed vacation rentals.

"Yup." Nakamura slipped a piece of gum between his teeth in that way of his. He'd hold it there, gripped lightly between thin lips like a cigarette. Constantly trying to quit, or so he told her. "About an hour ago. They recognized her from the pictures on the news."

That's when Alice had gotten the call. The phone had buzzed where it lay against her chest, loud in the quiet darkness of her bedroom. She'd been staring at the thin cracks that ran the length of her ceiling.

"Isn't this private property?" She scanned the long expanse of fine, white sand that gave way like powdered sugar beneath her boots. It was all trod upon now. Though the CSI techs did try, there was nothing worse than sand when it came to preserving a crime scene.

It was perfect in the eyes of a killer.

"No one listens around here." Nakamura shrugged.

It was hard not knowing a place. It was what made the best cops— knowing the people, knowing the streets, knowing the rules that were always broken just because. There weren't a lot of things she missed about DC, but she missed that.

Alice still couldn't get a handle on St. Petersburg, and she wondered if she ever would. The small city—which she thought of as Tampa's strange, alcoholic cousin—was an odd mix of overtanned, middle-aged Jimmy Buffett wannabes who beer-bellied up to the open bars that were a dime a dozen downtown, and smooth, moneyed upper-class families who jockeyed for prominence over pearls and finger sandwiches.

And then there was South St. Petersburg. The nonwhite, nonrich part of town that scared both the Miller Lite–swigging retirees and the pampered Southern ladies.

The combination gave Alice cultural whiplash. And made figuring out the underlying social currents harder to do.

"They called from a cell phone?" She paused, then clarified: "The jogger."

"Nah, didn't have it on him." Nakamura slowed his pace as they neared the police chief and the other officers huddled around the small bundle right at the edge of the water. The tide was coming in.

Nakamura nodded back toward the dunes. "Ran up to the house. Left the scene for about ten minutes before he came back with the owner to wait for the officers."

The owner. The jogger. She started a list of all the players in the game. It would add to the one she'd already been working on in the four days since Ruby Burke had gone missing.

"Was it the actual owner of the house or someone on vacation?" Alice asked. She could see it. Rent a place for a week under a fake name, pay in cash, drop the girl, and leave town. There would be no trace left other than a ghost who never existed in the first place.

"It's his," Nakamura said. Killers didn't tend to leave the bodies of their victims right outside their back door for the world to find.

She slipped her own sunglasses down to cover her eyes when the chief caught sight of Nakamura.

"The mother?" she murmured, one last question under her breath. Another player. At the top of the list. At the top of everyone's list. They always were in cases like this.

Nakamura tipped his chin toward the woman huddled against the early-morning wind coming off the ocean.

Charlotte Burke.

Her red hair tangled into itself around a pale, tear-streaked face. She wore light tan linen pants and a blue blouse beneath a cashmere cardigan. The ensemble was probably more expensive than Alice's car.

She looked away.

"Nakamura." The chief's deep-bass rumble cut through the background chatter and roar of the pounding waves. He glanced at her. "Garner."

Alice was still an afterthought to the big man. It didn't bother her. She liked that his eyes sometimes stopped before they reached her, that his thoughts didn't immediately include her, that she slipped like a shadow behind her partner.

It was preferable to the scrutiny she'd faced in DC, where her every move had been watched by those who had previously considered her one of their own. She'd been stamped with a reputation for being erratic and had never been able to shake the eyes that followed her with wary expectation after that.

Being overlooked wasn't so bad, really.

They didn't go through the niceties but simply nodded in greeting.

Then all that was left to do was look at the body. The reason they were there. The reason the entire city, the nation, hadn't breathed for the past four days.

"Ruby Burke," Chief Deakin said, putting voice to the thing no one wanted to name.

"A positive ID?" Nakamura asked, as they all stared at the tiny body crumpled just beyond their feet.

The five-year-old was wrapped in a peach silk sheet that was speckled deep orange from the mist coming off the ocean. Just her purple shoes with Velcro straps stuck out from beneath the fabric.

The shoes Alice's daughter had loved had been blue and white, with the face of the latest Disney princess smiling on the sides of them. Lila would wear them even with her fanciest dresses.

Alice wished she had a cigarette, even though she didn't smoke. It would give her something to do with her hands. Instead, she pinched at the fleshy skin of her upper thigh through the pocket of her jeans. If only she could draw blood.

"The mother," the chief confirmed. Like it was nothing. Like it was a throwaway.

"Charlotte," Alice said. Both men looked at her. "The mother's name is Charlotte."

The space between them stretched taut at her reminder. Then they nodded, and Deakin cleared his throat, running a hand over his smooth, shaved head. In her mind, she heard the whispers that still clung to her even states away. *Emotional. Erratic.*

"It's Ruby Burke," Deakin said. "She's identifiable. There wasn't much . . . damage."

They all paused to absorb that.

Then Nakamura broke the silence. "Has the grandfather been contacted?"

Another player on the list. Judge Sterling Burke, St. Petersburg's reigning king. If he wanted to, he could have all their jobs, and he'd made that very clear several times over the past four days that his granddaughter had been missing.

It wasn't the first time she'd had to deal with a threat like that. DC was the land of lawyers and politicians, where what you did and whom you could intimidate were the only currencies that really mattered. This was the first time that an entire police station gave two shits about what some blowhard thought, though.

The power of Judge Sterling Burke was not to be underestimated. Deakin checked the time on his phone, then sighed. "He's on his way."

The chief said it with the resignation of someone who had long acquiesced to the inevitability of the interference.

"Head him off, yeah?" Nakamura directed.

"You guys have"—the chief glanced down again—"six minutes. Tops."

At that warning, Alice shut everything out—the low hum of unease that fluttered along the particles in the air disrupting the tiny hairs at the nape of her neck, the broken sobs coming from the now-broken woman to her left, the smack of Nakamura's gum in her ear. Everything other than Ruby.

She slipped evidence gloves on with no intention of touching anything and then squatted down to sit on the backs of her heels. At thirty-three, it was no longer an easy position, but she ignored the screaming in her tight thigh muscles just like the rest of the distractions.

It was so small. The body. Ruby.

It hurt too much to give them names sometimes. They became people that way. If they had a name, they had loved ones. They had thoughts and feelings and wishes and silly daydreams and a family who sang "Happy Birthday" in loud, embarrassing voices, and maybe a sibling who stole crayons and other prized possessions. They became real, instead of just another mystery to solve.

But the girl deserved one. A name.

Alice couldn't look at the shoes any longer. She wanted to cover them up, make sure they were completely hidden from prying eyes, from people who didn't realize those may have been the girl's favorites. Maybe Ruby would have even refused to leave the house unless she was wearing them.

Something brushed her shoulder, and Alice realized that Nakamura had come to stand next to her, his leg pressing against the length of her arm. She leaned into the contact, thankful for the steadying presence.

Her eyes shifted up along the girl's body, which was draped in fabric. The wind caught the edge of the sheet, lifting it, and something scraped against the back of Alice's throat. She didn't want to see the girl's face. She knew what it looked like: the cheeks that were just losing the baby roundness, the upturned nose and bright blue eyes, the strawberry curls that always seemed to want to rebel from braids and ponytail holders. Alice had seen enough pictures, enough video footage, in the past few days that she even knew about the thin white scar on Ruby's jaw, from that time she'd jumped from the top of the slide at the playground.

She breathed deeply, and the salt in the air coated her lungs as she stood up.

"No tire tracks," she finally said, and Nakamura hummed in agreement, a low sound at the back of his throat.

"She's light."

It didn't account for the deadweight, though. She couldn't have been carried far.

Alice shifted to look back toward the dunes, back toward the pink-and-turquoise house that disappeared with the curving of the earth. It was an eyesore. A lot of things in St. Pete were, though.

"Is that the only road entrance?" she asked the group at large. It's where she and Nakamura had come through, a little path that ran alongside the house out onto a quiet cul-de-sac that was now bursting with cop cars.

"About a quarter mile down is a public parking lot," a voice chimed in. She didn't care whom it came from. The answer was all that mattered.

"A quarter mile carrying, what, forty pounds?" Alice lowered her voice so only Nakamura could hear.

"Or they came in through the house access here," he said.

"Which would require less strength, at least."

"Could you carry her?"

Alice looked back at the bundle. Remembered the weight of Lila when she begged to be hauled around like a toddler instead of the six-year-old she'd been. *"Please, Mama? My legs are so tired, I can't even take another step."*

"Yes."

They both shifted their gazes to Charlotte. The woman was about ten years younger than Alice but had a similar build: tall and thin with long limbs and shoulders that were a touch too broad. However, Charlotte, unlike Alice, carried her willowy frame with an easy grace that, combined with a delicate bone structure in her face, turned her into a dreamy Romantic painting.

Everything about Alice was sharper. Where Charlotte was lazy, pastel strokes, Alice was heavy, dark slashes, with high, defined cheekbones and toned muscles and harsh collarbones that overshadowed a flat chest. She was a short, dark chin-length bob, where Charlotte was a wild cascade of curls. She was narrow hips and long legs, where Charlotte had somehow conjured up a hint of curves.

"Could she? Carry her?" Nakamura voiced the direction both their thoughts had traveled in. There was doubt in the question, like he didn't think those slim arms could bear the weight of a dead child.

"You'd be surprised at what people can do," Alice said. "With enough motivation."

Nakamura knew that. Every cop knew that. They looked back at the body, and Nakamura knelt down to where Alice had just been. He lifted the sheet with the tip of his pen, and she tried not to look away.

If Alice didn't know better, she'd think the girl was napping; she'd think maybe those eyes were seconds from blinking open, bleary and crusted with sleep. There were no bruises on her throat, no cuts on her face, no scratches along her skin to suggest otherwise. A fading shadow on her arm was the only sign of a struggle. And even that was old.

"Chief says there's a wound at the base of her skull," Nakamura said.

"Must have happened somewhere else." There was no blood on the sheets, which would have been saturated from a head injury.

Her clothes were intact, her limbs arranged neatly by her sides. Care had been taken with her body.

Perhaps they'd find skin cells beneath her nails or lacerations hidden by her T-shirt, anything that would tell a story that was different from the one written out in front of them so clearly.

Because right now, it looked like the girl had known her killer. Had known the person well.

"Two minutes until Sterling's here." The chief's warning cut into the fragile web of their shared thoughts. It was funny, that. How quickly she'd slipped into trusting her new partner. She stepped away from Nakamura, severing the connection.

There would be photos, evidence, memories—distorted or not—from the jogger and the house's owner, a million minuscule details to examine for the tiniest hint of a clue. They'd have uniforms talk to the men who'd found Ruby and scour the rest of the neighborhood for more witnesses.

That would come later.

This wasn't the time for that. This was the time for impressions, quick and irrational and possibly faulty but authentic nonetheless.

Now. Now there was the rolling ocean lapping ever closer to those sneakers, there was the sand that embraced the tiny body, there was the electricity in the salt-heavy air that crackled around them, there was the sun that must have been only an idea when the girl had been left here.

Now there was just that one question, the one they'd all been asking since news of the missing girl had been splashed across every TV in the county.

What kind of monster could do such a thing?

CHAPTER TWO

CHARLOTTE

July 22, 2018
One week before the kidnapping

The tangy smell of sex almost overpowered the stale smoke that seemed to be a permanent feature of the dingy motel room. The combined scent would cling to Charlotte's hair, her clothes, her pores. No matter how many times she showered, it would be there.

Cigarettes and sex. It might as well be her signature perfume.

A manic laugh caught in her esophagus, and she swallowed hard before it could escape. Enrique was sleeping. Or pretending to. Sometimes she didn't care enough to figure out which it was. Sometimes she could hardly care enough to remember his name.

Charlotte pulled her knees up and shifted so she was sitting on the edge of the bed. Enrique didn't move at the sound, so she pushed to her feet and padded across the carpet that was matted with unknown substances and scarred by burns that had singed the discolored fabric.

She closed the thin bathroom door behind her and leaned back against the cheap wood. The air was cleaner in the tiny space, and she let it fill her lungs. Her heart, which had begun to race in that way it did before the darkness started closing in, steadied. And Charlotte concentrated on that—that even staccato—as the world became less blurry around the edges.

Why must her constant companion be panic? Why was it like this, always? Or, she knew why it was like this always, but why couldn't she wrap her arms around it and understand it? Better yet, why couldn't she bury it, hide it, shove it away?

She squeezed her eyes tight until the stars burst against her lids, then turned on the shower. It was dilapidated, like everything else in this godforsaken hellhole of a motel room. The walls of it were crusted orange with years of shampoo residue, the yellow tiles along the wall cracked into patterns that might have been pretty under other circumstances.

There was a part of her that wished she could blame Enrique, wished he was a prick who wanted to hide her away in places that charged by the hour if given the right incentive. But it wasn't on him. She'd been the one who'd picked the Flamingo for their seedy little rendezvous. She always picked the places.

So instead of thinking about the lipstick-smeared towel she would have to use, Charlotte stepped under the lukewarm spray and wished she could feel clean. For once in her life.

There was a waxy tablet of soap wrapped in impossibly thick plastic sitting on the rim of the tub. The packaging refused to relent to her damp, fumbling fingers, so she simply ripped it with her teeth. Then she dragged the bar along the ridges of her hips, scrubbed at the sweat-tinged skin under her collarbones.

The water turned cool, but she didn't step out until the first telltale shivers ran along her spine. If she gave in to them, she would end up curled on the floor, a whimpering mess, unable to stop shaking. So she climbed out and wrapped herself in the disgusting towel, the rough fibers of it an uncomfortable rasp over her skin.

Leaning against the brown-tinted porcelain of the sink, she forced herself to meet her bloodshot eyes in the fogged-up mirror. There were thick mascara tears smudged beneath her lashes, but the rest of the makeup she had so artfully applied was just a memory. Stripped of the painted facade, her pale face was all that was left—too needy and too desperate and too wan and too thin and too hollow and too much. Charlotte slapped her hand against the glass, wanting the image there to dissolve into nothingness as her palm hit it. Her face stayed, though, stubborn and defiant. So she turned and left the bathroom, left the bruised eyes and sad lips behind, no longer caring how much noise she made.

"Mmm, what time is it?" Enrique muttered from beneath the pillow he'd shoved over his head.

Charlotte glanced at the red numbers on the bedside clock. "Four in the morning," she answered without sympathy.

"Babe . . ."

"Don't call me that," she snapped as she started to dress.

"Charlie," he said instead, and that was far worse. She didn't bother to correct him this time. "Come back to bed. Another hour won't hurt."

She wrestled herself into her wrinkled blouse, smoothing a hand down over the fabric. It was hopeless. "No."

Enrique knew better than to argue further. Instead, he rolled onto his back so he was leaning on his elbows to watch her check under the bed for her shoes. "So, Wednesday?"

This was a game they played sometimes. One where she pretended this was the last time. Where she pretended she could say no.

But she was tired. The day had been unbearably long. And it was four in the morning. "Thursday," she countered.

"'Kay," he said, and pursed his lips as if blowing her a kiss before collapsing back into the blankets.

She slipped her purse onto her shoulder and pushed into the crisp early-morning air, letting the door close behind her without looking back.

It was that in-between time when it wasn't quite night but wasn't day yet, either. Charlotte liked it best, liked the uncertainty of it. The feeling that maybe the sun wouldn't rise, that maybe the night wouldn't ever end. If only she could live here in this hour, maybe she wouldn't feel like she was being held together by shoddy glue and a defiant streak that just wouldn't let them win.

A few cars passed on the mostly empty four-lane highway that cut through South St. Petersburg, and she ducked so her hair covered her face each time the beams caught her peripheral vision. She didn't think she'd be recognized. Not here. Not now. But it didn't hurt to be careful.

She started walking. The motel was snugged in between greasy fast-food joints that were just waking up for the morning crowd. Fat and oil hung heavy in their parking lots and crawled into her nostrils, coating the delicate hairs there.

Just three more blocks. Then she could take a cab. Three more blocks of desperation in the form of cheap gas stations and cheaper motels and storefronts that had long ago given up the ghost of caring.

The first catcall was almost a comfort. There were so many different types of monsters in this world, and sometimes being surrounded by the tame ones made her feel safe. The "Smile prettys" and "Hey, beautifuls" became almost harmless compared to the other shadows that crept up, quiet and fatal, a whisper of steel slipped beneath ribs in the dark of the night.

"Shake that beautiful ass for us, girl," one man shouted from a cocoon of blankets and cardboard on the street.

She ignored him and checked the intersection. It was far enough from the hotel; she hailed a taxi.

By the time she had the cab drop her off ten minutes away from where he'd picked her up, the sky was hinting at the coming sun. Charlotte was cutting it close. The judge was up not a second later than 5:30 every morning. There had been only two occasions in his life when he'd overslept. The first had been the day after Ronald Reagan had won the presidency. The second had been when Charlotte's older sister, Mellie, had run off with her high school sweetheart, leaving a note that she was four months pregnant and headed to Vegas to get hitched. The boyfriend had dumped her before they'd even made it to the altar.

So Charlotte decided not to risk walking to another location before getting her second cab. It was a slip in her normally regimented procedure that she would have to live with and hope she wouldn't pay for later. She was lucky; one pulled to the curb only minutes after she'd made the decision.

The house wasn't far. Charlotte touched fingers to the pulse that was wild beneath the nearly translucent skin of her wrist, and she counted. She counted to ten, and then she counted to twenty and then thirty as the run-down one-story homes with overgrown lawns and broken-down cars in driveways faded into a middle-class shabbiness that at least was coated with a thin layer of paint.

In another life, she could see herself living in one of those houses. Ruby and her. She liked St. Petersburg, for all its quirks, not that she'd ever known anything else. But the people, the real ones, the ones who lived in these houses, not the ones who looked for creative ways to stab each other in the back, were nice. Carefree and simple in a way that came from living on the beach. They hung wind chimes made of spoons and beads on their porches and wore cheap plastic flip-flops when they went to restaurants.

Maybe in that life she'd work as a middle manager at some large office building and save up for the taxi rides they'd have to take to the ocean. Ruby would beg for toys and ice cream once there, and Charlotte would have to make her choose which she wanted more. Maybe they'd be happy. In that life.

She had the cab stop four blocks away from the house, then checked her phone: 5:05. Close but doable.

It wasn't until she was on the steps leading up to the porch that she realized she wasn't alone.

"Sinning on a Sunday." The quiet, mocking voice slapped at Charlotte just as her foot hit the wood. "Out early praying, were you, dear Auntie?"

Trudy. Charlotte should have known, though she could barely keep track of the girl's whereabouts these days. Charlotte sometimes wondered what had happened to her sweet little niece, the one who would hunt seashells and build secret forts and lie in meadows of flowers with Charlotte and tell knock-knock jokes that made no sense. Gone was that round-faced eight-year-old, and in her place was a bratty, moody eighteen-year-old little shit who did things like wait on the porch to catch her aunt coming home.

"Or were you on your knees for another reason?" Trudy continued while Charlotte just stared at her.

Charlotte finally snapped out of it, not sure if the rush of heat to her cheeks was rage or humiliation. "Watch your mouth."

"You're right, I shouldn't be so disrespectful to my elders," Trudy said, touching her toes to the porch, enough to push the swing into a lazy arc. The chains protested, a grating squeak that rubbed already-frayed nerve endings raw. Trudy smirked. "Perhaps you should tell the judge all about it."

Charlotte took a step closer, her fingers itching to slap that mouth.

"Or maybe you could explain where you were two hours ago when Ruby woke up crying for her mama."

It was the death blow, and Trudy knew it had landed.

All Charlotte's anger collapsed on itself, melting down into self-loathing and fear and hate. "Is she . . ."

"I got her back to sleep." Trudy's voice softened for the first time. If nothing else, she loved Ruby.

Charlotte nodded once. It would have to be thanks enough.

"Oh, and Charlie dear," Trudy called out just as Charlotte's hand closed around the door. "Do be sure to change out of that dress. There's a stain on it that I don't think can pass as holy water."

Charlotte bit her lip until she tasted copper.

She was going to ignore the taunt, ignore Trudy. She was tired and emotionally strung out from a day that had pressed on all her bruises, and she had zero energy left to spar with her niece.

"Why are you like this?" Charlotte whispered, not even caring if the girl heard her. Because she knew. She knew why Trudy lashed out at her, why she used those razor-sharp claws to tear into the deepest of Charlotte's wounds. It was funny how two people in the same circumstance could cope in such different ways.

Charlotte's hatred had turned inward, sometimes to the point that it was paralyzing. Always to the point that it was destructive.

Trudy's had washed outward in waves, crashing over everyone, without mercy.

It had been a long time since Charlotte had even tried to get through to her. She didn't know why she was waiting now for an answer that wouldn't come. Charlotte turned the handle of the door.

That's when Trudy spoke.

"Wait," the girl said, a soft, plaintive plea, her voice stripped of the venom it had been drenched in only moments earlier. She sounded so young all of a sudden. "I need your help."

CHAPTER THREE

Alice

August 2, 2018
Four days after the kidnapping

After they left the beach and Ruby's body behind, Nakamura made no effort to break the silence on the short drive over to the Burke residence. She liked that about him. The way he could sit with his own thoughts without needing to fill the air with pointless words.

It was a different kind of quiet from what she'd become so familiar with back in DC.

Alice had never been particularly emotional. Her family members were middle-class New Englanders through and through, and they liked to express themselves with passive-aggressiveness rather than weeping and hysterics. Sports were the only acceptable excuse for passion.

It had prepared her, though, for the police force. To fit in, women had two options: out-guy them or slip into the role of station mom. She'd never liked picking up dirty socks or pouring coffee, so she went with the former option. She told raunchy jokes and smoked cigars when they were handed around and swore like a sailor raised in the gutter.

Tommy Hughes had been her first partner right out of training. He was a burly man, with thick biceps and tree-trunk thighs, who had won every beer-chugging contest he'd ever entered. Visually, they were quite the pair.

He'd been unhappy to be saddled with someone who had a vagina, though he couched the criticism in words like *new* and *inexperienced*. Working with him those first two weeks had been hell, filled with snide innuendo, like every time she disagreed with him she must be "on the rag," and wouldn't she prefer a nice desk job or a position with the sexual violence unit?

Alice had finally forced herself along on a night out with the squad. She'd matched Tommy drink for drink and then took a shot while he was slumped over the table. The next morning she'd had the type of hangover that bespoke of permanent liver damage and the respect of the entire station. Like a light had switched on.

Then Lila had been taken.

It had been one moment of distraction, a hectic day at the mall, a bored little girl. She'd found out later that the man who had killed her daughter hadn't gone there to take Lila specifically. He'd been looking for an opportunity, and she'd provided it to him.

Two days of hell had followed until they'd found Lila, discarded by the side of the road as if she hadn't even been worth the time to hide.

After that, there were no more nights drinking. No more high fives after cases. No more nasty insults that hid approval beneath filthy curses.

It had just gotten very, very quiet. As if they were worried she was one wrong word away from shattering and spilling the crazy everywhere. As if they were worried it would get all over them.

Hughes had requested a new partner not long after they arrested Lila's killer. The next seven had rotated out quickly, none of them lasting longer than three months.

The most galling part of it, though, was that she had not once cried, not once broken down in front of them. They simply thought they knew how she would act, but suddenly she was a different person.

Suddenly, Alice was roughing up suspects and pulling her gun when it wasn't necessary. "One of these days she's going to snap," a former partner had told the chief. Alice had overheard because he'd wanted her to. "Someone's gonna get killed, and you won't be able to cover it up."

As if she'd ever be so careless.

Alice pushed the thoughts away. Just like she'd pushed away the ones from the beach. Just like she pushed so many away. There was no room in her mind to deal with them. Emotions, as always, were the enemy, dangerous and deceptive. They clouded judgments, they altered reality, they directed focus from what was important.

Long ago, she'd learned the beauty of compartmentalizing all those messy feelings.

Instead, she thought about the crime scene. Not about the long days before when they'd all but lived and breathed Ruby Burke, and not about the impressions that came later. Just for now, she thought about only the crime scene. Clothes still on. Shoes still on.

No obvious signs of struggle aside from the single, violent blow to the head.

Face covered.

Nice sheets.

There was a direction this was headed. She'd read it on the chief's face. She'd read it in Nakamura's questions. She'd read it in the awkward distance the other officers had placed between themselves and Charlotte.

The woman was being tried and found guilty.

"You're sure you're okay to take lead?" Nakamura asked when they were five minutes away from the Burke house. She'd been running the case when it was a disappearance. But now it was a murder.

"Of course," she said. Her tone was sharp, defensive, and she didn't try to soften it. This wasn't a discussion.

"No one would blame you . . . ," Nakamura tried again. Unwisely.

They didn't know the details of Lila's case here in Florida. It hadn't caught national attention, perhaps because Lila's skin had been light brown instead of lily white. Or maybe it was because Alice had struggled to afford the little one-bedroom apartment they'd shared instead of owning three mansions with a vacation home to spare. Whatever the reason had been, Nakamura and the others knew only the basics of what had happened.

It was enough, though. Even when it was just a kidnapping, Deakin had pulled her aside after giving Nakamura the case, told her no one expected her to work it under the circumstances.

"No one would blame me," she repeated.

Nakamura pounced, misreading the reason her voice had turned slow and circumspect. "You've only been here a few months. No one even expects you to take lead on a murder investigation, let alone on one like this."

"One that hits so close to home, you mean," Alice said.

"Yeah." Nakamura nodded.

"No one would think I was too weak or too emotional to handle important cases if I sat this one out, right?" Alice said. "And since this will be the only little girl to ever be murdered in this city, I don't have to worry about being passed over for cases in the future."

He glanced at her, but his eyes were hidden behind his sunglasses. By now, he'd caught on.

"No one would leave tissue boxes in my locker because cops are well known for respecting delicate sensibilities, right?" Alice continued. "No one would watch to see if I was going to the shrink more than was necessary. No one would dare start telling stories about my shaking hands when I drew on a suspect. Because it's normal to need to sit out some cases, right? Because it's not just me being emotional."

The car was silent. Whether he suspected she was drawing on personal experience or not didn't matter. He could picture it; he'd been a cop for more than twenty years.

"Yeah, no one would blame me," Alice said, turning her attention back to the road. "Just shut up and drive."

They didn't speak again until Nakamura pulled to a stop a few doors down from the Burke house. "This place, man," he said when he threw the car into park.

They'd been there off and on since Ruby had been reported missing, but it seemed that neither of them would get over the sheer absurdity of its grandeur.

The mansion was a story higher than its neighbors, a visual representation of the pissing contest it was engaging in. The style, with its thick, prominent columns and wraparound porch, was more suited for Alabama plantations than St. Petersburg's quirky architecture, and something told Alice that was the whole point.

She'd been on the job only a week before someone mentioned Sterling Burke. A particularly gossip-addicted desk clerk hadn't even paused for a breath after his introduction before he was spilling the details on the judge, who had a reputation for going easy on frat boys while sentencing anyone to the max with a skin color darker than pure white snow.

"Southern boy, through and through, our dear Sterling," the clerk had drawled, with just the right hint of affection that Alice was learning meant pure disdain in these parts.

It was true what they said. But it was also true that Sterling was a born charmer, a politician without the politics, a charismatic preacher type proselytizing about better times gone by, but without the manic religious slant.

The first time she'd met him had been at a fund-raiser for the police department, two months ago. Her attendance had been mandatory, and she'd spent the majority of the night holed up in a dark corner behind a plant, eating bacon-wrapped shrimp she'd bribed a waiter to bring her before anyone else.

But on her way back from the bathroom, the chief had grabbed her elbow, pulling her into a little gathering of people. One that happened to include Judge Sterling Burke.

From what she'd heard and knew about the man, she'd expected something else: a sleazy veneer, perhaps, to hide his rotting, putrid soul.

Instead, he was pleasant. He was handsome, distinguished.

"Welcome to St. Pete," he'd said as he shook her hand. His had been warm and dry, and he'd pumped her palm a few exuberant times to show just how welcome she should feel. She was good at spotting snakes, even ones who wore the careful camouflage of charm, but he didn't ring any alarms for her. "We're a little nutty here, but once you're in, you're in. It's like family that way."

Alice had murmured something that may have been taken as agreement as she slipped her hand back in her pocket.

"How are you finding it?" he pressed.

Alice shifted but kept her face neutral. "Hot."

Sterling laughed as if it was actually a funny joke and nudged her ribs with his elbow.

He was kind. Friendly.

He'd treated everyone in their little circle the same, with that warm, attentive gaze. Even when the governor stopped by to hover at his elbow, a pup waiting to be acknowledged, Sterling had finished listening to the story a uniformed officer was telling him.

The judge was likable without trying too hard, engaging without coming off like he was climbing ladders. It threw Alice off-balance.

That was also the night she'd met the matriarch. Hollis Burke.

Where Sterling was warm, Hollis was ice. Where he schmoozed, she intimidated. Where he joked, laughed, teased to ease any tension, she reveled in the anxiety, the nervousness, the fear being in her presence caused those around her.

When the governor's wife, a tiny bird of a woman who stuttered through her introductions, moved into Hollis's target range, she was spared no mercy.

"Julia, hello, dear," Hollis said, kissing the air above the woman's hollow cheeks. "Should you be out tonight?"

"What . . . what do you mean?" Julia tugged at the hem of her ill-fitting blazer.

"Surely, you're ill, dear?" Hollis's voice dropped to an exaggerated whisper. She wanted everyone to hear.

"No," Julia said, her eyes flicking to each nearby face of each person who was trying to ignore the put-down.

The exchange had been sour and petty and had reminded Alice of countless others she'd overheard in DC. She'd felt pity for the delicate woman, but mostly she'd felt like she'd actually found her feet for once. This, she understood. Human nature at its finest.

"Oh." Hollis's red-slicked lips formed a perfect O, and she let her gaze slide down over Julia's beige suit that even Alice knew wasn't appropriate for the ball. "My mistake."

They were a pair, Sterling and Hollis. People flocked to them, to bow and scrape and kiss at their knuckles in order to receive just a hint of acknowledgment. That's all it seemed to take.

That had been apparent two days ago when the governor and his wife had planted themselves in the chief's office, demanding to know why the station's newest cop had been placed on such an important investigation as Ruby Burke's disappearance. It was after they left that Deakin had called her in to ask if she was sure she was all right handling the case. No one would blame her if she needed to step aside.

Never underestimate the power of Judge Sterling Burke. And his wife.

She wondered how many times she would learn that lesson.

CHAPTER FOUR

TRUDY

July 1, 2018
Twenty-eight days before the kidnapping

The absolute quiet in the mansion did little to reassure Trudy Burke that her family was asleep. So she held herself still, curled on the cold, harsh hardwood floor of her bedroom, her back against the wall. Moonlight filtered in through her white lace curtains, and she watched the patterns it created dance along her furniture as she controlled her breathing, syncing it with the steadiness of her heartbeats.

It had been a long time since she'd been scared of the dark, a long time since she'd realized the monsters that lived there were just shadows. The real ones stayed around long after the sun came up.

But there was always the nervousness that lingered in her fingertips, which made her realize that her room wasn't actually her space. It could be—and frequently was—invaded with the ease of a slowly turning doorknob. So she waited. She waited while the house settled in for the night, and waited while Charlotte snuck out to wherever she was running off to, and waited until her mother, Mellie, collapsed into an alcohol-induced sleep. The thin walls had never been able to keep secrets.

And then she waited longer.

Only when she was as sure as she could be that she wouldn't be disturbed did she finally move. Shifting to her knees, she shuffled over to her closet, avoiding the squeaky places in the wood that could betray her.

She dug past clothes that had fallen off their hangers and mismatched shoes that no longer had their mates until her thumb ran along the groove she knew so well.

Beneath the loose board lived a safe. It was a cheap thing she'd bought for twenty bucks at Walmart, but it was all she really needed.

Once she pulled it free from the small, dark space under the floor, she sat back on her heels and twisted the knob in circles until the little door popped up. Nestled against the black velour inside was a slim, silver laptop.

No one in the family knew about its existence, and Trudy prayed it would stay that way. If any of the girls wanted access to a computer, they had to use the one Hollis left in the living room, or venture into the judge's office. Only Mellie ever did that.

So Trudy had saved up for hers.

Their bank accounts were monitored for any extra withdrawn cash, but all the Burke ladies had found ways to squirrel away money. It had taken Trudy two years to hide enough to get the laptop.

She shuffled over to the darkest corner of her room, her back once again pressed along the wall, with the laptop balanced on her bare legs. While she powered up the machine, Trudy listened for any new signs of movement. The house was quiet.

By muscle memory, she opened various sites and windows before clicking over to her blog. The very first day she'd bought her computer, she'd created the site. It was her baby, the only thing that kept her sane sometimes.

There were a few messages waiting for her; there always were. Sometimes she'd go days between feeling comfortable enough to bring the laptop out of the safe, so she wasn't able to check as often as she'd like.

She scrolled over the past few weeks' posts. They were standard—information on safe houses for victims of domestic violence, hotline numbers, answers to calls for help because of abuse-related suicidal thoughts. Those were the hardest ones. Because many of the messages she received were anonymous, she never knew what happened to the lost souls, the ones who knew the monsters too well.

The uncertainty was worth it, though, if she could help even one girl, if she could make a difference to someone who was even now curled beneath a comforter with wide eyes watching a slowly turning doorknob.

She'd answer the messages that had come in later, before she stowed the laptop for the night. But for now, she clicked over to the in-box she had set up to connect to the blog.

The address for it was just a string of letters and numbers that meant nothing and couldn't be tied back to her. Somehow the email had ended up on a Pottery Barn subscription list, but other than spam from them, the only mail she'd received at the address was forwarded messages from her blog.

Except for recently.

Recently another address had been popping up with some frequency. The name the person used was nbeckett, but Trudy assumed it was as fake as her own. She'd googled it anyway and had come up with too many results to sift through.

The first email from N, as she had started thinking of the person, had come in through her blog. It had just been a list of resources in St. Pete for victims of sexual abuse. Trudy had known about most of them and kept a similar list linked on her site for anyone seeking help. But a few had been new to her, so she published it.

A few days later, another message came in with more information that looked legitimate. It took two weeks after that for N to send her an email address along with a note:

I have something I want to share with you, but
don't want it to be public. Message me? – N

Trudy wasn't an idiot. It was Internet Safety 101 not to give out information just because some stranger behind a fake name asked for it. But she was somewhat secure behind her own anonymity. And N had proven to be a reliable source.

So she'd emailed.

After that, she began to realize N was leading up to something. From her blog, the person seemed to figure out that she had personal experience with the subject matter. *Have you checked out any of these places?* N had asked one time. *It's hard to save enough money to get away, isn't it?* A throwaway line at the bottom of another list. Probing, gently, to try to figure out Trudy's situation.

Trudy never answered the personal questions. But she also didn't try to hide as much as she normally would have.

There was an email from N now, bold and unread at the top of her in-box. The name was almost a comfort, after more than a month of correspondence.

She clicked into the message and squinted at the string of numbers. It was an address in Tampa, one she didn't recognize.

Beneath it was just one sentence.

Trust me.

CHAPTER FIVE

ALICE

August 2, 2018
Four days after the kidnapping

Alice and Nakamura paused just outside the front door of the Burke mansion. She raised an eyebrow at him, and he shrugged for her to take the lead, his decision made. Sometimes she wished he was an asshole, so she wouldn't have to like him. He never was, though.

After Alice rapped on the thick wood, they waited for several minutes in silence until the door finally opened. Mellie Burke stood on the other side, draped from head to toe in black, even though it had only been three hours since they'd found Ruby.

Mellie, Charlotte's older sister, was a miniature version of Hollis. She and her daughter, Trudy, shared the signature platinum-blonde hair of the matriarch, though the older women probably relied heavily on the skill of their hairdresser for the look. And like every other member of the family, she was as slim as a reed.

But whereas Alice had found Charlotte and Hollis to be reserved, Mellie was wild dramatics tumbling out over thick mascaraed eyelashes toward a neck that was bedecked with thousands of dollars' worth of diamonds. Expensive, but somehow gaudy. That was Mellie.

She was a good ten years older than Charlotte, closer to Alice's own age than her sister's. The extra years had carved lines around the corners of the woman's eyes and lips. She would not hold up as well as Hollis had.

"Oh, Detective." Mellie ignored Alice to drape herself over Nakamura, her long, painted nails digging into the front of his shirt as she buried her head in the nook of his shoulder. "I just heard."

Ever the professional, Nakamura disengaged himself from Mellie's grasp without actually appearing to do so, holding her by the shoulders at arm's length.

"Ms. Burke." He nudged her upright before letting his hands drop completely. "We're very sorry for your loss. We're here to ask Charlotte some questions."

"Of course." Mellie cast one last appreciative glance over Nakamura's lean body, then sighed and turned, gesturing them to follow. Alice rarely thought about it, but she supposed the man was attractive, in an older-gentleman sort of way that called to women who were looking for an authoritative figure.

He was average height but had toned muscles that gave him a certain presence. His hair was jet-black and threaded through with silver. Broad shoulders tapered down to a narrow waist. This wasn't the first time he'd been hit on in the course of an investigation.

Alice glanced away from his questioning look.

They'd been in the house several times, so it wasn't unfamiliar to her. It was sparse, like rich houses often were. Knickknacks were kept to a minimum, and white was the overpowering decorative choice. There was a large oil painting of the entire clan hanging in the entryway. Sterling sat in the middle of it with Hollis standing at his side, one dainty hand resting on his shoulder. She wore an ice-blue suit to match his dark charcoal one. Mellie and Charlotte were in shades of gray while Ruby and Trudy matched their grandmother.

Alice's eyes lingered on Ruby's smile, the dimples that dented in those round cheeks.

These types of ostentatious paintings were for rich people. But there was a sentiment there that Alice recognized. *This is us, this is our family,* it said.

The one Alice had hung up in the living room had been a charcoal caricature of Lila and her that she'd bought for five dollars at a local fair. The edges of their faces were a bit smudged from her four-year-old's grubby hands, but the message was the same: *This is us. This is our family.*

When Lila had looked at it months later and asked why there wasn't a daddy in the picture, Alice had wrapped her arms around the girl's chest and pulled her into a tight embrace. She'd whispered the lie, "Because I love you too much to share."

Nakamura bumped her shoulder, and she realized Mellie was half-way down the hall to the study.

She flushed at her own distraction.

"The poor love," Mellie was saying as they caught up with her. Mellie didn't seem to realize they hadn't been there the whole time. "She's almost inconsolable. Not that I blame her, of course."

"Where were you last night?" They'd have to wait for the autopsy to have an official time of death to confront suspects with, but it didn't hurt to ask.

The question stopped the woman midstep, and she teetered on six-inch stilettos as she tried to collect herself.

"Out with some friends," Mellie said, her eyes shuttering. The shadows of the hallway hid half of her face. "I would never hurt Ruby, Detective."

Alice ignored the second part. "They'll be able to corroborate that? And how late were you out?"

"Of course, yes," Mellie said, and she shifted so the light fell along her face once more. It was too harsh against the woman's pale skin. "I'll give you a list. I didn't get home until about four in the morning."

"Is that usual?" Nakamura asked from where he'd settled by Alice's shoulder.

"Not . . . every night." The answer was slow, uncertain, despite the lack of censure in Nakamura's voice. It was strange, though, for her to go partying three days after her niece was kidnapped. "Charlotte said . . ."

She trailed off, the corners of her mouth tipping down.

"Charlotte said what?" Alice asked.

"That I should go." Mellie was back to being defensive for her own sake, not for Charlotte's. It was selfish and stupid when talking to the detectives leading the case. "She said it would help me relax, after a stressful few days."

Stressful because her niece was missing and possibly dead. Alice's gut told her that the alibis would come through. But it was interesting that Charlotte had been the one to tell her to go.

Mellie looked between them, her fingers playing with the expensive jeweled ring on her hand.

"Please get us that list," Alice finally said.

Mellie nodded, then stepped toward the closed door to the study, her hand hovering over the knob. She leaned in to Alice as if they were confidantes.

"I've never seen her look so dreadful," Mellie faux-whispered, the oversweet scent of her perfume making Alice dizzy. "It would do wonders for her if she would just run a comb through her hair. Not that I blame her, of course."

Alice dismissed the woman from her mind. She was vicious but in a way that was neither clever nor intelligent. Alice didn't have the patience for stupid cruelty.

Mellie, her smugness dropping a bit at Alice's lack of response, finally turned the handle to the study.

The room was dark, the blinds blocking the harsh morning rays. It was decorated for a man who considered himself an intellectual. Thick books lined up like soldiers on the shelves running along the back wall; deep burgundy chairs stood sentry by an old-fashioned drink cart that offered up a variety of brown-colored liquors in heavy crystal decanters; and a massive, shiny desk that was surely a metaphor about compensating for something stood prominently in the middle of the room.

Charlotte, by contrast, was a tiny, hunched figure that was all but swallowed up by the dark masculinity of the room. Her legs were tucked against her chest, her thin arms wrapped around her knees, her cheek resting on the tops of them. The long fall of red curls tumbled around her shoulders, partially hiding the vulnerability on her face.

She was barefoot, her toenails painted a bright, shimmery pink. Perhaps it was an inane thing to notice. Alice noticed anyway.

Everything about the woman was fragile, it seemed—the curve of her shoulder, the wet lashes that clung to pale cheeks, the hitch of each breath as if it were painful to drag in oxygen.

This was the worst part. The questions. Alice knew them well.

"Where were you when it happened?"

"What was going on?"

"Did you get distracted? Look away? No? Not even for a split second?"

Those were innocent enough.

The doubt, the judgment, the blame began to creep in with each progressive ask—subtlety giving way to thinly veiled accusations.

"Were you drinking?"

"Were you distracted by a man?"

"On that note, when was the last time you had sex?"

Because that somehow related to how her daughter had been kidnapped.

Alice had taken it, just as Charlotte had that first day Ruby went missing. The repulsion, the disbelief, the confusion, and then the resigned acceptance on the woman's face had been a mirror of Alice's so many years ago.

This was what it was like to be a mother who had just lost her child.

"Ms. Burke," Alice said, keeping her voice even and low so as not to startle the woman.

Charlotte turned damp blue eyes on them. They locked with Alice's, and Alice could read the pure emptiness that was there. This was not the same woman who had sat across from them in that chair four days earlier.

That's what people didn't understand about this grief. It was fundamental. The person you were before this happened was eviscerated, destroyed. In its place was someone unrecognizable.

"We're sorry for your loss," Nakamura said, glancing at Alice before settling into one of the seats in front of the desk. It scared him, this new Charlotte.

Charlotte blinked at them, then lifted one slim shoulder. The movement was enough to get Alice to sit.

"Charlotte, we'd like to ask you a few questions." Alice kept her voice soft in a way she wouldn't have in any other investigation. Kindness was easily read as weakness. "Charlotte. Do you have any idea who would want to hurt Ruby?"

They'd asked her the question already. They'd asked her many times, and they'd asked everyone who came even into the brief periphery of the case. *No, of course not.* That was the standard answer.

But sometimes shock rattled repressed memories loose. That man who stood too close at a store, that woman who was a bit too helpful so she could talk to Ruby, the family acquaintance who focused a bit too much on the little girl. So they had to ask again.

Something flickered across Charlotte's face, but she pressed her mouth tight and shook her head. "No, of course not."

Nakamura stilled. He'd seen it, too, that flash of something, come and gone so quickly.

"Anything at all you can think of, Charlotte," Alice said. "No matter how silly or little it may seem to you. It could start us down a path we hadn't been considering."

Charlotte's eyes lingered on Alice, searching. The scrutiny was unnerving, but Alice held her gaze, willing her to say something, anything that could direct the investigation.

"Anyone in this household, perhaps?" Alice said. Quiet, so quiet. She didn't want to frighten Charlotte into silence.

There was a brief moment, as Charlotte's lips parted, when Alice thought, *Maybe*. Maybe this was when the secrets would finally slip out, the ones that confirmed this family was a nest of vipers desperate to sink poisonous fangs into one another. It would be easier if Charlotte verified what they all knew anyway.

But what came out was: "No, of course not."

Alice covered her disappointment by flipping to a new sheet in her notebook. Charlotte had to already know that it wouldn't be long before every single officer in the precinct thought she was guilty, and that the rest of the world would be quick to follow. Public opinion, once it took root, was hard to overturn.

"How about Ruby's father?" Alice prodded. They'd already gone down this rabbit hole in the hours following the kidnapping. *Who was he? Was he in Ruby's life? No? Why not?*

Charlotte had given them only the briefest answers. It had been a one-night stand, someone passing through the city on a business trip. He didn't even know about Ruby.

Alice had pressed. *"Are you sure he didn't find out? Would he be angry if he had? Enough to come down here and do something about it?"*

Whatever color had been left in Charlotte's cheeks at the time had drained, and she'd flinched. *"I'm absolutely certain that's not what happened,"* she'd said. There'd been a conviction in her voice that Alice was inclined to believe despite the fact that she was so clearly lying about the father.

Charlotte studied her now but had slipped behind a mask that even Alice couldn't read. "No. It wasn't him."

Nakamura shifted, and Alice knew he wanted to pursue that line. Alice sympathized with Nakamura's frustration but also recognized a brick wall when she saw one.

So she pivoted in a different direction.

"Where were you last night, Ms. Burke?" Alice asked. If the woman wasn't willing to play ball, she'd realize their sympathy extended only so far.

Unblinking, Charlotte placed her hands palms down on the wood of the desk. "I didn't kill my child," she said finally, everything about her flat, detached.

The words hung in the air as if Alice could reach out and touch them, stroke the downward slashes and curves of each letter.

"Who said you did?" Alice asked.

Charlotte looked away, toward the window that was completely blocked off by the curtains.

"You will."

CHAPTER SIX

CHARLOTTE

July 22, 2018
One week before the kidnapping

The air conditioner in the church was broken, and the heat sat like a heavy hand on Charlotte's chest.

The ladies in the pew in front of her had thick paper fans they used to move the stale air, as if that would offer some relief.

She was using every bit of willpower within her not to swipe at the beads of sweat along her temple. Hollis would be livid, and it wasn't worth the lecture. Charlotte had always wondered if her mother equated sweat with weakness, discomfort with vulnerability.

Hollis, in her perfectly tailored blazer, was immobile beside her, eyes locked on the priest. But that didn't mean she wouldn't see even the smallest movement from any one of the Burkes. That didn't mean she wouldn't catalog the grave offense in the little scorecard she kept tucked away in her head.

But Charlotte was functioning on almost no sleep. When she'd crawled into bed to curl around Ruby that morning after talking with Trudy on the porch, she hadn't been able to still her thoughts long enough to slip into the darkness. Instead, she'd watched the light as it crept across the carpet, up along their legs, until it cradled Ruby's face. The girl had blinked awake, disgruntled for the second before she realized Charlotte was there with her. Then she'd smiled—bright, happy— Charlotte's absence in the night forgiven or forgotten.

Now, Charlotte pressed the tip of her finger to the white painted wood of the pew, searching for the sharp point of a wayward splinter. Perhaps the pain would let her focus on something other than the loose board of the lazy fan above them that rattled at each turn, and the dampness under her breasts. Ruby banged the back of her heel against the underside of the seats in a rhythm that was off, just slightly, from the beat of Charlotte's heart. It raced trying to catch up and then trying to slow down, but Ruby's foot stayed at that same steady pace, and Charlotte couldn't quite match it.

Everything was itchy. If only she could dig her pointer finger into her scalp and let the jagged nail do its work. To let it scrape at the dried skin cells there, to leave raw, angry red lines, to draw blood, to create scars. Anything to stop the fire that burned just beyond her actual reach.

The waistband of her skirt cut into her hip bones, and she arched her spine, shifting to ease at least that discomfort.

Hollis's fingers found Charlotte's wrist, her thumb pressing against the pulse point there. It was a warning, and Charlotte stilled immediately, the memory of countless bruises a strong incentive to listen.

But the tension in her muscles remained, the fibers nearly tearing from the bones with the tightness of it all.

The grip on her wrist didn't release, so she couldn't move and she couldn't relax and she couldn't breathe and she couldn't think and she couldn't, she couldn't, she couldn't.

Then she was floating. The air became soft, and it glittered in the light that streamed in from the windows. She chased one of the dancing sparkles with fingers that weren't her fingers and giggled when it escaped her. Her body was wrapped in a cool sheet, and her lashes kissed her cheeks in delight. The fabric caressed her limbs, draping itself along her thighs that were no longer slick with sweat, over the stretch of her ribs, into the valleys of her collarbones. It was lovely. Everything was so lovely.

It was Hollis who brought her back with a simple tug. Charlotte blinked. The fogginess lingered, but it was no longer pleasant. All that was left was a grogginess that weighed on her spine, and she didn't know what had just happened.

She'd been in the church. But she hadn't been.

Her first instinct was to scoop Ruby up and run. Run and never stop. She looked at her baby girl, who was watching Charlotte, her little bow lips turned down at the corners, her foot paused midair, her head tipped to the side. It was like Ruby could see her so clearly.

Something caught in the back of her throat. Children were not supposed to see their parents clearly.

So instead of pulling her from the pew in a panic, Charlotte crossed her eyes and stuck out her tongue. She was rewarded with a giggle that was easy and relaxed. Wind chimes on the first day of spring. And everything snapped back into place.

The odd tension drained out of Ruby, and she was once again a five-year-old, bored and hot and uncomfortable, quiet only because of the threat of her grandmother and the whispered promise of ice cream if she held on a little longer.

Charlotte's fingers, her teeth, her knees—they were all hers again. The waistband that had been the final trigger still dug into her flesh. The heat was still unbearable.

The world hadn't tilted along with her, it seemed.

Each of the final minutes of the Mass were heavy and loaded. Charlotte counted the seconds in her head, and the task kept her tethered to reality. That floating place stayed in the back of her mind, though, seductive as any drug-induced oblivion. It was a terrifying desire, to go back there, but she wanted it anyway.

Hollis said nothing on the way home, but Charlotte knew without being told that her presence would be required in the study. It was Hollis's battlefield of choice.

When they walked into the house, Charlotte grabbed Ruby's shoulder, spinning her around.

"Hey, petal." Charlotte bent down so she was crouched in front of her. "Why don't you go play upstairs?"

Ruby's eyes went wide, and she leaned in so her nose bumped against Charlotte's. "Are you in trouble with Grandma?"

Charlotte pulled at the end of one of her braids. "No, sweetheart. We're just going to talk a bit."

Ruby's lips pursed and then flattened. "That means you're in trouble."

Out of the mouths of babes. There was something both funny and tragic about it, and Charlotte was too tired to find the line so she could know whether to laugh or cry. Instead, she stood up and turned Ruby by her shoulders. "We'll get ice cream later."

"Can Dee-Dee come?" Ruby asked, the slippery soles of her polished white dress shoes already hitting the steps.

The memory of harsh words in the early-morning light lingered, but so did the soft moment when Trudy had stopped her. *I need your help.*

"We'll ask her," Charlotte promised, and the grin it earned her was worth the sacrifice.

She stared at the empty staircase after Ruby disappeared.

The house had gone quiet. Mellie and Trudy had beelined for their rooms the minute they'd walked through the door, neither of them willing or interested in being pulled into whatever storm was headed Charlotte's way. Sterling was God knew where. He said golfing, but for all she knew, he was screwing his latest mistress into the mattress. His version of church.

And Hollis, well, Hollis was always waiting. Waiting for Charlotte to mess up, waiting to punish her, waiting to take out on Charlotte the bitterness that seemed to fuel her very existence. Sometimes she directed that anger at Mellie, but rarely. It was always Charlotte who seemed to displease the most. Who drew the venom so often she didn't even try to guess the cause anymore. Or she knew the cause, really, and had long given up on rationalizing it.

It wasn't complicated. Sterling had never looked at Mellie the way he'd looked at Charlotte. The way he'd looked at Trudy. The way he was starting to look at Ruby.

Hollis wasn't an idiot. But rather than doing anything to stop it, she just steeped in her own resentment, directing the toxic hostility that ran through her blood toward the very girls she should have protected.

The thought was an echo to the earlier one Charlotte had had while bearing the brunt of Trudy's verbal assault. The Burke women were the snakes who couldn't bite the foot that stepped on them. In Hollis's case, that meant she went after the mice that had been dropped in the cage instead.

Charlotte's heels clicked on the slick hardwood floor, and her stomach pitched with each step. There was a little voice prodding at the very base of her brain that wondered if she would go back to that floaty place now. If this would be enough to send her there. That same voice asked if that meant she was going crazy. It was a question she was terrified to answer.

She took one final breath before pushing the door open and stepping through the threshold.

Hollis stood by the corner of the desk and nodded to one of the chairs. Charlotte would sit; Hollis would loom. A clear visual reminder of their power dynamics in case Charlotte ever forgot.

There were so many times they'd sat like this. Some might call them natural adversaries, the fading mother, the attractive daughter, but Charlotte had never wanted it to be like that.

On Sunday afternoons when she was young, she would slink into the study, tuck herself into the chair, and listen to a list of things she'd done wrong all week. It was instructive, Hollis had told her. The grooming it took to become a Burke wasn't soft or easy. Crying over the corrections wasn't allowed, not at first.

Later, when Charlotte was a teenager, Hollis seemed to revel in it when she broke down.

There had been exactly one time when Charlotte had tried alcohol, outside of wine, at formal functions. She'd come home with liquor on her breath that she hadn't been able to hide with mints. Hollis had dragged her by the wrist, her fingers digging into the bones there, through the house, paying no attention to Charlotte's efforts to break free. She'd thrown her to the floor once they'd made it to the study and then knelt before her. Hollis had captured Charlotte's chin in her hand to force her mouth open, and Charlotte had relented only when the edges of her vision had gone blurry.

When she smelled the Scotch, Hollis had slapped her. Burkes don't get drunk like homeless men on the street. Burkes don't disrespect their family like that. Did Charlotte not know who she was, what was expected of her?

The punishment had been isolation, unrelenting isolation. Charlotte had never had many friends, not like other girls. But she'd had one. A person she could trust and whisper secrets to under blankets and not worry about the tiny confessions becoming weapons in cruel hands. Once Hollis realized this, though, the connection had been quickly severed on the premise that the girl was a bad influence. Burkes had to be choosy about the people they surrounded themselves with.

Seven years later, Charlotte recognized the tactic for what it was—just another way to keep her controlled. Helpless.

"Explain yourself" was all Hollis said, a pink nail tapping on the desk.

Charlotte watched the sharp edge of it hit the wood, the fast rhythm the only outward indication of Hollis's annoyance. "It was hot."

"I'm not talking about your embarrassing display at the service," Hollis snapped out.

Startled, Charlotte met her eyes. "Trudy?"

Why would she have told, though?

Hollis smoothed down a nonexistent wisp of her hair. Not a single strand of the platinum-blonde shell was actually out of place. "As if I need a child to inform me of what's happening in my own house."

She must have seen Charlotte coming in. Trudy had delayed her only a few minutes on the porch, but it had been enough, as she'd already been running late.

"It's nothing," Charlotte said, knowing it wasn't the right answer. But there wasn't a right answer for Hollis. There never was.

"Whoring around town is nothing?"

Defending herself would be pointless. A waste of energy and breath. Hollis wanted to attack, and so she would. If not for this, it would be for something else. Charlotte's shoulders hit the back of the chair as she sagged against the smooth leather. Would this ever end? This cycle they were caught in, with Charlotte forever being punished for something she'd never been able to fight off in the first place.

Hollis stepped around the desk, her eyes cold as she stopped in front of Charlotte. She sank her fingers into Charlotte's smooth hair and yanked in one brutal movement, wrenching Charlotte's head to the side. The position exposed her neck and the small bruise Enrique had left there.

Hollis dug the tip of her nail into the spot, then leaned over so that her breath was warm against Charlotte's ear. "Did this one try to stop when you called him 'Daddy'? Or did he like it?"

Bile pressed at the back of Charlotte's throat, and she surged to her feet as she tried to swallow the vomit. The quick movement knocked Hollis back a few steps, forcing her to let go of Charlotte's hair.

They stared at each other as Charlotte panted, her stomach heaving, the ragged breaths the only sound in the otherwise-silent room.

Hollis's face was passive, a mask of smooth perfection. But her eyes were hard and unrelenting as she watched Charlotte's reaction. The taunt had been crude, vulgar. So unlike Hollis.

And it was the only time she'd ever alluded to the fact that she knew. The only time she'd so blatantly thrown it in Charlotte's face, and there had to be a reason. Had to be. The purpose must have been to provoke Charlotte, to shock her into doing something. But what? What was it supposed to accomplish?

If only Charlotte could think beyond the urgent need to curl into the fetal position and protect all her vulnerable organs from blows that weren't even coming.

"Why?" She forced the word out between lips so chapped they hurt. Everything hurt.

Hollis knew what she was asking, and when she answered, her voice was cool once again. Gone was that hot, derisive whisper that would now forever live in Charlotte's memory.

"Your behavior is reckless and dangerous," Hollis said. "And it's a bad influence on my granddaughter."

All the muscles in Charlotte's body seized. Ruby. Of course this was about Ruby.

"Winning custody of her wouldn't take much," Hollis said. "All we care about is her welfare and her happiness."

It was a threat, one Hollis had been keeping up her carefully tailored designer sleeve for five years. The one that had never been uttered until now, even though the idea of it had always been enough to keep Charlotte in line. Each time she brought up moving out, Hollis would simply look at Ruby. Each time she started withdrawing just a little extra money from her account than what Hollis knew she needed, she'd drop in a casual question. "What are you planning to do with it?" Hollis would ask, her hand resting on Ruby's thin shoulder. And then she'd make Charlotte turn over any cash she had on her.

But now Hollis was putting it into words.

"Why do you hate me so much?" Charlotte choked out, her voice weak and small, even though she knew it was the wrong response. Hollis didn't react to emotion.

"Darling, I don't hate you." Hollis stepped closer again, her fingers trailing down Charlotte's cheek. It was grotesque in its gentleness after the violence that had just occurred between them. "I just want what's best for you. And your daughter, of course."

Charlotte flinched. But didn't say anything further.

Hollis hummed in approval of what she saw as obedience. "You're unstable, Charlotte. Don't think I haven't noticed. Us taking care of Ruby while you take some time to recover is the only reasonable path forward."

"Recover from what?" Charlotte forced herself to ask. Her mind wasn't keeping up. And a little part of her wondered if the words rang too true.

Hollis leaned forward. "It doesn't even matter, darling."

A mental breakdown, drugs, alcohol. It could be anything. That's what Hollis meant. If her mother decided to whisper encouragement in the right ear, Charlotte would be unable to do anything about it.

Charlotte closed her eyes, to block out the sight of Hollis's face, and breathed. She needed to think.

This wasn't an idle threat; Hollis could make it happen if she wanted. Another way to hurt Charlotte.

It would be a blow to the family's reputation, but not one it couldn't weather. They'd already absorbed the whispers about two unmarried daughters with bastard children living in the house; it would surprise few people if Charlotte checked into rehab.

Panic clawed at her rib cage. She needed to act, she needed to plan. She needed to talk to Trudy again. *I need your help.*

She opened her eyes to find Hollis watching her, red lips turned up at the corners.

It was hate, pure and uncomplicated, that thrummed through Charlotte's veins. It fueled her, gave her a strength she'd never had before.

"You'll never take my daughter away from me," Charlotte said, her voice even. "I will kill you myself first."

CHAPTER SEVEN

ALICE

August 2, 2018
Four days after the kidnapping

"You don't think she did it," Nakamura said as he knocked the back of his hand against the corner of his lip, going for the glob of pizza sauce that clung there.

Alice chewed on her straw. She had no appetite, even though she couldn't remember the last time she'd eaten. The only reason she'd stopped was that Nakamura had pled starvation, and she'd known he'd be useless to her if he didn't get food in his stomach.

"I don't know." It was all she was willing to commit to.

"You don't think she did it," Nakamura repeated, this time keeping his eyes firmly on her face.

She shrugged, looking away. The pizza joint was mostly empty, except for a pair of teenagers in the back, racking up points on the ancient pinball machines. It smelled of oregano and grease, and the floor was sticky from beer that must have been spilled the night before. Sometimes she thought all the floors in St. Petersburg were coated with a thin layer of Coors Light.

They had gotten little from Charlotte Burke in the latest round of questioning. No more, certainly, than they had in the previous four days. After her dramatic declaration, she'd clammed up and slid a card with the name of her lawyer over to them.

Even after reassuring her there was no need for one yet, Charlotte had refused to say anything further.

So they'd left, with nothing else to do but eat pizza and wonder if the case had just been solved for them anyway.

"Do you?" She paused, then clarified: "Think she did it." At the moment she didn't really care what Nakamura thought. His impressions were his to have.

"I don't know," he said, and that got her attention.

"Asshole." She laughed and chucked her partially shredded napkin at him. "You're giving me shit and—"

"And I really don't know. You, on the other hand . . . you've made up that brilliant little mind of yours already. And that, my dear partner, is the difference," Nakamura said, finishing off his last slice.

Her eyes tracked the smooth contours of his face. For the most part, he was open and easygoing. But he was a veteran cop and could use that to his advantage to hide what he was really thinking.

"You want me off the case, then?" She had to ask.

"Did I say that?"

He hadn't, but it wouldn't be surprising. Too close to home. That would be the excuse. Something with a slightly nastier undertone would be whispered behind her back, though. She'd heard it before.

She spread her palms on the tabletop. "I think if she'd done it, she would be laid out right next to Ruby."

Nakamura's eyebrows shot up. "You think she would have killed herself, too?"

"Seems the type," Alice said, watching the teenagers as they grabbed a discarded slice from an abandoned table and headed for the door.

"The type?"

Alice shifted her attention back to her partner. He was watching her with a quiet, thoughtful expression she found disarming. Most of the time, eyes slid over and past her face, unwilling to linger in case they got a glimpse of a tragedy they didn't want to think about. She was no longer a person who had thoughts or opinions. For others, she was forever and perpetually in grief. For the rest of her life.

"Mothers kill their children all the time," she said. Saying it aloud almost felt taboo. "It's not this mystical bond that can never be severed. But there are types to it."

Nakamura nodded and then tipped his head to the exit. They both pushed out of the booth. He held the door for her, and she didn't make a thing of it.

The day had turned just as hot and muggy as the warm morning had promised, and she immediately missed the pizza place's weak air conditioner. Even walking to the Buick parked three spots away felt overwhelming as the sun cooked the hot black pavement under their feet.

"You have the mentally ill. The type who think their children belong in the house of God, and such," Alice continued, eyeing the door handle warily. She didn't particularly fancy losing skin to the hot metal. "You have the neglectful ones, the ones who shake their babies when they won't stop crying or who forget to feed them when they're in the bathroom shooting up."

"Charlotte Burke doesn't really strike me as either," Nakamura said, sliding into the car. Alice followed suit.

"No," Alice agreed, shuddering as the cool air blasted her damp skin. Goddamn Florida. "Which leaves the type who kill their child and then kill themselves."

There was a beat of silence as Nakamura backed out of the spot. "And yet Charlotte is still alive."

"Points to the detective on that one." Alice smirked, and Nakamura flipped her off.

"Are those the only types?"

Alice shrugged. "Who knows? I could be pulling this all out of my ass."

Nakamura barked out a laugh and took a sharp right, heading in the direction of the station. "You're a good liar, Alice Garner."

"It's all in the confidence."

"It sounded legit, at least," Nakamura said, still chuckling. He didn't even slam on the horn when a white pickup truck with a Confederate-flag bumper sticker cut him off. The king of being unruffled.

"Mostly it is," Alice said, watching the strip malls and fast-food restaurants blur by. It was better than watching him drive. "I simplified it. But the point stands."

Psychologists had talked about Alice when Lila was killed. Not in so many words, because ethics didn't allow it—diagnosing someone who wasn't a patient was a no-no. But talking shit in vague terms to the local papers let the shrinks clutch at their fifteen minutes of fame while they tore her apart. Consequently, she knew a lot about women who killed their children.

"So how do you explain that little announcement, then?" Nakamura asked, though his voice was more curious than anything. She liked that about him. His willingness to consider ideas that didn't come naturally to him. "That we're going to think she murdered Ruby."

"As cliché as it may sound, grief does strange things," Alice said. Sometimes clichés were there for a reason—to lend words to a universal truth. Grief could warp reality into something unrecognizable. She knew that too well.

Alice remembered watching as the man who had killed Lila was pulled from the police car outside the courthouse. She remembered the stubble on his jaw, the red chapped skin on his nose. She remembered the weight of the gun in her lap as she ran her fingers lovingly along the length of it.

Grief did strange things.

"She also feels guilt over something," Alice continued. "But to assume it's for killing Ruby is making a leap that's not necessarily there for us to make."

"Just . . . ," Nakamura started, then trailed off. One hand was cupping the gear stick, the other cradling the steering wheel, and his eyes, hidden behind dark sunglasses, were on the road.

"You don't need to tell me," Alice said.

He glanced at her. "You need to be careful."

"I just said you don't—"

"I know what you said." He cut her off as he downshifted and made the left into the police station parking lot. "And I think I did."

———

Exhaustion throbbed through the police station, a tangible thing that clung to the faces of everyone there. It may have been only hours since Ruby Burke's body had been found, but they had all been working nonstop since the girl had been reported missing four days ago. It was starting to show.

Clothes had gone unchanged, jelly and mustard stains ignored. The comb-overs had wilted into sad wishful thinking, and oil saturated the strands of those who had hair. A vague mustiness permeated the air, and they all universally decided not to acknowledge it.

Alice wasn't the only one with deep bruises beneath her eyes that betrayed a severe lack of sleep. There were only two cots in the back storage room, and they'd taken them on a rotating basis.

It wasn't that they'd never had a missing-child case—now a murder case. They had plenty. The ones they were familiar with, though, involved poor black kids whom the general public didn't care about.

Ruby Burke, though. St. Petersburg royalty? A beautiful strawberry-headed cherub with bright blue eyes and a smile that spoke of innocence that needed protecting? She brought out the vultures.

There was the media with a twenty-four-hour news cycle to fill and clicks to gin up for advertisers. An army of white vans had set up camp outside the station's doors, and Alice found herself tripping over bored, shellacked news anchors with disturbing frequency. She hadn't been able to walk by a TV in days without seeing Ruby's face.

There were the concerned citizens. Both the ones who made hushed phone calls at 3:00 a.m. with "tips," and the mothers, dressed for PTA meetings, who had many thoughts on children that they believed needed to be shared with overworked and stressed police officers immediately.

There were the genuinely disturbed. Men and women who thought they were guilty, who turned themselves over for crimes they hadn't committed, hoping for notoriety, hoping for shelter, hoping to quiet the incessant voices in their heads.

Then there were the rest. The curious, the frightened, the ones who wanted to be told it couldn't happen to them.

They were all the same. Vultures picking at scraps of rotted flesh.

A crime board had been set up in one of the conference rooms, away from the windows, away from any prying cameras, and the chief was ushering all the available officers into a semicircle. She and Nakamura perched on the table running along the back wall, their feet swinging a few inches off the floor.

Deakin clapped his large, meaty hands, and the sound snapped through the low-level chatter. The silence that followed pressed into her eardrums.

"No ransom note," Deakin started, turning to face the board full of pictures and layouts and timelines. He tapped on one of the pictures of Ruby, his finger hitting the middle of her forehead. "No contact with the family for four days."

That didn't look good for Charlotte.

"We had an Amber Alert out within two hours after she was reported missing from the beach," Deakin continued. "Charlotte Burke last saw her daughter at one in the afternoon on Sunday, July 29. They'd gone to St. Pete Beach for the day, leaving their home at around five in the morning."

It had been an unusual trip, Charlotte had told them. She'd had the urge to take Ruby for a special day but hadn't wanted to go to one of the ritzier beaches they normally frequented.

"This morning, a jogger found Ruby Burke on a private strip of beach just north of the city. Wrapped in a sheet, her clothes still intact, with no signs of trauma," Deakin said. They were the facts. But that didn't mean Alice had to like the way they were being presented. Nakamura sensed how she'd tensed and leaned his shoulder into hers. It might have been a warning. It might have been an offer of comfort. She moved away.

Weakness was not to be tolerated. No matter how small the gesture.

"We've put a rush on the autopsy report, but that's still hours if not several days from telling us anything," Deakin continued, his mouth tight at the corners. Alice knew from experience that if there was one person in this town who would refuse to bend to Sterling Burke's pressure, it was their coroner. "I've put in a search warrant request for the house, too, but that's taking a bit of time."

Alice and Nakamura had been in the place often over the past few days, but it had always been limited to the rooms the Burkes allowed them to be in. They'd always been watched, accompanied, and then swiftly escorted out when their interviews were over.

They needed that search warrant. Alice needed it. There were secrets in that house, and she wanted to find each one of them.

"Nakamura and Garner are taking point on this, but I can't stress enough how important the case is." The chief's eyes flitted to them and then away again. It didn't even need to be said. They'd all felt the pressure over the past four days. They'd seen the governor in the chief's office. They knew the media was just waiting for them to fail. "This is all hands on deck."

"It's gotta be the mother, right?" one of the uniformed cops shouted. He was young, still had the pimples and the cocky attitude to show for it. "Gotta be."

Deakin tipped his chin toward them. "Did you get anything out of her?"

Nakamura shook his head. "Lawyered up."

"Might as well have confessed, then," the cocky little shit chimed in again.

Alice pushed off the table and walked over to the kid, her movements slow and deliberate. The room's eyes were on her, but she didn't care. Let them watch.

Emotional. Erratic.

She didn't stop until her knees were almost pressed up against his thigh, her boots nudging his. He was forced to twist his neck into a painful angle to look up at her.

She let her eyes drag over him—a slow, derisive sweep—let the air become taut between them. Let the words he'd so carelessly tipped out into existence replay in his head as he was forced to remember exactly who she was.

"You seem to be under the mistaken impression that anyone in this room gives two shits what you think when time and again you've proven you don't even have enough IQ points to rub together," she finally said, low and calm. "If I hear one more word from you other than 'Yes, ma'am, how do you take your coffee?' I will personally shove my foot so far up your ass your tonsils will be bruised."

And then she turned and walked out of the room.

CHAPTER EIGHT

Trudy

July 3, 2018
Twenty-six days before the kidnapping

The hot, muggy air turned Trudy mean. Or meaner. She didn't necessarily consider herself to be a particularly kind person to begin with. But the water that clung to each particle of oxygen she dragged in along with the nicotine clogged the passageways of her lungs and turned her tongue vicious.

"No one likes you here," she said, shifting her gaze to the quiet boy perched on top of the picnic table beside her. He'd sat silent through her first two cigarettes, and she was bored, waiting for him to speak.

There was something about Zeke Durand that people might call beautiful. His skin was dark brown and smooth; his hair, close-cropped; his jaw, strong. The shoulders she let bump against her own uncovered ones were broad, and the muscles of his biceps strained the ink of the tattoos that danced with each shift of his arm.

His eyes, though, were what made him different from the rest of the cookie-cutter teenage boys who thought blond tips were something to swoon over. He turned them on her now, and the sunlight caught the edges of his irises where a deep blue ring dissolved into crystal teal. They slanted down at the corners, except when he smiled.

"I'm aware," he said, his voice too smoky for such a summer day. Then he went back to reading his thick leather-bound book, ignoring her once more. People didn't ignore Trudy.

She shook her curtain of white-blonde hair so that it bared her throat to his view as she pressed her palms against the table. The position wasn't subtle, but it rarely failed to get her what she wanted.

Zeke's gaze dipped to her exposed flesh, traveled over her body to the chest that only hinted at cleavage, paused at her smooth, naked midriff where a diamond glittered in the dip of her belly button, then caught again at the frayed edges of her cutoff jeans.

There was supposed to be hunger on his face when he looked back at her. But there wasn't. Instead, his expression was blank—a neutral mask, with only a slight upward slant of his lips that was far more mocking than aroused.

"Not interested, sugar," Zeke said, holding her gaze.

"Screw you." She straightened. "As if I'd let you fuck me." It was probably a lie. But there was her pride to maintain.

He didn't call her on it, just lifted one dismissive shoulder in a lazy man's shrug. "What do you want?"

She hopped off the picnic table. If there wasn't any reason to press her body against his, she preferred to be pacing. The dirt was dry, and her black Chucks kicked up dust as she trod over the worn earth of the old playground.

People had mostly forgotten it existed. It was in the wrong part of town. Families like her own would never step foot here, thinking their precious babies would get hep C just from looking at the rusted equipment. For the less fortunate, exhausted parents, well, they didn't have the time or energy to drag their kids to the park anymore. They plopped them in front of *SpongeBob SquarePants* and then went to their second jobs or went to get high or went to get drunk.

The seniors from the public high school used the park at night for screwing and drinking and smoking, and the cigarette butts and used condoms that littered the ground when the sun came up attested to that. But during the day it was usually abandoned.

Except for Zeke Durand.

Trust me. The simple command from the email was on a constant loop in her head. But it didn't matter if she did or didn't trust N. The address that had been in the message was in Tampa, and she had no way to get there that wouldn't alert her grandparents. She'd been trying to figure out a solution to her problem for two days. It was only this afternoon she'd thought of Zeke.

Zeke Durand had shown up in town a few months earlier. Normally, Trudy wouldn't have had any interactions with him. They weren't in the same social circle—he went to public school, he lived in the wrong part of town. If her grandmother found out that Trudy even knew his name, she'd be grounded for weeks.

But one day not long after graduation, she'd been out with a few girls whom she tolerated for the sole reason that they were Hollis approved and provided an excuse to leave the mansion. One of them was having a fling with a poor kid from the public high school and had dragged the rest of the group to the beach to meet up with him. Zeke had been there, quiet and brooding and keeping to the far edges of their little circle. People talked about him behind upturned palms as if he couldn't hear the whispers that weren't whispers.

Trudy had mostly ignored the gossip, except for a few details she'd filed away for safekeeping.

"You have a car," she said now, one of those tidbits she'd kept.

"I'm aware," he repeated, his honeyed accent a little different from the lilt to her own words. But it was just as dry, just as slow. New Orleans, if she had to guess.

"Don't be rude," she said, but really she appreciated his saltiness. He'd need it around here. As long as he didn't mouth off to the wrong person.

"Ah, ma'am, I am so sorry, ma'am." He let his voice turn deep Alabama and held his hand over his heart in fake contrition. There was something hard in his eyes that Trudy recognized as a mirror of herself. This was someone with hard edges, who suffered no fools. This was someone who was intimately familiar with how awful life could be. This was someone who carried on anyway.

She shook her head, wanting to rid herself of fanciful thoughts of camaraderie and friendship. Neither had a place here. "So you have a car."

"Ah, you've remembered you need something from me." He didn't look up. "I've seen what you have to offer in return, and, again, I'm not interested."

When she was turned down, it was usually from uppity jackasses who thought she was essentially walking syphilis. But there wasn't that same slow condescension in his voice they used when passing on any unspoken offer.

So the rejection, his just slightly on the wrong side of a polite no-thank-you, didn't hurt coming from Zeke Durand. She didn't really know him, hadn't really spoken to him on the few occasions their groups had collided. But there was something about him, something in him that made the jitters that forever crawled along her skin calm just a bit. It wasn't sexual. There was just a recognition there. One damaged soul to another.

"I'll get you money," she said. She didn't have it yet; that's why she needed him. But it was unlikely he'd notice her careful wording, that he wouldn't just assume things because of who she was.

He glanced up at that, his finger holding a line on the page as if he had actually been reading. She rolled her eyes.

"I'm not selling you my car," he said, but there was curiosity there. It was a victory in and of itself. Curiosity she could work with.

Trudy popped her hip, finally feeling in control of the situation. "I'm not asking you to."

———

The sky had turned a dusty rose by the time Trudy started back to the house. The long summer days had a way of stretching the colors and light so that there were always a few hours that the world lingered in a golden time. Everything was soft and slow and gentle. It reminded Trudy of bare feet on warm grass and cool glass firefly jars in grubby hands.

Innocence.

She tripped over the word but didn't let her thoughts loiter along the syllables. Instead, she focused on the way the air licked at the delicate layer of sweat that coated her lower back despite the lack of fabric there, the way the scent of the lilacs that crawled up a decaying fence coated the inside of her nostrils, the way the sugar from her Coke turned her tongue lethargic and syrupy. Anything to forget how she used to believe there was such a thing as innocence.

Just as she had the thought, a small body crashed into her legs.

"Dee-Dee." Ruby's voice was muffled against Trudy's thighs, but the delight in it was unmistakable. It was as if she hadn't just seen her a few hours ago.

"Baby." Trudy peeled Ruby's fingers from her flesh so that she could kneel in front of the girl. "What are you doing out here?"

Ruby's eyes went wide, and she glanced back down the block. The house was visible, but still much farther away than the distance Ruby was allowed to venture by herself.

"I was on an adventure," Ruby said, her smile going mischievous. Trudy couldn't help but grin in response.

"Oh yeah?" she asked, taking Ruby's hand and tugging her along. It was unlikely Ruby was in any real danger, but she was only five years old. Jesus Christ, Charlotte was a horrible mother. And Trudy knew horrible mothers—it wasn't exactly like Mellie was much better. Or Hollis, for that matter. "Where were you off to, then, little one?"

Ruby giggled, swinging their hands, then leaning her weight into Trudy. "The ocean. Wanted to see the dolphins."

"And their underground palaces?" Trudy asked, knowing the answer.

"Uh-huh." Ruby nodded, letting Trudy's hand drop so she could skip ahead. "And to rescue the prince who's stuck in the tower."

Trudy watched the girl's strawberry curls catch the fading sunlight as she bounced away, still chattering on about the stories Trudy liked to tell before bedtime. They'd cuddle up in Ruby's big bed, surrounded by stuffed animals in the neon glow of the plastic stars glued into pretty constellations on Ruby's ceiling. Trudy would whisper stories of brave princesses rescuing princes in distress, and Ruby would shriek and laugh and gasp at all the right places.

They rounded the side of the house to enter through the kitchen. Less chance of catching questions that way.

Ruby was still talking, as she tended to do with zero need for an attentive audience, when Trudy saw Charlotte. Her aunt was a slim figure curled into one of the chairs on the back porch, a full glass of wine caught between two delicate fingers.

It was her eyes, though, that spooked Trudy. They were empty, staring at some point in the distance, unblinking.

"Go inside, baby." Trudy cupped the back of Ruby's head and nudged her to the door.

"But . . . ," Ruby whined, clearly caught midstory.

"Now."

It was only at the sharp tone that Charlotte looked up. The black of her pupils ate up most of the crystal-clear blue of her irises, and it took a second for her to focus.

"Shit, Charlie." Trudy dropped her voice so that it wouldn't carry. "Are you high?"

Charlotte rubbed the heel of her hand against one eye before bringing the wineglass to her thin lips to gulp at the straw-colored liquid.

"No," she finally answered, the denial almost disappearing into the wind.

Trudy scoffed. "It would be a hell of a lot more believable if you didn't need to drink half a bottle before answering."

She didn't wait for her aunt's response. She didn't even care if there was one coming. It didn't matter. What mattered was Ruby and the way she was dipping her finger into the bowl of icing the cook had left out on the counter as Trudy walked into the kitchen. The thick, pink substance was caught halfway to her mouth, and Ruby's dimples deepened as she realized it was Trudy, and not Mrs. Blake, coming to redden her behind. She plopped the glob in her mouth.

"You started without me," Trudy accused, digging her thumb into the bowl.

"Whose fault is that?" Ruby sassed back in a perfect imitation of Mellie.

Trudy had no shame in resorting to kindergarten tactics, as she was fighting a kindergartner, so she stuck out her tongue, blowing a raspberry at the girl.

Ruby dissolved into giggles and then darted off the stool when they heard footsteps in the hallways. They were both laughing as they crouched behind the laundry so as to avoid the wrath of Mrs. Blake for ruining dessert.

So maybe there was such a thing as innocence. Maybe it was little girls with untied shoes and scrapes on their knees who went on careless adventures on warm summer nights and stole pink icing out of bowls and laughed with their whole bodies.

Maybe Trudy had been that girl once upon a time.

That didn't matter anymore, though. What mattered now was protecting Ruby.

CHAPTER NINE

ALICE

August 2, 2018
Four days after the kidnapping

"What did Charlotte do with the four days? If she *did* kill Ruby." Nakamura's fingers curled around the black-and-yellow bumblebee stress ball. Its happy, smiling face smooshed into something unrecognizable, and Alice had never related more to an inanimate object.

Every minute she kept breathing during this case she counted as a victory. Her very cells felt stretched and contorted to fit some narrow image she had to portray lest she get yanked from the investigation. Shoving her trembling hands in her pockets to hide the telltale signs of wear would last only so long.

"Exactly," Alice said, adjusting her head so she could better watch him from where she was sprawled on the old, musty couch that was more stained than clean fabric. Nakamura perched a couple of feet away on a stack of evidence boxes.

They'd sought refuge in the basement of the station, needing to get away from the ringing phones and the baleful stares. Few others dared venture into the damp space, so Alice often used it as her escape.

Nakamura had asked a few weeks ago where she was always sneaking off to, so she felt she had to tell him about it.

"She was being watched almost continuously," Nakamura said, his eyes fixed on some distant location she doubted he was even seeing.

"We still don't have time of death," Alice said. "Goddamn lazy coroner."

Four days, though. In some ways it almost didn't matter what the coroner reported. There was a gap to be explained to the jury. Would they buy that the girl had been held for that long? Or would a quick death go over better? There was a story to be told. Alice just had to find the right hook.

"So." Nakamura stood up and began pacing. His dress shoes left tracks in the dust on the floor. "Charlotte Burke, what? Takes her daughter to the beach for a spontaneous girls' day."

"We only have two eyewitnesses who even place Ruby there," Alice said. Nakamura's jagged movements were too much for her exhausted brain. Instead, she shifted so her eyes were tracing the cracks in the ceiling once more. "And that was earlier in the day."

"The hot dog vendor guy." Nakamura's voice came from somewhere over her left shoulder. "And that brunette woman."

Witnesses were notoriously unreliable. People thought memory worked like a video recording, something they could play back and pick apart. But it was more like a puzzle with missing sections. Even the suggestion that a little girl had been there could become reality for someone trying desperately to make the pieces fit.

"Do we put it past her to stage the whole thing?" Nakamura asked, and she could tell he had stopped moving. "The witnesses were just susceptible to what we suggested. They couldn't even remember what she'd been wearing."

"I can hardly remember what I was wearing yesterday, let alone a random child whom I barely interacted with," Alice pointed out. There was a spiderweb in one of the corners, its silver strands catching the light at certain angles. A bug had flown into the sticky threads, its wings fluttering uselessly against the trap. It was strange how that worked—how a spider could just lie in wait, knowing the fly would ensnare itself.

"Fair point," Nakamura said. "But what if—"

"What if she'd already hid Ruby's body at some other location, then went to the beach and faked a disappearance? Is that what you're saying?" Alice sat up to find Nakamura watching her. He blinked and looked away, almost guilty. But she knew the feeling of eyes settling on her, judging her. *Emotional. Erratic.*

"I'm not ruling it out," he said, continuing his pacing. He tossed the ball in the air and caught it with the easy grace of an oft-repeated action. Stress was becoming their not-so-friendly companion.

"That seems elaborate," Alice said, tucking her feet beneath her. "And psychotic."

"Or she was desperate," Nakamura countered, his voice low.

Desperation was a powerful force. It was an animal backed into a corner, snapping its frothy jaw at every hand, even the ones that wanted to help. It was a snarling mindlessness that lacked logic.

"Let me get this straight," Alice said, her fingers tangling together. "In this scenario, the killing was an accident. Charlotte then hides the body—"

"Could have just been in her car," Nakamura cut in. "Doesn't necessarily mean it was a separate, planned-out location."

"Shit," Alice said, holding up a hand to stop him. "Let me call Bridget before we go down this route."

Bridget Mullaney was the best crime-scene tech Alice had ever worked with. She was Irish, with all the pale skin and temper and drinking ability that entailed, and most people lived in fear of her. But for some unknown reason, she liked Alice. Since it earned her preferential treatment, Alice didn't question it.

Nakamura rolled his eyes, but mostly because he was jealous that Bridget made him go through proper channels to get his reports.

"'Lo," Bridget answered on the third ring.

"Hey, it's Alice. Have your boys finished with the prelim on the beach?"

Bridget snapped her gum on the other end of the line. "Yup. Whoever it was, was a clean mother-effer."

Alice's lips tipped up. "So there's nothing?"

"There's always something, yeah?" There was some shuffling, and all of a sudden, the background noise was gone. "Sorry, little bastards are so loud."

Anyone meeting Bridget for the first time would think she hated everyone. She mostly did, but she was protective of her crew. When she called someone a bastard, it usually meant she liked them.

"We're going over the cars again now," Bridget said. She must have stepped into her office, and Alice glanced up to the ceiling as if she could see her working through the cement.

"Thought you did a full sweep before," Alice said.

"Did," Bridget confirmed. "Want to find something."

"Your lips to God's ears, yeah?" Alice said, amused when she found herself slipping into Bridget's abrupt speech patterns. "So you have no presents for me?"

"No goodies for now," Bridget said. Her voice turned stubborn. "We'll find something."

"Know you will," Alice soothed. "Let me know when you do?"

"Course," Bridget said and then hung up.

Nakamura was watching her, eyebrows raised. "Let me guess. She was delightful, as always."

"I don't know why you aren't nicer to her," Alice said, slipping the phone back in her jeans. "You wouldn't have to rely on me to get you all your info."

"Why would I put myself through the pain when you two have that charming rapport?" Nakamura said. "She's working on the cars?"

Alice wrinkled her nose. "Yeah. I don't think she'll find anything, though. She doesn't, either."

"She said that?"

"Of course not." Alice shot him a look. "Nothing from the beach, either. Maybe the coroner will have something for us."

"You mean the goddamn lazy coroner?" Nakamura asked, deadpan.

"I'll call him by his name when he starts doing work." Alice shrugged. "All right, so Charlotte kills her daughter, puts her in the trunk of some secret car, drives to St. Pete Beach, a place she's not known to frequent. Spends an hour there, grabs a hot dog, apologizes to the brunette lady for the errant Frisbee—which she's, what? Tossing to herself?—then alerts the Coast Guard that her daughter's gone missing."

There was a beat of silence. "I've seen stranger things," Nakamura said slowly.

"So then, with her daughter still in the trunk, she waits around for hours, goes through questioning with the police, is generally distraught."

"Some people can act their ass off, Garner. You know that."

"Point to you. Then, she gets a ride home with an officer and has near-constant supervision from then on until this morning."

"How'd they get to the beach?"

"She said she took a taxi."

Nakamura was watching her. "Which makes no sense. It's unnecessarily expensive, when they have cars they could have used."

"God, who the hell cares?" Alice surged to her feet, her pulse racing for no logical reason. "Maybe she took a bus instead and forgot."

"Charlotte Burke on a bus?" Nakamura prodded, gentle enough to annoy her.

"Christ, come on." Alice started pacing. "You know it doesn't . . ."

"It doesn't what?" Nakamura asked when she trailed off.

"Fit."

Alice sank back down to the couch, her head in her hands. She pressed the heels of her palms into her eyes. The headache that had started as a low thrum had worked its way up to miniature elves Riverdancing on her frontal lobe. "It doesn't make sense."

"Because things like this so often make sense?" Nakamura countered. Despite the sarcastic lilt to the words, there was something softer beneath them. An understanding that maybe she didn't deserve.

She couldn't deny his words, either.

When had anything made sense? Lila's murder hadn't made sense. That had been random, all the wrong moments in time aligning. The weak sentence for her killer that stopped far short of what was fair hadn't made sense. Sometimes even Lila hadn't made sense.

Lila, her wild girl who had no fear, who was always chasing adventures in a world that should have been scary. Lila, who cried over shoelaces that weren't tied right but giggled as she balanced atop monkey bars and laughed at an ocean that shouted back with rogue waves that could so easily sweep a little girl away. *"You'll be the death of me,"* Alice had whispered time and again into soft baby hair as Lila's body wiggled against her tight grip.

No, Lila hadn't made sense, but, paradoxically, in the way all things with children were, Alice also thought she may have been the only thing in the world that had.

Alice blinked back to the present. Her throat was dry, so she didn't say anything, just sat and watched Nakamura pace.

They were both in their natural environments of guarded thoughts and contemplation they kept tucked behind pressed lips. And the silence beat in time with the pulse beneath her wrist.

"What *does* make sense?" Nakamura finally asked.

Alice shook her head. "I can't see it yet."

"There was no ransom note," Nakamura reminded her.

"That means it wasn't financially motivated," Alice said. There were clichés and predictable behaviors that cops relied on. But that didn't mean they were the truth. "Nothing more."

"It means it was probably one of the family members, and you know it. You're too good of a cop to ignore this shit, Garner," Nakamura said. It was a rare show of agitation.

She stood up so she wasn't at a disadvantage. Feeling small and weak and vulnerable tended to make her lash out.

"Do you know my daughter was found covered in a sheet?" Alice said. The words were knives to her throat, their serrated edges slicing the pink tissue there until it bled down her esophagus into her belly. "Do you know what that means? In copspeak?"

Nakamura was frozen on the spot, the bumblebee stress ball forgotten and dangling from the fingers of one hand.

"It means that whoever killed the victim felt guilt and remorse for their actions," Alice said. "And that they wanted to treat the body with respect."

They stared at each other. They both knew this.

"Which means a family member or loved one," Alice continued when Nakamura didn't fill in the blanks. "Which meant me."

"You were the exception," Nakamura said, almost without voice. She still heard him.

"Was I?"

What she was accomplishing, she didn't know. And it was time to end the confrontation.

She shook her head, the curtain of short, choppy hair falling into her eyes. "I've got to go. Cover for me?"

"Cover for you to who? Me?" Nakamura tried to joke. It fell flat on the floor between them. "Go."

For the second time that day, she walked out of the room.

"You're doing all the wrong things," Alice said as she closed the distance between herself and the woman standing at the edge of the ocean.

Charlotte Burke didn't look at her, didn't even startle. She just kept her eyes on the gentle waves as they crested into white foam and then died along the shoreline. "Isn't it funny, that?"

Alice's heels sank into the damp sand as she rocked back. She'd been raw from the back-and-forth with Nakamura and had been seeking escape when the text came in.

At the beach, it had said. An invite, an escape, a mistake.

Now they were shoulder to shoulder but not touching. "What's funny?"

"How we're always doing the wrong things," Charlotte breathed out. The wind had died completely, and the woman's long, messy locks hung around her face, shielding it. "Nothing we do is ever right."

"Who is 'we'?" Alice asked, not sure she wanted the answer. It hurt to look at her, this woman who was balanced on some precarious, unknown ledge. Alice swallowed the saliva that gathered in the back of her mouth, the way it did just before she had to throw up.

Charlotte finally looked over, a small smile at the corners of her lips, her eyes sad and clear. "Mothers."

Alice closed her eyes against the truth of it.

The judgment—the cuts—happened with a frequency that was almost not even worth noting.

"She wouldn't do this if you didn't feed her goldfish."

It was some random passerby, a woman with her own toddler who was watching Lila with wide eyes. Alice's daughter was sprawled, legs akimbo, in the middle of the grocery store, her face pinched and red and covered in crocodile tears. The words she howled from deep in her belly could barely be called words, more just absolute discontent made into sound. Sound that reverberated against the low ceilings. Damn the bad acoustics.

The woman who had stopped was preening. Her child might be sucking his thumb, but at least he wasn't on the floor screaming.

It was more than just one incident. It was a lifetime of them that clung like burrs, just waiting to cut into sensitive skin.

The barbs had become especially sharp after Ricky had left. Before, the jabs had been subtler and had often revolved around her decision to not let her husband be the primary breadwinner so she could stay home with Lila. After Ricky had taken off to wherever less than a year after Lila's birth, the insults had turned cruel. The ladies who sent their children to the same preschool as Lila couched their criticisms in gentle concern, well aware they didn't have a leg to stand on when it came to leaving their children with strangers. But there was plenty else to correct. What Lila ate. How she behaved. How Alice punished her. The scrutiny was constant, and that was from women she knew.

Out in the real world, the one full of grandmother wannabes and veteran know-it-alls and well-meaning newbies with just one month more experience that lent credence to their slight arrogance, it was far worse.

The ways Alice had ruined Lila's future had been endless. If only they'd known there would be no future to ruin, maybe they would have left Alice in peace. To enjoy the years she'd had.

There was no peace. There never would be.

"Why did you take your eyes off her?"

"Why were you distracted?"

Even after all the questions, even after she'd been cleared of any suspicion, even if they didn't know there was a time she had been blamed for killing her child, there was a shadow that appeared behind their eyes. One that blamed and judged and wondered.

"Why couldn't you keep her safe?"

The sun was suddenly too hot on her upturned face, the air too thin for her greedy lungs. Her pelvis throbbed, like a missing limb. She fought with everything inside herself to remain upright, not to crouch into the fetal position and rock at the feet of this woman who'd just lost her only daughter. The woman who was watching her.

"So what am I doing wrong now?" Charlotte asked, gathering her hair into a bun at the top of her head.

Alice glanced past her, down the strip of beach that had been so ominous and deserted that morning. Where they stood now, on the public part, they couldn't even see the turquoise house that had been the most tragic of landmarks.

"Returning to the scene of the crime," Alice said, knowing she shouldn't. Knowing that even talking to Charlotte here, with Alice's careful defenses scattered around her in pieces, wasn't the best course of action. "It doesn't exactly scream innocence."

Charlotte's eyes slid over the lines and contours of Alice's face, searching. She relaxed at what she must have seen there, turning back to the water that stretched out before them. There was nothing to break the horizon, so the ocean simply became the sky, which dipped right back into the ocean so that they blended into their own reality where borders didn't exist.

"I guess it will be our little secret, then, won't it?"

CHAPTER TEN

CHARLOTTE

July 24, 2018
Five days before the kidnapping

"This is you, right?" The cab driver shifted in his seat, throwing her a glance in the rearview mirror. Charlotte wondered what he saw. A woman paralyzed, unable to move? A woman having an affair, a secret made obvious by the enormous sunglasses that hid most of her face and the bright red lipstick Charlotte Burke would never be caught wearing? A woman on the edge of a breakdown?

Maybe he didn't think anything. Maybe the world didn't revolve around her. Maybe he just wanted her to get out of his cab so he could go on to his next fare and then the one after that and the one after that until he was done for the night and the woman who couldn't bring herself to climb out of his car was long forgotten.

"Sorry," she murmured, slipping him a twenty. It was precious, that tip, but maybe it would make him think kindlier of her. It was unclear why she cared.

After a final bracing breath, she pushed the door open and stepped onto the hot black pavement. The slight burn of it seeped in through the thin soles of her flats, but she didn't hurry to cross the parking lot.

She stopped on the sidewalk and pulled a scrap of paper from the pocket of her linen pants, as if it wouldn't confirm that she was exactly where she thought she was. The bold scrawl of her own handwriting forced her to admit the truth. This was what it had come to.

A horn cut through her hesitation, and, jolting, she clutched at her purse before starting toward the row of storefronts that were slotted next to each other in the low-rent strip mall.

The psychologist's office had an inexpensive "Open" sign hung in the window. Like a car-service place or a pet store would have.

If she wasn't desperate, she wouldn't have even forced herself out of the cab. But the memory of that moment in the church prodded at her. She thought about it too much, wanting to sink back into that floating place. It terrified her to think that Hollis might be right. That she might be losing her mind.

As Charlotte Burke, she had few ways to get an answer to that question. Any doctor who worked with her family would inevitably report back to Hollis as if privacy ethics didn't exist. So that left her with cheap shrinks in strip malls or staring at her own ceiling, wondering when the day would come when she'd completely shatter.

She pushed through the door.

A cold blast from the overworked window-unit air conditioner hit her, and a little bell tinkled overhead as she stepped inside.

The woman at the desk looked up from her gossip magazine. Charlotte guessed she was in her fifties, though the crocodile skin aged her into the next decade. She topped off her tan with bright orange hair, styled into a bouffant more commonly found in the 1950s. Then she jumped a few decades in style with a skintight leopard-print leotard she wore under whitewashed jeans.

As she took the purple lollipop out of her mouth, she looked Charlotte up and down with the same confused appraisal. "Can I help ya, hon?"

Charlotte licked her dry lips, wishing she had water to soothe her sore throat. "I made, um, an appointment. Smith. Rose Smith." She was proud of herself for not tripping over the name.

The receptionist's eyes narrowed, but then without pressing Charlotte further, she flipped through the appointment book, one long bright pink nail dragging over the paper. Clicking her tongue, she looked up. "There you are, hon." She took in Charlotte's purse, her shoes, her blouse, before her gaze snapped back to Charlotte's face. "No insurance, then?"

"No, I'll pay in cash." It was painful, but necessary. She'd learned long ago how to squirrel away money here and there, but it never added up to much. It was never enough. A threadbare safety net that would never actually hold her weight.

They had family credit cards, but those were monitored by Hollis. All expenses were to go on them, and there had to be a good explanation if the girls withdrew cash from the debit accounts they had. Not that Hollis kept any more in there than could cover a nice lunch.

Carrying five one-hundred-dollar bills turned her hands shaky.

"Hmmkay." The receptionist handed over a blue plastic clipboard. "Fill this out, and I'll let you know when Dr. Harrison is ready for ya."

The psychologist's waiting room was empty save for a middle-aged man dressed in a long trench coat, despite the heat. Charlotte took the farthest seat from him, right next to the old-fashioned popcorn machine that was churning out those pieces of yellow fluff that tasted like stale cardboard.

The forms were daunting. Medical history. Social Security number. Address. She wrote nonsense answers, and the ink blurred beneath her eyes. It was strange how easy it was to become someone else, if even just on a meaningless sheet of paper.

She signed her fake name, and the pen left a heavy splotch where it rested on the last letter. Staring at it, she felt for her pulse and knew it was too fast.

The receptionist slid a cursory glance at the forms, then asked for payment up front. Since Charlotte was using cash and all. Charlotte reluctantly parted with two of her one-hundred-dollar bills.

"Won't be long," the woman said, sorting the cash into a drawer beneath the counter, then slipping the lollipop back in her mouth.

Charlotte sat.

She supposed the room was meant to be soothing. There was even a large fish tank that spanned the length of one of the walls, gentle bubbles the only thing disturbing its peaceful waters. A muted TV in the corner was turned to a nature documentary, and the notes from a flute were piped in over some sound system.

But the lights were too bright, and the music was grating. And a single, solitary goldfish bumped against the rim of the tank in time with the mild current, no longer alive to swim against the pull of it.

Charlotte turned her attention to a loose thread on her slacks, her fingers plucking at it. The fabric gave beneath her insistent ministrations until the thread was hanging to the side, down along her thigh. It wasn't free like she'd hoped but caught in the firm grasp of the rest of the stitching.

A giggle caught in her throat. She had to be losing her mind. Did people who were losing their minds realize it, though?

"Ms. Smith."

The name didn't register at first, but by the time the small man standing in the doorway called her again, she recognized it.

She stood up, her fingers tight around the leather straps of her purse. "Yes," she said simply.

The psychologist smiled and held out a hand. "Dr. Harry Harrison."

She'd found his name in the yellow pages, as obsolete as those were these days. It hadn't been just a listing, either. There'd been a tacky ad next to it, with a cartoon version of his face. The more garish the better, was her reasoning for writing down the address. The less likely that someone she knew would see her there.

"Pleasure," she said, sliding her hands beneath her armpits so as not to have to shake his. He dropped his arm, without any hesitation, and stepped back to let her into the darkened space.

"Ah, you're the first one today not to say anything about my name," Dr. Harrison said, easy and light as he followed her in. He settled into a deep leather chair she hated on sight, then gestured for her to sit on the rose-patterned couch opposite him. "I usually get the whole 'What were your parents thinking?' shtick." He laughed, a high-pitched wheeze that she imagined he thought was congenial. It reminded Charlotte of broken glass.

Everything about him was just slightly off. Bent in a way that made it feel like there were bedbugs crawling along her skin when she looked at him.

It was nothing in particular. He was short but well dressed. He'd discarded his jacket, so he was just in shirtsleeves, but the fabric was clean and wrinkle-free.

The dimensions of his face were wrong, though. His eyes were too small, too beady, and his lips too plump. If he had a chin, it wasn't noticeable where it faded into neck skin that was wrinkled and speckled with errant scruff. His nose, a bulbous, protruding thing, made up for the shyness of any of his other features.

"Asking what parents were thinking in any regard is usually not a wise course of action," Charlotte finally said. *This* had not been a wise course of action.

"Touché, Ms. Smith." Dr. Harrison smiled with all his teeth.

"Rose, please," she corrected, fiddling with the sunglasses she now held in her hands, wishing she could slip them on, wishing she had at least that to hide behind.

He paused. "Rose, then. So what brings you in here today?"

There was a small journal perched on his tweed-covered thigh, and his pen poised over the pages. His features, his just-wrong features, had arranged themselves into something that was supposed to pass as interested concern.

"How do you know?" The question tumbled from her mouth before she realized it was formed. But once it was out, there was no use pulling it back, no use swallowing it down and redirecting. This was why she was here. This was why she was sitting too close to a man who smelled of beets and heavy cologne.

"How do you know what, Rose?" the doctor prompted.

"If you're crazy."

Tap. The pen against paper. Tap. Tap. It was a beat that was not quite right. Like Ruby's shoe against the wooden pew. Tap. It didn't match Charlotte's pulse.

"Well," Dr. Harrison said, sliding his tongue around the word until it was too long. "Why do you think you're going crazy, Rose?"

Tap. Tap. Tap.

"No," she said, stretching her neck so the taut muscles there could get some relief. "That's not what I'm asking. Don't turn this around on me."

"I need to know what's happening, though, Rose."

He kept saying her name. Every time he spoke. Like he was soothing a wild animal.

"I wasn't there." Her fingernails dug into her thighs, through the protection of her trousers. "I mean I was and I wasn't."

Tap. Tap. "It felt like an out-of-body experience?"

Ruby's shoe against the wooden pew. The church. Hollis's fingers on her chin. The hot accusations in her ear. "Yes."

"Have you been having any increased levels of anxiety?" he asked. "Depression or thoughts of suicide?"

"Yes," she whispered. "Yes."

Tap, tap, tap. He cleared his throat. "Well."

"You've said that," Charlotte snapped. Then she reached out, in a quick, smooth movement, and snatched the pen. She threw it, and it hit the wall before dropping to the carpet with a small, unsatisfying sound. "Am I crazy? Please. Please."

She was begging. Because she was weak. Like Hollis said she was.

"There's no answer to that, Rose." The doctor hadn't even blinked at the outburst, just folded his hands above the journal. "It sounds like you had a dissociative episode. Though let me reiterate, that does not make you crazy."

She twisted her fingers together, trying to make sense of what he'd just said. "What does that mean?"

"Well—" he started, but then cut himself off. His lips twisted and then straightened out again. "A dissociative disorder involves an involuntary escape from reality, characterized by a disconnection between thoughts, identity, consciousness, and memory."

He was watching her, watching the way the muscles in her face ticked as she took in the information. "Okay."

"It's usually brought on—" He stopped. Took a breath. "It's usually brought on by a traumatic experience. Or abuse."

He leaned forward when he said it, his forearms braced against thick legs. She skittered back, drawing her thighs up to her chest. He wasn't touching her, but he felt too close anyway. And he was still watching her with that same focus, his gaze sliding over her face.

"Does it happen often, Rose?" The question was soft, begging for confessions. But his eyes were sharp and glittering, assessing.

"Could I hurt someone?" Charlotte asked instead of answering. This was why she was here. "During one of those periods. Could I hurt someone?"

Dr. Harrison blinked, reeling back a bit as if he were surprised. "No one needs to get hurt, Rose."

"That's not what I asked."

He tipped his head. He hadn't looked away once. "Are you worried about hurting someone?"

Everything was tight, and it was hard to breathe. Tap. Tap. The echo of the pen was still there, beating in her chest, in her mind. She rubbed the heels of her hands over her eyes, pressing until stars popped behind the lids. "Just. Christ . . . ," she said on a sob. "Just answer the goddamn question."

The office was quiet, so quiet. There was no pen, no foot against a wooden pew. No racing heartbeat. Just silence.

And then a quiet intake of air. A rustle as he shifted closer. "It's possible, yes."

She scrambled to her feet, no longer in control of her limbs, but knowing she needed to get out. To leave.

"I have to go." There was a frantic pounding in her chest. It wouldn't ease until she was away from this, away from those eyes and these questions and these truths that she'd known all along.

"Why don't I get you some water instead?" Dr. Harrison said, his hands held out in front of him. "Then we can talk about what happened."

"Nothing happened," she said. Desperation was a wild thing, clawing at her throat. She spun toward the door, her heel catching on the carpet, throwing her off-balance.

"Wait," he called to her back.

A mistake. This had been a mistake. Useless fingers fumbled against the metal of the handle, as he loomed behind her. Logic told her that he wasn't dangerous, but she couldn't reason with the intense urge to flee.

"Rose," he said. And then: "Ms. Burke."

She stopped, and the world tilted, then righted itself. As it did, she finally closed her hand around the doorknob. After wrenching the door open, she staggered into the waiting room.

Charlotte was at the swinging door when she heard the receptionist click her tongue.

"I can always spot the runners. What did I tell ya, Harry?"

The unbearable heat was a slap to the face as she tumbled out onto the sidewalk. She gulped in air, even though it was heavy with water and did little to calm the panic.

Stumbling back against the brick wall behind her, she then scanned the parking lot while keeping the door to the doctor's office in her peripheral vision. It didn't burst open, but lingering any longer would be foolish.

She walked—she didn't run because that would draw attention—away from the office, down the sidewalk past the Chinese restaurant and discount shoe emporium.

There was a coffee shop at the end of the row of stores. That was her safety. She just needed to keep it together until then.

The teenager manning the cash register greeted her, but Charlotte didn't hesitate as she headed toward the back. She cut off a middle-aged man on his way toward the bathroom, squeezing into the small space between his body and the hallway wall, and stepped inside before he'd realized what had happened.

Flipping the lock, she grabbed a handful of paper towels from the dispenser by the door. Then she crossed the room to the sink, where she tossed them into the cool basin. She ran the water, letting the stack soak until it was a step away from disintegrating into pulp.

Using the sopping mess, she scrubbed at the heavy makeup, which she had so foolishly thought was an adequate disguise, until her skin was raw and pink.

Only when there was nothing but abraded skin left did she drop the towels into the trash can.

Leaning her hands against the porcelain, she met her own gaze.

Could I hurt someone?

Her legs gave out, and she crumpled to the floor, where she curled into herself, her thighs pressed to her chest, her cheek against her knees.

The knocking when it came was jarring at first, but she found it easy to ignore.

CHAPTER ELEVEN

ALICE

August 2, 2018
Four days after the kidnapping

The parking lot for the bar was overflowing even at the late hour. Journalists had been flocking into town since Ruby had gone missing, and Alice expected even more, now that her body had been found.

The thing about reporters was that they easily got bored of being sober. Especially when there wasn't much movement on a case. The bar was the perfect hunting ground for what she needed.

Alice swung through the door of the dive, her eyes scanning as she went. Always in cop mode, Ricky used to say. Accuse, really.

There was only one table left, a misfit among overflowing booths that were laden with pints and pub food. She ignored it and instead grabbed one of the few remaining stools at the end of the long, scarred bar. It was next to an older gentleman whose beard dipped into his shot glass, as his hungry eyes caressed the bottles of tequila, rum, gin, and whiskey behind the guy working the taps.

"What are you having, love?" The bartender didn't even look up when he asked.

"Ginger ale," Alice said, and his brows shot up as he passed off a cocktail to the waitress whose wrinkles stood out in sharp relief from the strain on her face. A few profanities followed the woman as she dodged sloppy drunks and asshole reporters on her way toward the back corner.

"On the house." The cool glass slid to a stop just where her fingertips rested against wood.

She smiled. "Impressive."

He smirked back, running a hand through his shoulder-length black hair. There was something light and mischievous in his eyes that promised fun with no strings attached. Once upon a time, she would have found it appealing. In another life.

She shook her head, he shrugged, and life went on.

It didn't take long to get what she wanted. Only a few minutes after she'd sat down, she felt the lightest brush of fingers against the small of her back.

"What's a girl like you doing in a place like this?" Ben Wilson's voice was pitched low and sleazy, his breath hot in her ear.

Bingo.

She shifted so that he was forced to step away or absorb a sharp elbow to the stomach.

"More like, what's a boy like you doing in a nice establishment like this?" she asked, leaning her forearms back against the bar to look at him. She hadn't been aiming for Ben in particular, but he would do.

They went back a ways. She'd met the reporter in DC when he was writing trash-fire stories for tabloids that favored pun-heavy headlines. It hadn't taken her long to realize, though, that beneath the requisite scum in his articles, there was good information. She'd made friends with him.

When he shifted to the *Washington Post*, they'd stayed in touch. It was the kind of symbiotic relationship that was hallmark in DC, and she didn't mind because it had helped her out on a case or two. All it had cost was a little bit of insider information every once in a while.

"Ah, don't wound me like that, Alice." He grinned at her, that golden-boy grin, as he slid his lanky body into the space between her and the pickup station. He already had a tumbler of some amber liquid in his hands, but he held it up toward the bartender and took the last swallow. It was refilled with quick competency.

"Detective Garner," she corrected absently, even though she knew the tone would piss him off.

"Yeah, well, I don't call women whom I've slept with by their last names," he countered.

"Such a gentleman . . ." She waved a hand, unimpressed.

"Well, as fun as this has been," Ben said, shifting as if he was going to leave. He wouldn't. She was the lead detective on the case he was here for. But there were those games to play.

"You're not leaving before the main event, are you?"

"When you ask so prettily? Never," he said, amusement crinkling in the lines around his eyes. "So what do you want from me, Alice?"

"Who says I want anything."

"Oh, come on now." Ben nudged at her arm. "As fun as it is, you didn't come here just to banter, darling. And you certainly didn't come for the drinks."

They both glanced at her half-empty glass.

"Unless you're waiting for someone else," he said, looking around. He lowered his voice into a conspiratorial whisper. "Should I make myself scarce?"

She considered it. But Ben was as good as the next guy. Better, even. Off the record with him meant off the record. And there was something to be said about the devil you know. Plus, he was here, and reeling in another reporter all of a sudden seemed draining.

"What's the word on the street?" she finally asked.

Tipping his head, he studied her. Trying to read her as she read him. The games were so tiring. But it was a decision he'd have to make to tell her, one he'd weigh before revealing any of his cards.

"General consensus?"

"Yeah."

He shrugged, his body relaxed and open, surveying the room. "It's the mother."

Just what she'd expected. "What do *you* think?"

The last time she'd seen him had been two weeks after Lila had died. It had been at a bar just like this one. Dives were like that, the same anywhere in the world.

"They caught him," she slurred. She'd lost track of the amount of liquor in her system after she'd finished off the handle she stored in her fridge. The woman behind the bar was keeping an eye on her, which meant she'd had more than a few here as well.

"That's a good thing, yeah?" Ben clinked his glass against the rim of hers. Like a cheer.

"Is it?"

He sipped the whiskey, his eyes sharp. "Why wouldn't it be?"

Lifting a heavy shoulder, she signaled for another refill. The woman watched Alice's face, but she poured anyway. Everyone was watching her face. "Can't kill him if he's in jail, can I?"

"All right," Ben drawled, grabbing the glass from her hand. "That's enough for you, I think."

Ben had been there during her darkest days. He knew why she was asking about the mother.

"I'm here, aren't I?" he said, an odd response to her question.

Then it clicked. Ruby's disappearance had caught the attention of the national media. Pretty white girl kidnapped during a beach day with her pretty, rich mother. It was a compelling story. But the *Post* wouldn't have sent Ben to cover it. Not if that's all they thought there was to it.

"Why are you in St. Pete?" she asked, and maybe that was actually the right question.

He didn't say anything at first, then glanced around. They were being watched from the corners of eyes and talked about behind shifted hands. The media world was a small one, and they'd all been living in each other's pockets for the past four days. People knew who Ben was, and they certainly knew who she was.

"Not here," he said, and then dropped money onto the bar before sliding from the stool. He walked toward the door without waiting to see if she was following.

Ben looked over his shoulder as he slipped into the dark alley running alongside the bar. It was lit by a single bare bulb casting a soft glow against exposed brick. Otherwise, it was dark, the shadows winning the war with the light.

They stopped close enough to the dumpsters so they'd have a few seconds of muffled privacy if someone looking for a smoke or looking for them stumbled out the exit door. The pavement was damp from whatever was leaking from the bottom of the bins, and she was careful to breathe through her mouth.

Ben wasn't the type to be pushed. There was a certain melodrama to these meetings that he enjoyed, and if she rushed him, she ran the risk of getting nothing. So she waited, arms loose by her sides.

"I have a buddy on the sports desk at the paper down here," he finally said. She couldn't see his eyes. She wanted to be able to see his eyes. "He's been here for . . . I don't know . . . twenty years. One of those."

A lifer.

"There's been some rumblings," he continued. "Nothing concrete, just talk."

Just talk. She'd learned that "just talk" was usually more than just nothing.

"About?"

"There's a kid who's been hanging around the family for the past month or so," he said, scratching at his nose.

"What?" she snapped out, then dug her fingernail into the soft flesh of her palm in penance for the show of emotion.

Those sharp eyes were watching her, and she forced her shoulders to relax.

"I mean, what are you talking about?" Her voice was calm again.

"Seems like it's been a bit under the radar," Ben said slowly, as if he were reconsidering his decision to tell her. "Zeke Durand. He's friends with the girl. Trudy Burke."

She shook her head, her eyes slipping to the pavement. It wasn't possible. They'd pored over lists, studied family trees, interrogated every Burke for details of their friends and acquaintances.

Not once had a Zeke Durand come up.

Ben stepped closer when she looked up again. "Apparently she's been spotted hanging out with him a few times. Wouldn't even be anything to notice except she's a Burke in St. Petersburg, and he's . . ."

Ben paused, and she dug the fingernail in deeper, wanting to draw blood.

"He's what?"

He pressed his lips together and then sighed. "Black."

"Oh shit." She scrubbed her hands over her face. It was one thing to have a missing girl on her hands. It was another if race became involved. A pretty little white girl and a suspicious black man? The facts were tinder poised to explode into a bonfire at the least provocation. And she would have just as much success containing that type of inferno as she would containing the story if the media caught hold of it. The facts didn't matter. They never did. It was all about the narrative. "That's why you're here."

"Yup," he said, leaning heavy on the *p*. "This could turn into a circus. No matter if he did it or not."

"It's going to be a witch hunt if this gets out."

"Just here to document it, darling." Ben shrugged. "You get the honors of trying to control it."

It was a wet dream for any producer who wanted the next made-for-TV-movie script.

"The black kid killing the little white girl, or the mother gone crazy," Ben continued, a hard edge to his voice. Chasing a twenty-four-hour news cycle had made him a cynic. That was, if he hadn't been one before. "She did have a wild look in her eye at the press conferences."

"She just lost her kid, asshole," Alice said, but her mind had already moved past the conversation. Why hadn't they known about Zeke Durand?

Trudy. Trudy Burke.

Alice called up an image of the teenager.

The girl was pretty in the way of her grandmother and mother. Where Charlotte and Ruby were red tinted, the other women of the Burke family were frosty blonde. Trudy was a willow reed like her aunt, and Alice guessed she hated it. She'd never spill out of dresses the way her mother did.

Alice didn't have a strong impression of her otherwise. She tended to fade into the background whenever the family was gathered, easily overpowered by the other women. Often, she was sent from the room when the discussion turned too serious.

But there was a constant whenever she was mentioned: Trudy had adored Ruby. It was to the point that the relationship had created tension between her and Charlotte.

"Are you going to run with this?" she asked Ben.

He considered, then lifted one shoulder carelessly. "Nothing to run with yet."

"But when there is?"

"I'm not losing my scoop," he said.

Alice chewed on her lip. It was fair. "Just . . . let me know?"

"Yeah."

She was surprised by his easy acquiescence until he continued.

"But, Alice? I'm not going to be the only one giving head here."

Rolling her eyes, she shoved at him, dissolving some of the tension between them. "Why must you be so vulgar?"

He smirked. "Because you like it."

"Asshole."

"Seriously, Detective." Ben sobered. "I'm not telling you this just because you asked so nicely."

In those games they were playing, reciprocity was the biggest rule. "I know less than nothing."

"When you do?"

She shrugged. He was a smug bastard who needed a slap every once in a while.

"Apparently, your mama didn't teach you about not giving the milk away for free, dear Benjamin."

CHAPTER TWELVE

TRUDY

July 7, 2018
Twenty-two days before the kidnapping

"I wouldn't have pictured you as a Willie fan," Trudy said propping her feet on the dash of Zeke's car.

It was a pristine white Honda that didn't seem to fit him any more than the music pouring from the speakers. She'd pictured him with an old 1970s muscle car, maybe one that he'd lovingly worked on until it purred just like when it was brand-new. But he'd pulled up in the generic four-door sedan looking far too modern and not nearly mysterious enough.

Zeke Durand was like an idea that drifted through her consciousness but never really materialized. Dangerous and beautiful and enigmatic. Not from St. Petersburg.

This person who drove a Civic and sang along, off-key, to "Red Headed Stranger" was anything but a fantasy.

The sun was coming up, and the sky was losing that deep cobalt color she loved. An old boyfriend had once tried to capture it with a cheap pair of earrings, and they'd turned her lobes green.

The way the rays caressed Zeke's face created shadows beneath his high cheekbones and turned him back into a riddle she would never solve. She liked it better that way.

They'd kept the windows rolled down because it was early, and the coolness from the morning still lingered in the air. The black leather seats stuck to her thighs a bit, but it wasn't unbearable yet.

The filmy skirt she'd worn pooled around her hips, exposing the long length of her thigh, but Zeke had spared it only the briefest glance before returning his eyes to the road. So she didn't bother adjusting it, just tilted her seat back, easing into a half-asleep haze as they crossed the bridge heading into Tampa.

"You never told me why you needed to go into the city," Zeke said as Willie's twang melted into a beat of silence before the next song.

As if they were sharing confidences. She didn't answer him; he couldn't have expected her to.

Trust me. N.

If she told Zeke she was going to check out an address an anonymous stranger on the internet had sent her, he wouldn't let her go. Or he'd try to come with her. She couldn't explain even to herself why she was trusting N. Maybe desperation had turned her careless, stupid. But she couldn't risk not taking the chance. Too much was at stake.

She gathered her long, wind-tangled hair into a bun and then shifted so she was facing him entirely. The seat belt cut into her shoulder, so she pushed it behind her.

"Come on," she poked. "Why'd you move to St. Petersburg? There had to be better places."

"Less racist, less bigoted places, you mean?"

"Uh, yeah, that's exactly what I mean, dude."

He puffed out a breath of air, somewhat amused. "I didn't have a choice."

"You always have a choice," she argued, despite knowing how deeply her own feet were buried in the cement that built the city.

He glanced at her as if he knew, too. "It's that easy, huh?" Not really calling her on it. But sort of calling her on it.

She tilted her head so that her temple touched the leather of the seat. "If you feel like you don't have a choice, you're just ignoring the options that you don't want to consider."

"That's naive," he shot back, fire in his voice for the first time since she'd met him. Maybe, maybe, she was finally getting under his skin.

"It's not. Take *me*." She waved a hand down her front. "You'd think I have the life, right? Rich, privileged girl, the world at her feet."

Zeke shrugged in agreement.

"My grandparents track every move I make," she said. "My money, my schedule. Who I talk to. Who I associate with. If it's not the right people, it's corrected immediately. If I don't give in, I'm punished."

There was more she could add but knew she never would. Secrets like those were meant to be kept locked away, deep in the darkness.

"My aunt and my mother are both idiots, so neither of them are any help. Mellie, I get. She's not exactly playing with a full deck. But Charlotte. God, she's just let herself be locked into this life she hates. She likes the velvet handcuffs."

It was something Trudy had never been able to understand. Why Charlotte hadn't just left. Why she hadn't snuck out at night or when Hollis was on a trip—anything. There were so many opportunities, and instead, Charlotte just stayed. A lot of things made Trudy angry, but that had to top the list, because now Ruby was involved.

"I say I'm stuck, but that's not true," she said, her voice stronger now. She wasn't stuck, Charlotte wasn't stuck. "I have other options. I could hitchhike out of town, change my name, get away from them. Maybe I'd need to steal to do it, maybe I'd need to sell myself. Live in a homeless shelter, even. There are plenty of choices if I really wanted to get out. It's just all about the ones you can live with."

And as circumstances changed, those ones that had seemed so impossible before became the only ones that made any sense. She didn't say that, though, but just let the words hang in the silence between them.

"Moving to St. Pete was the only choice I could live with," he finally murmured, easing the tautness that had stretched for far too long. "My mother asked me to."

A small piece of this puzzle that was Zeke Durand snapped into place. It was like she'd just won a prize, and she didn't know why getting the information out of him felt that way. "Why would she do that?"

He breathed in deeply, possibly weighing how much he wanted to tell.

The morning was clear and quiet, and the vaguest hint of friendship snaked between them and tugged at secrets as the highway stretched out before them. It was alluring and dangerous, this desire to let all her hidden truths tumble out to be devoured by a stranger.

Perhaps he felt the same. Perhaps that's why he spoke.

"She's dying."

"Well." That was all Trudy could manage. She licked at her dry lips.

"Yeah," he said, an almost silent exhale.

"The choice you could live with," she said. "Where were you guys before?"

He'd pushed his sunglasses up on top of his head a while back, so when he turned to her, she could see the crinkles around his eyes. "New Orleans."

"Was it better?" She'd never been, and the name alone conjured images of voodoo practitioners and little-girl ghosts who haunted plantations.

"In what way?"

"In the not-being-assholes way."

"There are assholes there, too," he said. "But there are assholes everywhere."

"Ain't that the truth," she said, finally shifting back around so she was sitting normally, her eyes on the shiny skyscrapers that were coming ever closer. Sharing time was over.

———

Zeke dropped off Trudy five blocks away from the address N had sent. It was a quiet little neighborhood a bit of a ways from downtown, so there wasn't anyone else on the sidewalk with her.

Before he'd driven off with a promise to meet her back there in a few hours, Zeke had given her a look like he knew she was about to do something stupid. She'd pulled back her shoulders, bracing for a fight if needed, but he'd simply shaken his head and pulled away from the curb. Maybe he thought he'd never see her again.

Maybe that wasn't an unfounded fear.

Trust me.

Her flip-flops slapped at the ground, loud against the hush that enveloped the street. Earlier she'd looked up how to get to the place, so she moved on autopilot now, her fingers playing with the strap of her purse, adjusting her hair, tugging at her clothes. She was anxious.

But like she'd told herself every five minutes last night, she didn't actually have to do anything once she found the place. She could just keep walking if something seemed weird or off about it.

When the numbers on the houses finally started getting closer to the address she'd long since memorized, she slowed. The one she was looking for was three in from the end of the block, its facade more subdued than its colorful neighbors. If the owners had wanted to blend in, they should have gone with obnoxious colors instead of bland neutrals.

Trudy glanced around for the best place to conceal herself so that she could watch without drawing any attention. There was a small park a little down the way, nothing big, just a triangle of grass for dogs. But there was a bench, and a few palm trees she could duck behind if needed.

Once she sat down, she positioned herself so that she could keep the front door of the house in her periphery without actually staring at it. Then she dug out a cigarette—not to light but to give her nervous energy an outlet. She turned it over in her hand, running her nail along the seam where the smooth paper disappeared into itself.

And she waited.

Two hours later her legs were restless and her back was stiff, but she'd watched three ladies go into the house and not come back out. They'd all been middle-aged and matched the staidness of the place, with their conservative trousers and mom-cut hairstyles.

If this was a den for serial killers, they certainly had good covers.

Still, she wasn't stupid. She stretched, enjoying the slight pull on the muscles in her shoulders and back, then resumed her spot, slouched against the bench.

One more woman approached the house in the next hour. This one was different, though. She was wearing jeans and a coat despite the weather; she was younger, too, and had long brown hair that she'd pulled up into a ponytail.

But it was the way she walked that rang familiar with Trudy. Her shoulders were sloped forward, her arm wrapped around her waist like she was holding herself up. She kept glancing back, tucking her chin to her shoulder so she could see behind her.

The woman didn't even slow at the foot of the stairs to the house. As she passed a narrow driveway a little ways down the block, she twisted and ducked into the shadows the opening provided. The movement was fast, practiced, and unexpected.

Long minutes passed, and the street remained empty. Trudy tried not to watch the spot where the woman had disappeared, in case eyes were watching her from a distance. It was an instinct honed from years of experience.

Just when she was about to give up on the woman, write her off as someone unimportant, someone taking a shortcut to work while Trudy had projected onto her, she came back to the sidewalk.

She was still glancing around, still a bit caved in on herself, but this time her stride was purposeful. She paused at the house, checked something in her hand, then jogged up the steps to the front door. Trudy couldn't see the person who welcomed the woman inside, but the little details she'd been gathering since she'd arrived started to click into place.

Trust me.

It was a safe house.

———

Trudy needed money. She always needed money, an irony of her life that she did not find amusing. But now she needed a lot of it, fast.

The women at the safe house had been exactly what she'd expected once she realized what it was. They were nice, boring ladies who probably all had ridiculous savior and superiority complexes that would annoy the living shit out of Trudy in any other circumstance. But that didn't matter now. What mattered was that they told her they could get her fake IDs, new names, backgrounds that would hold up at least to a little scrutiny.

What they couldn't give her was money. Not much, anyway. Not nearly what she would need. And if she wanted to leave soon, Trudy would have to figure out a way to get her hands on some.

She didn't dare linger in front of the house after she skipped down the stairs. Nor did she go back to the park. Instead, she just started walking, not really knowing where she was headed. She slid her phone out of her purse and opened up the maps app. Her grandmother had access to her password and often checked what she'd been looking at, so Trudy didn't risk googling anything. It took a while, but she finally found what she was looking for.

There was one easy way for a girl who looked like her to get fast cash.

She zoomed in on the name of the little gray building situated in the middle of a long line of fast-food restaurants, tanning salons, and dry cleaners.

Mac's Strip Club.

CHAPTER THIRTEEN

ALICE

August 3, 2018
Five days after the kidnapping

"If it wasn't Charlotte who killed Ruby, then who was it?" Nakamura asked.

That was the question, the one they were missing. Juries didn't want to know who hadn't committed the crime. What they wanted was to be told a story. A good one at that. Facts didn't really matter to them, but narrative did. There needed to be an engaging plot, a hero if possible, and, the most important part, a villain. Someone to blame.

Alice just had to find hers.

It was three in the morning. She'd been left talking to walls in her own apartment, and once they started talking back, she'd realized she needed a change of scenery. Halfway to the station, she'd made a detour to drag Nakamura out of bed, too. A healthy sleep pattern was a foreign concept to her, so she didn't even blink at the hour. But now her partner was slumped in the lone chair in their little makeshift basement office.

His eyelids drooped as he watched her tape pictures to the empty cinder-block walls. "This is getting out of control, Garner."

She pushed her hair back into a low ponytail that was mostly just a stub and wrapped a rubber band around the strands. "You didn't have to come."

Nakamura rolled his head once to each shoulder, stretching his neck. "You realize when I get three calls from you in quick succession I'm not just going to sleep through that."

Alice shrugged. "You didn't have to come."

"So," Nakamura said, switching the subject, "if it's not Charlotte Burke, who killed Ruby?"

Zeke Durand. He was a new player, and she added him to her mental list. The jogger. The owner. The Burkes. Zeke Durand. How long would the list become? How many more did they not know about?

She told Nakamura what she'd heard from Ben, but at three in the morning there was little to do about the new information.

"What if it was a classic kidnapping gone wrong?" she asked. Her hand twitched by her side, and she brought her thumb to her mouth to gnaw at the nail that was already bitten down to the quick. It kept the shaking to a minimum, though. "It wasn't supposed to go down like this."

"I think we'd still have gotten a ransom note," Nakamura said, and when she looked over at him, he was looking at the wall instead of at her. She dropped her palm back to the outside of her thigh. "Even if they'd grabbed her and then she'd died in the process, they would have pretended she was still alive."

"But they would have had no proof of life."

"Do you think the Burkes wouldn't have paid anyway?" Nakamura tipped onto the back legs of the chair. "They wouldn't have taken the chance, even without a guarantee that she was alive."

Alice stepped back away from the wall of suspects, hands on her hips, her gaze bouncing from each picture to the next.

"What if it's not about money?" Alice asked. "What if it's about . . ."

"About . . . ," Nakamura prodded when she paused.

Alice tapped her fingers against the seam of her jeans, considering whether she wanted to put the thought out there, into the world. She took a deep breath, making the decision because she was tired, and it was exhausting holding all her thoughts in check.

"What if it's about revenge?"

Nakamura was silent at that. She turned when it dragged on.

"Could be," he finally said, his eyes shifting away. "Doesn't rule out the family, though."

"No." She returned her attention to the photos, then grabbed a thick black marker from where it rested on top of a stack of evidence boxes. "But if it was revenge from an outsider, it would start with Sterling."

She circled the patriarch's face with her Sharpie.

"Why?"

Alice clicked the cap back on the marker, her gaze locked on the judge's face. "The rest of them"—she waved a hand toward the wall—"they're so controlled they have almost no contact with the outside world."

The iron fist with which Hollis ruled her family was apparent in each interaction Alice and Nakamura had with them. Alice wasn't sure quite how cut off the women were, but when she'd asked for the names of friends and acquaintances, the lists had been almost embarrassingly short.

Neither Charlotte nor Mellie had a job, outside of a few select charitable boards, which had probably been approved by Hollis. Trudy had school but didn't seem to do much beyond what was required. No sports, no extracurriculars.

"Okay, so not the younger women," Nakamura said. "What about Hollis, though? She seems the type to inspire rage."

Alice pressed her lips together, considering. She remembered the governor's wife at that party, flustered and mortified because of Hollis. Humiliation was a powerful force. It was more often than not the primary emotion that spurred on mass violence. Kidnapping and killing a little girl wouldn't be an unbelievable leap.

"I think," Alice started, slow and careful, "Hollis tends to inspire rage in women. She doesn't tend to direct that venom toward men."

Nakamura made a little surprised sound. "You're saying you think our perp isn't a woman, then?"

"I'm saying this doesn't feel like a reaction to some society lady feeling bitter that Hollis stole her venue location for a party," Alice said.

"Your gut instinct is out in force on this case, isn't it?" It sounded like Nakamura was teasing, but there was something underneath the words that set her on edge. Before she could bristle, he moved on and the moment was broken. "So, Sterling."

Sterling. Despite the fact that he hovered over the case like a threatening, dark cloud, they had barely seen him at all.

"The snake himself," she murmured. They'd had to question him, of course, the day Ruby had gone missing, and he'd played the part of concerned grandfather convincingly. That didn't mean anything, though. They were all playing parts.

Nakamura thumbed at his chin. "You have a real problem with him."

Alice shook out her shoulders, the tension there pulling at the delicate tendons of her neck. "I don't trust him."

"That's probably a good call." Nakamura laughed, and the remaining tightness dropped from her back. "But we've scoured his cases and got zip."

That was true. The junior officers they'd assigned to that duty had found little in the search. Despite the well-known fact that his sentencing practices weren't quite fair, anyone who was likely to hold a grudge was still in jail.

There was one man whom the officers had gotten excited about. But it turned out he'd moved to Michigan and had a solid alibi.

"They could have missed something," Alice said, not sure why she was pushing. "A connection that was overlooked because it wasn't obvious."

"Schaffer and Lowe are still searching," Nakamura said. "If they find anything, then we can chase it. But if it's not a blatant link, then we're kind of screwed trying to come in from that angle."

Nakamura slid a hand into his dark hair, then lifted the, by now, lukewarm cup of coffee he was clutching to his lips. He swiveled his jaw after he swallowed.

"Alice." It was coming. The tone, the way her name was weighted, the way it slipped off his tongue like an apology. "What does that gut of yours say?"

"It says, going into an investigation with a preconceived assumption of guilt blinds you to any other options," she said.

Everyone wanted it to be Charlotte.

The facts didn't matter, the narrative did. Alice said it enough to know it to be true. There were gaping holes in the evidence that everyone was just going to ignore because of course the mother did it.

Nakamura scratched at his scruff. "But we're cops, yeah?"

"Thank you for reminding me. I would have forgotten otherwise," Alice shot back.

He squeezed one eye shut. "You seem to have, though."

"Because I refuse to give in to the laziest option possible without considering others?"

It annoyed her that Nakamura was hopping on the bandwagon. It annoyed her that it brought up the ghosts of those whispers that had haunted her before they'd found Lila's killer. It annoyed her that she still let it affect her. Fragile emotions had no place here.

She had to remember that.

"No," he said slowly, not rising to her tone. If they were going to fight, she wanted a brawl. But he kept his same measured, easy voice even as he accused her of being shit at her job. "We're all considering other options."

"Are you?"

"You think we're all steering this investigation to go down a certain road," Nakamura said. "But what you're not seeing is that we're not directing it. We're following the path already there. You just don't like where it's taking us."

"Why are you so sure I don't like where it's taking us?" Alice pressed, wanting him to say the words. Needing him to.

Nakamura tipped his head, studying her face. "Because now you're running the investigation that you couldn't when your daughter was killed."

There was a beat of silence.

"Then why haven't you asked for me to be taken off the case?" Alice asked.

This wasn't the time to be having this argument. They were both exhausted, and it showed in the way they'd lost the carefulness with their words, with each other. Her own had become sloppy, spilling out into the hushed, darkened space in a way they wouldn't have in the bright light of day.

"Who do you think did it, Alice?" Nakamura asked instead of answering the question. She released a breath she hadn't realized she'd been holding.

"I don't know," she said, repeating her assertion from earlier in the day, turning to the wall again.

Nakamura paused, and she could feel his eyes on her back.

"Who do you think did it, Alice?"

"What do you want me to say?" she asked.

"I want you to say what's in your gut."

Everything in her was coiled tight, ready to shatter.

She walked up to the picture she'd circled and tapped the capped marker against it.

"Sterling Burke," she said, throwing it down like the challenge it was.

Nakamura smiled, and the tension that had been holding them both in its ugly claws dissolved into nothingness. "And that's why you're on the case."

———

There was a twenty-four-hour convenience store four blocks away, and by 4:00 a.m. neither Alice nor Nakamura had been able to continue resisting its neon lure. The sludge at the station that passed as coffee wasn't cutting it.

Alice leaned back against the counter, cringing as a spill she hadn't noticed seeped into the fabric of her jeans. Nakamura was busy carefully peeling the tops off his fancy creamers, lining them up next to his cup. She didn't have the patience for all that.

As the caffeine started to clear the fog from her brain, she studied her partner.

"You don't think it's Sterling," she said, keeping her voice low. There were three other people in the store, one of whom was the bored teenage cashier twirling his phone on the counter. The other two were some college kids with bloodshot eyes, giggling over potato chips. None of them were paying any attention to the detectives.

Nakamura shrugged. "No."

"Then why does it matter that I do?" Alice asked.

In a practiced move, he dumped the sweet cream into his black coffee, the pure dark color of it turning milky. She winced at the sacrilege of it all.

"Why do you think it's him?" Nakamura asked instead of answering her question.

Alice knew the kind of man Sterling Burke was—evil, manipulative, power hungry. None of those things made him a killer, though. If Alice based her suspicions on the quality of his character alone, she'd be just as bad as the rest of them desperately snatching at the low-hanging fruit that was Charlotte Burke.

"Process of elimination," she said, following Nakamura as he walked toward the front. They paused as he made a slight detour to the doughnut case, where he plucked out three with pink sprinkles.

"So you think it's someone in the family?" Nakamura asked as he arranged his bounty in the little brown paper bag that he'd grabbed. "Weren't we just talking about revenge?"

"Either way, we should be looking at him more than we are." Alice shrugged off the semantics as they headed toward the front counter. Did it matter if he'd been the one to actually strike the blow? There were other ways he could be responsible for Ruby's death.

"Maybe you're right." Nakamura held up the doughnuts and the coffee to the kid behind the register and then gestured to hers as well.

The boy didn't even look up from his phone as he tapped their orders in. "Five sixty-three."

Nakamura slipped him a ten. They were silent as the kid counted out the change. Nakamura only started talking again once he'd pocketed the bills and they stepped away. "But you know there's a big difference between Sterling killing her and someone doing it because of him."

"Is there?" she asked, sipping at the coffee. *Stupid.* It was a stupid thing to say. Nakamura had already called her a shitty cop at least once tonight.

Emotional. Erratic.

The words were all but branded into her skin. They also came with the implication that she couldn't be rational or logical or be trusted to do her job. There was a thin line between the way Nakamura was watching her now and those memories.

Alice didn't really want to ask the question that was nagging at her. The coffee hadn't hit her system yet, and the case was rubbing her raw in all her most vulnerable spots. But she was never one to hide or cower. "Why is my thinking it's Sterling the thing that's keeping me on the case?"

They pushed through the door, leaving behind the harsh fluorescent buzzing for the cool morning air, and Nakamura smiled back at her. "That's not all there is," he said gently.

Alice fell in step next to him. "But?"

"No one else would dare consider it," Nakamura said as their shoulders bumped.

"That's scary."

"It's reality," he said.

He was wrong, though. People would consider it; they just wouldn't say any of those accusations out loud.

"Oh, come on." Nakamura gulped at his coffee, a desperate man. "It's not like you're exactly fresh off the bus, Garner. You know what it's like."

Alice shook her head. "DC is bad, but not like this," she said. "Everyone there is a power player. You don't go there to live in DC. You go there to own DC."

"See, not so strange."

"But it's an even playing field because *everyone* there has power," Alice corrected, wanting him to understand how messed up this situation was. "Here, though, it's just Sterling Burke. He holds the keys and has no reason to negotiate anything."

He dug in his bag for a doughnut, but she could tell his attention was focused on what she was saying. "He's not the only player in town."

"Oh yeah?" Alice raised her brows. "Because the police chief bows and scrapes to him. The governor is up his ass. From what I hear, he gets lunch with the state speaker every other week. He's the godfather of one of the Supreme Court justices' kids, and literally no one will get us a fucking warrant to search his house even though his granddaughter was murdered. You wanna tell me that's not what's happening here?"

Nakamura sighed, a small sound that disappeared into the lingering darkness. "Well, thank God we have you."

There was a sarcastic bent to the words that she saw reflected in the tilt of Nakamura's lips.

"Oh, screw you," Alice said.

He shook his head. "Honestly, though, I'm glad you're on this case. There are a lot of people in this town who would work very hard to make sure not even a suggestion of suspicion falls on Sterling Burke. If you start yelling about all of this too loudly, you're slapping the target on your own back. Not a lot of people are willing to do that."

"As we've seen," Alice said, frustrated. "I can't tell if you're warning me or encouraging me."

Nakamura grinned at that. "A little of both?"

"Can I ask you a question?" *Will you be honest?* was the subtext underneath.

He seemed to understand. "Yeah."

"Do you not think it was Sterling because you don't think it was Sterling? Or do you not think it was because you don't want to be the one to have to arrest him?"

There was a moment when she thought she might have pissed him off to the point of silent treatment. But then he slid her a look. "You're still on the case, aren't you?"

She could press, but she wouldn't. "What do you think about this Zeke Durand thing?"

Wrinkling his nose, he stared off in the distance as his hand rummaged in his bag for a doughnut. "We should be talking to him."

"Yes," she agreed, quick and easy.

"And it means Trudy Burke withheld information."

Tilting her head up to the sky, she sighed. "Yes."

"Makes you wonder . . ."

She let her chin fall to her shoulder, her eyes on his. "What else aren't they telling us?"

CHAPTER FOURTEEN

CHARLOTTE

July 26, 2018
Three days before the kidnapping

"Can you get me a gun?" Charlotte asked, her voice small in the darkness. Once upon a time, the question would have been ludicrous.

Enrique pushed himself up onto his forearms, his face red-tinged from where it had been pressed into the pillow. "Are you okay?"

If she could answer that, she wouldn't be in this mess.

"Can you?" She'd already shifted her eyes back to the popcorn ceiling of the cheap motel room.

There was some rustling that she didn't pay attention to, and then Enrique coughed. She looked at him. He'd slid from the bed and pulled on his black boxer briefs. He scratched at his six-pack and then dragged his nails down farther, an idle, distracted movement, until they slipped under the elastic waistband. A part of her recognized that he was gorgeous. All smooth skin and tattoos and muscles, dark eyes that promised nights of depravity. His jaw was sharp, his lips lush to the point of feminine. The contrast was appealing.

It wasn't his looks that drew her, though. It was the way he didn't care about the bruise marks he left on her hips in the shapes of his fingers, and the way he dragged his thumbs over her windpipe sometimes. It was the way he didn't treat her like she was a girl made of glass.

"Yeah," he said, slapping his stomach as if he'd just decided on something. "You have to tell me why."

It was a pointless ultimatum, one he wouldn't follow through on if she pushed. But, God, it was tempting. The lure of letting it all spill out.

Enrique had no connection to the Burkes, no connection to her real life. If he knew who she was, he'd never let on. Perhaps it was safe to tell him—not all of it, never all of it. But some.

They'd met six months ago on the waterfront. There was a bench there she liked to call hers. She pretended no one else knew about it, and whenever she went shopping, she'd get a cup of ice cream and take it to her spot.

On that day Enrique had been sitting there, legs spread so that they took up half the bench, arms stretched along the back so that his very presence took up the rest.

An hour later she'd been splurging on a nice hotel room for them. She'd later had to explain the charges by saying she'd been struck with a sudden migraine midday and hadn't been able to do more than crawl into the closest Hilton and book herself a room for a few hours.

Enrique Lopez, it turned out, was a doctor at an underserved clinic on the south side of St. Petersburg. He'd moved to town only a few weeks earlier and had no idea the Burkes were to be treated differently. That hadn't changed in the six months they'd known each other.

He was watching her now, though she knew he didn't expect anything. That was another draw: his pure acceptance of what she had to offer without a demand lurking behind every easy word.

"I think I'm going crazy," she said, the confession lifting the weight that had taken up a permanent residence on her rib cage. The freedom of it made her giddy, became a rush and pop in her blood, which tickled a giggle from her throat.

She arched up, her spine coming off the bed, until she was clutching her knees to her chest. Laughter, uncontainable and light and edging on manic, filled the room until tears ran unchecked down her cheeks.

"Hey, hey." Enrique's voice was tinged with panic as he knelt on the bed. Arms came around her, strong and warm, and she flinched.

"Don't touch me," she gasped out with the little breath that was still in her lungs. He knew the rules. He wasn't supposed to touch her after. The chemicals that flooded her brain during it all helped her forget her terror. But the crash afterward always yanked her back to a reality where the weight of a body was too familiar, too horrifying. The memories that came with *it* would send her to her knees, swallowing against bile.

"Sorry. I'm sorry. Char." He sat back on his heels.

"Don't . . . touch me," she said again on a gasp, forcing the words out because it was important. So important.

"I know, I'm sorry." Enrique moved so he was no longer in her space, so that he was across the room, leaning his weight against the wall. He sank down to the floor so that he was still watching her but was no longer such a threat. "Talk to me, Char."

She'd always liked the way he said her name, the way he caressed it with his tongue before letting it slip out. Char. No one else called her that; it was just him. Her father called her Charlie, a habit Trudy had picked up once she realized how much Charlotte hated it. Her mother never called her anything but her full name, leaning heavy on the last syllable, without a trace of her Southern accent. Mellie sometimes called her Lottie, because she was silly. But to Enrique she was Char.

Sometimes she wished she was always Char. She imagined that woman was wild and uninhibited. She ate street food with her fingers and went skinny-dipping in the ocean underneath full moons. She slept with hot Latin men and danced in clubs where sweaty bodies rubbed against each other to a relentless, pounding beat.

Char said things like "I think I'm going crazy," but in a way that could be remedied over bottomless mimosas at brunch.

Charlotte, on the other hand, had breakdowns that caused said hot Latin men to stare at her with eyes that understood too much.

"Char, talk to me," he said again, but it was a plea more than an order.

She swiped at the wetness beneath her eyes and laughed again, this time at herself for being ridiculous. All of a sudden, she remembered she was naked. She pulled the sheet from beneath her so that she could wrap it around her shoulders. It wasn't much, but it provided the illusion that she wasn't completely vulnerable.

"I, um. I have a daughter," she said, refusing to think about the amount of trust she was putting into this man. Into any man, really. He only nodded for her to continue, as if the moment wasn't fraught, as if it hadn't taken walking to the edge of some sort of cliff to get her to talk to him about Ruby. "She's . . . she's the wind. You know?"

"Yeah," he said softly, though he couldn't actually know. She wanted him to. She wanted him to know how Ruby made ships sail and windmills turn and carried the smell of lilacs to far-off places. She wanted him to know that Ruby could bring down buildings as easily as she could let birds dance and dive through the sky. She wanted him to know that Ruby was the wind, but she was also the sun and the rain and the moonlight on a crystal-clear night. She was everything.

"They want to take her away from me," she said, licking her lips. It hurt, even saying the words.

"What? Why?"

She laid her head on the tops of her knees. "My mother hates me."

"They can't just do that, though." Enrique sounded sure, so sure. If only she could believe him.

"You don't know my parents," she countered.

"Maybe so," he said. "What started this?"

You, she wanted to say, to see how he would react. Would he feel those sharp barbs of guilt bite into his skin? Would it sink in, settle in, find a place in his soul, a dark malignant thing that ate at the purity of not knowing?

But it wasn't the truth, not really. "I lost her."

"Your daughter?"

She nodded. "Last Saturday. We were in a store, and she disappeared. I couldn't find her. I kept trying to and I . . . I couldn't find her." The sob was wrenched from her. It was broken and painful.

"It happens, Char," Enrique said. "You're not the first person to lose track of her kid in a busy mall."

She shook her head. He wouldn't understand. "It doesn't matter. It's an excuse. She's been waiting for one." He was another. Or, the fact that she was sleeping with him was another. They were all just excuses.

It was a final punishment, the ultimate one. Complete and total control over her life hadn't been enough. Hollis wanted to burn her to the ground and salt the earth.

"What's with the gun, then, Char?"

"Have you ever felt powerless?" she asked, sure that he hadn't. He carried himself with an easy confidence that bespoke a life of getting what he wanted. Not through the privilege of being born into the right family, but through being the kind of man he was. She didn't wait for his answer. "I've spent my whole life feeling powerless. I don't want to feel that way anymore."

"A gun is the easy answer," he said, slow and deliberate. "But don't think that makes it the right one."

"I don't think I asked for your opinion," Charlotte snapped.

"No, you just asked me to get you a gun. So I kind of think I get to have an opinion on it," he said, his voice going sharper than she'd heard it before.

They both backed off then and sat in silence. A fight broke out just on the other side of the door, and they listened to the mix of Spanish and English cuss words as the languages warred for dominance.

"Why do you think you're going crazy?" he asked once the chatter moved off to interrupt someone else's conversation. Perhaps it would be well timed for them, too.

"I'm not a strong person," she said, not sure how to actually put into words what was happening. But this thing she knew. This one fact.

A protest scraped against the back of Enrique's throat. "You're the strongest person I know, Char."

"Don't say that," she said. "Don't say something that's not true because it sounds nice. Because it fits what you want it to be. Say I'm not crazy. Say I'm normal. Fine. Don't say I'm strong when I'm not."

The demand pushed into the empty spaces of the motel room, filling it with something other than the residue of smoke.

"Okay," he said, and she relaxed without realizing she'd gone rigid.

How to explain it anyway? It wasn't possible. Why had she thought he would get it? Why had she thought she could tell him?

"I'm not a strong person," she tried to start again. This time he let her talk. "And when things get hard, I break. You know some people, they're like diamonds, right?"

"Pressure makes them beautiful," Enrique said, and for the first time all night she remembered why she'd picked him. Why she hadn't let this thing between them die after that one afternoon at the hotel.

"You're like that, aren't you?" Somehow she knew it to be true, even though he didn't answer. "I wish I was. Sometimes I wonder what it would be like. Do you ever do that? Have arguments in your head long after the fact? The words you wanted to say, wished you were brave enough to say, rattling around there as if they meant something? As if they weren't just empty thoughts that will never see the light of day?"

"No."

It was harsh and easy all at once. "Of course you don't," she said. "Because you're like a diamond. But me? I shatter like glass."

"What are you going to do with a gun, Char?" he asked.

There was nothing to say that would make sense to him.

She didn't want to be glass any longer. She didn't want to be power-less. She didn't want to bow her head and say the right words to soothe a hatred she had never asked for in the first place. Was that so hard to understand? She thought it must be.

Why would someone who had never known what it was like to fall apart understand the need to feel like it could all be put back together?

She bit her lip, sinking her teeth into the flesh. "Do you really want to know?"

CHAPTER FIFTEEN

ALICE

August 3, 2018
Five days after the kidnapping

"We want to bring in Trudy Burke," Nakamura said as soon as the chief walked into his office. They'd been squatting in it since getting back from coffee an hour and a half ago, going over their game plan for day two of the murder investigation.

Deakin's eyes flicked up briefly before returning to the file he was holding as he rounded his desk. "What? Who?"

"Charlotte Burke's niece," Alice said.

"Well, I want a million dollars and a nice little place on Key West." Deakin looked between the two of them. "It ain't happening. What's going on? You think she had something to do with it?"

"No, not necessarily." Alice leaned forward, her arms braced on her thighs, and filled him in on Zeke Durand.

"So a teenage girl lied about the boy she was seeing to cops who would have told her mother and grandparents?" Deakin asked. "Just trying to understand the suspicious part here."

Alice plucked at a loose thread on the inseam of her jeans. She hadn't had enough sleep to deal with people being obtuse on purpose. "She lied."

"Everyone lies," the chief shot back.

"I have heard that a time or two," she said, and Nakamura coughed. It was a warning, and it was reflected on Deakin's face. She pulled an apology from the depths of her belly and hoped he wouldn't care that it wasn't sincere. "Sorry, sir."

"I think the point we're making, perhaps poorly, is that from every indication we've gotten from the girl, she cared about Ruby deeply," Nakamura said. "If there was a relationship she was withholding that could have informed the investigation, it's suspicious that she didn't disclose it."

"I don't have any intention of interrogating her," Alice said. There would be no dramatic scene of the young woman handcuffed to the table in a cold room. "I just want her away from Hollis Burke."

"She's a minor. You'd be working around lawyers and her mother anyway," the chief said. "Go try to talk to her at the house first. Then we'll see."

"I also want a search warrant on the residence," Alice pushed.

"Working on it," Deakin muttered, his attention back on the file. "Apparently, all of the city's judges have conveniently misplaced their phones."

"This family, man," Alice muttered as they pushed to their feet. It would be pointless to try to talk to Trudy at the house, but that seemed to be the option they'd been left with.

"And you wonder why it's so weird that you think it's Sterling who killed her," Nakamura said, keeping his voice pitched lower than hers so the chief wouldn't hear as they walked from the office. "You haven't really explained your reasoning for that yet."

"Process of elimination," she said again, though she knew that wasn't what he wanted.

He growled in annoyance but didn't say anything more in the crowded bull pen. Everyone was watching them.

They stopped by their desks. Alice leaned over her computer without bothering to sit down as he snagged the car keys from the drawer.

The autopsy report wasn't there yet.

She slammed shut the lid of her laptop, then followed him along the narrow path between the desks. "I want to know immediately when the coroner's report comes in," she yelled to the room at large, not even bothering to look back, and Nakamura laughed.

"You have a real specialty for pissing people off, don't you?" he said.

"It comes naturally," Alice said. "I wasn't even trying that time."

"Such a Yank." Nakamura shook his head.

"Like you weren't born in Chicago." She shoved at him, reveling in the brief moment of levity. "And didn't spend most of your life walking the beat in LA."

Nakamura kept a straight face, though she could see a spark of humor in his eyes. "Yeah, but I'm a nice guy in general."

They pushed through the back doors of the station into the sunlight. It was becoming habit now for all the detectives to enter and leave from the back, where it was blocked off from the streets. It helped avoid the vultures camped out in the front.

"Are you saying I'm not nice?"

"That's exactly what I'm saying." He bumped his shoulder against hers, and she bit the corner of her lip, amused.

"Yeah, well, Southerners put far too high a premium on what they call nice," she countered. "And not enough on actual kindness."

He laughed again. "There you go pissing people off again."

She looked around before sliding into the passenger seat of the car. "No one to offend but you, and I don't care about your feelings."

"Do you care about anyone's?"

No. If she said it, she could play it off as a continuation of the joke. But something told her he'd see it as the truth it was. No, she did not care about anyone's feelings. That ability had died a long time ago.

Awkwardness crept up between them as the silence stretched, devouring the teasing air that had sparked with their banter.

"Tell me about the process of elimination," he said, because he had an ease about him that could cut through even the worst tension.

"Like I said, I don't buy that Charlotte did it." She held up her palm as he shifted in his seat. "I'm not ruling her out. But there are some things that don't make sense to me."

Nakamura waved his hand to get her to expand.

"We've been watching her too closely since the day Ruby disappeared for her to have moved the body," Alice started.

"She could have hidden her first, somewhere closer to where we found her," Nakamura countered. "We probably would have noticed if she'd started disappearing for large amounts of time, but slipping out one night to get the body to the beach if it was already near there? I could see that."

"So she hides the body somewhere around the turquoise house, and then . . . ," Alice prodded.

"Then she drove to that public beach to be seen," Nakamura said.

"With which car?" Alice asked. "The family ones were clean. I doubt she knew enough to get all the DNA out of the fabric. Not with that head wound Ruby had."

Nakamura shrugged. "Borrowed from a friend." He cut her off before she could say anything to that. "Just because they say they don't interact with many people outside the family doesn't mean they don't. She could have some secret accomplice."

Alice tipped her head in acknowledgment of the point. "So she snaps, kills Ruby. Calls this secret friend to come get her. They hide the body, then cook up a plan to make it look like a kidnapping."

It wasn't necessarily an impossible scenario.

"But then why dump her body to be found?" Alice asked. And that's what had been sitting at the edge of her thoughts whenever she considered Charlotte. That's what someone trying to convince a jury to sentence her would have to explain: Why would they have gone through that elaborate ruse if four days later they were going to put Ruby out on the beach?

Nakamura sucked his lower lip in. "Yeah, good point." She poked him, and he glanced over at her. "Doesn't rule her out, but okay. Keep going."

"So then we have Mellie Burke, who is an idiot who can't string two sentences together. She's tipsy half the time and drunk the rest of it."

Nakamura smirked at that but didn't say anything to interrupt.

"Trudy Burke," Alice said, tripping over her thoughts about the girl. "She reminds me of myself."

"Are you saying you could never kill anyone?"

"No. I'm not saying that at all," Alice said, a spike of ice drilling into the top of her spine. "We're all capable of it. Under the right circumstances. You are."

He tipped his head. "I never said I wasn't."

"I mean she's . . . she's not a bullshitter." Alice kept her eyes on the road in front of them. She hadn't meant to say it—hadn't meant to compare herself to Trudy—but now that it was out there, she had to explain. "There's not really any pretense with her. She wears her emotions on her face. I think . . . I think we'd see it if she'd killed Ruby, presumably by accident. I think she'd be breaking down."

"You're not like that," Nakamura said, and Alice flinched despite the fact that she knew it was the truth.

"I used to be," she said quietly.

Before Lila. It hung in the air.

The silence all but vibrated until Nakamura broke it.

"She could just be a fantastic actress."

There was always that possibility. But if "Everyone lies" was the maxim to define the case, then to an extent they were all acting. It just came down to figuring out who wore the best mask.

Alice didn't like people, but she knew people. She knew their little insecurities and their quirks and the way their limbs moved in reaction to strong emotion. There was something going on in Trudy's life that pushed at her, pulled at her, slapped at her when she was around her family. There were secrets buried in the very core of her being that influenced the way her body bent and collapsed and fortified itself when it was around any of the other Burkes. But it didn't do that when she was asked specifically about Ruby.

Explaining that, though, felt far more vulnerable to both herself and Trudy than saying it was a gut feeling and moving on. Somehow it would expose both of them.

"Do you think it's her?" she asked instead. Deflection was her friend.

Nakamura tilted his head. "No."

"So that leaves Hollis and Sterling, the queen and king, if you will," she continued, but then her phone rang from where it was tucked into the pocket of her jeans. She held up a finger. "To be continued."

"On the edge of my seat," Nakamura said quietly as she answered.

"Bridget, tell me you have something for me," Alice said without preamble once she saw who was calling.

"Depends on what you define *something* as," the woman said, snapping her gum to emphasize the cryptic comment.

"I'm pretty sure I define it like the rest of the world does," Alice said.

Bridget hummed. "Ya wanna hear or nah?"

"Tell me."

"There's nothing," Bridget said.

Alice closed her eyes. "So how do *you* define *something*?"

"Now that's the right question." Bridget laughed, big and boisterous and too loud. "It's strange, isn't it? That we found nothing. And I'm not talking smudged, invalid fingerprints. Or brushed-away shoe prints. I'm talking nothing."

"When nothing becomes something," Alice murmured.

"I knew I liked you for a reason, Garner." Bridget cracked her gum again. "It takes a pro to get by my team. This wasn't some spur-of-the-moment thing."

"It was calculated," Alice said.

"I mean, above my pay grade, darling," Bridget qualified. "But someone who just snaps? 'Cause they've gone 'round the bend? They don't know how to do this. How to keep it this clean."

"All right," Alice said. "Hey, thanks. For working on that." She knew Bridget must have been up all night.

"Course." Bridget brushed it off and hung up without any goodbyes.

Nakamura sighed while Alice repocketed her phone. "I heard some of it."

"Someone knew how to cover their tracks," Alice said. "Still think that sounds like Charlotte?"

The Burke house came into view as she waited for an answer. He pulled into the only free space of curb several blocks down from the house. "Whoever killed her had up to four days to figure out how to hide the evidence. It doesn't take a genius to realize sand wipes a lot of it out. Other than that, as long as there wasn't much of a struggle, it's not like they had to destroy that much DNA."

"A little bit of luck, and what? A Google search?" Alice asked as she climbed out of the car.

She eyed the news vans parked two deep on the quiet residential road. Something about the contrast made the scene even more unsettling. "God, they multiply like a virus, don't they?"

The journalists squawked at them as they passed, rivaling the seagulls that circled above looking to scavenge scraps of dropped food. Alice paid them just as much attention.

"Here goes nothing," Nakamura said with just a shifting of his brows before ringing the bell. It was early, a little past 7:00 a.m., and surprise was the only thing on their side.

That and the fact that it was Mellie who answered the door. She was in a blue satin robe that ended above midthigh and was left gaping to reveal the valley of creamy flesh between her breasts. She also had on a full face of makeup, and her hair was pinned back into some kind of fancy coif. It was as if she was about to head off to a lingerie shoot.

"Detectives," she murmured, her voice scratchy. "I'm sorry, unless you have a warrant, you'll have to leave."

It was more backbone than she'd expected from the woman, but Alice supposed she shouldn't be surprised. There was clearly a party line that had been drawn, and the Burkes, if nothing else, seemed to fall into form.

"We just have a few questions for your daughter, actually," Alice said, as an attempt to confuse her into agreeing. "Perhaps we could talk to her? With you there, of course."

"Trudy?" Mellie turned wide eyes on Nakamura. "What could you want with Trudy?"

"Just a few questions," Alice repeated, keeping her voice as soothing as possible. "Nothing to worry about."

"No, I'm sorry. No, that won't do at all," Mellie said, starting to shut the door in their faces.

"Wait."

They all shifted to the young woman standing just out of the stream of sunlight that was pouring in through the door. The darkness from the rest of the house hugged her narrow shoulders and threw her face into deep relief. The only bright spot was her long blonde hair that shimmered like liquid silver in the shadows.

"Trudy, that's not a good—"

"I want to. Let them in," Trudy interrupted her mother. Her arms came around her thin waist, her fingers smoothing over her own skin. It was a protective, self-comforting gesture in conflict with the defiant confidence of her voice. Again, it was all right there to read, if one only looked hard enough.

"I don't think this is a good idea," Mellie said under her breath but stepped back anyway, cowed by the daughter half her age.

"Yeah, well, you got up in the morning and thought that outfit was a good idea, so I don't really put much stock in your judgment, Mells," Trudy said.

Instead of fighting back, Mellie yanked the loose fabric over her breasts, her eyes damp when she looked back at them.

The little interaction spoke volumes about their relationship dynamics—the way Trudy called her mother by her name, the way Mellie had cowed so easily before the young girl, the derision Trudy had for the woman.

"I'm going to get Hollis," Mellie said, and then she took off toward the back of the house.

They all watched her walk away, and then Trudy turned. "You have three minutes, tops. Don't waste it."

"Tell us about Zeke Durand."

Trudy glanced toward the hallway. "Be more specific. There's not enough time."

"Why didn't you tell us about him?" Alice asked.

The girl shrugged, a pure embodiment of teenage dismissiveness. It was easy to forget how young she was with the way she carried herself. "He didn't even meet Ruby. He doesn't have anything to do with this."

"How did you know him?" Alice fired off. There was no reason to argue with her.

"He drove me into Tampa a couple times. I can't . . . They monitor how much money I spend. I couldn't just Uber."

Alice filed that away. "What were you doing in Tampa?"

"It's not relevant," Trudy said.

"You don't get to determine what's relevant."

"Actually, I do." Trudy straightened, dropping her arms, and Alice could see the Burke training fall into place. The arrogance that came with having it as her last name. "Or would you like me to start scream-ing for my grandmother?"

Nakamura laid a hand on Alice's back between her shoulder blades.

"Did you approach him first, or did he approach you?" Nakamura asked.

"I approached him. He had something I wanted, and we traded for it," Trudy said, this time tipping her chin up to challenge them to assume the worst. Which was . . .

"Sex?" Alice asked.

There was a gleam of triumph in those cold eyes, as if they'd fallen into some kind of trap she'd set. "No."

"Then, what?"

The question was interrupted by a sharp click of razor-thin heels on a polished floor.

"It's not him, don't waste your time," Trudy muttered, then turned and faded into the darkness that lingered just beyond the foyer.

"What are you doing in this house?" Hollis's voice preceded her, as if those seconds before she could properly enter the room would make all the difference.

"Had a few questions, ma'am," Nakamura said, easy and slow.

But Hollis wasn't one to be charmed.

"You need to leave immediately," Hollis said. "And do not come back without a warrant. Or you'll be hearing from my entire army of lawyers."

Alice stared at the space where Trudy had disappeared, but they had no choice. Neither she nor Nakamura said anything to the matriarch as they turned to leave.

The moment their feet hit the porch, the door shut behind them.

"And why exactly do you not think it was Hollis?" Nakamura asked, sliding his sunglasses onto the bridge of his nose.

"If it had been Hollis," Alice said, keeping her voice pitched low enough so that it wouldn't be picked up by any of the vultures, "we wouldn't have found the body."

CHAPTER SIXTEEN

TRUDY

July 13, 2018
Sixteen days before the kidnapping

"You look like you ate some bad shrimp, honey," the woman next to Trudy said. Her name was Candy, she'd told Trudy earlier with a wink, like they were all in on the joke. "Gotta unclench or you're gonna scare them away."

Nervous laughter tripped out even as Trudy tried to swallow it. The way the other performers were watching her made her wary. Turned her bitchy.

She shifted in the director's chair so that her back was to the small cluster of girls lingering by Candy, the clear matriarch of the group. It probably wasn't a good idea to piss them off by ignoring them, but her tongue was thick in her mouth, and she wasn't sure engaging with them would be any better.

Instead, she met her eyes in the mirror. Flaws would not hold up well under the scrutiny of the two rows of bright, uncovered bulbs that lined the glass. She shifted her wig, appreciating the fact that fake neon hair was in style.

The purple bangs slashed in an asymmetrical diagonal across her forehead, changing the shape of her face, and the ends, which faded into a teal blue, slanted just below her chin. Where her longer hair kept things soft, the bob cut made everything sharper—the line of her cheek, her jaw, her nose. The makeup and glitter she'd applied with a heavy hand did the rest of the job. Her disguise wouldn't hold up to someone who knew her well, but for any of her grandfather's acquaintances who wandered into the third-rate club, they would see what they wanted to see. Just another girl on the pole, desperate for the damp one-dollar bills they clutched so tightly in their sweaty palms.

"You've got bruises, baby?" The girl who called herself Brooklyn popped her ass on Trudy's counter, knocking the old eye shadow and crusted bronzer the girls had given her out of the way.

Brooklyn was short, with curves that challenged the bra she wore beneath the pink silk dressing gown. Her midnight-black hair was dyed to bring out the violet streaks that made it interesting, and the strands settled against flawless skin. She looked like an evil Snow White, and Trudy guessed she was the most popular dancer in the place.

She wondered why Brooklyn was at such a shitty joint, where her closest competition was Candy, whose skin was turning that special type of Florida leather brown, and Lola, whose features would just never add up to anything other than passable.

"Who doesn't?" Trudy shot back. She knew girls like Brooklyn. *She* was a girl like Brooklyn. And the fact that the question had been coated in sympathy didn't hide the fact that her eyes were predatory.

"True." Brooklyn pouted a bit. "Only bruised girls end up at Mac's."

Mac's. The strip club didn't even have a mysterious noir name, like the ones Trudy liked in movies. The Blue Moon. The Pink Flamingo.

But maybe if they'd used one of those names, people would have been pissed at what they got. Walking into Mac's Strip Club, you didn't expect anything other than what it was. The carpet was dark maroon, patterned with black stripes to hide unfortunate stains, while the walls were cheap wood paneling more popular four decades earlier. There was an all-you-can-eat shrimp buffet that ran along the back wall, but its best feature was the three fried pieces left to swim in the butter sauce that coated the cold metal bins. Drinks were plentiful, but they were only palatable by mixing them with copious amounts of juice or sugar. The only people Trudy had seen taking straight shots so far had been a large Russian man in the corner and Candy.

When Trudy had first seen the place, she'd known it was exactly what she needed.

"So you know the rule here, right?" Brooklyn slid off the counter, and the dressing gown draped down one shoulder to catch on her boob.

"I'm sure you're about to tell me," Trudy said, standing up herself when the bored, skinny dude with a clipboard pointed in her direction. Her cue.

Brooklyn stepped in front of her, blocking the way. "Oh, kitty's got claws, hmm?"

Trudy rolled her eyes, but all the familiar bitchiness was helping calm the nerves that tightened the muscles of her belly at the thought of stripping for the four bored businessmen she knew were out there. The greasy man who'd hired her had promised she'd make at least $500 if it was a good night. Given that it wasn't the weekend, she still hoped to pull a couple hundred. She had to; her plan depended on this.

"Stop being a walking stereotype," Trudy said, and pushed past the girl. "It's boring. You're boring."

The laughter of the rest of the girls followed her, and she knew she'd pay for the insult later. It would be something petty and stupid, and she just couldn't care about shit like that. She had to make it at Mac's for only a month. Maybe figure out how to talk Zeke into driving her to Tampa more than once a week to pick up an extra shift or two.

Time and money. There never seemed to be enough of either.

She pasted a sultry smile on her face when she heard the announcer over the static screech of the loudspeaker.

"And welcome to the stage, Mac's newest angel, Zoey."

———

Trudy's shift at Mac's had been an early one, so it was just before midnight when Zeke picked her up. Her face was mostly scrubbed clean of the makeup she'd worn, and just a little glitter lingered in the soft skin of her inner thigh. There was also $300 tucked into her purse—a slow night, she was told by the veterans who didn't know she was grateful for anything.

"One more stop," she said after sliding into the passenger seat. It was already later than he'd probably thought they'd be in the city, and there was a protest sitting in the downward tilt of his mouth. "Please."

He blinked—a long, slow flutter of dark eyelashes against his cheeks—and she realized that was the first time she'd said that to him. *Please.* She hated the word. It was vulnerable and begged for rejection. But it seemed to work, because he didn't reply, just lifted a brow in question. She rattled off an address before he could change his mind.

The club was in a shitty part of Tampa, and the bouncer waved them through without even pretending to check IDs.

"That shouldn't have been so easy to get in," Zeke murmured into her ear as they pushed through the darkened hallway, lured by the pounding bass of the music.

"I told you we'd be fine," Trudy said over her shoulder and laughed.

"You're crazy," Zeke said, but there was something in his tone that was light in a way that it usually wasn't. Maybe he was actually beginning to loosen up. Maybe he was beginning to like her. She wasn't sure if she wanted that anymore. At the start of it, that had been her goal. To get him to like her, trust her, so that he would be easier to manipulate. Now she wished he wouldn't.

"Stick with me, Durand," she said instead of the warning she wanted to scream. *Run. Leave. Don't tangle your future with mine, because all I do is sink. And I'll take you with me.*

The thoughts were drowned out by the thumping of the music. Which was how it was supposed to work. Clubs like these. The blue-and-green lights were the heartbeat that pulsed in sweaty bodies as they grinded against each other on the dance floor, lost in the pure sensation of lust and pleasure and anticipation. The undertones of samba turned everything fast and dirty, tongues finding tongues, hips teasing hips, fingers digging into flesh.

It was pure in a way that Trudy could appreciate. It was giving up control and promises and security in exchange for being free. Being free to live in that precious moment where only one second to the next mattered. Where ugliness and pain and memories didn't dare tread.

Getting to the bar was always easy. She was pretty and thin and young, and people made room for her. Zeke simply followed in her wake.

"Four shots of tequila," she shouted and held up her fingers just in case her voice got lost somewhere along the way.

The bartender looked like he was about to give a shit about her age for two seconds, and then he shrugged and lined up the glasses.

A small, turtlelike man on the stool next to her placed a damp hand on her arm and nodded to the guy pouring the drinks. "On me," he said.

She'd been expecting it. The bartender shrugged again and moved on while she handed the shots back to Zeke. "Thanks." She smiled at the dude before disappearing into the crowd.

"I don't drink." Zeke bent down to yell in her ear, his large hands easily accommodating the glasses.

"Thank God for that," Trudy said, taking the first one and tossing it back. "You would have had to go get some for yourself."

The implications of that fully set in only as she finished the second and reached for the third.

"Whoa, slow down, yeah?" Zeke said, touching her waist with his newly freed-up hand.

The liquor no longer burned its way down her throat, and everything was becoming a little slurred. It was probably too soon for it to actually be hitting her, but she liked this phase. Before her body caught up with her mind and she just let herself be for once, under the guise of alcohol, but not under its influence.

"Let's dance." She looped an arm around his thick neck as she licked at the rim of the last glass, her tongue desperate for the sticky drops that lingered in the bottom of it.

"I don't dance, either," he said with a laugh.

"You say that as if it matters," Trudy said, dragging him into the mess of bodies.

They were pressed together in an instant, his thigh slipping between her legs. She went with it, her hands running up the base of his neck, up along the back of his head.

The music didn't have a melody, but she didn't care. She found the rhythm and let the alcohol working its way through her bloodstream do the rest.

It was a moment before his hands rested against her hips, just lightly holding on or, if anything, nudging her away so there was distance between them. And that wouldn't do at all.

She plastered her body to his, letting the excuse of the crowd, the undulating wave of it, push her into the space that he usually kept so guarded.

In the next breath, the emptiness behind her was filled, and she was surrounded. There were hands on her stomach, on her pelvic bones, on her ass. A hot breath against her neck, and she let her head fall back against the stranger's shoulder. His mouth found the skin beneath her jaw immediately, nipping at it, trailing damp, open-mouthed kisses down the column. And the entire time, Zeke's hands didn't move from her waist.

Blinking was hard, so she kept her eyes closed instead. When she was little, she'd loved the ocean. She would beg Mellie to take her every day, and when Mellie got sick of it, she'd turn her pleas on Charlotte.

Trudy could barely wait until they dropped their towels on the sand before she'd take off toward the water, screaming at the way the coldness surprised her even though she was braced for it. She was never one to ease into the frigidness, preferring to dive under the first wave and take the shock of it.

It was better, she'd reasoned. Why prolong the pain when it was coming either way?

She would stay in for hours, until her skin was pale from the cold and her fingertips had shriveled into miniature mountains and deep valleys.

But just before she would get out, she would sink to the bottom, her hands keeping her under when the water wanted to rid itself of her presence. It was never quiet, like the pool was, with its silence pressing in against her eardrums.

No, the ocean talked to her instead. It murmured secrets and promises and wrapped her in an embrace and kept her suspended, weightless all the while.

That's what this felt like. The ocean. Their hands were the tide, pushing and pulling and returning her to where she'd been; the pounding of the music was the distant sound of waves on the shore; the manic edge to it all was the incineration of oxygen from full lungs that no longer knew if they would ever be able to pull in air again.

It was heady and reckless, and it made her feel alive, so she got greedy with it. Always wanting more. Always more than anyone was willing to give.

She tried to pull Zeke closer, ever closer, her mouth seeking his, desperate to forget who she was and why this could never work anyway.

"I'm not . . ." Zeke dodged, turning his face so that her lips caught his cheek instead. "I'm . . ."

He was yelling again in her ear, but he wasn't making sense, and she didn't think she was the one to blame for that.

But whatever it was, it was rejection, and it served as the push to the surface she needed. She gasped when she broke through, returning to herself, returning to a shitty little club and a hangover that shouldn't actually exist yet. Her limbs were heavy, though, and her tongue was sticky and her head was fuzzy, and it was no longer fun.

She broke away from hands that still grabbed at her and stumbled through the bodies until she found space to breathe. It was time, anyway, to do what she'd come here to do. She shouldn't have been distracted.

Zeke was behind her, mumbling something that was probably an apology. It got lost in the noise, and she was thankful for that. Pity wasn't something she was comfortable with. It wasn't something she would accept from anyone.

It was a good thing he was there, though. For the muscle.

She scoped out the back wall, bypassing the little neon signs for the bathroom and zeroing in on the swinging door that led back to the kitchen.

"Come on," she said, grabbing his wrist and pulling.

"I don't think we're supposed to be back here," he said as soon as they stepped through the doorway, the sound of the club behind them muffled.

"Good to know," she said, ignoring the glances from the short, balding man in front of the massive industrial stoves. It was even hotter in here, and the sweat gathered at the waistband of her cutoffs. She ignored the unpleasant feeling and maneuvered her way around the variety of obstacles that stood in her way.

Zeke followed, but she put him out of her mind when she got to the door. One more faceless, brawny man lounged against the wall, dragging on a cigarette. He straightened as they got closer, his gaze moving to Zeke, dismissing Trudy as a nonthreat.

"I'm here for a pickup," she said, taking the ciggy out of his surprised, limp hand and bringing it to her lips. She locked eyes with him as she hollowed out her cheeks on the inhale. He was no longer watching Zeke.

"You have an appointment?"

"Of course," she said, trying to sound as if this wasn't terrifying. Confidence was key. It was how she lived her life. Fake it till you make it. "Malone. Jane Malone."

Without looking away, he dropped his fist to his side so he could knock three times on the door behind him in quick succession.

It opened to reveal a small but bright and clean room. A few replicas of the giant at the threshold—right down to the faux leather jacket—were squeezed into the one sofa in the corner. A tired woman behind the sad oak desk was the only other person in the room.

She wasn't particularly pretty, and she wasn't particularly ugly. Her medium-brown hair was pulled back into a tight bun at the back of her neck, turning a face that already lent itself to harshness even starker. There were wrinkles not only by the corners of her eyes but also by her lips. They circled her neck like rings within a tree. She wore no makeup to cover any of the obvious flaws, making Trudy even more aware of her own, which were slathered in a comforting layer of foundation and eye shadow.

It made her like the woman and hate her at the same time. Not an unusual feeling for Trudy.

"Jane?" the woman asked, her lips smirking as they curved around the name.

"Yes," Trudy confirmed.

The woman watched her for a beat longer, then reached into the top drawer of her desk. She tossed the small yellow package so that it settled just on the edge of tipping off.

Trudy held herself back from rushing for it. Desperation in situations where she didn't know who held the upper hand was dangerous. So instead, she took her time, grabbing the packet as if it wasn't her entire future. She opened the clasp to pull out one of the passports. Her face stared back at her, under the name Jane Malone. Tucked into the crease was a Social Security card. It looked legit. There was nothing to do but trust that it was.

"Okay," Trudy said. "Thank you."

The woman who had never introduced herself inclined her head, and her face softened. "Take care of yourself, Jane."

"It's not me that I need to take care of," Trudy said, perhaps unwisely. Something about that slight relaxing of the woman's stiff mouth made her want to confess everything. Like she was a child holding on to a secret that was much too big.

"Yes," the woman said with a nod. "I know."

Because she did.

Trudy didn't properly breathe again until they pushed through the exit door at the back of the kitchen.

"What the hell was that?" Zeke seemed to regain his own stability as the warm night air hit them in the face.

She didn't answer him, instead trying to get her bearings. They were in an alley behind the club, but it looked like they could hop a low wall to get to the parking lot where they'd left the car.

"Come on," she said, taking off for it.

"No." Zeke followed anyway. "A fake passport? What the hell are you involved with?"

"Don't worry about it."

"What the hell, Trudy? How can I not worry about it?" Zeke leaped over the stacked stones with ease, pausing as he turned back to help lift her over. They were almost running at this point. "You dragged me into this. Don't get me caught up in your illegal shit."

Trudy stopped, grabbing on to his elbow to bring him to an abrupt halt. His feet stuttered, but then his entire attention focused on her, still and unblinking in the darkness.

What could she even say?

"The choices we can live with, yeah?"

CHAPTER SEVENTEEN

ALICE

August 3, 2018
Five days after the kidnapping

"Where the hell is my autopsy report?" Alice slammed through the door of the police station. "And get Zeke Durand's ass in here immediately."

"Who are you talking to, exactly?" Nakamura was three paces behind her, his voice amused.

She spun around. "Anyone who will get it done."

Nakamura gestured to the bull pen, which was empty save for that pimply little asshole from the briefing. He sat in the far corner, his feet kicked up on his desk, sipping coffee.

"Get *him* to do it," Alice said without pausing on her way back toward the basement. The hallways were blessedly quiet as well, and she only had to nod curtly at one passing officer before she was swinging through the door and skipping down the stairs to her makeshift head-quarters. She crossed the concrete in a few long strides.

The pictures that were stuck on the wall stared back at her. All she saw were distractions.

She heard Nakamura coming a few seconds before he spoke.

"I'm having him go pick up Durand," he said, coming to a stop next to her. "His address was in the system. Misdemeanor."

She didn't bother to ask the question he was about to answer.

"Bar fight," he filled in.

"He's a teenager, though, right?"

"It was in the parking lot. I don't know," Nakamura said. "I don't have the details."

There was no picture for Zeke Durand yet, so she found a piece of scrap paper and wrote his name in thick marker. She hesitated and then put a question mark on it before taping it up alongside the family.

"What do you make of it?" Nakamura asked, picking up his little stress ball as he watched her.

"Don't know," Alice said. "He might have a car."

Which meant he could have helped Trudy or Charlotte hide the body if one or both of them had killed Ruby. It might also mean that he could be acting on his own. He could have followed Charlotte to the beach and made his move then.

"We should look into his history," Nakamura said. "Maybe you're onto something with that connection-to-Sterling thing."

Alice nodded.

"There's something off with this family," Alice said. "Why would this teenager kidnap his girlfriend's cousin, keep her for four days, and then leave her on the beach to be found?"

"See, that's your problem. You're trying to tell a story again," Nakamura said. "Sometimes things just don't make sense. Especially when you don't have all the pieces."

Patterns. Connections. They were just there, waiting to be made.

"What do you think we are if not storytellers?" Alice drew a line between the piece of paper with Durand's name on it and Trudy's photo. She paused and then drew another line to Sterling's.

"Tell me a story, then, Garner."

"So what if Zeke isn't just showing up at the wrong time, wrong place," Alice started. "He put himself in Trudy's way. Made himself available for something she wanted. Got her to trust him. Maybe, if he's good, even got her to think she was working him."

She glanced back at Nakamura, who had stopped throwing his stress ball.

"Go on."

"Bided his time, for what seems to be about a month. A couple options there. Could have been the plan, could have had a date in mind in the first place. It could be he saw an opportunity and seized it. It could be something set him off. It would have taken some planning, though, either way."

"So was it a kidnapping or a murder?"

"Revenge," Alice said, the word slipping past her chapped lips again almost without her permission. It all came back to revenge. "There are only so many reasons someone would commit murder, right?"

"Money," Nakamura began, always game to follow her down the conversational rabbit hole.

"Which we ruled out because of the lack of a ransom note," she said. "Humiliation. I think the violence would have been more direct and personal, though, if that were the motive. They would take out Hollis. Or Sterling. Why go after Ruby?"

"Jealousy," Nakamura said. "A crime of passion, then."

She shook her head. "That motive falls under the umbrella of humiliation."

And that still didn't feel right.

"To protect a secret," she said quietly.

"Ah." Nakamura shuffled a bit behind her, settling into the seat. "Tell me a different story."

She plucked at another thread. Patterns. Connections. Just waiting to be made.

"So maybe it *is* a crime of passion, but not inspired by jealousy or an affair," Alice said circling back to that, still focused on Sterling. "Rage."

"This doesn't look like rage, though," Nakamura said. "Nothing about it looks sloppy."

"Exactly," Alice said. "It looks like control."

"Rage and control."

"Who does that sound like?" Alice asked, moving closer to the wall now. "Rage," she said, answering her own question and pointing to Sterling. Then she tapped the marker against Hollis's face. "Control."

"So tell me the story," Nakamura repeated.

"Sterling Burke, esteemed member of St. Petersburg society, bases all of his self-worth on being respected. He and Hollis run their family with an iron fist. The daughters are adults and still live in the house—"

"But they also both have children out of wedlock," Nakamura interrupted.

"Which must have been quite a blow to good ol' Sterling and Hollis," Alice murmured.

The father. Ruby's. That had been the first path they'd run down when Ruby was first reported missing. Statistically, it was the obvious choice.

But Charlotte had been adamant it had been a one-night stand that had left her with a souvenir. She'd never even told him that Ruby existed, didn't even know his full name. With only a vague description of a middle-aged man with brown hair and an average build, they'd had nothing left to go on.

"Do you think she's lying about it?" Nakamura had asked her after the interview.

"Yes," Alice had answered.

Now, Nakamura was back to pitching the ball from hand to hand. "But Ruby was five."

"If Sterling was going to snap over them getting pregnant, he would have done it when it happened." Alice followed his train of thought.

"Yeah, I could see one of them"—Nakamura waved a hand at Hollis and Sterling—"going after the girls when they were first told. But now it feels like old news."

Alice nodded. "What if they found something out?"

"And that would be?"

She shrugged. "Who the real father was?"

There was a beat of silence, and then: "Shit," Nakamura said.

She turned around. "See the power of a good story?"

———

An hour later they were parked outside the closest fast-food joint.

There was a long to-do list for the day, but they'd gotten to the point where they were no longer functioning human beings, so they'd dragged themselves off to get food.

It was becoming their pattern for the case, one they settled into with the familiar ease of working countless other investigations. Work, eat, drink coffee, don't sleep. Rinse and repeat.

"There's a flaw in your theory," Nakamura said as if no time had passed.

"Only one? Aces," Alice said around the massive bite of burger she'd just taken. "And it's not my theory."

"What?" Nakamura smudged at the bit of ketchup that clung to his lips.

"I never said it was my theory on what's going on." Alice handed him a napkin. "You asked me to tell you a story. I did."

Nakamura waved that away. "Okay, in that scenario, there's a flaw."

"Edge of my seat here, Joe."

He polished off the rest of the bun he'd been holding. "Charlotte would have had to play along."

141

She hummed in agreement while digging into the white paper bag that sat in the space between them for some now-lukewarm fries. Better than nothing. The salt sent a pulse of pleasure through her, and her brain immediately craved more. Anything to fight the fatigue that was settling, camouflaged as numbness, in her bones.

"Say Sterling snaps and kills Ruby," Nakamura said, ripping into another ketchup packet. He squeezed out a portion directly onto a fry and devoured it before repeating the process. "And then Hollis goes into damage-control mode. That requires Charlotte to pretend she'd taken Ruby to the beach that day and lie about her being kidnapped."

"It was always weird, the kidnapping, though," Alice argued for the sake of arguing. "It's a lot harder than people think to just walk off with a kid that's not yours."

He shot her a look that she decided to ignore. Yes, it was harder than people imagined, but it wasn't impossible. She was living proof. "Don't start."

"Was I starting?" Nakamura held up his hands in mock innocence even though his eyes shifted away in guilt.

"I'm really okay," she said, despite not wanting this conversation. "It's not like I've never dealt with a missing-child case before."

"But have there ever been quite so many similarities?" he asked, gentle and soft. It was off-putting when he did that, when he stripped away that ever-present friendliness for this. This kindness.

"I'm fine," she repeated, and she wondered if those words would ever hold meaning again. She couldn't remember the last time she'd said them and it hadn't been a lie.

"I'm fine," Alice said to the chief. The woman's eyes were deep brown and sad.

"You're not fine, Alice." Chief Hughes didn't even bother to soften the words. She had a policy against calling female detectives by their names, claiming it created an unprofessional intimacy that didn't exist with the men on the squad. But she'd called her Alice.

Hughes was right, though. The words were empty. She wasn't fine. She would never be fine again.

"I think you should take a break, Alice," Hughes said. Gentle, but firm. There would be no arguing here.

Alice rolled her shoulders, the tips of her fingers finding her gun. "No."

Hughes sighed and settled deeper into her chair. "Alice. You've physically assaulted two suspects in the past thirty days. If you were anyone else, you'd be off the team. But you're one of my best detectives. And . . ."

And you just lost a child. It wasn't spoken out loud, but it dropped into the silence anyway. Of course you've gone crazy. What mother wouldn't?

She licked at her lips. "I'm not crazy."

"We've never said you were," Hughes said, but she had that look. The one that people wore when talking someone off a ledge. "I just think a break might do you good. And appointments with the shrink."

The fucking shrink. Hated and ridiculed at large by the detectives, yet she was supposed to go spill her guts to this person. "No."

"The shrink or the suspension becomes permanent," Hughes said. "I'm sorry, Alice. But it's your choice."

"Okay, so Charlotte makes up the kidnapping," Nakamura continued, jolting her out of her memories. "But you don't think she's guilty."

"I didn't say that," Alice said, snatching the last of the fries before Nakamura could, a victory despite the fact that he simply let her do it. Pity was a powerful force no one should underestimate. Even if it was employed just to get a cold french fry. "I said I don't think she killed Ruby."

That stopped him. "What?"

"Abusive relationships are complicated." She shrugged. "If Hollis told her to, I wouldn't be surprised if she'd go along with it."

"You think she'd lie about her own child's murder to placate her mother?"

"Don't act like you haven't been a cop for more than a decade and a half, Nakamura," Alice said, turning a bit in her seat. Nakamura raised his brows in question.

"Those relationships follow a logic that outsiders can't understand," she continued. "How many times have you seen the wife drop charges while still sporting the bruises?"

"You think Hollis hits her?" Nakamura asked. "That's a serious accusation."

"'Abusive' isn't limited to the physical," Alice said. "You need to be around that family for thirty seconds to realize there is some sort of control and emotional manipulation happening. It doesn't seem like a stretch to me that Charlotte would do what needs to be done."

"You know I'm a fairly capable detective," Nakamura grumbled as he crumpled up his trash, stuffing it back in the now-empty bag. He shoved the key in the ignition, glancing in the rearview mirror.

She patted his forearm in a deliberately patronizing manner. "Sure, you are. You were just distracted by Mellie's cleavage."

He shook his head but was smiling. "People are cagey, aren't they?"

Shrugging again, she shifted so she was facing forward once more. The station was only a few minutes away. "Maybe. But they're obvious, too, you know?"

"Yeah?"

"Find what makes them fragile, what makes them vulnerable. What lengths they would go to in order to keep the world from discovering their secrets," she said. "That's where you find the cracks in the foundations behind the pretty facades. That's where you'll find motivation."

She glanced at him. "That's where you'll find your story."

"And what's that for Charlotte?"

Alice thought for a moment.

"That she's just as weak as her mother has made her believe she is."

CHAPTER EIGHTEEN

CHARLOTTE

July 28, 2018
One day before the kidnapping

If Charlotte didn't force herself to move, she'd be late for dinner. It was a Saturday-night ritual in the Burke residence that only Sterling and Ruby were allowed to miss. Sterling, because he was Sterling, and Ruby, because Hollis didn't tolerate children at the table.

Ruby swung her little legs against the bed now, watching Charlotte with wide eyes. "You look pretty, Mama," she said.

Everything in Charlotte went soft at that, even the part that was tightly coiled in a fist and slamming against her rib cage. She sat beside her daughter, taking her chubby face in her hands. "Thank you, baby," she whispered into cheeks as she pressed a kiss to each one.

"You're crying," Ruby said in that matter-of-fact way of children.

Charlotte swiped at the moisture and then widened her eyes at the girl. "Are you ready for our adventure tomorrow?"

Ruby threw herself backward on the bed, sprawling out on the thick comforter and punching her tiny fists in the air. "Yes," she cried out to the ceiling. Charlotte resisted the urge to shush her, even knowing Hollis would be downstairs already, unable to hear the disruption.

"And remember, it's our secret." Charlotte bent closer to her so she was whispering. Ruby was terrible at keeping anything quiet, but it was unlikely she'd see any of the rest of the family for the remainder of the night. And then they would leave before anyone was up.

"Shhh." Ruby pursed her lips, holding a finger up to them. "Like I have with Grandpapa."

Charlotte's stomach clenched, quick and violent, and she swallowed against the bile that rose in her throat. She tried to keep her face neutral.

"Not quite, baby," she whispered, a bit dizzy with the attempt to keep herself from giving over to the sick wave that crashed into her. She breathed deep, in through her nostrils and out through her mouth. Ruby tilted her head, still watching her.

"All right, my little petal, bath time with Isla and then bedtime, yes?"

There was a mutiny brewing in the squint of her eyes, but it wasn't Charlotte's problem, because the knock on the door came just as she was expecting it.

Isla popped her head in. "Sorry to interrupt, but Mrs. Burke is requesting your presence at the dining table."

"Yes, of course." Charlotte stood up, smoothing a hand over the cotton of her patterned dress. It was a simple sheath that ended at her knees and was fancy enough to fit Hollis's strict dress code. Ruby hopped off the bed and skipped her way across the room. "Actually, hold on. Rubes, where's my good night?"

Her daughter paused midstride, stumbling a bit as she caught herself to swing around back toward where Charlotte crouched, ready for her.

Her little body crashed into Charlotte's, and only years of practice wearing stilettos stopped her from tumbling onto the floor. She held tight to her little girl, though, burying her face in her soft curls. They still smelled of strawberry even though her bath from last night was a distant memory. She wondered if it was still there, the scent. Or maybe it was one of those ingrained things, where Ruby would always smell like strawberries and always be a baby and always fit in her arms just like this.

"Good night, Mama." Ruby pulled back a bit, and Charlotte had to let her go.

"Good night, petal," Charlotte said, and pressed the back of her hand to her lips to keep anything else from pouring out.

"Ma'am." Isla had let Ruby run by her and was watching Charlotte attempt to gather herself.

"I'm fine." Charlotte smiled as brightly as possible. Come tomorrow, it wouldn't do for staff to be talking about how she had fallen apart in her room the night before. "Just getting sappy, you know her birthday's coming up and all." She waved a hand. Silly. She was being silly, she tried to convey.

Isla hesitated but then offered up her own small smile. "She's getting so old."

"No," Charlotte said, and realized how harsh the denial rang in the room only when Isla flinched. She forced herself to chuckle again. "See. Look at me. I can't stand to see her grow up."

"It's normal, ma'am," Isla said. "I'll just . . ."

And with that, she disappeared again, presumably to follow Ruby to wherever she'd run. It certainly wasn't the bath.

Charlotte made her way downstairs and took the last minutes of freedom to pull herself together. This was not the time to fall apart. This was a time for masks. The ones she'd spent years, decades, crafting.

Everything would be easier if she could trust herself. But she'd never learned to. When other girls were testing their confidence, hers had been continually undercut.

"You're mistaken," Hollis said. "My daughter's not smart enough to be in that class."

"You think you can live on your own? But you don't know how to do anything."

"Raise a child? As if you can even take care of yourself."

147

Countless moments could be called up with ease, each one defining Charlotte in a way she wished she was strong enough to combat.

What she was left with was smoke and mirrors. Deflect, hide. Survive. It was what she knew.

Hollis's eyes skimmed over her when she stepped into the dining room, cataloging every way in which Charlotte was wrong.

The air was already thick with tension, as was normally the case for this farce of a happy family dinner. Trudy was watching her own plate, while Mellie gestured toward Charlotte with a wineglass that was already mostly empty.

Hollis was at the head of the table, swallowing whatever scolding words she had for Charlotte arriving late. Sterling was absent. Relief slammed into Charlotte, almost bringing her to her knees.

As she sat down, she realized they were all waiting for Hollis's reaction. The woman was at war with herself: desperate, always, to scold Charlotte like a child, but at the same time loath to make a scene.

At this point, Charlotte didn't even care. She just had to make it through the next hour without breaking down, and there was only so much Hollis would do with Mellie and Trudy present.

"Trudy, tell us how your tutoring is going," Hollis said finally, and the muscles in Charlotte's neck relaxed.

Charlotte's fingertips inched toward the stem of her wineglass, the cool white liquid a siren's song.

"Are you getting tutored, peaches?" Mellie slurred.

Hollis tut-tutted but didn't issue the harsh slap-down Charlotte would have received. "Trudy is tutoring an underprivileged boy."

"You are?" Charlotte asked, surprised. It was out of character for Trudy. Or maybe she just didn't know her niece as well as she thought she did.

Trudy snorted, an unattractive expulsion that Charlotte leaned away from on instinct.

"He's not, like, some illiterate kid without shoes, despite what Hollis would like you to think," she said, her disgust for them, all of them, dripping from her tongue.

Hollis's mouth tightened. But there would be no scene.

Two people, in the same circumstances. And yet Trudy handled Hollis with all the fire and confidence Charlotte had always wanted to have. The girl was a diamond, sharp and hard and beautiful and flawed. It was so easy to forget how young Trudy was; it had been so long since Charlotte had thought of her as anything other than grown.

Charlotte sipped at the wine and wondered if she would ever have even a little bit of the girl's courage.

Maybe. Maybe that's what tomorrow was about. Finally pushing back, finally tearing at the velvet restraints that had held her paralyzed her entire life. An act of rebellion twenty years too late for herself. But maybe it was just in time. Just in time to save Ruby.

"What are you tutoring him in?" Charlotte asked. Even in situations like these, she was looking to ease the tension, play the diplomat. Appease, soothe. Take the hit and thank them for it.

Another difference. Where Trudy challenged each blow, Charlotte bowed beneath it.

But they still both ended up bruised in the end.

Trudy flicked her gaze toward Charlotte and then just as quickly looked away. Dismissive. "Math."

"I'd like to meet him," Hollis said, but it wasn't a request, and they all knew it. If she hadn't been watching her carefully, Charlotte would have missed the way Trudy's shoulders went taut, the way her fork paused for a second on the way to her mouth. "He's been taking up so much of your time, it's only right for us to know who you're spending it with."

And that made more sense. It wasn't tutoring, it was an excuse. A place to hold hours that would otherwise be unaccounted.

"He's busy," Trudy said.

"On all the days?" Charlotte couldn't resist. Old habits died hard.

Trudy tipped her chin up as if ready for a fight.

"Some people don't have the luxury to lounge around all day doing absolutely nothing with their lives," Trudy countered.

"Because you wouldn't know anything about that?" Charlotte murmured.

"Charlotte, you are an adult. Act like it," Hollis said, each word a slap. "Trudy, watch your mouth when you talk to your aunt."

After that, the conversation portion of the evening was over. The rest of the dinner passed with a quiet soundtrack of silverware on fine china and the clink of wineglasses being refilled.

It was only when dessert was served that her reprieve was interrupted.

"I talked to Dr. Sterett today," Hollis said, bringing a spoonful of mousse up to her mouth. "He's going to see you next Tuesday, Charlotte."

"What?" Charlotte was caught off guard. It wasn't a feeling she particularly liked when it came to Hollis. "For what?"

"Your erratic behavior as of late," Hollis said, like it was obvious. Like she wasn't just planting the seeds to convince Charlotte and Trudy and Mellie that Charlotte was indeed having issues.

"Oh, what have you been up to, then, Charlie?" Mellie asked, almost gleeful. Charlotte hated her in that moment. More than she hated Hollis.

For the most part, Charlotte had always thought of her sister as harmless. Almost helpless. She treated her with the same kid gloves everyone did.

But it was so unbelievably unfair. Somehow Mellie had skated through a life that had been so absurdly hard for Charlotte, and the inequity of it all bubbled into an anger so fierce her blood was lit with it.

"Go drink another bottle of wine, Melissa, and leave the grown-ups to their conversation," Charlotte snapped. Mellie paled and shifted back in her seat like she'd been struck.

"Oh shit," Trudy said, settling into her seat as if she were watching a boxing match.

"That's enough." Charlotte pointed at her. The rage that had been so pure and strong when it came to Mellie tempered and bent when it came to Trudy. "That brat attitude that you think is derision isn't cute. It wasn't cute when you were nine, and it certainly isn't now. You're not even clever."

"Charlotte," Hollis said, not even raising her voice. It was more effective that way.

But she couldn't stop. Those emotions she no longer seemed to be able to control with the easy grace of a skilled conductor were scattering and popping and fizzing in the space behind her eyes. Her body all but vibrated with it, and she knew if she didn't walk away, the implosion would come.

Her entire life narrowed down to that moment. A life of cowering beneath blows and making herself small so as not to attract attention, because she'd learned early on that attention was the worst possible thing. From Sterling, it meant nightmares and hot breath against her neck, and from Hollis, it meant bruises, both emotional and physical.

But right now it was her mother who looked small. Small and mean and vicious, her body rotting away beneath designer clothing and too-red lipstick.

"And you," Charlotte said, her voice soft and unrecognizable to her own ears. "You're a failure of a human being and a mother. If you think I would ever let you raise my daughter . . ."

She didn't finish the thought, didn't need to. Hollis's eyes were locked on hers. Looking away, Charlotte stood and left the room.

Charlotte stopped walking only when she made it outside.

The humidity hadn't burned off from the day yet, and her lungs struggled to scrape oxygen from the water-laden air. She leaned against the porch railing, and a splinter pierced into the soft flesh of her palms. It helped, focusing on that small pain.

"Why are you freaking out?" Trudy's voice was soft but still carried an edge to it. Charlotte didn't look up. "It's all going to change after tomorrow anyway."

If everything went as planned. If they didn't screw it all up. Maybe. Maybe things would be different. With the morning creeping ever closer, it all of a sudden felt so foolish, though. Like when grown-ups were caught playing a child's game. Or when kids dressed in their mothers' clothes.

What were they thinking?

"You know, you're doing a really good impression of someone who's on the verge of a breakdown."

Charlotte barked out a laugh at that, the sound so unlike her they both froze, statues separated by only a few feet that somehow felt like an ocean. "Yeah. Doing an impression."

She felt more than heard Trudy step closer, start to say something, and then stop herself. Turning, she found her niece watching her with wide eyes, her face stripped of the carefully constructed expression she usually wore.

What was left was a vulnerability that couldn't be countered by the bravado in her voice. What was left was the girl Charlotte had helped raise, the one who asked for rainbow sprinkles on her ice cream and cuddled against Charlotte during thunderstorms.

Without overthinking it, or dwelling on the reasons why Trudy was no longer that little girl, Charlotte reached out, circling her wrist to pull her into a hug that was so reminiscent of the one she'd given Ruby only an hour ago that it brought fresh moisture to her eyes.

Trudy didn't smell like strawberries, though. She smelled of cigarettes and a perfume that was just on the wrong side of sweet. Her body wasn't soft baby fat, either, but long and willowy, sharp hip bones and exposed ribs. It was all Trudy.

"Take care of my baby," Charlotte murmured into her hair.

And neither of them said anything about the fact that Trudy was just a baby herself.

CHAPTER NINETEEN

ALICE

August 3, 2018
Five days after the kidnapping

By the time Alice and Nakamura got back to the station from the fast food joint, Zeke Durand had been brought into the station and was waiting for them in the interrogation room.

"Want to take the lead?" Nakamura asked as they walked back down the hallway from where they had just come.

She nodded. It was unspoken between them, but she was running the investigation at this point. It was the first time she'd assumed the role since she'd been in St. Petersburg, but she slipped into it like a well-worn leather jacket.

The stark room was intimidating even before they started in on questioning. It was designed to put its occupants on edge, to make them question their own reality, with its single metal table and the mirror that was so obviously not a mirror.

That silvery glass was a threat—people were watching. Even if they weren't. Suspects couldn't help but look at it, their eyes drawn to the idea of someone they didn't know scrutinizing their every movement, twitch, sigh.

Zeke Durand was no different.

The kid's shoulders were turned in, protective and defensive. His head was bowed, his hands gripping each other as if that grasp was the only thing keeping him from falling apart. But his eyes. His eyes kept shifting to that mirror.

"Hello, Mr. Durand." Alice slid into the chair across from him, putting them on an equal level. Nakamura arranged himself into one of the corners, leaning against the wall with his feet crossed at the ankles. "I'm Detective Alice Garner, and this is my partner, Detective Joe Nakamura."

He looked up at her introduction, his eyes a startling blue, but just as quickly he went back to staring at the table. "Call me Zeke."

"All right, Zeke," she said, easy and friendly. It was important to build a rapport in these situations, to coax him out of his shell. It would be a waste of time if they couldn't provoke any true reactions from him, if the only thing they could read were nerves and not answers. "Do you want some water? Coffee?"

"I'm set," he said, though his mouth remained a grim line.

"Great. Well, we just have a few questions we thought you could help us out with," she said, letting her shoulders open up and her legs relax.

"I want to help."

"Well, that's wonderful to hear," Alice said. "Is there anything in particular you'd like to tell us?"

Zeke licked his bottom lip, but then after a minute shook his head.

"That's okay," Alice said. "Do you know what this is all about?"

He glanced up, and once again she was taken aback by his eyes. It wasn't just the unexpected color. Pinned under his gaze, she struggled to keep her arms resting on the table, not to bring them up across her chest to protect all her secrets.

"It's about Trudy," he finally said.

There was relief in not having to sidestep into it. "Could you tell us a little bit about your relationship with her?"

He shook his head. "There was no relationship."

Nakamura shifted behind her, but she didn't take her attention off Zeke. "Friendship, then?"

"Maybe," Zeke breathed out. "I don't know anymore, to be honest."

"That's okay," Alice reassured once again, taking some of the pressure off the question.

He lasted with the silence for all of one minute. "She, uh, she wanted my car," Zeke said.

"To buy it?"

"No." Zeke shook his head, and one of his broken nails picked at the dry skin of his knuckles. "She wanted me to drive her. Places."

"Would you pick her up from her house?" she asked.

He ran a hand over his head. "No. Never," he said. "Her grandmother is psycho. Apparently, she would freak if she saw us together."

"She told you that?"

"Yeah," he said. "It was part of the deal."

Her eyes slid over his face. "And where'd you take her?"

Zeke shrugged. "Tampa, mostly."

"Where did you take her in Tampa?"

"She'd always have me drop her at a street corner," he mumbled. "Wouldn't tell me what she was doing."

Alice tilted her head. "And you didn't press her on it?"

Zeke looked up again. "She's allowed her secrets."

She hummed a bit. "Any guesses, then?"

There was a minute where it seemed like he was warring with himself. And then he took a little breath. "She'd sometimes have thick makeup on. Glitter. Smell like heavy perfume."

Which could add up to sex work of some kind. Stripper, hooker? A quick cash grab.

"And . . . um . . ." Zeke trailed off, shook his head. Then nodded once. "One time we went to a club."

That wasn't the grand announcement she'd been expecting. "Okay. Was there anything particular about this club?"

"No, but . . ."

Alice could all but see his mind working—how much could he tell without screwing Trudy over? "We danced a little bit. But then we went into this back room. It was straight out of a movie."

"Did she pick something up then?" Alice asked.

"Yeah. Fake passports." He grimaced when he said it.

Trudy had been planning an escape.

"How many?" Were they all planning on leaving? Or just Trudy?

Zeke took a beat. "Two, I think. But I didn't get a good look."

She nodded. "All right. Did you take her anywhere else?"

"She asked . . ." With a sudden burst of movement, Zeke unlocked his hands, dropping them to the tops of his jean-clad thighs. He raked his fingers up and down the rough fabric, looking between her and Nakamura. "That day."

Her pulse fluttered, but she worked to keep her face relaxed. "The day Ruby was kidnapped? That day?"

He flinched at Ruby's name but didn't react much beyond that. "She borrowed my car."

And, shit. "Zeke . . ."

"I know." Zeke's eyes were wet with unshed tears when he looked up at her. "I don't think she hurt Ruby."

"That's not for you to guess," Alice said, not feeling very sympathetic. "Why didn't you come forward with this?"

"She brought it back. Like an hour later," Zeke said as if it were justification, but it dug the hole only deeper. Someone could do a lot in an hour. It was plenty of time to hide a body.

"Was this in the morning?" Alice asked.

Zeke licked his lips. "Early afternoon."

Ruby had been kidnapped at 1:00 p.m. "Zeke."

He shook his head. "Trudy wouldn't hurt her," he said again. "She would never hurt Ruby. And nothing was messed up with the car. I checked it later. Once I'd heard . . ."

"Used your homemade forensic kit and everything?" It was a pointless jab, and it made Nakamura shift against the wall in subtle warning. She rubbed a thumb along her eyebrow, trying to regain control of the conversation. Zeke was just blinking at her, sad and slow, like a kicked puppy.

"So she just returned your car, no explanation? Did you hear from her after that?"

He paused. "No."

"Don't lie to me, Zeke," she warned, putting some authority in her voice.

"I haven't."

"Then, what are you thinking?" Alice asked. He was easy to read, and there was clearly something. She'd already picked up on a baseline for his cadence, for the way he hesitated because of his accent and the way he hesitated when there was something he didn't want to say.

"I didn't hear from her," he said, like he was trying to say something more than that.

So she guessed. "That was unusual?"

"Yes."

"How often did you hear from her before that day?" she asked.

"Every day," he said. "I drove her into Tampa about twice a week, sometimes three days. But she liked to text." It was said as if he was betraying a confidence.

"And the two of you weren't . . ."

"Dating?" he finished for her.

She nodded. Two attractive teenagers talking every day? It was unlikely that something hadn't happened.

"I'm gay, Detective," he said. "It was never like that. We were just. Yeah, I guess we were friends."

She hummed. "Did she know? That you're gay?"

His lips tipped up again. "Eventually."

"Was she upset to find out?"

"No, not at all." Zeke smiled this time. It was still restrained, but it was a real smile. "Trudy isn't—I mean. You could look at her family and assume things."

"Like what?"

He shrugged. "You know. She likes to come off as tough," he said. "And maybe she was kind of a bitch in the way that girls call each other that. Like she's not going to say nice things just to say nice things, you know?"

Alice nodded.

"But when push came to shove? She was . . . God, she would kill me for saying this." He seemed to realize this as he said it. He gave a rueful shrug. "Well. She's kind."

They were quiet.

"Look, I know this doesn't look good." Zeke pressed his hands flat on the table and really looked at her, his body tense and urgent. "Everything I've said . . . I know this doesn't look good for her . . . but . . . she wouldn't do anything to hurt Ruby. She loved that kid."

She felt for him, she did. Sighing, she shook her head. "That doesn't guarantee anything, Zeke."

There was something incredibly sad in the way he deflated into himself once more, his chest collapsing, his shoulders hunching. "I know." It was so soft, that admission, but it must have been hard to make.

"Did you ever meet Ruby, Zeke?"

The tension was back in his body. "No."

She nodded and then let the silence take over. If there were secrets to spill into the space, it was easier to do without someone else's chatter taking up the slack.

He remained quiet, though, head still bowed.

There was an itch between her shoulder blades as she watched him, one that had been there since they'd talked to Trudy at the house.

"What was your deal?"

He lifted his head, but his face was blank, his blinking slow and confused.

She continued, "With Trudy. What did she give you in exchange for driving her around?"

He paused. It was one of those hesitations that was weighty. One where he was choosing the words with care, with a thought toward the ramifications each would have. "A favor."

"You know I'm going to need more than that, Zeke," she said.

Shaking his head, he kept his eyes on the table. "An unspecified favor. When a Burke offers you that, you don't say no."

St. Petersburg royalty. "Even though she's just a teenager?" she asked.

One finger tapped a staccato beat against the metal top of the table. "Didn't matter."

"Why are you so sure?"

He looked up at that, his hands stilled once more. His gaze snapped over to Nakamura and then back to her face, pulling his bottom lip into his teeth. "The rumors."

She leaned forward. "Come on, Zeke. Don't make me work so hard here. What rumors?"

"Everyone talks about the Burkes, yeah?" Zeke said instead of answering her. Then he took a breath. "People say messed-up things."

"What rumors, Zeke?"

He exhaled, and it was loud in the room, which had gone quiet. "They say she has influence over her grandfather. Trudy," Zeke finally said.

"Like he dotes on her?" Nakamura asked.

Alice knew the answer, could read it in the set of Zeke's shoulders, the reluctance of the words, the disgust that pulled at the bridge of his nose. "No," she said with barely any voice behind it.

He heard her, though. Shaking his head, his eyes not leaving hers, Zeke repeated the simple word that said far too much.

"No."

———

"Did you know?" Alice asked, but she could read the answer on Nakamura's face.

His lips pinched downward. "Of course not."

"Come on," Alice said. She'd known, she had. But there was something about it being confirmed out loud that set her blood on fire. It was rage—fierce and hot and ugly—that poured through her now. The helplessness she felt in the face of Sterling Burke's power only threw gasoline on the flames. "There're always rumors, right? You're telling me this family? This family got away with something like that without anyone knowing?"

He slapped a hand against the mint-green tile that lined the wall outside the interrogation room. "No. Jesus. Do you think I wouldn't have done something?"

"You know what? I don't know what to think." Alice threw her arms out. "This town is so far up his ass, it's unbelievable. We can't even get a warrant, and you want me to think you would have, what, moseyed up to his house? Knocked on his door like a good little Boy Scout?"

"We're not all like that," Nakamura bit off. "This town's not all like that."

"Get me a fucking warrant and maybe I'll believe you," Alice said. "Bring that asshole in here. None of that 'Can we have a minute of your day, sir?' I want him handcuffed to that table."

"You know what? I get it." Nakamura pushed off the wall, got in her space a little. She held her ground. "I get that you're pissed. But getting irrational isn't going to help the situation."

And, no. "Irrational? You think I'm overreacting? My emotions getting a bit much for me to handle?"

Emotional. Erratic.

"I think this case is a lot," Nakamura said, pitching his voice low. "And I think you haven't slept in days. You're running on stubbornness and black coffee right now, and cuffing the city's most prominent judge to an interrogation table *without cause* is irrational. The fact that you can't see that is telling enough."

Her fingers curled, begging to hit him. She wanted to hear bones crack, and she didn't even care whose they would be.

It was scary, the way she felt right now. Wild, angry, and as emotional as they always said she was. The control she had on the wildfire gathering in her chest was tenuous at best. She knew she needed to get out of this situation, but she couldn't quite make herself walk away.

Instead, she pushed him. Hard. So that he wasn't looming over her anymore, and when he stepped back, she followed. She pushed him again, and then again and once more until his back was up against the wall.

"Don't you ever talk to me like that again," Alice said, her voice calm. His eyes were dark and steady. "Sterling Burke is a child molester and a rapist. And you're telling me I don't have cause."

"You don't even know that," Nakamura said. "They're rumors, Alice. You have nothing even confirmed."

Her brain was foggy, and it took the words too long to make sense. "What?"

Nakamura didn't try to get around her, didn't try to get her out of his space. He just watched her with a calm expression. "All of that stuff? It's based on rumors and unfounded allegations."

Her lungs heaved, struggling to keep up with her breathing. "Please. You know it's true. If there are rumors like that going around, it's true."

"No . . . that's not . . . You can't say that," Nakamura said. "You're not thinking straight."

She wasn't. She didn't even know why it had set her off, except that everything seemed so fragile and raw these days.

"Alice, you can't charge based on rumors," Nakamura said, and she hated him for being rational. "You know that."

"We don't need to charge him."

"What do you mean?" he asked.

"We need a warrant and we need him in here," Alice said, frustration eating at her stomach lining. "Show me you're better than I think you are right now."

Nakamura's lip tightened. "You know what this looks like."

"It looks like a child molester's granddaughter turned up dead." She knew that's not what he meant, though. "Connect the puzzle pieces."

"No." Nakamura shook his head, still calm. "You know what this looks like. It looks like Charlotte snapped after she found out her daughter was going through the same abuse as she had. You want me to pull my head out of his ass? Pull yours out of your own."

It was too much. She stepped away, her hand dropping to her side.

"Stop being the woman who lost a child, and start being a cop," Nakamura said, and it was the harshness of it, coming from him, that broke her.

She was on him, her hand a hard edge against his windpipe. He was larger and stronger, but she had rage coursing through her, and he wasn't struggling anyway.

There was something in his eyes that looked like satisfaction. Like he'd wanted to push her off the ledge so that she would finally fall.

She moved back again, releasing him. His hand came up instinctively to his throat, rubbed there. "Fuck off," she said.

"What does it look like, Alice?"

"It wasn't Charlotte," she said.

"You don't think it's Charlotte because you don't want it to be Charlotte," Nakamura said. "You have to stop investigating Lila's murder."

"I'm not," Alice said, and for once she felt on solid ground. "I know who killed Lila. I don't need to investigate it."

Nakamura shook his head. "You're still investigating it."

There would probably be a bruise where her fingers had dug into his neck, and he still said it. Maybe he did have enough backbone to actually get her the warrant after all.

"I have to go."

"Where are we going?" Nakamura asked.

"No," she said. "Just me. I have to go."

He looked at her. *Don't do anything stupid.* He didn't say it. He didn't have to.

She ducked her head, turning toward the exit. "Get me my warrant. And we need to talk to Sterling Burke."

Not waiting for an answer, she headed down the hallway toward the exit and reached into her pocket for her phone.

She opened a new message. Her fingers were shaky as she typed.

Meet In 10?

The response was almost instantaneous.

Where?

Alice texted an address, pausing only for a second on the station's back stairs to do so.

It was time for damage control.

CHAPTER TWENTY

TRUDY

July 19, 2018
Ten days before the kidnapping

The Burkes' summer party was the invite of the season. Hollis was meticulous in planning it, with no detail left untouched.

Mellie had selected Trudy's outfit for the day, a light pink thing that was reminiscent of one she'd worn when she was five. If Mellie was trying to convey purity, she would have to pull out more than just a high-necked sheath dress.

The pearls were a step too far. They were the collar Southern ladies locked around their own necks as if they were a badge of honor. Trudy had little interest in playing those games. She left them on the dresser where Mellie had laid them.

It was midday by the time Trudy made her way down the long curving staircase. Her fingers dragged against the polished wood, the smudges from the oil on the tips marring its gleaming perfection.

Guests were being routed to the back gardens where the tents blocked the worst of the sun. Air-cooling units set up in the corners did their best to battle the humidity, but there was only so much they could do.

After nabbing a glass of champagne from a passing waiter, Trudy wove her way toward the little crab cakes stacked high on one of the cocktail tables. She washed the expensive meat down with a swig of the wine, and the bubbles were sharp against her tongue, coating her throat in sugar.

The flute was yanked from her hand before she could take another sip.

"Trudy. Absolutely not." Hollis's voice was drenched in censure but pitched low so no one would overhear. "At least pretend you are not misplaced trailer trash for one day. I think even you can handle that."

Trudy turned and walked away without answering her grandmother, without even looking at her. Finding another waiter would be easy. Disappearing into the crowd even easier. Hollis would be distracted by some tiny flaw that would itch at the back of her neck until it was fixed.

Mellie, meanwhile, was at least halfway to sloshed herself, pressed up as she was against an uncomfortable businessman in a seersucker suit.

Sterling sometimes watched Trudy at parties like this, his eyes on her skin, her hair, her shoulders. Others probably saw a devoted grandfather. She'd learned to stick to the shadows.

But today he would be somewhere cozied up with the legions of ass-kissers who were gagging for the smallest crumb of attention.

That left only Charlotte to deal with.

Her aunt was nursing some pretty lemonade concoction out of a mason jar, and Trudy would bet good money there wasn't even a whiff of alcohol in the drink. Ever the perfect lady in public, that was Charlotte.

She was in a light blue wraparound dress that played into her strengths, her hair slicked back into a low chignon with not a single strand out of place, her makeup subtle, highlighting her sharp cheekbones and downplaying the slight slope to her eyes that, with a smoky shadow, could turn her wide gaze into a sleepy bedroom invitation.

From the outside, Trudy knew most people thought Charlotte was the favorite.

It was curious how so often people saw only the surface of one another. They filled in the blanks they didn't know or couldn't understand with preconceived notions that had no grounding in reality. They thought Charlotte was the beloved, perfect daughter because that's what she presented to the world. And nobody questioned why a twenty-four-year-old unmarried woman with a five-year-old daughter still lived with her parents.

No, for them it simply made sense that Charlotte was the heir apparent in the social dynasty that was the Burke family. She was sleek and controlled where Mellie was messy and wild. Her hostessing skills were second only to Hollis's, and she had an innate way about her that made others feel relaxed in her company. Grace, some people might call it.

Charlotte was Hollis, but prettier, nicer, and with a warmth the older woman could never understand.

And that's why Hollis hated her.

It had taken a long time for Trudy to realize it. There had always been little barbs directed at all the women in the Burke family beneath Hollis's reign of terror. When Trudy had been younger, she'd assumed it was just how families talked to each other. Everything from subtle put-downs to vicious hostility.

Then Trudy slowly began to realize it wasn't normal. The constant barrage of corrections and veiled insults toward first Charlotte and then Trudy were the manifestation of the ugliness of her grandmother's soul.

Mellie, for the most part, was immune. Only in recent months when Ruby, sweet baby Ruby, became the newest target of Hollis's rage did Trudy start to wonder why that was.

Her brain circled the truth, shrinking back when it touched the deep, pulsing darkness that awaited her there. Sterling had never paid attention to Mellie.

Charlotte glanced up as if she could hear Trudy's thoughts, as if there were a line of silk thread between them, pulling her aunt's attention.

It would have made sense for the venom that was directed at them to bond the two, but it hadn't. Instead, it had turned them mean against each other. Well, it had turned Trudy mean. Charlotte was much too good a person for that kind of behavior. It had turned her icy instead.

Trudy blinked first, and when she broke the moment, Charlotte moved away.

"Look at you." The deep, booming voice surprised her enough that she didn't back away in time to avoid the dry lips that landed just a bit too close to the corner of her mouth. The dodge did nothing to deter the older man they were attached to, who was still invading her personal space.

"Mr. Cooper," Trudy murmured, stepping out of the circle of his arms. He was her grandfather's age, but the years had not been as kind to him as they had been to Sterling. The thick shock of white hair was the only saving grace to draw attention away from the rolls under his chin and the craggy deep orange skin that he absolutely thought made him look younger.

"You've grown up well, girl," he said, slicking his tongue along his bottom lip before taking a deep sip of his drink.

"Not quite yet," she reminded him.

"If you'll excuse us, Mr. Cooper." Charlotte came up behind Trudy, her arm going around Trudy's shoulder. Her fingers dug into the bones there, but Trudy hid her wince. "I have to borrow my niece."

Cooper smacked his mouth but didn't put up a fight. "Of course, of course, ladies."

Despite the relief coursing through Trudy as Charlotte directed her away from the man, she bristled. She'd never been particularly good with gratitude. "I don't need you to protect me," she said instead of "Thank you."

Charlotte's body stiffened against hers. If she had Trudy's personality, she would have lashed out with a thin whip of emotion. But she had no actual backbone, so she simply dropped her arm and stepped away.

"I didn't do it because I don't think you can take care of yourself, Trudy," Charlotte said, only a bit of the exasperation on her face seeping into her voice. They were in public, after all. "I know what it's like, though."

And wasn't that the crux of the problem? They both knew too well what it was like.

"Well, you can take that savior complex of yours and shove it up your tight ass. Do you think it will fit?"

Charlotte's eyelids slipped closed, her cheeks pale despite the heat of the day, and Trudy wondered if her fingers itched to slap Trudy right across the face. The smack might make them both feel better. It would relieve some of the guilt Trudy had for the need that throbbed within her to make her aunt hurt. To slice at her skin with jagged words, to try to make marks on a psyche that was already thick with scar tissue.

It would make Charlotte feel better, too. Because that control she employed with such a steady hand was killing her. The energy she dumped into making sure she kept all the pain and grief and anger and pettiness and sadness bottled up was slowly draining the life from her body. Soon, she would be left with nothing.

One way or another, it would break her.

But Charlotte was Charlotte. Instead of her fingers leaving angry red imprints on Trudy's cheeks, they turned into themselves. Trudy could almost feel the way those nails dug into her palms.

"Be more careful next time" was all Charlotte finally said when she opened her eyes.

"Because it's my fault some creepy guy cornered me?"

"In this world? Yes," Charlotte said, her eyes locked on Trudy's, and something that felt like dismayed understanding fluttered between them.

"Wow." Trudy turned away, breaking the moment. "You always manage to live down to my worst expectations for you, dear Charlie."

She stepped away but hesitated when Charlotte puffed out a small breath of air. "Right back atcha, babe."

It was so quiet that Trudy wondered if Charlotte had even meant for her to hear. She glanced back over her shoulder and smirked, for once impressed with her aunt. Then she turned to grab a half-drunk glass of champagne from the nearest table, not caring that there was already red lipstick on the rim.

She needed oblivion and she needed it immediately.

———

Two days after the summer party, Charlotte dragged Trudy and Ruby to the mall to buy replacement panty hose for ones she'd ripped.

They were in the food court when a man in a stained wifebeater brushed against Trudy's arm. He left behind a layer of sweat and body odor so pungent that it cut through the thick Cinnabon scent that clung to the air around them.

"Why are we even here?" Trudy asked Charlotte again, to be obnoxious. There was something inherently cheap and disgusting about being in a mall that made Trudy want to scrub her skin clean of other people's sadness.

"You could have stayed in the car," Charlotte said in the same measured way she'd answered the past five times Trudy had complained.

"But we gotta get ice cream." Ruby hung off her mother's hand, and Charlotte spared her a distracted smile as she navigated them all toward the department store at the end of the building.

"Trudy, can you get the ice cream and meet us?" Charlotte asked.

"Cash." Trudy held out her hand.

Charlotte shot her a look but started digging in her Louis Vuitton. "You could put it on your card."

"Like Hollis wouldn't ask what I was doing in a mall?"

There was a reluctance in handing over the ten-dollar bill Trudy knew too well, but she was unsympathetic as she snatched the crisp paper out of her aunt's fingers to tuck underneath her bra strap.

"Panty hose section" was all Charlotte said as she turned and pulled Ruby behind her.

"'Nilla, Dee-Dee," Ruby called. "With sprinkles."

Trudy made little finger guns at her to signal she'd heard, then tried not to breathe too deeply as she navigated the grease-laden air of the food court. There was a pimple begging to break through one of her pores just from the secondhand contact.

She flirted with the teenage boy who was scooping the ice cream and lingered in the warmth of his admiration. He had pretty green eyes and a mostly forgettable face, which made it easy to concentrate on the approval in his gaze instead of any actual interest on her part.

Eventually, the ice cream in Ruby's cup slipped over the side of the flimsy cardboard container, the melted sweetness sticky against the inside of her finger. She licked at the edges to contain the damage as she made her way toward where Charlotte had disappeared.

The nondescript music and cheap fabric and saleswomen with thick eye shadow distracted her so that she didn't realize something was wrong until she was almost right next to her aunt.

"Hey." Trudy nudged her shoulder, and Charlotte whirled on her, pupils dilated and face devoid of color.

"Ruby," Charlotte gasped, the tips of her fingers digging into the exposed flesh of Trudy's arms.

The undiluted panic on her aunt's face, in her voice, cut through any lingering confusion. Something was wrong. So very wrong.

"Where is she?" Trudy asked, the fear turning her voice sharp enough to cut through Charlotte's hysteria. "Charlotte."

"She's gone." Charlotte breathed the words out on an exhale, and though they'd just confirmed what Trudy had suspected, they still lodged themselves somewhere in her windpipe so that it was almost impossible to breathe. The ice-cream cup spattered against the tile, and the cool, melted liquid slinked into the spaces between Trudy's toes.

"Charlotte." She forced the name out. Concentrating on the points of Charlotte's fingers where they pushed bruises into Trudy's skin helped her focus. "She's not gone. She's just lost. I'm sure she wandered off. You know her."

Giving in to the fear right now would be fatal. She needed Charlotte with her, not useless on the floor, which was where she was currently headed.

She snaked a hand up to the vulnerable skin of Charlotte's inner arm and pinched hard, pulling up and twisting, almost drawing blood. The mark she left behind was red and pulsing, and Charlotte flinched. But her eyes lost some of their glassiness.

"Here's what we're going to do," Trudy said. There was a clock in her head, white and black and simple, and it was counting each second that Ruby was missing. "You're going to take this half. I'm going to take the other and then work my way toward the toy section. She'll find it if she can."

Trudy pushed Charlotte's arms out of the way and grabbed for her purse, palming the weight of her aunt's cell phone. She held it up in front of Charlotte's face. "You're going to call me the second you find her, and I'll do the same. Keep this out."

She pushed the phone into Charlotte's lax fingers and then took off without waiting for a response. If her aunt was going to go catatonic on her, that left only Trudy to find Ruby.

"Would you like to try Sweet . . ."

Trudy turned toward the voice, only to find one of the perfume ladies with an intricate pink bottle clutched in one hand and an empty smile approaching her, ready to spray. Knocking the perfume out of the way, Trudy grabbed her shoulders. The plastic mask faltered, her eyes going wide.

"My baby has gone missing," Trudy said, not willing to waste time on the complexities of the relationship. "Go find an intercom and make an announcement. She's five and has curly red hair."

Again, she didn't wait for confirmation before jogging a few steps back and spinning, her eyes at knee level, searching for familiar pigtails.

Ruby was fine. She was probably just hiding. She wandered off like she always did, and Charlotte had never learned how to actually keep an eye on her. Trudy repeated the loop of reassurances, turning up the volume on it to be heard over the rush of blood past her eardrums. Ruby was fine.

But the seconds kept slipping by, one into the next, and her hands tore at racks of clothing and at pretty purses and pillows fluffed on beds, and still no Ruby. Her breathing had turned shallow minutes, hours, days ago, and there were spots popping at the edges of her vision. Her phone remained stubborn and silent in her hand despite her desperate inner pleas for it to ring, for Charlotte to laugh in her ear no matter how manic that laugh might be, and they'd yell at Ruby and squeeze her at the same time until she tried to squirm away.

But still nothing.

It wasn't until she'd finally admitted to herself that Ruby wasn't in the toy section that her phone buzzed.

Got her. Dresses.

She'd thought she'd feel relief, but she didn't. She didn't feel anything but an emptiness that was left behind from the waves of fear that had kept her upright for the past fifteen minutes.

Trudy found them sitting on the dirty linoleum floor in the middle of an aisle, surrounded by dresses that had angry red sales stickers hanging from their arms. Charlotte's face was buried in Ruby's hair, and the girl's arms were tight around her mother's back.

A movement caught Trudy's peripheral vision, and she tilted her head just a bit, still keeping her family in sight. There was a woman, tall and slim with brown hair, walking away from their group, her long legs swift and confident. Just as she turned the corner at the end of the aisle, she dipped her chin to her shoulder for one last glance at the scene. Then she was gone.

"Who was that?" Trudy asked. Neither Charlotte nor Ruby answered, and she doubted they'd even heard.

She dropped to a crouch, her hand shaking as she placed it between Ruby's shoulders. "You scared us there, shortcake."

Ruby burrowed her head deeper into her mother's neck. Charlotte looked up at Trudy, the rims of her eyes red, her lashes thick, damp clumps. There was something bordering on a thank-you there in her expression, and Trudy hated it.

"I can't believe you let this happen," Trudy said, and the words burned like acid even as they formed in the soft spaces of her mouth. "God, you're such a failure."

Ruby stiffened underneath Trudy's palm, and that only added to the guilt that was like sandpaper against an open wound.

Trudy straightened so she didn't have to meet Charlotte's now-blank expression, the flicker of gratitude doused by the unwarranted cruelty.

"Come on, petal." Charlotte shifted her grip on her daughter so she didn't have to let go of her as she stood. Trudy leaned down, cupping her elbow to help her, a silent penance that was nowhere near enough of an apology. But it was what she was capable of.

Adjusting Ruby so that most of her weight was supported by Charlotte's hip, her aunt shifted so that she met Trudy's eyes.

You're such a failure.

There was an echo of her hateful words ricocheting in the space beneath her skull, and Trudy saw it there on Charlotte's face as well. It would take a long time for that echo to go silent for either of them.

Finally—without dropping her gaze—Charlotte murmured, "I know."

———

Later that night, Trudy waited for Charlotte on the porch, in the dark, for an hour. When Ruby had crawled into Trudy's bed, her face damp with tears, Trudy had known that Charlotte had gone off to God-knows-where to ease the self-hatred that was slowly killing her. Trudy didn't know if the solution was sex or drugs or alcohol for her aunt, but whatever it was, she was seeking it far away from anyone in the Burke household.

"Tell me a story," Ruby had whispered into the nook of Trudy's shoulder, and so Trudy did. It had taken only minutes for her breathing to even out as she snuffled a bit and rolled into a comfortable position. Only when she was confident Ruby was truly asleep had Trudy slipped out from beneath the comforter, her feet padding across the hardwood. She'd grabbed a cigarette she kept hidden in her birth control packet and had tucked it behind her ear. It wasn't like she would be able to smoke it, but it would give her something to do with her hands.

Then she'd crept downstairs, making sure to gently close the screen door that liked to slam at the most inopportune of moments. When she'd been satisfied she hadn't awoken the entire household, she'd settled onto the swinging bench that hung just off to the right of the stairs.

She pulled her legs up to her chest, then stretched her baggy, well-worn T-shirt out to cover her knees. It was cool enough to have goose bumps but not cool enough to go searching for a blanket.

And then she'd waited.

The night was always so quiet. Trudy liked to think they lived close enough to the ocean to hear the waves breaking, but it wasn't true. It was just something she told herself, and she didn't even know why. There were so many things like that.

Instead of lingering on the thought, she'd concentrated on the plan that had started as just a wisp of an idea earlier that day when Ruby had gone missing. They'd all been silent on the way home, crashing down from their fear, torn panty hose long forgotten. In the confines of the car, with her hand petting Ruby's hair, Trudy had admitted they'd overreacted. The girl had simply wandered off and been found by a "nice lady" who helped Ruby locate Charlotte. But the terror was easy to ridicule in the moments after. Panic, however, knew nothing about rational thinking.

Trudy was also on edge. There were the passports she kept on her person at almost all times. There was Ruby's birthday trudging ever closer, when Ruby would pass over an invisible line none of them dared mention. And then there was Charlotte, who seemed to be held together with cheap glue and frayed strings and perhaps a few promises to gods she didn't believe in.

They were going to have to act, sooner rather than later, it seemed. Now she just had to get her aunt to trust her again. If she ever had trusted her.

When Charlotte crept back up the stairs, Trudy fell into old patterns, flinging mud at her just to see if it would stick. It was habit at this point.

"Do be sure to change out of that dress. There's a stain on it that I don't think can pass as holy water," Trudy said. Christ, why couldn't she stop being a bitch? For once in her life?

Her aunt didn't react, just went for the doorknob.

And Trudy was about to miss her opportunity because she couldn't keep the barbs that bit into her own soul to herself. She had to watch them slice into Charlotte's skin as well, because only then was it justified in how much it hurt.

This, though—Ruby—was too important. It was so much bigger than either her or Charlotte, so much bigger than pettiness and anger and frustration. It was so much bigger than her pride.

Trudy swallowed hard. "Wait."

Charlotte turned, slowly, so slowly, exhaustion in every collapsed angle of her body.

"I need your help."

The laugh that came out of Charlotte was ugly and broken and spoke of the years of animosity that festered between them. "You're asking for my help? After that little scene?"

Trudy winced. At herself. At her aunt. At their screwed-up situation. "Yeah."

Still, it was that simple because she knew Charlotte. If Trudy asked for help, Charlotte would help.

Charlotte pressed the heel of her palm into the space between her eyes, but Trudy could tell she wasn't going to ignore her and walk away. Looking up with those cool, judgmental eyes, Charlotte sighed. "What do you need?"

Where to start? "I don't hate you, you know." And that's not what she had meant to say. She pressed her lips together, biting into the flesh as if it had betrayed her for letting that confession slip out.

This time Charlotte's laugh was dry and brittle. Disbelieving. "I honestly don't care if you do, Trudy."

That wasn't true. Charlotte cared, and she cared too much, which was part of the problem, wasn't it?

"Ruby's turning six," Trudy tried, because that really was the start of it, wasn't it? Ruby's birthday and the ever-ticking clock as they moved closer to it.

Charlotte paled in the weak glow of the streetlamp. "I know."

"What are you going to do?" Trudy asked, not hopeful. Charlotte had done nothing to protect the girl up until this point. Why would she suddenly start acting like a mother?

Her aunt shook her head, looking helpless as always. Rage, swift and fierce and familiar, shot through her.

"Why haven't you taken her away yet?"

Charlotte's eyes were wide and damp and scared. Haunted. Hunted. "He wouldn't let me."

"That's bullshit." Trudy wanted to yell it. Wished they were having this out, finally having this out, somewhere other than their front porch where anything over a whisper was dangerous. "Come on, Charlie. Do better than that."

But her aunt was shaking her head. "You think he'd let me take her? She's his daughter."

Trudy blanched at the stark truth of it, her stomach heaving. No one ever said it out loud, though they all knew. She pushed to her feet and took the few steps necessary to lean over the railing. Her body rid itself of bile as if it could purge itself of every terrible thing in the world.

When Trudy was done, she straightened, wiping a hand across her mouth. Charlotte hadn't moved, was still watching her with quiet, resigned eyes.

"We have to get her out," Trudy said, surer than she'd been of anything in her life.

"I tried to leave when I was fourteen," Charlotte said. "A friend of mine was going on vacation to Miami, and I lied and said Hollis and Sterling were letting me go with her family. Hollis was waiting for me when we got there—she'd flown ahead while we drove. She broke my wrist."

Trudy swallowed hard. She hadn't known. She'd never known Charlotte had tried to escape.

"I tried to leave again when I was sixteen," Charlotte continued. "Mellie had gotten out that one time, just left in the middle of the night with Tommy. So I thought, that's what I'll do. I'll take a bus to Vegas. I didn't even care what would happen when I got there. All I wanted to do was leave."

The choices you can live with.

"It took Hollis two weeks to track me down." Hollis. Always Hollis. Sterling would never get his hands dirty. "We couldn't leave for three days, though, because of how bruised my face was after she found me. When I tried to leave at eighteen. Well, that's how we have Ruby."

And with Ruby came complete control over Charlotte.

"Why?" It was too much, and Trudy could barely push the question out between trembling lips.

Charlotte's laugh this time was hollow and desperate. "If I knew why . . ."

"Hollis hates you," Trudy said, like it was a revelation, except it wasn't. They all saw how Charlotte was treated. Even worse than Trudy.

"Hollis doesn't hate me," Charlotte corrected. "She hates herself."

"She hates Sterling."

Her aunt shrugged, one delicate shoulder. "I don't know. I think it's more complicated than that." She paused, then continued, "I was the first, you know? Mellie. Well, he didn't look at Mellie. But me? I used to think I was special. Our little secret."

Whispered in the night. Trudy remembered the thrill of it. The idea of it. "Hollis should have tried to protect you."

"She didn't know."

That wasn't true. "She knows everything."

"She didn't want to believe it," Charlotte conceded. "Denial is a powerful thing."

It was almost surreal that they were talking about this. After all these years of silence and misdirected anger, here they were whispering on the porch at 5:00 a.m., ripping open old scars and pouring salt in the wounds.

"We have to get Ruby out," Trudy said again.

"I know," Charlotte said, but her voice was hesitant. "I just don't know how. I've saved some money. I've been trying to come up with . . . something. I don't know what to do, though."

She sounded so young. Lost and unsure. Nothing like the poised Southern lady she portrayed to the public. And Trudy remembered in that moment that Charlotte was only twenty-four.

All of a sudden, Trudy was exhausted. Tired beyond anything she'd ever felt before. It was in her bones and her muscles and her limbs. But this was important.

"Well," Trudy said, "lucky for you, I have a plan."

CHAPTER
TWENTY-ONE
ALICE

August 3, 2018
Five days after the kidnapping

Alice stared at the address she'd just texted Charlotte, trying to consider her options. But the rage that swept through her, ruthless and uncontrolled, had died as sudden as it had come, leaving behind a thick fog that turned her thoughts sluggish.

Damage control. Think. Move.

The car would be too easy to spot. She would have to go on foot instead.

Alice took a breath, ignoring the shaking in her fingers. Then she started forward, across the parking lot. Once she got to the small plot of dirt on the other side, she slipped through the crack in between the fences lining the street and the station's closest neighbor, a run-down Victorian that was the proverbial sore thumb of the area. She'd always liked it, and she liked it more when it provided her cover to move through the shin-high grass of its backyard into the alleyway on its far side.

She dipped into the shadow of one of the garages that lined the graveled road and scrolled through her contacts until she found the right number.

A little misdirection to keep the wolves at bay.

Ben Wilson answered on one ring. "Couldn't get enough of me, could you?"

"You should run what you have on Zeke Durand," she said, not bothering with foreplay.

There was a bit of shuffling on the other end, and when he spoke again, Ben's voice was harder. More professional and less relaxed banter. "What do you have for me?"

She ran her hand through her hair, and the tips of her fingers caught in the knots. "Nothing."

"Tease," he said, and just like that, the easiness was back.

"Write it or don't, I don't care," she snapped. "Consider this your heads-up."

There was no guarantee that he'd run with it, but if he thought there was enough for her to call him, he might take a chance.

She didn't wait for him to answer, just thumbed the power off completely and slipped the phone in her pocket before taking off at a slow jog. The diner was close, but she was going to be late. Even later since she planned on taking several wrong turns, ducking into side streets she knew led nowhere. It was paranoia at its finest, but her tolerance for sloppiness had plummeted in the past twenty minutes.

She knew she needed to get control of herself; she couldn't risk another outburst like the one she'd just had at the station with Nakamura. There were too many eyes on her as it was, wanting her to fall apart, wanting her to break down. Just so they'd be right.

It had felt good, though, letting go just for once. Terrifying and exhilarating, seductive despite the consequences.

God, she was walking a fine line with this case.

By the time she reached the diner, Charlotte had already arrived. The familiar strawberry hair was easy to spot even though it was mostly hidden under a faded gray baseball hat.

The woman had chosen her seat well, tucked as she was into the back-corner booth that was mostly obscured by the large neon jukebox right beside it.

She blended into the background that way. It was more than how she disappeared amid the garishness of her surroundings, though. It was how she sat, how she breathed, how she avoided anything to draw eyes in her direction.

Attention was fatal. Alice guessed she'd learned that lesson the hard way.

Charlotte's shoulders were thin and collapsed into themselves, the knobs of her spine showing through her thin cotton T-shirt. She kept her chin tilted toward the wall and down so that there was only the faintest outline of her cheek visible to the majority of the patrons. Even her breath seemed shallow so as not to disrupt the air around her.

There was a sadness to her as well. One that kept eyes from lingering too long in case it was contagious.

Alice looked around, scoping out the place. Neon and Elvis were the main decor choices—perhaps the *only* decor choices. It wasn't kitschy enough to draw the tourists, and it was too much for the locals. It was perfect.

In classic diner fashion, the cook, a small man with too much white hair, was visible through the causeway between the restaurant and the kitchen. Behind the counter, a middle-aged woman was wiping a frayed rag over and over on the same spot while she flipped through a comic book. She hadn't looked up at the bell.

Besides the two workers, there were three shabby businessmen huddled into one of the booths closest to the doors. They'd glanced over in unison when she walked in, the light catching on the thick plastic rim of the blond's glasses, before they hunched over their table once more.

She moved, as quietly as possible, toward the back and didn't say anything as she slid onto the cracked vinyl bench across from Charlotte.

The woman's eyes were wide, and she startled when she noticed Alice. Perhaps that was just her default expression now, with the world coming at her faster than she could process.

Charlotte's fingers slid up to her eyebrow, plucking at the skin around a tiny bald spot, the fine strawberry hairs apparently victims to nervous hands.

"Hello," Charlotte whispered, ducking even deeper into the shadows beneath her cap.

This was a mere ghost of the woman Alice had met a week earlier. Gone was the quiet confidence, the elegance in the way she moved replaced with jittery sorrow. Gone were the expensive dresses and flawless accessories; in their place were faded jeans and a cheap tee.

The waitress interrupted them before Alice could say anything. She handed over laminated menus with pictures of food and then walked away.

Once she was gone, Alice turned her attention back to Charlotte. "I know you can't actually talk to me."

"I can't." Charlotte touched fingertips to her throat as if she was surprised by her own voice. That it was working.

"I know," Alice said, wrinkling her brow like she really understood. It was an act, but so were so many things. Her patience had already been devoured today by talking to Ben and talking to Nakamura and talking to Zeke. Fake sympathy was all she had left to offer. "I know. Your mother won't find out."

It fascinated Alice, always, how willing people were to trust where none had been earned. Trust in a uniform, trust in a person's story, trust in promises that were empty and hollow but dressed in pretty clothes. She could see it on Charlotte's face. She believed Alice for no other reason than that Alice said it was true.

There was power in that.

"Why are you helping me?" Charlotte asked, her fingers going for her eyebrow once again.

"Who says I am?" Alice answered, because sometimes honesty grounded lies in reality.

"Oh." The woman dropped the leg she'd had pulled up against her chest back down to the floor. There was something disjointed in her movements, in the way she was processing information, the way she was watching Alice with just a sliver of iris visible beyond her dark pupils. It was as if she was a half step behind.

Maybe if Alice were Nakamura, she'd be suspicious. This was a woman in the middle of a breakdown. She was showing signs of emotion beyond grief. Like guilt. That's what really ate at a person.

"You helped us, though," Charlotte said, her words going soft at the pauses between them so that they blended into each other.

"Whatcha getting, hons?" The waitress was back, her pen and pad held at the ready.

"Tea, with honey," Alice ordered for herself.

Charlotte merely shook her head, nudging the menu she hadn't even looked at away from her elbow. The waitress rolled her eyes but then left them alone again.

They didn't speak until Alice had her hands wrapped around a tiny, chipped white mug that had stains of drinks past smudged near the handle.

"You helped us," Charlotte said again.

At the department store. "That doesn't mean I'm helping you now."

"You never told anyone." It wasn't a question. She was right, though. "You helped find Ruby that day at the mall. I was . . . I thought I'd lost her."

Charlotte brought her knees back up against her chest and wrapped her arms around her shins. Where she'd been thin before, now she was just bones, and Alice wondered if that fragility had always been there, hidden under loose blouses and forgiving trousers. Here in the shivering fluorescent light of the diner, the sharp lines and juts were harder to ignore.

"You should order something to eat," Alice said, surprising even herself. What did it matter if Charlotte wasted away? It wasn't Alice's responsibility. The woman would have to learn to force herself, learn to remember that food had purpose beyond pleasure. It let you get up another day. It let you find the prick who put you in that state in the first place. It gave you fuel to fight them.

It was predictable that Charlotte shook her head. Alice shrugged off her own concerns, let them fall to the dirty floor to take up residence with the Coke and salt that coated the tiles. It wasn't her problem.

If she told herself enough times, she might actually believe it.

"Why didn't you tell anyone?" Charlotte asked, turning her cheek so that it rested on her upturned knee. Her gaze was surprisingly steady.

"It would have looked bad for you," Alice said, taking a sip of the tea. Redirecting attention to Charlotte would keep her worried, would keep her from thinking about coincidences.

"And you care?"

"Not about you," Alice said. Again, honestly. It was possible no one would have blinked if Alice had disclosed that she'd had a prior run-in with Charlotte and Ruby before taking the case. Maybe, though— maybe it would have been an excuse to kick her off it. "But I want the right person to be punished. That's not you."

"Isn't that against"—Charlotte paused, her eyes fluttering closed, perhaps struggling to find the right word—"ethics?"

Alice lifted a shoulder. "Ethics are relative."

"You believe that?"

"Of course." Alice pushed the mug away. The tea was tepid anyway, and clumps of honey stuck waxy to the rim. "But justice. Justice is immutable."

Charlotte blinked, that slow sweep. "I used to think I had ethics or some sort of moral compass, at least."

Alice used to as well. "And then Ruby . . ."

Charlotte nodded. "Now I have none."

"I know," Alice said. Because she did.

There was a thin string of understanding pulsing between them like a live wire. They both knew how one second, one heartbeat, could shatter years of living a life as a good person.

For Alice it hadn't been the heartbeat when Lila had slipped from her grasp. No, it had come later.

"Life in prison." The news was delivered like a Band-Aid being pulled off skin. Quick, efficient, painful.

Alice curled tighter into the fetal position, wrapped around Lila's favorite stuffed animal. It was soft and warm and still smelled of her even though it probably didn't. The fur, matted now from tears she'd been unable to stop, brushed against her cheek.

Alice hadn't been able to force herself to the court for the sentencing. Instead, she'd asked Jimmy Barstow, an old friend of her mother's and one of the few people she could stand being around these days, to go for her.

"I'm sorry, Alice," he said now in his radio-smooth voice. "I know you wanted . . . Well, I know you wanted it to turn out differently."

The death sentence. It was what he deserved; it was what she'd expected. How was he allowed to remain in the world, breathing and laughing and crying and living, when Lila had been so cruelly ripped out of it?

"Alice . . ."

"No," she said, then hung up.

She didn't shatter despite the fact that this sentencing had felt like the only thing holding her together for months. Instead, all the softness that had been left in the nooks of her body turned hard. The grief, the sadness, the memories, the love—it tightened into a jagged rock that sat heavy in her chest. It had taken only a moment.

Gone was the pain. Gone was the helplessness. Gone was the pounding injustice that had held her paralyzed only seconds ago.

Gone was Alice. The person she used to be who thought there was right and there was wrong, and that somehow it was a worthwhile pursuit to strive for the light.

What was left was a darkness she knew had only one purpose.

"What answers do you need?" Charlotte asked now, and Alice focused her attention back on the woman.

"Tell me about Sterling."

Charlotte tensed, her shoulders going rigid under her soft cotton fabric, her knuckles white where her hands were clasped around her knees. "Why do you want to know about my father?"

"I think you know the answer to that," Alice said.

Charlotte plucked at that bald spot again. "We wanted to get Ruby away."

"We?"

Alice watched the muscles pull tight in the woman's face, at the corners of her lips, across her otherwise-smooth forehead.

"Trudy."

"Ah," Alice said, and then glanced around the diner once more. An old man had situated himself at the counter and was working over a bowl of soup, but no one else had come in. "I'm going to need the details."

"She'd been planning it for some time," Charlotte said. "We actually were going to do it later in the week, but we found out that both Sterling and Hollis would be out of the house that day."

Four days. Ruby had been held for four days. A reaction to a plan that had been altered.

"We set up the beach trip," Charlotte continued. "Trudy, actually . . . She came up with the idea. A little girl gone missing at the beach? It was believable enough."

"Why the ruse?" Alice pressed. "Why not just take her? Leave the state."

Charlotte's lips turned down at the corners, those patchy eyebrows rose. "You don't know my mother."

"But if Trudy was gone with Ruby, wouldn't Hollis immediately know you two were behind this staged kidnapping?" Alice asked. It had been so foolish of them, two young, naive girls plotting schemes that were so much bigger than themselves.

Charlotte swallowed, the lines of her neck working to adjust to the saliva. "That's why I couldn't . . . go. They would be watching me, not Trudy." It was said like she was repeating well-rehearsed lines, and Alice could picture Trudy coaching her aunt, persuading her that this was the only way. And for someone who had never learned to question or say no, Charlotte would have been an easy mark.

"Trudy would have left a note saying she was running off," Alice guessed. "Ruby would be enough of a distraction that she could get far enough, lose herself, before Hollis started paying attention again."

They didn't know Hollis as well as they thought they did. A woman like that, she wouldn't let Trudy out of her control any more than she was willing to let Charlotte. Girls playing dress-up in adult clothing.

There was hopelessness in Charlotte's eyes as she nodded. "We had a plan."

It was a whisper that cracked along the edges.

"What happened, Charlotte?"

The woman's chapped lips turned in on themselves, the skin around her mouth going white.

"What happened, Charlotte?"

"I don't—" Charlotte paused, dragged in a shaky breath. "I don't know."

"What do you mean you don't know?" This was different from the careful answers the woman had given before. In the days after Ruby's kidnapping, Charlotte had given them a complete timeline for the day. Had she lied about it?

Charlotte shook her head. "I don't remember. I just . . . I don't know. I don't know what happened to Ruby."

The name came out on a sob, and Alice glanced around. They'd drawn a few eyes, but none that were anything more than curious.

Alice's pulse notched up. Charlotte shouldn't be telling her this. If she'd been in a different frame of mind, she wouldn't be.

"What's the last thing you remember from that day, Charlotte?"

If possible, the woman collapsed even further into herself. "I remember sitting on the porch in the middle of the night. I was thinking about Ruby. I don't . . . Nothing else."

"That morning? Getting to the beach? Anything?" There hadn't been very many solid details in the timeline Charlotte had provided them, but she had described the morning.

Charlotte paused, but then: "No. I told you and the other officers what we had planned. But I don't remember getting there. I don't even remember getting in the car."

It happened. In traumatic situations, the brain, desperate to protect, erased memories. Full hours, full days. Moments in time that would be lost forever.

But it looked bad. It looked like Charlotte had either had a psychotic break and killed Ruby or she was covering for someone else.

"You should have told us this, Charlotte," Alice said, but she knew why the woman hadn't.

Charlotte's eyes were more shadows than anything else. "You would have thought . . ."

They sat in the heavy silence, both knowing what the cops would have thought.

"It all fell apart," Charlotte finally said, so quietly. A young girl confused at how reality interfered with her carefully constructed fantasy.

The waitress was watching them now, and Alice didn't like the interest on her face.

"I'm going to leave," Alice said, and Charlotte merely nodded at the abrupt declaration. "You won't follow for another ten minutes. Order a sandwich." Alice knew she wouldn't. Perhaps trying anyway was her weak attempt at penance.

"You asked about my father," Charlotte said, stopping Alice from shifting from the bench. "Does that mean, do you think . . . Did he have something . . . ?"

"Just"—Alice paused, counting the seconds so it would seem just long enough to appear hesitant—"let me know if you remember anything that could be relevant about his behavior."

Charlotte nodded, her expression blank and her attention turned inward.

Alice paused, her hip bumping into the laminate tabletop. "You wanted to know why I'm doing this?"

She waited until Charlotte's eyes met hers so Alice could see there was still a person in there, not just some empty shell. Then she pulled a small photo from her pocket where she always carried one. She had plenty, so after tracing the pad of her fingertip over the girl's cherub face, she placed it on the table, right in front of Charlotte.

It was a stupid and careless thing, on top of already stupid and careless things, but she wanted Charlotte to understand. To know. If this was her only chance to try to make her understand, Alice couldn't pass it up.

She tapped her hand over the picture, just once. "That's why."

CHAPTER TWENTY-TWO

CHARLOTTE

July 29, 2018
The day of the kidnapping

The white rectangular pill nestled into Charlotte's palm. It sat along her life line, which she knew because three years ago she'd dipped into a dank little tarot shop and paid all of five dollars to have her future told to her through her hand.

The woman's purple, bedazzled turban had been knocked askew so that wispy raven-blue hair had peeked out from underneath, and the thick plastic rims of her Coke-bottle glasses had all but obscured her eyes. When she'd taken Charlotte's hand, her own had been warm and dry, not slick with sweat as Charlotte had feared. There was no urge to recoil even as they sat in silence in a room that was draped in black velvet and smelled of incense used to cover the sour tang of pot.

Madame Clara tut-tutted at whatever she'd seen, her thick tongue clicking against her palate. "You are going to have a tragic life, my dear."

Weren't they supposed to lie to you? Take your money and tell you pretty things, soft things, happy things?

"I know," Charlotte said, tapping a French-manicured nail on the dark cherry wood of the table that separated them.

"Very tragic" was all the woman said again.

And then she'd shooed Charlotte out of the shop.

Charlotte looked down at the pill now, unfocusing her eyes so that the *X*'s and the *A*'s and the *N* smudged into each other. Then she tossed it back into her throat and chased it with the pinot grigio that had lost most of its chill. The glass was slippery under her fingers, the condensation collecting into beads of sweat that dripped down the expensive crystal.

It was late or early or whatever that middle part was where people still thought it was yesterday even while living in today. She was curled into her favorite chair on their back porch now that the rest of the household had gone to bed and she could be left alone. Left alone to sink into the scary places in a brain she no longer trusted.

She really had to keep it together only for another day. Then she could fall apart, she could weep, she could scream, she could collapse to the floor, and she would be excused her hysterics. If there was any time it would be considered acceptable, it would be after Ruby disappeared.

The plan. The plan. The way Trudy said it was with the confidence she'd always had, because she had a beautiful face and a slim body and long full-moon hair that drew eyes wherever she went. She said it with the confidence she'd always had because she had a grandfather whose name was synonymous with power and had the money to back it up. She said it with the confidence she'd always had because she'd built a tough persona for herself to survive the abuse she'd been put through.

She said it as if both words were capitalized in her head. The Plan. When Trudy had hatched it a month ago, it had been nothing more than a frustrated desire to do something, anything, to stop the oncoming train they all saw barreling down on them.

It had morphed and changed and developed, which Trudy had been cagey about when pressed. Charlotte had the impression someone had helped her, but it didn't seem important. What was important was that Ruby was going to be free. Free of this shitty life that Trudy and Charlotte had to live, and also free of her.

There was no doubt, no maybe, no but if. Charlotte was a terrible mother to her baby.

At first she'd hated her. The heartbeat. The flutter of movement on a black-and-gray screen. Then that same feeling, but beneath her belly. A foot kicking against her spleen. A thumb that was sucked even in the womb. Charlotte had hated her.

She'd had the kindest nurse the day she'd been able to find out the gender. The woman had blushed pink in happiness, all but crawling onto the table in her excitement.

"Do you want to know? Or be surprised?" she'd asked, with a teasing lilt in her voice that spoke to the fact that she had a secret. And a fun one.

"I don't care," Charlotte had said, and some of the light in the nurse had dimmed. She'd felt guilty for taking this joy from this stranger in a moment that held no joy for her. She'd plastered a fake smile on that looked genuine from years of practice. "I mean, yes. I'd love to know."

It was a girl, the nurse gasped out with the enthusiasm of someone achieving a lifelong dream. Charlotte had wondered if the nurse had children of her own, if she wanted them. That had been her first thought after finding out she was carrying a girl.

Then there had come that day at the pool. Ruby was due in three weeks, and it had been unbearably hot and humid, so much so that the air was mostly water and every part of her hurt and her skin had felt stretched to breaking and her body had felt stretched to breaking and she'd just wanted it to end.

She slipped beneath the water, her fingers pressing up against the ledge to keep herself submerged. The air bubbles formed, stealing oxygen from her lungs and carrying it back up to the surface. Eventually there would be nothing left to feed her needy blood, or the baby's needy blood, and then it would end.

Even as her throat began to throb and her eyes burned from the chlorine, she'd felt peace for the first time in years.

Seconds later, burly hands had fit themselves under her armpits and hauled her up and out of the quiet place. She'd dragged in air because her body demanded it, not because she'd wanted to.

So Charlotte had hated Ruby. Until she didn't.

It wasn't at birth, like some said it would be. She'd been tired and weak and exhausted and still hated the tiny bundle of flesh and bones and mucus that wanted something from her when all she wanted to do was sleep.

Then three days later, everything in the world tipped and righted itself, and when it did, she was in love. They'd been struggling with breastfeeding because of course Charlotte would be terrible at every aspect of being a mother. But she was being stubborn because Hollis was demanding she use a bottle, and giving in on that felt like a preview of a lifetime of giving in on everything. So she'd suffered through Ruby's red little face scrunched in frustration, her mouth rooting around for sustenance she didn't seem to actually want to take, for hours and hours and hours. She didn't hate her because of that. But it didn't make it easier.

It had been that same in-between time of night, and she'd been in that extraordinarily expensive rocker Hollis had bought her so she didn't have to use Mellie's old one. Ruby had been howling for an hour straight, and Charlotte had wondered when her vocal cords would just give up. And then she'd latched.

There was science behind it. Endorphins and oxytocin flooded the brain when the baby suckled. But she didn't care why or how or for what purpose it had happened; all she knew was that she'd looked down and for the first time hadn't seen Sterling.

She'd seen Ruby.

So she loved. She loved with all of herself that she was able to give; even the broken parts, jagged and splintered as they were, she gave. It was never enough, though.

Because she lost her daughter in malls and yelled at her when she got frustrated and numbed her own pain at the expense of Ruby's happiness. Which made her sad enough to want to go get laid or down a bottle of wine or shake out more than one of the Xanax she kept so carefully hidden under the loose floorboard by her bathroom. Relief, no matter how fleeting, was worth the crash.

She was a failure.

She'd failed Trudy. Her beautiful, stubborn, sassy niece. With Trudy, it had been love at first sight, easy in a way it had never been with Ruby. Mellie had come running home, abandoned on the side of a dusty road in Vegas for the lure of slot machines and red sparkly cocktail dresses on women who weren't pregnant. She'd taken a Greyhound bus with the forty dollars she'd had left in her purse.

Maternal love for Mellie was fashionable onesies and an around-the-clock nanny interviewed and paid for by Hollis. It was light and fun and showing off pictures of matching dresses at a mommies' brunch where no children were allowed.

They had both been so young, she and Mellie a decade apart and still both so young, when Trudy had come along.

And then Charlotte failed her. Because she'd known what was happening. She'd only been a teenager herself at the time, but she'd seen the shadows come into Trudy's eyes and the sunlight dip behind clouds. She'd seen Hollis go rigid with rage at the girl for the merest offenses the same way she had with Charlotte. There had been nothing she could do, she'd told herself. Powerless, her hands tied, she'd watched, she'd sat back, she'd let Trudy push her away. And she'd failed her.

If not for Trudy, she would have failed Ruby, too. She wasn't like her niece. There was no plan, just fear and helpless panic and a desire to hold on to the pieces even as she felt herself spinning off into nothingness.

Trudy was strong, though. Where Charlotte had failed, she had found a way.

Or at least that was the hope. And there was nothing left but hope, so she would wrap her arms around it and hold it to her rib cage and breathe it in, and perhaps it could make her strong. At least strong enough to get through today.

The door opened behind her, and she didn't even need to turn to know who it was. The tap of small feet against the porch's hardwood was warning enough.

It was only seconds later that she had a young girl in her lap, warm and drowsy and snuggling underneath Charlotte's blanket.

"Couldn't sleep, baby?" she murmured, sliding her fingers through the soft curls.

"Mmm, too excited," Ruby whispered her confession into Charlotte's neck.

Charlotte dropped her chin to the top of Ruby's head. "Yeah? We're going to have so much fun today."

CHAPTER TWENTY-THREE

ALICE

August 4, 2018
Six days after the kidnapping

Nakamura was already sitting at Alice's desk when she came in the next morning. She hadn't turned her phone back on until 1:00 a.m., and there hadn't been any messages waiting for her, so she didn't know what to expect from him.

If she'd thought he'd be pissed that she'd walked out after she'd pushed him up against the wall and then shut off her phone for hours, she would have been mistaken.

There was nothing to read off his face, either, or from the relaxed way he'd settled back into her chair, his left foot resting on his right leg. He was tapping a thick bundle of folded papers against his thigh.

She slowed, her boots dragging along the linoleum, reluctant to face the possible confrontation.

But he surprised her instead. "We got the warrant for the house."

"No way," she said, the tension she'd been holding in her shoulders dissolving, only to be replaced by a giddy sort of excitement.

Instead of answering, he pushed himself to his feet, keys dangling from his middle finger on one hand, the papers held high like a bounty in the other. "Let's go."

"How?" she asked, trailing him, her equilibrium thrown off.

He looked back, cocking an eyebrow at her. "Does it matter?"

"Nope." Fire crackled along her nerves as her brain caught up with her body just as they stepped out into the fresh air of the morning. It was quiet. Even the vultures had to sleep sometimes.

As if sensing the direction of her thoughts, Nakamura paused, resting his arms against the roof of the car to peer over at her. "Durand was front-page news this morning. Did you see?"

There was something about the casualness of the question that put her on alert. "No. I didn't have time to check."

Nakamura hummed and then disappeared from sight, sliding in behind the steering wheel. She pulled her own door open and climbed into the passenger seat.

"Interesting how it's directing the public's attention away from Charlotte," Nakamura said, not catching her eye as he glanced over his shoulder to back out of the spot. "Did they call you for comment?"

"Nope," Alice said again, fumbling in her purse for her sunglasses. It helped her avoid his scrutiny. "I would have directed them to the communications department if they had."

"Would you?" Nakamura asked. It was almost a relief, the question. Passive-aggressiveness didn't suit her personality.

"Do you have something to say?"

"You threw him to the wolves, Garner," Nakamura said.

"I told you, I didn't do anything." Alice watched his face. A small muscle at the corner of his eye twitched. "You don't believe me."

"I want to believe that you wouldn't lie to me." He took the left too hard, and her shoulder slammed into the window.

"This isn't about Durand," she said. "Any one of those reporters could have gotten the jump on the story."

"Funny how it happened to be the one you know."

Once again, she wished Nakamura was a jerk. She wished she'd gotten saddled with someone like those boys back in DC who'd flipped on her in an instant.

Maybe then the guilt wouldn't taste like acid on the back of her tongue.

But she'd gotten Nakamura instead. Chill, open-minded, quick-to-defend, and slow-to-judge Nakamura, who looked like he cuddled puppies and rescued orphans on the weekends.

Lying to him nudged at that moral compass she used to have in a way that it wouldn't have if her partner had been a complete ass.

She lied anyway because it wasn't an option not to, but she did feel guilty about it.

"You either trust me or you don't. But if you don't, this won't work."

"Aah." His lips tipped up at the corners, but it wasn't from amusement. "So you'll request another partner? Run away from your problems like you always do? Is this how you've cycled through so many?"

"What, are you my shrink now?" Everything was hot and itchy all of a sudden, and she knew she wasn't completely in control of the words tumbling out of her mouth. Which was dangerous.

"No, I'm your goddamn partner," he said, and it was chilling how he kept his voice even while he was spewing annoyance. He was an aberration. "And right now, it doesn't feel like that."

"Say the word."

"Stop." He cut himself off. Took a deep breath. "Stop saying that. And start acting like you know what you're actually doing. I don't want you off the case. But you can't be pulling disappearing acts like you did yesterday. Don't pretend that was the first time, either. Going MIA for hours at a time."

There was nothing to say to that, and it didn't matter anyway because they were pulling to the curb in front of the Burke residence. The white vans with outrageous satellite dishes signaled that the media hadn't given up hope on getting a glimpse of the mourning family, but the rabid energy in the air was missing. Maybe some of them were chasing the Zeke Durand angle.

Tell a story. Create a villain.

"The rest of the cavalry coming?" Alice asked as they climbed the steps. They were back into professional mode. Now was not the time for anything else.

Nakamura nodded. "I didn't want this to be a show of force. But they'll be along to help execute the search."

It was funny how they'd so seamlessly switched roles. He was now taking point on the case, without there being a decision made. She wondered if that moment had come when she'd held him up against the wall, her hand at his throat.

Nakamura knocked on the thick door, and it opened as soon as his knuckles left the wood. Hollis. She'd been waiting for them.

"Good morning, ma'am," Nakamura said, as if it wasn't unusual for her to be standing there decked out in a power suit with a face full of makeup and her hair shellacked into submission this early in the day.

"Detectives," Hollis said. In her mouth it sounded like an insult.

Nakamura went through the motions of serving her the warrant, but it was clear that she not only had been expecting them but also was familiar with the legalese of it all. Her husband wasn't the most prominent judge in the city for nothing.

"Is anyone else here?" Alice asked when Nakamura finished.

Hollis turned to her. "Yes. Charlotte and Melissa are still sleeping."

"And Trudy?"

There was a crack in the facade for the merest of moments before the mask was firmly back in place. "She's not here."

Alice's attention sharpened. "Where is she?"

"Is that in your warrant, Detective?" Hollis countered, even though she had to know it made no sense. It still shut them down on that line of questioning. Simple and effective.

Alice hummed, but the question settled in under her breastbone. Where was Trudy? It was a missing piece, and Alice didn't like missing pieces. She had players she needed to keep track of, chess pieces she was overseeing.

She locked eyes with Nakamura, and the distance he'd been keeping up all morning dropped. They'd have to figure out where she'd disappeared to.

"Please know, Detectives"—Hollis interrupted whatever silent conversation Alice and Nakamura had started having—"I will be personally overseeing this entire search. Make a single wrong move and the governor will be hearing about it."

"Hmm, but that would require him to actually pull his head out of your husband's ass," Alice said pleasantly before walking down the hall toward Sterling's study.

———

Alice stood in front of Ruby's bedroom door, fingertips resting against her thighs. She didn't want to reach for the knob, didn't want to turn it, didn't want to push against the wood so it would swing open to reveal its secrets.

She'd already been in Sterling's office and Trudy's room, the two places she'd thought would have the most to offer. In the study she'd found the security codes to the mansion, written in an easy and clear scrawl, and had tucked the piece of paper away in her jeans before anyone else saw. But Trudy's room was clean. There was no secret laptop to find, as far as Alice could tell, even though she suspected the girl kept one. After that room had been cleared, she'd drifted into the hallway, drawn to the door that was still closed.

The knob burned like something bright, like something she couldn't touch unless she wanted her skin to peel away from the bone.

There was a great deal of noise and movement around her, bodies pushing through the space, disrupting the perfection that was so carefully cultivated, but it didn't register fully. It was as if everyone else was in real time, and she was stuck in seconds that had slowed to minutes that had slowed to years that had slowed to an eternity.

She was cold. The slope of her ear, the end of her nose, the skin at the top of her spine. She wanted to rub each spot, warm it up until it burned beneath her hand, until she could feel the blood again, hot and pulsing, telling her she was alive.

It wouldn't. Maybe she was destined to be reminded constantly that she really wasn't. Alive.

The drag of oxygen into her nostrils, the way it caught in her throat and trickled into her lungs, was there to remind her that she wasn't quite dead yet, either.

It took three more breaths before she was able to force her body to move. Her hand touched the door, and everything snapped back into focus. The officers around her, the click of Hollis's heels on hardwood, the subtle smell of freesia sweetening the air that had turned sour from the number of sweaty bodies occupying the space.

"That's my daughter's room." The voice was soft and confused, not accusatory or demanding like it might have been. Alice glanced at Charlotte over her shoulder. She was wrapped in a silk dressing gown, and her hair was down around her shoulders. There was no makeup to ease the shadows beneath her eyes or to cover the hollowness of her cheeks.

Alice sensed, more than saw, Nakamura come up behind her, and it felt like he was backing her up, giving her his trust once more, if only in the form of knowing when she needed help and offering it.

"I know." Alice pitched her voice just as soft. Charlotte was a skittish animal who needed soothing, who needed gentle pats and reassurances, and Alice would give them if it meant getting what she wanted in the end. "We won't disturb it."

Charlotte brought a nail up to her teeth to gnaw at the skin of her finger as her gaze bounced between Nakamura, Alice, and the room. Then her chin dipped once, and she was gone.

"She's getting so weird," Nakamura muttered. It was out of character enough that Alice didn't react immediately, didn't punch his arm or shove a finger into his sternum in chastisement. And by the time she processed the words, he'd already pushed by her into Ruby's room.

Alice followed quickly.

It was a little girl's room in a way that she hadn't been expecting, not in this household. There were pretty murals painted on the walls and stuffed animals piled into baskets and books scattered on a bright rainbow-colored desk. Where the rest of the house had been devoid of any personality, this room burst with it.

She walked to the dresser, where little white porcelain figures depicted a scene from a circus, with a delicate lion jumping through a ring of fire, a trapeze walker tipping precariously to the side, an elephant balanced on a ball, and an intricate conga line involving bears in tutus.

Alice ran her finger over the top of the elephant, her nail coming to rest against the tip of his trunk. They had been Lila's favorite, elephants.

The animals had always been able to cheer her up. Even on the worst days when Alice thought the crying and screaming would never end.

The zoo was mostly empty. It was the middle of the day, and it was cold in the way only February could be—where the wind cut through layers of jackets, and the grayness of the sky sapped any sun warmth from the air.

But Lila bounced along beside her, happy and eager, her hand in Alice's, as if impervious to anything that might ruin her adventure.

That morning's tantrum was long forgotten for the girl. But the memory of curling up on the cold tile of the bathroom behind a locked door as Lila wailed and pounded on the wood would haunt Alice. Lila had been begging for Alice to open up, let her in, let her spill every desperate emotion that the little girl's body couldn't quite contain into Alice, to absorb like all mothers were supposed to do.

It had been too much, though, the little-girl screams and the thick, vicious tears that turned eyelashes clumpy and dark, and Alice hadn't been able to make her legs work.

The storms came so quickly, always had with Lila. One moment's happiness was so fleeting, so precarious. So unlike Alice. Where she was steady ice, Lila was erratic fire.

Everyone said that's just how toddlers were. She'd grow out of it. But Alice knew Lila wouldn't, and worried. Because sometimes she thought the girl might burn into embers and then into fire dust, to float away in the air.

"Wanna see the 'phants." Lila smiled now. She was a few months from turning four, and nothing was permanent. Not even sadness.

Alice met her own eyes in the mirror and had to look away, had to walk away.

They searched the room with a smooth efficiency after that, one born from years of being cops. She hadn't had to serve a warrant since she'd been in St. Pete, but it had occurred with frequency in DC.

There was nothing to find. She hadn't expected there would be, but the process was important. The Burkes may have power, but they weren't above the law. It would have been helpful had they been able to impart the message before the family had time to completely sanitize the entire household to hide or destroy anything they didn't want found.

"Well, they at least know how to clean behind themselves," said a voice from the doorway.

Alice turned to see Bridget leaning against the wall, her feet crossed, snapping away at the gum in her mouth. The woman was watching her tech team sweep the room for body fluids and DNA samples.

"Just like the crime scene," Alice said.

Bridget glanced over at her, eyes searching. "Not really."

"What do you mean?" Nakamura asked, stepping closer to both of them.

"The crime scene was . . ." Bridget waved a hand, and she still hadn't taken her eyes off Alice. "Perfect."

"And this isn't?" Alice asked.

"Different kind of clean," Bridget said, finally looking away. She still didn't really acknowledge Nakamura. Instead, her eyes touched on the corners of the room—the bed, the sheets, the opened closet doors where pretty dresses and skirts hung neatly on hangers.

"Different kind of scene." Alice shrugged, and it was humor in the lines of Bridget's face now instead of annoyance.

The woman pressed her hands together as if praying and then bowed slightly. "So wise, Socrates."

"Screw you." Alice laughed but kept it quiet. There was a sadness, a reverence, in the air that she didn't want to disturb. "You're just pissed you haven't found anything."

"Science will come through for me. She is my lover and has yet to let me down," Bridget said, but didn't disagree with the reason for her bad mood.

Alice shook her head. "It's all about narrative." It was an argument they'd had many times in the back booths of dark bars.

"Why the four days?" Nakamura asked, a non sequitur that stopped whatever bickering was about to erupt between her and Bridget. The woman took the hint and turned, leaving them without a goodbye.

The abrupt departure amused Alice, and she watched Bridget until she was no longer in sight. Then she turned to Nakamura. "What?"

Like Bridget, he was monitoring the tech guys. "I keep getting stuck on the four days."

Alice thought back to the diner. A plan altered. She didn't mention it.

"Because there was no note," she said instead.

"Well, that." Nakamura lifted his shoulder, dismissive. He wasn't hung up on a note, because he thought Charlotte was their perp. "The logistics of keeping someone against her will for four days are complicated at best."

"Maybe it wasn't against her will." Alice stepped closer, letting their shoulders touch. A physical reassurance that they were okay again. Even if it was reluctant from his end and manufactured from hers.

"The family is all accounted for during that stretch of time," Nakamura said, drawing out the thought. "Which means if it was the family, they had outside help."

"So who helped the killer?" Alice asked. "Find them . . ."

"Find our perp."

CHAPTER
TWENTY-FOUR

TRUDY

August 1, 2018
Three days after the kidnapping

"They don't know what the hell they're doing." Trudy wanted to break the glass her grandmother held between her slim, elegant fingers. She wanted to break every fragile thing in this house and then move on to the nonfragile things.

Ruby was missing. And no one was doing a goddamn thing about it.

"Trudy, language," Hollis snapped.

"No," Trudy shot back. "The police are sitting around with their thumbs up their asses. It's been three days. And what do they have to show for it? They just keep asking us the same questions over and over again."

Anger. It was familiar, so familiar. An old friend. It was better than the guilt that had been trying to devour her from the inside.

The anger hurt, too—always had. But where guilt was acid, anger was fire. Fire could fuel her. She could use it to help her move limbs that had grown lethargic and numb, she could use it to unleash vocal cords that had gone silent, she could use it to spur action where before there had been only static confusion.

"You aren't doing enough," Trudy said. Anger was also easier to turn outward. This, she was used to. "What good is all that power if you can't use it?"

"Trudy, honey." Mellie laid a gentle hand on her arm, and for the first time in a long time, there was no alcohol lingering on the whispered words.

That didn't make it better, though. Maybe it made it worse. It was like Mellie was trying to parent Trudy after sixteen years of forgetting she was a mother.

"Go back to being worthless, Mellie dear," Trudy said, pushing her away. Mellie went with the momentum and fell back into one of the dining room chairs. It was dramatic in the way Mellie was. Over the top, ridiculous, absurd. Her eyes were damp and red rimmed as she watched Trudy with betrayal.

Trudy ignored her and turned back to Hollis. But just as she was about to go at her again, a quiet voice cut through the manic energy that had settled into the room.

"Stop."

It was Charlotte, and for no one else would Trudy have listened. That one word, though—it took the righteousness from her, drained the rush that had made her head fuzzy and light. All that was left was an emptiness she'd been trying so desperately to ignore.

Her aunt untucked her legs from the chair, pushed to her feet, and then walked from the room.

"You will apologize to Charlotte, after you've collected yourself, Trudy," Hollis said.

Trudy turned to her, her eyes sliding over her grandmother's slicked-back hair, the flawless lipstick that had not seeped even a little into the groove at the edges of her lips, at her goddamn string of pearls.

"You wanted this to happen," she said, meeting the woman's hard gaze. "You're just happy your little problem is taken care of."

Mellie gasped, but Hollis didn't flinch. Instead, she stood and walked over to Trudy. Hollis reached out, grasping Trudy's chin between her thumb and finger to the point of pain. "You will collect yourself," Hollis said. "Then you will apologize to Charlotte."

Hollis squeezed as she said it, the pad of her thumb pressing a bruise into Trudy's jawbone.

"And if you ever again question the lengths I would go to in order to keep this family protected, you will no longer be considered a part of it," Hollis continued. So soft, so deadly. "Do I make myself clear, child?"

The agreement tasted like rotting meat where it sat on her tongue, but she forced it out. "Yes, Grandmother."

Hollis dropped her hand and stepped back, smoothing a palm over her suit. "Very good. Now leave my sight. I am tired of you tonight."

Trudy fled.

———

Trudy didn't search out Charlotte. The idea of trying to comfort her aunt was draining to the point of exhaustion.

And there was something in Charlotte's eyes these days. As if she was broken beyond repair. Glass shattered, the shards so tiny they were almost dust, never to be put together again.

That look scared Trudy sometimes in ways she didn't realize—that she could still feel fear. It made her wonder.

It made her think of that day on the porch after Trudy had found Ruby on the sidewalk, and those vacant eyes. It made her think of the mall and the way Ruby had slipped so easily out of Charlotte's attention. As if she were hoping it would happen. It made her think of the way even the love Charlotte had for Ruby was tainted with an edge of hate. Because of where she'd come from.

It made Trudy wonder.

If Trudy was wondering, the police had to be as well. Trudy wasn't blind and she wasn't stupid. She knew what the questions meant. She knew the look the detectives shared when Charlotte didn't know the answers. Trudy knew what Garner and Nakamura thought, knew what the public would think.

Her mind skittered away from the idea and those vacant eyes staring into nothingness. The thought was almost as repulsive as their secret, the one they kept so close, tucked away from all the bloodsuckers who would be giddy at finding out something so damaging to the great Sterling Burke.

But long ago, Trudy had learned that things that seemed like nightmares were sometimes much more. They were sometimes reality.

In a flash, she was up off her bed, digging into the back of her closet, beneath shoes and blankets and clothes that had fallen off hangers, until her fingers hit metal.

The safe. The one that hid her laptop.

After opening it, she tossed aside the passports, the money from her stripping. It felt so stupid now, and her cheeks burned with the shame of it.

Her grand plan. The thing that started this all.

The laptop was slim and silver and sat against the bottom of the safe. She flipped it open and powered it on. Her finger tapped against the casing of it as she waited for the email to load.

Trust me.

It was still there, the message, sitting at the top of her in-box.

Her mouth went dry at the sight of it.

The safe house N had told her about had been there. N provided her almost everything she'd needed to get Ruby out. So why would someone send her there if they'd been meaning to hurt her, hurt her family?

It wasn't like she had trusted it completely. Nothing came easy, not in this world. There had to be strings attached. But she'd thought that maybe she'd be able to use it all and get out of Dodge before they came calling for their favors.

So she'd taken the help, as foreign a concept as that had been. She'd gone to the club the women at the safe house had told her to go to and picked up the passports they'd told her to pick up. She'd saved the money from her shifts and figured out the bus station she'd have Zeke drive her to on the day they got Ruby out of there.

She'd planned. She'd planned. She'd planned.

And then it had gone to shit.

Haunted, vacant eyes. Charlotte's tearstained face. The long, elegant fingers that dug into flesh and left bruises there. What had happened that morning? Where had it gone wrong?

Stop.

Charlotte hadn't killed Ruby, she hadn't. Trudy wasn't quite sure why this was the thread she was holding on to, but she knew, somehow, deep down, that if it started to unravel, it would take her with it.

Whatever had screwed up their plan, it hadn't been her aunt. She wouldn't believe—couldn't believe—it had been Charlotte.

Survival had never been a choice—it was just something that was. She would get up every day, her heart would beat, her lungs would expand, her muscles would stretch, and she would survive. This, though, would take her down; it would peel the layers back until there was nothing but the emptiness that lived at the center of herself.

She wished she could press her fingers in her ear and scream like she did when she was little and didn't want to hear what someone was saying. She wanted to be young again so that she could.

It wasn't Charlotte. It couldn't be.

Trust me.

Why had she come up with the plan in the first place? She'd known she'd wanted to act but hadn't known what to do. Then, like a miracle, the email had arrived. Why hadn't she questioned it? Why hadn't she remembered that prayers like hers weren't answered?

This had to be something. Or it had to be ruled out, at the very least. Every other lead, the police were investigating—the family, an old grudge, a random psycho. Even Sterling.

But they didn't know about this email.

It had been nagging at her. In the dark, when she couldn't sleep and all she could think about was Ruby's soft body snuggled up against hers, it nagged at her. When the detectives stood in doorways and watched her with eyes that were too searching, it nagged at her. When Charlotte blinked too fast under the blinding bulbs of the news cameras, it nagged at her.

Would they have been at the beach if it weren't for that email? What would have happened if she'd ignored the advice, if she'd simply deleted and removed it from the trash like she did with every other message that came in?

Was she grasping into the void, hoping her fingers would connect with anything even remotely solid?

But Ruby had disappeared on the day they had been trying to get her out of this hell. If that was a coincidence, it was a big one.

The email.

Trudy kept an IP address tracker running on her blog.

Sometimes, when she received strange messages, she checked the timing of the emails against the tracker. It wasn't refined enough to differentiate into neighborhoods, but she could tell which cities and states her visitors were from, if there weren't too many people on her website all at once.

She'd gotten lucky with N. The messages had mostly come in during weird hours, so there hadn't been many other people on her blog. There were a few other cities, including Tampa, that popped up once or twice.

But only one that came up routinely.

Jacksonville, Florida.

CHAPTER TWENTY-FIVE

ALICE

August 4, 2018
Six days after the kidnapping

"You missed the turn," Alice said, in retrospect perhaps nonsensically. Nakamura knew these streets better than anyone. He didn't get lost.

But they should have been headed to the police station instead of driving along the coastline.

"I think we should check out the owner," Nakamura said, turning onto the road that she now realized would take them back to the beach where they'd found Ruby. She flashed hot, then cold. Goose bumps danced along her arms, and it had nothing to do with the air conditioner that was on blast. When she was prepared, when she was braced for it, it didn't bother her. But the surprise of it threw her.

Especially after just coming from the girl's room.

She wondered if that was part of the plan, if he was watching her from his peripheral vision to see if she'd react, to see if there were any cracks in her armor. Any excuse to call her unstable, erratic, emotional.

It would help him undermine her case if he got fed up with her defense of Charlotte. *Can't be trusted,* he would say.

They would believe him, too. Why wouldn't they?

Her mouth was dry, and her tongue scraped along the roof of it.

"We already talked to him," she said, looking out the window so he couldn't see her face. The houses blurred into a pastel of colors as she unfocused her eyes.

"For about five minutes," Nakamura countered. "The team did a sweep of the house, but we didn't properly interview him. Not really."

"They did a sweep of the house and didn't find anything," she reminded him.

"Do you want to sit it out?" Nakamura asked, and she could hear the frustration in his voice.

"No," she said. That was unacceptable. "I just don't want to waste our time on a dead end."

"I hate to be the one to break it to you, but it's not like we are bursting with options," Nakamura said. "We don't have anything on the family. Nothing but speculation, at least, and that's not worth a damn."

Still watching the street, she nodded to show she was listening.

"Zeke Durand is interesting," Nakamura mused. "But my gut says he was telling the truth about him and Trudy. The story is just incriminating enough for it to be real."

"Bridget's checking out the car. But we should stay on him," she said, even though she agreed. Durand's story gave enough details, without being rehearsed, and was vague enough to prove that he was probably being kept in the dark for most of it.

"I think the media will have that covered for us," Nakamura said. She listened for the bite, but it wasn't there. Perhaps he was over it. More likely he was better at masking his thoughts than she was giving him credit for, and those little slips in tone had been deliberate.

"So we're back to the accomplice angle," Nakamura continued. "And who better to start with?"

There wasn't anyone else, and they both knew it.

Nakamura was relaxed, one hand easy on the wheel. "We keep thinking about those lost days. What if they were just keeping her at the house?"

"Why dump her right outside it, though?" she asked. "We'd immediately suspect the owner."

"But we didn't," Nakamura pointed out. "It's been two days, and this is the first we're really considering it. And even now you're not exactly raring to interrogate the guy."

"Because it doesn't make sense."

"Not everything has to make sense, you know," Nakamura said. "You're a little too attached to that idea, Garner."

"Yeah, me and my crazy need for logic." She smiled. The banter that had become a staple in their partnership eased the tension, if only for a few minutes.

They drove in silence through several stop signs before he cleared his throat. "I actually do think it makes sense, though."

"The owner?" she clarified.

"Yeah." Nakamura tipped his head to the side, thoughtful. "Access being the biggest thing. We said on the first day that it would be hard to get Ruby to that location. Imagine walking on the beach for any length of time carrying that much weight."

"It would be difficult," she murmured. "Especially if it were Charlotte."

He slid her a look but let it go. "But if the person had access to that house. Imagine how easy it would be. There aren't any other ones next to it, so it's that or the public-access road."

They both paused a beat.

"So we talk to the owner," she finally said.

Enrique Lopez was an attractive man with dark slicked-back hair and smooth caramel skin that was covered with tattoos.

He poured Alice and Nakamura lemonade out of a plastic pitcher into glasses that had chips on the rims, while they sat on his Ikea two-seater couch. There was one other foldout chair in the room and then the coffee table.

There was an apology in the way he shrugged and the self-deprecating tilt to his mouth as he handed them their drinks. "Sorry. I feel like I've just moved in, but I'm not sure that excuse qualifies anymore."

"How long have you been here?" Nakamura asked while taking a sip of the lemonade, puckering a bit before setting it aside. She put her own on the table.

"About six months, now, wow." Enrique laughed a little at that, running a hand through his hair. "Feels like yesterday. I just get so busy at the clinic I don't have that much time for furniture shopping."

"The clinic?" she asked, feeling the need to contribute something.

He met her eyes, then looked back at Nakamura. "Yeah, I work at a health clinic in South St. Petersburg."

"Tough gig?" Nakamura asked while reaching inside his suit jacket for his little notepad. He jotted something down.

Enrique watched the smooth glide of pen on paper but smiled easily when Nakamura glanced back up. "Rewarding."

They all hummed. There was nothing to say to that. A clock ticked away the seconds in the other room, and Alice's chest tightened with each beat.

After a full minute had passed of them simply staring at each other, she pushed herself to her feet and walked to the sliding glass window that led out to the dunes. She could just see the ocean over the tall stalks of wild grass that acted like wind catchers on the mounds of sand.

"So," she heard Nakamura start, and she could tell by just the one word that he'd shifted into professional mode. She wondered if they were both looking at her, or if they would ignore her sudden urge to no longer be trapped on that overstuffed couch with the too-sweet lemonade and a lingering scent of a chemical cleaner and the empty house that was too similar to her own and far too close to a particular strip of beach.

"We'd like to ask you a few questions, if you don't mind," Nakamura continued. She should turn around, she should watch. Body language was so telling, and Nakamura would ask her about it. But she couldn't tear her eyes from the thin sliver of blue-green waves and white foam.

"Of course," Enrique said, his voice smooth like rich coffee, almost as if he were comforting them out of awkwardness. "Anything I can do to help. I assume this is about Ruby Burke."

At that, she was finally able to move, though she didn't go far. She leaned up against the wall, crossing one ankle over the other. It wasn't the best location to read the scene, to interpret the tension in both men's bodies, or the way their faces twitched or smoothed out or creased at certain questions. But it would do.

"Yes," Nakamura confirmed, shifting forward so he was on the edge of the cushion. "Can you tell us where you were the night of August first and the morning of August second?"

"Uh, yeah." Enrique looked around him as if he were searching for something, but there was nothing there. He shook his own head and laughed. "Sorry, I was checking for my calendar just to make sure, but, yeah, I was out of town all day Wednesday."

Nakamura's spine arched as he leaned forward. "Where did you go?"

"Just over to Tampa. A buddy of mine was passing through. We rented a boat, did some fishing, got some grub. I left Tuesday afternoon and got home really early on Thursday morning. Maybe sixish," he said. "Next thing I knew, that guy was banging on my door. The jogger who found the girl."

"You went out of town in the middle of the week?"

The other man shrugged. "Doctor's schedule."

"We'll need his number to verify that," Alice spoke up.

Enrique was already on his feet, walking over to the desk in the corner. After checking his phone, he jotted something down on a piece of paper. He crossed the room, and his fingers brushed against hers as he handed it to her. His eyes were dark, but his mouth was tipped down in that concerned Good Samaritan frown. She'd seen it a million times in her career. "Of course. Here. His name's Lou. I wrote it on there."

She slipped it into the back pocket of her jeans as he sat down again.

"When you got back, was there anything suspicious you noticed?" Nakamura asked.

Enrique scratched at the spot behind his ear. "I can't say I did, no. I was pretty tired from being up so early, though."

Nakamura wasn't deterred. "And the days before that, did you notice anyone coming by? Even someone you're used to seeing?"

"Man, there's that jogger guy," Enrique said. "And a few other usuals. I get kids, teenagers, every once in a while, sneaking out on the beach. There's a path just over there that leads out to the public road."

Both she and Nakamura nodded.

Enrique shrugged, looking between them. "They're pretty harmless, though. I've only had to chase them off once, and that was because they tried to throw a school-wide party down there."

Nakamura slid his eyes to her, then looked back at Enrique. "Do you ever recall Trudy Burke hanging around? Was she part of this group?"

There was no spark of recognition on his face, and Alice let the breath she hadn't realized she was holding slip out between her lips.

"Trudy Burke?" Enrique shook his head. "I don't know who that is. Other than she must be related to that little girl, right?"

Nakamura's shoulders relaxed a bit at that, and he hummed neither an agreement nor a denial. "So nothing strange or out of place, even in the past couple weeks?"

Enrique slicked his tongue along his lower lip, looking lost in contemplation. When he looked back at them, he was again shaking his head. "No, I can't think of anything. I'll be happy to keep trying to remember, though. Terrible thing about the girl."

That was a clear dismissal, but Alice waited for Nakamura to accept it or not. This was his ball game. When he braced his hands against his thighs and pushed himself to his feet, she straightened off the wall.

Enrique led them through the darkened hallway to the front door, stepping back to let them through onto the porch. Alice slipped her sunglasses over her eyes as she stopped and turned back to him.

"One more question, Mr. Lopez," she said, and she could feel Nakamura pause, one foot already on the stairs leading down to the driveway.

"Sure," Enrique said, his face open and eager.

"Do you know Charlotte Burke, in any capacity?"

His eyes remained blank at the mention of the name.

"No," he said. "Not at all."

CHAPTER TWENTY-SIX

CHARLOTTE

August 1, 2018
Three days after the kidnapping

It was harder to escape these days. There wasn't just Hollis and Sterling to avoid, but with Ruby missing, there was the media now, too. They camped out in front of the house, just far enough away to maintain a semblance of privacy, but it was a smoke screen. The journalists lounged on camping chairs or squatted down to sit on the burning asphalt and ate stale ham sandwiches and had pizza delivered right to their vans. Restless hours filled with boredom and card games, broken up with only tiny stretches of excitement when one of the Burkes moved behind drawn curtains.

If she left the house, they scrambled up like a flock of disgruntled pigeons, all ruffled feathers, until they settled again. Then they would start the yelling. It hadn't been awful things at first. During the press conference, they may have zoomed in too close on her tear-streaked face, but the tone of the questions had been sympathetic.

It had changed, though. Subtle at first. By evening there had been an edge to the voices that hadn't been there before, an accusation only thinly veiled. Maybe they believed she did it, but probably not. Most likely, they were looking for a sound bite that she'd yet to give them. A grieving mother was good for ratings, but a diabolical one was even better.

The one she could portray, the one she'd been groomed into for years, was composed. She knew it didn't play well for public sympathy, but there was nothing she could do about it. Even as her muscles trembled beneath designer silk in their effort to keep her from crumbling to the floor, even as her heart's rhythm blurred so that she could feel it as a constant reminder in her neck, even as snot and unshed tears ran down the back of her throat, she held it together for the cameras. There was no other acceptable option. Not as a Burke.

She'd walked by a television earlier in the day and heard one of the hosts say her name as if it was a rancid thing, unpleasant and disturbing at once. The woman had decided Charlotte had not cried enough at the press conference, but her cohost had chimed in that Charlotte had cried too much. Clearly, she was faking the grief. By the end of the program, they still hadn't agreed on just how many tears were appropriate when your child had been kidnapped.

That, she could turn off, though, power down. She hadn't, but she could have. It was more difficult to ignore the questions as they were hurled in her direction each time she stepped foot outside the house.

It had already been her cage. Now it was her prison.

Only when she got to the hotel did the specter of them chasing her dissolve into the nothingness that was actually behind her.

Enrique already had a room, like always, so she ducked past the front office, pulling her baseball cap low to cover her face. She had never worn one before, but she was quickly finding out how useful it could be in helping her hide in plain sight. People knew her as a body draped in expensive clothes, as long, wild hair that was a contradiction to her personality, as a face painted to perfection. Jeans and T-shirts, snagged from the back of Trudy's closet, had become her camouflage.

But it still wouldn't do to be caught outside a third-rate motel with Ruby missing, so she knocked, quick and quiet, on the flimsy door.

It swung open four seconds later, and she skirted in past Enrique, making sure not to touch him on the way in. He would try to hug her, offer her comfort, and she didn't want that.

She shucked off her canvas shoes and dropped the hat to the floor, then turned to find him sliding the little gold chain into place even though they both knew it would do nothing to stop someone who really wanted into the room.

They locked eyes as she crossed her arms, gripping the hem of her T-shirt, and their gazes broke only when she pulled it over her head so that she was left in a plain white cotton bra and jeans.

"Char," Enrique whispered, hesitant and careful as if she were fine china balancing on a table's edge. This wasn't what she wanted. He wasn't supposed to be like the rest of them. He wasn't supposed to think she was going to shatter. It wouldn't do.

Her thumbs stumbled over the button at her waistband, but eventually she got the metal unhooked from the thick fabric, which she then pushed off her hips. She kicked her feet free.

His eyes swept down her body, over the sharp juts of her hips and the outline of her ribs, both more pronounced than they had been months ago. She wondered if he still found her attractive, and she wondered if she cared.

"Char, I don't think . . ." He backed up against the wall as she took a step closer. "This isn't . . . Should we talk? Are you okay?"

No. Of course she wasn't okay. She would never be okay again. Why was he asking her that? Why would he think for even one second that she would want to talk to him about it? That wasn't what this was.

She moved closer, and then closer still, until her body was flush up against his fully clothed one, her hips canting into his. Then she pushed up onto her toes and slid her mouth over his.

"Come on, baby, no," he mumbled against her lips. "Let's just . . . Here." And then the worst happened. His arms came around her back, and one hand rested on her head, nudging her face into the crook of his neck. It was an embrace that had nothing to do with sex, and her skin crawled in the places he touched her.

"I'm so sorry, baby," he was saying into her hair. Whispers of condolence and reassurance and nonsense that meant nothing and could mean nothing. Each word pressed against her scalp, searing the already-dry skin there.

In desperation, she opened her mouth against his neck and sank her teeth into the tendons that ran along the thick column. His hands fluttered against her back like he was going to push her off, but then she tasted copper against her tongue, and he broke. Instead of stopping her, he swore in Spanish and then hauled her even closer against him.

Everything was hard and fast. The pleasure of it was tinged with darkness, but it was what she was used to, and she let herself sink into it, an old friend welcoming her home.

When it was over, he pushed to his feet. She just stared at the cracked ceiling as the toilet flushed and then the sink ran. By the time he came back out, she'd shifted enough so that she was lying on sheets that she could pretend were clean, instead of the blanket, which she knew wasn't.

"You know who I am," Charlotte said, not looking at him.

He slid in beside her, and though she could feel the heat from his body, he didn't touch her. "Of course."

"Have you known this whole time?"

There was a pause. "Babe. You told me your full name."

That wasn't the same as knowing who she was. "You know what I mean."

"I don't know what you want me to say," he said.

"My daughter was kidnapped," she said. It was surreal, forming the sentence, telling someone that. Maybe it was the only reason she could, because it didn't feel like reality.

"I know," he murmured, and his pinkie shifted so that it brushed against hers. She moved her hand.

"My daughter was kidnapped," she said again, and this time the words were shards of glass in her mouth, and it was too much. Too hot, too sticky, too empty, too tight. Everything at once crashed into her, slamming into her weakened body until she broke, like everyone thought she would.

The sobs came even before the tears—ugly, panting, desperate heaves that ripped through her, tearing the delicate fibers that held her together.

Pain. There was so much pain, everywhere, and she was in his arms again, with no strength left to push him away. She pressed the palms of her hands to her eyes, wanting to escape into the black velvet behind her lids, but there was only more pain there.

It was only when he rolled her, his body coming over hers, his hands pinning her wrist above her head, that she realized she'd been screaming and clawing at her own skin. She could see the angry red marks decorating the white flesh of her arm, but she couldn't feel them, and so she thought maybe she hadn't dug in deep enough.

Now it was impossible, with him holding her down as he was.

"Shhh," he murmured, his thumb rubbing gently against the inside of her wrist. "Breathe."

The weight of him made it impossible to move, impossible to do something wrong or bad, and it was freeing in that she could let go of the part of her that always worried she would mess it all up. She couldn't right now, and there was nothing she could do about it. The knowledge of that let her regain control of her lungs and her eyes and her brain.

He felt her come back to herself, and his body relaxed, just a fraction. "That's it," he said. "You're all right."

Time passed, but neither of them watched the clock. He continued his soothing strokes along her forearm and kept his hips pressed against hers, holding her body still even as she calmed beneath him.

When she shifted her arms, he let her go instantly, rolling off onto his back on the other side of the bed.

She tucked her legs against her chest, then rested her cheek against her knees and looked over at him. "Thank you."

His pupils were dilated when he looked at her, and she realized the amount of adrenaline that had to be coursing through him. "Don't thank me." His voice was rough.

A small smile tugged at her mouth, and she was amazed that she remembered how to make her lips curve at all. "I'm going to anyway."

"Do you . . . ?" He ran a hand over his head, cutting himself off.

"Do I what?" she prodded, still raw, still sore, but feeling stronger. "Do I know who took her?"

He glanced at her, and the shadows hid his eyes. "How could you, though?"

She lifted one shoulder, then let it drop. *How could you know?*

"You think it's someone you know?"

"It could be anyone, right? There's been no ransom note." Her voice wobbled over the last part, and she swallowed hard.

"Char." He sat up but kept his distance. "Do you think it's someone you know?"

Was it? What had happened that morning? Why couldn't she remember? Why was there only the sound of waves and seagulls when she tried? Why was her last memory of Ruby that soft moment on the porch, her warm weight against Charlotte?

Why was there nothing else after that?

She shook her head. "I don't know. Maybe. I think so."

"You have to go to the cops, babe." Enrique leaned his palms against the mattress, his body swaying toward her in his urgency. "If you suspect someone, God, someone in your family? You have to, Char."

It wasn't that easy. "It's not that easy."

"You said you wanted to be strong, yeah?" Enrique's eyes were on fire, and she flinched. She wanted to be strong, but she wasn't. He knew this. "You have to do something."

She pressed her thumb into the pulse point on her wrist. "I didn't say I wasn't going to do something," she said. "I said it wasn't as easy as going to the cops."

His whole body paused as he considered what she'd said, and then on the next breath, he was moving again, pushing to his feet. "You need that gun I promised you."

Meeting his eyes, she nodded slowly. "I need that gun."

CHAPTER TWENTY-SEVEN

ALICE

August 4, 2018
Six days after the kidnapping

"Hey, Garner," Nakamura said, breaking the silence that had settled between them on the drive back to the station.

She hummed in acknowledgment but didn't look over at him.

"Tell me a story," he said.

"What would you like to hear?" she asked.

They smiled at that, the both of them, probably because it hit too close to home.

"Sterling."

"Why I still think it's him?" She shifted toward Nakamura.

"Yeah."

Tell a story. Create a villain.

"They were trying to get away. Ruby and Trudy, at the very least. Probably Charlotte, too," she said. "Sterling is worried about few things, but one of them is appearances, and the other is power. If he learned they were up to something, it might have made him snap."

"So he discovers they're leaving and kills Ruby in a fit of rage," Nakamura prompted. "But there were no signs of struggle."

She tapped her foot against the floor of the car. "Controlled rage."

"I thought that was Hollis," Nakamura countered.

"Maybe," Alice admitted. She was just telling a story, after all. "But he hasn't gotten to where he has by being sloppy."

"You know what actually makes sense more than your obsession with Sterling," Nakamura said, ignoring her murmur of protest, "is Hollis pulling the puppet strings."

She waved a hand in a gesture for him to continue.

"Hollis has been aware of his behavior for some time but thought he'd stopped," Nakamura said, clearly warming to his theory. "Then when it becomes obvious that he hasn't, she breaks. She can't go after him, so she goes after the victim instead. It fits with the care shown to the body, the lack of damage, the control. And the perfect crime scene that's apparently a bug up Bridget's ass."

"And I can't imagine Hollis is a woman who lets her warmer emotions stand in the way," Alice said. "But why drop her off at the beach to be found? Four days later?"

"She's the one who found out they were planning on escaping," Nakamura said, altering the story. "Something wasn't ready, some part of her plan, but they were leaving, so she had to grab the girl when she could. She kept her somewhere. I'm sure she could afford to pay someone off until the day she'd actually planned on killing her."

Alice swallowed hard. A plan altered. "That would explain the four-day gap."

"But not dropping her at the beach." Nakamura tilted his head in her direction as if awarding her a point. "You're right on that front."

Tell me a story.

"Maybe she knew that if the body was never found, they would never move past this."

"The scandal of it?" Nakamura asked.

"That, yeah. The attention of the town and the social scene they both prize so highly. There would always be the suspicion that they had something to do with it," Alice said. "And then there's the media. They'd do a special every anniversary. Follow-ups on if the family could move on knowing their granddaughter had never been found. They would be caught in a perpetual state of mourning."

"If they acted like they were over it, they'd be shunned because it would be expected they'd search for the rest of their lives for her," Nakamura said.

"Yeah. So she makes sure the body is found. They can grieve and move on and be applauded for their strength instead of ostracized for their callousness," Alice continued. "But."

"But, what?"

"If Hollis was the mastermind," Alice said, just as they turned into the back parking lot of the station, "who is her scapegoat?"

Nakamura pulled the key out of the car and looked at her. "She would have set someone up to take the fall."

"Especially if she had been planning this for a while. Enough time to maybe even have a specific date in mind that they threw off by leaving early," Alice said. "And there's nothing that would indicate she planted anything to make us suspect anyone."

"Durand?" Nakamura suggested.

The sun streaming in through the windshield was making quick work of the coolness that had lingered from the air conditioner, and her T-shirt stuck to her damp lower back when she shifted to escape the greenhouse effect of the car. Nakamura followed her out.

"There's no evidence, though," Alice said. "Wouldn't we have found something? Anything that made him seem guilty?"

"We haven't got the autopsy yet," Nakamura reminded her. "Maybe something's there . . ."

The heat from the burning pavement sank into the soles of her shoes as they crossed the parking lot in silence. The darkness of the station was a welcome relief when they stepped inside. "What do you think of Lopez?" she asked.

"It's weird he went out of town in the middle of the week," Nakamura said. There was a shrug in his voice. "And his house smelled of cleaner."

"But?"

"The team didn't find anything suspicious," Nakamura said. "We should call the buddy in Tampa to verify he was there. But if he was, it makes more sense that someone took advantage of his house being empty for the day."

A plan altered.

"I'll call him," Alice said, her fingers slipping into the pocket where she'd put the number. "I agree, though. Could explain the timing of it. They knew he was going out of town."

Nakamura stopped just before swinging through the door to the bull pen. "We're no closer to who it could be."

Alice chewed on the flesh just inside her mouth. "Even if it was Hollis, which I still don't think it was, she had to have had help," she said.

"Charlotte," Nakamura murmured.

"Why does it always come back to her?" Alice asked.

Nakamura laid his hand on her shoulder, his long fingers cupping around it in sympathy. "I think you know why."

———

The man was short and ugly, to the point that it was unpleasant to look at him. Alice and Nakamura were sprawled at their joined desks, plotting their next moves, and she groaned when she realized that Liam Shaw, one of the young uniformed officers, was leading the person their way.

"Detectives Garner, Nakamura." Shaw greeted them with a nod. The small man hovered behind the young officer, his hands picking at each other. "This man says he has some information that might interest you on the Burke case."

Alice raised her brows at the officer, and he flushed.

"I thought you might want to hear him out," he stuttered. It was his job to weed out the crazies, and if this wasted their time, he would be held responsible for it.

She slid her eyes to Nakamura, who was already getting to his feet.

"Dr. Harry Harrison," the man said, coming out from the shadow of the young cop. His grip was weak and his palm damp when he took Alice's hand to shake. When he let go to turn to Nakamura, she wiped it against the outside of her leg.

"Perhaps we could chat in the conference room," Nakamura suggested, waving the way for the doctor.

The light bounced off the bald spot on the back of the man's head as they all walked down the hallway. When they got to the room, Alice set a water bottle in front of him when he'd settled into one of the seats. Then she rounded the table.

"You have something to share with us?" she prompted when he simply sat there fiddling with the plastic white top of the bottle.

He twisted it off and gulped at the water. Then he looked between them. "I've been battling with my ethics for the past week."

In her experience, when a doctor said something like that, it usually meant he had no ethics and was simply waiting the appropriate amount of time so as not to be skewered by the media. But she just murmured something sympathetic to get him to continue.

"I, uh, I've seen the coverage of the Burke case," he said. "I don't know if this is important or not, but, uh, Ms. Burke came to see me only a few days before her daughter disappeared."

It was what she'd been expecting. "What kind of doctor are you, Harry?"

His shoulders pulled back, and he straightened. "I'm a psychiatrist, Detective," he said, leaning heavy on the professional title. She resolved to call him only Harry from there out.

"And why did she come to see you?" Alice asked. If he was going to shrug off all his ethics, they might as well take advantage of it.

"She was having dissociative events," Harry said.

Nakamura pled ignorance. "Dissociative events?"

There was a smugness in the way he held himself. "It's when a person has, in layman's terms, an out-of-body experience. It's rare, but more common in victims of abuse."

"And could this . . . experience . . . last for an extended period of time?" Nakamura asked. Long enough for her to kill her child? The last part of the question was the elephant in the room, trumpeting and begging to be noticed.

"It could, yes," Harry said.

"This is different than a psychotic break, though, is it not?" Alice chimed in. "And is it common for there to be violence associated with these . . . events?"

Harry tilted his head, studying her. "Yes, it is different. And no, it's not common. But it's not impossible, either."

"Did she say anything, anything at all, that might have made it seem like she was a threat to herself or to others?" Nakamura leaned on the table.

"No. I just wish—" He broke off, swallowed, and pressed his hands to his chest. "I just wish I could have helped her. Maybe this all could have turned out differently. If only I could have stopped her from running away."

There was a pause as if he expected them to rush in and comfort him. Neither of them did.

"Is that all?" Alice asked, and he lifted his head from where he'd dropped it into his hands.

This was not proceeding as he'd expected. She could read it in the way his beady eyes widened and then narrowed. "Well. She used a fake name."

Again, that was almost a given. Charlotte Burke would not be so careless as to go to a psychiatrist in St. Petersburg and use her real name. "If you could get us the paperwork she filled out, that would be great," Alice said, pushing away from the table.

The sudden dismissal caught the doctor flat-footed, but he quickly recovered. "I just hope by sharing this I could rectify any part I played in this tragedy."

Just another vulture. There were so many of them on cases like these. She walked away without thanking him for his time. Nakamura would see the man out.

It didn't take long before her partner was back, leaning against her desk. "So I wouldn't say that was nothing."

"A victim of abuse is seeking mental health services?" Alice posed it as a question, but it wasn't one.

Nakamura didn't back down, though. "Days before her daughter was kidnapped and then killed? Yeah," he said. "The timing, Garner."

It didn't look good. She wondered if the doctor would take the information to the press. "Circumstantial."

"These dissociative events might explain something." Nakamura tapped a finger against his knee. "If she's having them, she could have had one that day. She might not have even realized she killed Ruby."

What happened, Charlotte?

"That's quite a big leap," Alice said.

But he just shrugged. "We need to bring her in, Garner."

They did need to bring her in. The question remained, though, if she would come willingly.

"You know what we need?" Alice said suddenly, swiveling to her computer.

"The autopsy report." Nakamura had followed her train of thought easily.

She touched the tip of her nose. "Exactly."

"If she was murdered the day she was kidnapped, it would make a stronger case for some kind of break," he said. "Then she had to cover her tracks for the days in between that and when we found Ruby on the beach."

"If Ruby was killed the day we found her, it was planned," Alice said. "And that negates everything the doc just told us, because he was certainly trying to make the case that she snapped. Where the hell is my report?"

She tilted her head back and yelled to the room at large, "Someone better fucking get me the fucking autopsy report. Right fucking now."

"Simple," Nakamura murmured, as three young officers jumped to their feet. "But effective."

———

St. Petersburg's medical examiner was a seventy-year-old man with a thick, white handlebar mustache, seventeen visible tattoos, and a prosthetic leg, which he'd gotten because of a motorcycle accident one week after returning without injuries from Vietnam.

William Byrd, who went by Birdie, took no shit and was intimidated by no man—or woman, for that matter. He was the only other person in the station Bridget adored outside her own team, and Alice thought that spoke volumes for his character.

In the few hours since Harrison had left, Alice took to pacing outside Birdie's office, but she had a growing suspicion that whenever he saw her, he actually moved slower. He'd also sent at least one of the young police officers who had hastened to do her bidding back to her in tears.

Three hours after that failed mission, he finally pinged them that the report was ready.

She didn't bother taking a seat across from his desk, when he slipped on reading glasses to scan over the papers he held. Her arms itched as his lips moved silently over the words, as if he were practicing them before saying them.

"The cause of death on Ruby Anne Burke, age five, was a subarachnoid hemorrhage," the man finally told them.

Nakamura had been lounging against the wall, his patience a far deeper well than her own. "Suba-what now?"

Birdie pushed the bridge of his rims back up along his nose. "Subarachnoid hemorrhage," he said slower.

"Not helpful," Alice said, and he flashed her a grin.

"Bleeding in the brain." Birdie rolled his eyes as if annoyed he had to dumb it down so much. He liked the dramatics. "Usually caused by trauma to the head."

"What kind of trauma?"

Birdie tipped his head to each side. "For young people, you see it in car accidents most frequently."

"Did you find anything else?" Nakamura asked.

Birdie nodded. "Contusions on her upper right arm."

"Bruises?" Alice clarified, earning another eye roll.

"Yes. Like she was"—Birdie lashed out with one hand suddenly, yanking at an invisible something in the air—"grabbed and then pulled."

"So she was handled with some roughness," Nakamura said.

"Well." Birdie circled a finger in the air. "Yes and no. The bruises were healing. And they were the only other markings on her."

"Maybe one incident, then," Nakamura filled in. "She's grabbed, her wrists are bound, but then after that she was kept without being restrained."

"That's above my pay grade, bucko," Birdie said. "I'm here for the facts."

"Could the, um . . . ?" Alice licked her dry lips and then abandoned any attempt at the medical jargon. "Head injury. Could that have been accidental?"

"Not my—"

Alice waved her arm, cutting him off. "In your *expert* opinion, could the head injury have been sustained in a fall? On a ledge or something? If there weren't any other injuries around the time of death?"

Birdie nodded, slow and thoughtful. "Could be. Could also have been pushed." He held both palms out to them and then slammed them forward. "For a child her size, it wouldn't have taken much force. So it could be possible not to see any contusions or lacerations from a struggle."

"Are you ruling out that she was hit with something, then?" Alice asked.

Birdie sucked in his top lip between his teeth, then let it go. "Because of the location of the wound, a deliberate strike with a blunt object from an average-size adult would be unlikely."

"Why's that?" Nakamura asked.

"You would normally see a wound at the temple if that had been the case"—Birdie touched the delicate spot near his eye—"or closer to the crown of the head. If she was curled up with her knees and arms underneath her, with the top of her neck exposed, you might see this wound. Or if it was a low swing of the arm that connected underneath the base of her skull while she was turned away. But it's not the most natural movement if you're attacking a child."

"All right," Alice said. She looked down at her hands gripping the sides of the chair. Her knuckles were white splotches against the rest of her skin. Unfurling each finger from the wood, she relaxed back into the seat. "Time of death?"

"That would be between midnight and four in the morning, August first," he said, glancing back down at the papers. "So three days ago."

Nakamura shifted. "So not in the hours directly before she was found on the beach."

They had been operating under two possible assumptions. One, that Ruby might have been killed the day she was kidnapped. The other was that she was killed the morning before she was found. This TOD fit neither scenario.

"Could the beach environment have skewed those readings?" she asked.

Birdie glared at her over the top of his lenses. "Are you questioning my results?"

"Never," she said. "I'm a city girl, though. Gotta be slow with me."

He thumbed over his mustache. "There's always a window," he said.

"By a day?" she asked, even though she knew what the answer was going to be.

"No." It was definitive. "That set you two off, huh?"

Alice ignored the question. "Did you find any skin under her nails? Fibers? Errant hair?"

Birdie whistled, long and low. "She's clean. Cleanest I've seen in a long time."

"And . . . any signs of sexual abuse?" Alice asked, wishing she didn't have to.

In a surprisingly quick move, Birdie tore the reading glasses off and dropped them on the desk. His eyes raked over her face, searching her expression for something he wouldn't find. She'd learned long ago to hide her emotions. She wondered if he'd heard the rumors about Sterling Burke.

"No," he finally said.

"Email me the report." Alice pushed out of the office into the cold, sterile hallway.

"Already in your in-box, lady," Birdie called out as Nakamura followed her.

Neither of them talked as they made their way out of the ME's building. But when they stepped into the sun, Nakamura stopped her, wrapping his long fingers around her arm, just above her elbow.

"What if it's not the family?"

The skin above her upper lip was already slick with sweat, and she licked at it, the salt sharp against her taste buds. "Can we not do this in the sauna that y'all call weather down here?"

Nakamura laughed, as she'd meant him to, and let her go. The thing was, he was somehow immune to the heat, the humidity. He wore light blue button-down shirts without fear of stains turning them a shade darker; his hair never frizzed or stuck to his forehead in a damp mess of strands. And then she was a perpetual mess who always looked like she'd just climbed out of a swamp.

They didn't speak again during the short drive back to the station, and by some unspoken agreement, they kept quiet until they were in their makeshift war room in the basement. The pictures she'd hung up were still there, as were the arrows connecting them all.

She stood looking at them, her back to Nakamura, when she finally prompted, "So what if it's not the family?"

"Want me to tell you a story?" Nakamura asked from behind her. He'd settled into the foldout chair, and she knew without having to look over her shoulder that he was squeezing his stress ball.

"No," she said, wrapping her arms around her waist. "I want you to tell me what you actually think happened."

Nakamura hummed, a low, surprised sound.

"The bruises," he said. "I think that signals that there's a chance she wasn't led away by someone she cared about."

"There was at least a small amount of struggle," Alice agreed.

He nodded. "The death was also somewhat violent."

"We don't . . ." Alice trailed off, shoving her free hand in her pocket. "It could have been an accident."

Nakamura nodded. "True. But the timeline is kind of weird, right?"

It was what had thrown them the most in Birdie's office. "If it was a fit of rage or a psychotic break by someone in the family, time of death probably would have been the day Ruby went missing." Alice laid out what they both were thinking.

"But why fake the kidnapping, hold her somewhere for three days, and then snap?" Nakamura asked.

A plan altered.

"It doesn't rule out the family," Alice corrected.

"How do you figure?"

Trudy had borrowed Zeke's car on the day of the kidnapping.

Bridget had reported back that there were no traces of blood or DNA in the fabric, but what was more interesting was that there was no sign it had been cleaned recently, either. So why would Trudy have taken the car when every other time she'd had Zeke drive her?

"What if Trudy and Charlotte both wanted Ruby out? If we go on rumors, Sterling Burke is a danger to women in his household. So they hatch a plan to escape." She paused. "But what if their plan went wrong and they got desperate?"

"Wait." He held up his hand. "Do my ears deceive me, or did you actually just admit it could be Charlotte?"

She flipped him the bird, though without any heat.

"All right." Alice started pacing. Her legs were restless, her body needed to move. "So they plan the kidnapping. Charlotte takes Ruby 'to the beach,' but in actuality, Trudy takes her in Zeke's car to some place to hide her."

"Enrique Lopez's house," Nakamura chimed in. He shrugged when she turned on him. "It would be perfect, right? No one in the family knows he has any connection to Charlotte or Trudy."

"It's a huge leap to say that he does," Alice said.

"Think big, Garner." Nakamura grinned a little, then pointed at her. "Keep going."

"They're planning on holding her there a few days until every-thing calms down a little." Alice went back to stalking across the floor. "Something happens, Ruby falls, or is pushed. They didn't mean for her to die."

"Shit." Nakamura whistled, and the sound scraped along her nerves. "That's interesting."

But Alice was already shaking her head. "Why keep her in the city?"

"They didn't expect there to be so much attention?" Nakamura suggested, but she heard the doubt in his voice, too. It didn't make sense.

Two strides had her in front of the pictures, and she slapped her palm against the wall. Hard enough so that it stung, so that it reverberated into all the bones in her hand. She wanted it to hurt more, wanted to feel those bones break. "We're going in circles."

When Nakamura spoke, it was careful and soothing, as if she were a wild animal. "Lopez. Let's go back and talk to him."

"Why?" Alice hadn't removed her palm from the wall, and she thought that maybe it was the only thing holding her body up.

"We didn't know what we were looking for before," Nakamura said in that same awful tone. She hated when people talked to her like that. He thought she was breaking.

The terrible thing was that he might not be wrong.

"What are we looking for now?" she asked, trying to get her hands to stop shaking.

"The wound's on the back of her head," Nakamura said. "From what Birdie said, that seems to mean it's more likely she fell or was pushed than straight-out attacked. Slammed against something on the floor. A fireplace, maybe. I don't know. Let's go see if he lets us look around."

"I want it to be noted that I think it's a waste of time."

He laughed, easy as always, but there was something watchful about his eyes. "Noted. Come on."

It was late in the day, but there were still a few people milling around the bull pen. Alice and Nakamura stopped through to direct them to start searches on Enrique Lopez before they made the drive back to the beach house.

The car that had been parked in front of it was gone, but that wasn't surprising. They pulled up and got out anyway.

"Not here," she said, stating the obvious even as they climbed the stairs. Nakamura's hands were relaxed, but they hovered near his holster, and she could tell by the way he was glancing around that he was on alert.

He hummed but didn't say anything. With one more sweeping glance around the porch, he knocked on the door.

As predicted, there was no response. He knocked again anyway, and she cocked an eyebrow at him when he looked over at her. "Think he ran out to the market?"

"It's late." She shrugged.

"Popped out for a beer?" Nakamura suggested, but she heard the doubt there.

On a normal day, it wouldn't be unusual for a person to head out for the night, run errands, continue with his life. For a day when said person was interviewed by the police about a murder outside his house? Well, that wasn't the best picture to paint.

Nakamura stepped to the side, cupping his hands so he could peer into the big living room windows. "I can't tell if it's different," he said. "It wasn't exactly well furnished before."

It didn't matter. There was an air of abandonment to the place that was palpable. What little clutter there had been was removed. The desk and table were empty; the shirt that had been draped over the railing was no longer there. They moved to the other side, the dining room. It was a similar scene. The table was still there, but it was the only thing left.

They'd need to get a warrant to confirm it, but Lopez was gone.

Nakamura knocked her with his elbow, catching one of her ribs in the process. "Still think this was a waste of time?"

CHAPTER TWENTY-EIGHT

TRUDY

August 3, 2018
Five days after the kidnapping

"What did you tell them?" Trudy asked Zeke. They were back at the park, back to that first conversation. She wished she could return to that night, when she still thought she knew what the right thing was.

Zeke's eyes were downcast. Shame. It was so much a part of her that it didn't take long to recognize it on the faces of others. "I'm sorry, Trudy. I had to tell them."

"I know," she said. She did. Who was she to blame him for sharing the secrets that he knew, when she had given him no reason to trust her and every reason to doubt? "What did you tell them?"

"Everything," he murmured. "All of it. I even told them the rumors."

No.

She didn't need to ask what rumors those were. They'd never talked about it. He'd never hinted that he knew, but sometimes it was in his eyes when he looked at her. It had been there when she forgot to scrub her face clean after a shift at Mac's, and it had been there in the club, beneath the pulsing lights.

Pacing away from Zeke, she watched the dust that kicked up beneath her Converse shoes. The police knew, then. How long would it be until everyone did? "Okay."

"I'm sorry," he said again, as if repeating it would compensate for the utter meaninglessness of the words.

She breathed in and then out, inhaling the smells of night and summer and flowers and stale air. There was nothing to do about it. The cops hadn't burst into the house to drag her off in cuffs, so whatever Zeke had said hadn't been enough to ruin her. But that also meant she had to act. And quickly.

"I need you to drive me somewhere," she said, turning back to the boy. He was sitting on the picnic table, just as he had before. But instead of the blank expression he wore so well, his eyes were filled with concern and a bit of helplessness.

"I think we've been here before," he said, smiling for the first time all night.

Trudy didn't smile back.

"Are you running, Trudy?" Zeke asked, his own amusement sliding off his face.

She shook her head. "No." She wasn't. But it had been so long, living in the world of secrets, that sharing anything felt like slicing open her chest and letting someone play inside. Her tongue fumbled for the words, the right ones, the ones that would convince him. It would have to be the truth, and that was terrifying.

"It wasn't me, Zeke," she started, because she had to start somewhere. "I don't know if you think it was or not, but it wasn't me. I didn't kill her."

It would be a long time before she could admit that Ruby was dead without a vise tightening around her heart. But she pushed through the pain—she had to. Sadness wouldn't find Ruby's killer; only ruthlessness would.

"I don't think you killed her, Trudy," Zeke said, and a small part of her relaxed. "Remember, I saw you that day. I know you were planning on running away with her."

That day the dream had seemed within reach. The impossibility of it all had shrunk because they were actually doing it. They were going to get her away.

"It wasn't my aunt, either," Trudy said, with just a hint of desperation on the edges of the words. She couldn't prove it, didn't even know if she believed it, but if she said it enough? Well, maybe it would be true. Maybe those haunted eyes hadn't meant anything. Maybe Trudy would stop seeing them when she closed her own. "I know what people are saying. Even in our bubble, I know what people are saying."

"Trudy . . ." Zeke said her name like a plea. Like he was asking her to think reasonably.

"No." She shook her head. "She was helping me. That's why she was at the beach. She wanted to get Ruby away."

"But maybe." He paused. "Maybe that's why. She thought she could let her go, and then it was too much."

The day at the mall, melting ice cream. A tear-drenched face. It was like a loop, those moments, running in her head.

"No," she said.

"Did you see her at all that day?" he asked.

Trudy hadn't. That was part of the plan, though. "She didn't do it, Zeke."

It was only then that she realized she was panting, that she realized she'd pressed her heel into the top of her other foot to the point where the fragile bones beneath cried out in pain. He noticed, too.

"All right, okay," he said, his palms up and out. "Who did it, then, Trudy?"

"You're going to think I'm crazy," she said, consciously relaxing her muscles one by one.

"The bus has left the station on that one, hon." Zeke laughed a bit.

So she told him. She told him about the person who'd contacted her, the one who'd given her directions to the women who helped victims of abuse, the one who had deleted their account before she could get any more information.

By the end of it, his eyes had narrowed.

"You think it was this person?" he asked, his slow drawl even thicker than usual.

"It's not that crazy." She spun away from him, not wanting to see the doubt. "It's not. Why would they have so perfectly led me down this path?"

"Because they were trying to help," Zeke said, soft like he was pulling a punch. "The information was good, wasn't it? They helped get you the passports. Helped set you up with those ladies."

Trudy shook her head. "Which made us vulnerable. Don't you see? It's perfect."

Zeke sucked his bottom lip in between his teeth but didn't say anything further.

"Get Ruby away from the safety of the house, this town, her family." The words were rushing out with hardly any space between them. "Create an opportunity and then seize it."

"Trudy . . ."

"No." Not wanting him to see her eyes, she looked down at her fists and uncurled her fingers. There were bright pink half-moons where her nails had dug into her palm. There were three heartbeats of silence and then four heartbeats more. Each one pounded in her chest.

"What about the cops?" he finally asked. "They're going to notice you're gone. They're going to want to come after you."

The breath she'd been holding escaped from her lips. "They're distracted."

"Enough not to notice one of Ruby's family members left the city?" Zeke asked.

No, not that distracted. It was a terrible idea to leave in the middle of the investigation. And she also didn't care. At least she'd know she'd tried.

"I don't think that's something you have to worry about," she said. Which was only partially true. The cops probably wouldn't look too favorably on Zeke if he helped her, but maybe they didn't have to know.

Zeke didn't bring it up, even though he could have. "So. Jacksonville."

She nodded.

"You want me to drive you there," he said.

"Yes."

He scratched at his neck. "What exactly do you think you'll find? Jacksonville may not be huge, but it's a city."

"I know," she said. "My grandfather was born there."

He studied her. "You think that's significant?"

Yes. But she just shrugged. "Out of all the IP addresses, in all the world, it happens to be one from the city where my grandfather was born? And Ruby was kidnapped on the day we were trying to get her away from him?"

"You think he has something to do with it?"

She tried to think about Sterling as little as possible. He would sneak in, though, sometimes. Like when someone ordered a Scotch neat at the bar, because that's what he'd drink after dinners with the family. Or when she spotted a Windsor knot, because he'd always loosen his when he came into her room. Or when she smelled peppermint, because he liked to chew on the leaves, and his breath always reeked of candy canes.

But day to day, she shut him out. That wasn't as hard. They lived in a big house, and he was almost never home. When he was, she could hide using the excuse of youth and rebellion.

She thought of him now, though. His empty laugh and his calculating eyes. No one ever seemed to see it; they saw the charmer and thought it was genuine. She thought of the cruelty in which he decided the fates of people he feared, and the leniency he gave to those who could help him. She thought of the way he shook the governor's hand after spending the evening planning to bring him down.

Could he kill someone? She had not a single doubt.

Did he kill Ruby? That was less certain.

"I think my grandfather grew up in Jacksonville," she finally said.

He nodded. "Well, it looks like we're going to Jacksonville."

———

They left that night. She'd hidden her backpack in a copse of trees right by the park, so all they had to do was swing by his place to grab clothes and supplies. Then they were on the road, chasing answers that might not even exist.

It felt good to do something, though. If she was wrong, if nothing came of it, and they crawled back to St. Petersburg with only receipts from gas stations, it would still feel better than staring out windows and wondering what she should have done differently.

Zeke left her alone for most of the drive. It was a little more than three hours between the cities, and even during the day there wasn't much to look at. Maybe it would have been the perfect time to think, to formulate a theory, but she couldn't. Instead, she took each thought as it came, unraveled it, and let it dissolve into the darkness of the night. Her head was blissfully empty by the time they crossed the bridge into the city.

"I'm guessing you didn't book a hotel," Zeke whispered as if he were scared of startling her out of wherever she'd sunk into. It was the first thing he'd said to her since they'd left St. Pete's city limits.

"No," she said. "Let's just look for a vacancy sign, yeah?"

It didn't take long. The *c* in the sign was out, but for the most part, the place seemed decent enough. In their price range, at least. Or in his, because she didn't have much money to spare for the room, and she couldn't use a credit card without being found.

Charlotte knew where she was but had been sworn to secrecy. And Trudy had no interest in letting Hollis know what she was up to.

He didn't even ask, though. Just told her to wait in the car as he took care of checking in, and she knew she owed him. In that moment, she remembered his mom was dying. She knew almost nothing about him other than that, and the fact that he was willing to do things for her simply because she asked.

Maybe that was why he was helping her. Maybe he'd rather be in a silent car driving to Jacksonville in the middle of the night than counting the cracks in his ceiling, waiting for the day to come when he would be left by himself. Maybe she wasn't the one who should be asked if she was running away.

He knocked on her window, and she gasped, thankful no one had been around to hear the noise fly out of her mouth.

"Come on," he said when she opened the door. "We're right here."

The room was nothing special, as the outside of the building advertised.

There was the faint smell of cat pee that lingered in the air, and the paint was chipping off the wall in large flakes in some places. But it had two beds that looked relatively stable, and a TV that was from the current century.

She dropped her bag and starfished onto the closest mattress. Something heavy landed in the space beside her. Her fingers touched metal, and she realized it was a flask. "Bless you, Zeke Durand," she said, sitting up and opening it to take a swig. Peach schnapps. Too sweet for her taste, but like the rest of this trip, beggars couldn't be choosers.

After tossing it back to him, she scooched up the bed until she was leaning against the headboard. It was nearly two in the morning, and she couldn't even imagine going to sleep.

"Why are you helping me, Z?" she asked, watching him grimace at the sweetness. He threw the flask over to her, and she took another sip, holding on to it for a bit. "You know that favor I promised you is about worth the paper it was written on now."

"Not everyone is out to get something from you, you know," he said.

That would be nice if life were a Disney movie, but it wasn't, so she just waited.

He sighed. "When you first talked to me. Well, there's this drug trial. My mom was rejected from it, but it's her only shot."

"You wanted my family to pull some strings?"

"Your grandfather golfs with the governor." He shrugged. "It was worth a try."

It probably would have worked. Especially if she'd played up the tutoring-an-underprivileged-kid thing. Good for the image.

"And now?"

He paused and then shifted so that he was looking at the ceiling instead of her. "You have sad eyes."

She tipped her head so the syrupy alcohol sat at the back of her tongue for a second before she swallowed. "You're helping me because I have sad eyes?"

A smile was in his voice when he responded. "I kind of like you a little, too."

"Just a little," she teased, feeling light and buzzed, though that was more from the stress and lack of sleep than from the schnapps.

"Not everyone's trying to get something from you," he said again. "Sometimes people want to help just to help."

And maybe life wasn't a Disney movie, and maybe he was just using her problems to forget about his own, and maybe that was all there was to it. But she'd take it.

CHAPTER TWENTY-NINE

ALICE

August 4, 2018
Six days after the kidnapping

"Who's coming in?" Alice asked, dumb with the surprise of it.

"Sterling Burke," Chief Deakin repeated, drawing out the name. "The man you've been salivating to drag into your interrogation room for the past two days."

She blinked, trying to get the words to make sense as she followed Deakin across the bull pen. "How?"

Deakin shrugged one shoulder. "Volunteered himself, actually."

"What? Why now?" The thoughts that had been encased in molasses moments earlier broke free. "He just called you? Out of nowhere?"

Nakamura bumped into her when she stopped just outside the chief's office. Deakin turned when he realized they weren't still trailing him.

"Are you really complaining, Garner?"

She shook her head, though her palms were slick with sweat. "No. It's strange, though, isn't it?"

"Does it matter why he's coming in? He's coming in," Nakamura said so that only she could hear.

"Understanding why a person does something is more important than what they actually do," she snapped, striding to her desk.

What nerve had they struck? The search warrant? Or maybe it was that they knew Trudy was missing. Alice had already set uniforms on the task of tracking her down; if it took longer than a couple of hours, she'd take over herself.

Whatever it was, Hollis wanted to throw a distraction at the detectives, as something shiny to look at, while she fixed the problem. That something shiny just happened to be her husband.

Nakamura tipped his chin toward the door. "Well, I guess we shall see shortly, won't we?"

She nodded once, her eyes on Sterling Burke as he walked in, watching him like she would a snake apt to bite.

Sterling was of surprisingly average build—only an inch or two taller than her own five feet eight inches—and had a delicate bone structure that should have made him appear petite. On a less confident man, it might have. Instead, the judge carried himself with a presence that took up space.

He was also fit in a way that spoke of daily workouts in an air-conditioned gym, and his hair was thick silver, which gleamed beneath fluorescent lights that turned others' greasy and limp.

Some might call him handsome, or dignified, at the very least. But it wasn't his classic good looks that drew the eye—it was the power, pure and captivating, that was draped over him like a cloak he wore with decades of familiarity.

The entire energy of the room shifted—tightened—when he came in. Young officers tucked in loose shirts and touched nervous fingers to scruff that had grown out of control. Older detectives played at being disinterested but gravitated toward where the chief stood waiting to greet the judge, their bodies pulled like magnets unable to resist.

She watched it all. She watched the way his palm slipped easily into the chief's as if they were old friends. She watched the judge's gaze traverse the room, landing on each face before dismissing it. She watched the way his smile came and went without disrupting the laugh lines near his eyes.

"We'll set you up in one of our rooms, Judge," Deakin was saying as he walked the man over. Or, really, the man walked him over, a hand firmly on the chief's shoulder. He dominated this interaction far more than Deakin ever would. "But if you're not comfortable in there, just say the word."

"I'm sure it will be fine," the judge said, turning toward Alice and Nakamura. Though the reassurance was benign, there was something dark in his tone.

"Our best are on the case, Your Honor," Deakin said, nodding at them. "Detective Nakamura."

Nakamura reached out a hand.

"And Detective Garner."

She nodded instead of holding out her palm, and the judge accepted it easily, his eyes on her face. "Ah. The new recruit," he said, his voice smooth Southern molasses.

The new recruit. *Welcome to St. Pete. It's like a family that way, isn't it?* He remembered her from that party months ago when they'd first met. It was a good skill to have. Recognizing faces. It spoke of the way he cataloged memories, slotting them into different files in his brain. *Useful. Not useful.*

"Judge Burke," she said, forcing the honorary out of her mouth. "Thank you for coming in. We just have a few questions."

"Of course." His face turned serious. "Whatever I can do to help move this investigation forward."

There was a threat behind the words, a right hook followed by an implicit jab that they weren't doing their jobs so he had to step in to help. The tone may have been couched in congeniality, but there was no mistaking the intention.

Nakamura led the way to the nicest interrogation room, the one they saved for innocent witnesses and well-meaning tattletales. The vent was kept clean of dust, and the walls were painted eggshell instead of stark white. She wished they were using a different one. This one was designed to put people at ease, and she wanted him on edge.

Sterling settled into the uncomfortable metal chair, thumbing open the button of his thousand-dollar suit as he did so. "I'm sorry it's so late, Detectives. I hope I'm not keeping you. My calendar was, unfortunately, impossible to clear."

Impossible to clear until it wasn't. Trudy. It had to be Trudy. Where was she? Why did they not want the detectives to look into her whereabouts? Why had the teenager disappeared in the middle of a murder investigation?

Was she running away, hiding? What did she know?

It itched at Alice's brain.

She tapped her fingers on the table while Nakamura took up his usual position against the wall.

Interrogations were battlefields. With the dumb, the lazy, the boring, it was easy to lay traps, to know how to play it. With the cunning, it was harder. There were personas to adopt, ones they kept as weapons in their arsenals. There were strategies to take, forged in countless wars.

The most basic was good cop, bad cop; it was a cliché for a reason. But it never seemed to work with her and Nakamura. The good cop fit him. But the bad-cop role felt too familiar, too welcome, for her to really embrace it. They'd learned early on it wasn't for them.

Instead, Nakamura would take the observer role, distancing himself from the action. He could read a room easily, but only when he wasn't engaging. She, on the other hand, thrived when she was parrying. Body language laid bare so many secrets, but it was best to read them when she was up close, where she could see the pearls of sweat form, where she could watch each muscle tick, where she could feel the way fingers tangled together to soothe themselves.

Sterling Burke was confident and at ease, with just a hint of sadness wrinkling his brows. He wanted to help; he was being honest. It was the story he told through his open palms, through his relaxed shoulders, through his wide, sincere eyes.

Trust me, I'm telling the truth.

He looked between them. "What can I help with, Detectives?"

Alice felt the chief's eyes from behind the mirror. If she screwed this up, she had only the amount of time it would take for Deakin to walk the short distance between the observation room and this one.

"You can start by telling us where you were the evening of July thirty-first and the morning of August first," she started. It's what she would have asked anyone.

The judge didn't react, beyond a quick glance up as if trying to remember something. "I had dinner at the club," he started slowly in that drawl of his that rubbed her nerves raw. "And then came home at about eleven. I went to bed around midnight and woke at five thirty the next morning, as always."

It was almost the exact window Birdie had given them for time of death. If they pressed for an alibi, Sterling would just direct them to Hollis.

The question had been a softball anyway. A man in Sterling's position would have an airtight alibi for when his granddaughter went missing, no matter if he was involved or not.

She needed to throw him.

"What about family members?" She watched him, watched the creases next to his eyes deepen.

"Excuse me?"

It was a warning: *Don't tread into that water.*

Then his eyes shifted to the mirrored window in case his message wasn't clear. He could end this at any time.

"Extended, of course," Alice said, as if that's what she meant all along, as if she hadn't been talking about the vipers that called the Burke mansion home. "Any long-lost, disgruntled cousins? An uncle who's bitter over your success?"

The question seemed to genuinely surprise him. His chin tipped up and his eyelids slid lower while his gaze tracked to the side.

"No," he finally said, but slowly. "My wife had a sister, but she passed years ago. No children."

A basic family tree had told them that days ago, but it gave her an interesting read on him. This was what he looked like telling the truth.

"Is there anyone you can think of who would want to hurt Ruby? Perhaps a business acquaintance? One who got too close, too often?" She let the suggestion coat her voice.

He shut down again, the mask slipping firmly back into place. His eyes were still sharp and focused on her face, though. It was a reminder that he was reading her, too. "If I suspected anyone, I surely would have let you know sooner than this, Detective."

"Would you have?" She tipped her head to the side, doubtful. She moved on before he could add anything. "Do you know where your granddaughter is?"

There was anger in his eyes, but he was too controlled to really let it slip out. This was the nerve they had struck. Here it was.

"She's staying with a family friend," Sterling said, as smooth and unruffled as he'd been earlier. He was still directing this conversation. Or at least he thought he was. "The media has become unbearable. We didn't want to put her through any more distress than she's already had to endure."

It made sense, but that didn't mean it was true. If it was as simple as that, Sterling wouldn't be here, wouldn't be forced to answer their questions so that they wouldn't look too hard in any other direction.

"We'll need the name of that friend," Alice said. Trudy wouldn't be there. All that giving them an address would do was buy the Burkes time, but she had to ask anyway.

"My secretary will send it to you."

They were parrying, but without any heat. The need to strike out, to draw blood, was burning in her veins, and Alice knew she needed to control the fire so she could use it, so that it wouldn't make her sloppy.

"And what exactly was their relationship like? Ruby and Trudy's."

It wasn't blood that she drew with the question, but it put him off-balance anyway; it forced him back a step to reassess the field.

His mind worked; she could actually see it. His lashes drifted down against his cheeks a beat too long as if he wanted to shield the confusion he knew his eyes would reveal. Why was she asking about Trudy? Surely the girl wasn't an active target in the investigation.

"I don't know what you're implying, Detective" was what he finally said. It was a stalling tactic.

"I'm not implying anything, Sterling," she said, opening her palms up to him. *Look. I can be sincere, too.* "Would you say the girls were close?"

There was a hesitancy in his manner that hadn't been there before, not even when she'd asked about the family as a whole. He didn't have a prepared answer for this. "You could say that."

"Would you say it?" she pressed.

"You would have to ask their mothers or my wife," he said. "They would have a better idea."

It was the perfect opening. "So you weren't close with the girls?"

"We're a close family, Detective," he said. His body language was the opposite of what it should be. He tensed when telling the truth, relaxed when he lied. It was a sign of someone more comfortable with deceit. She knew it well.

"But you don't know if the girls liked each other?"

Sterling shifted. "The softer things they shared with their grandmother."

"So they came to you with problems, instead?" Alice asked. "Did you spend a lot of time with them alone?"

It was the accusation they'd been inching toward. She pulled it out and laid it on the table between them so that he could see, so that he could realize. Alice knew the darkness in him, knew his dirty secrets, knew what he did when he thought no one was looking.

He didn't react to the gauntlet thrown, but she knew that he would now be looking for an opening, a vulnerability.

"Not often," Sterling said, his hands still relaxed on the table. The man's body language was that of utter control. Rage and control. The echo of her conversation reverberated along her skull. Rage. Control. "They would talk school. Their various projects. Trudy was tutoring an underprivileged boy."

"And Ruby? What did she talk to you about?"

He leaned back into the chair, crossing one leg over the other, finally closing himself off. Here was another nerve. If they'd had any doubts. "Trivial things, as five-year-olds do. You must know what that's like."

There. The counterattack. He'd found his footing. "Yes."

"You had a daughter, didn't you, Detective?"

There was a rustling behind her, Nakamura straightening against the wall. She wished he wouldn't move.

"I did," Alice said. The bile burned in her throat. It was tempting to scrape her fingernails along his face, draw blood so that it oozed thick and viscous over the smooth skin. So that everyone could see what lay beneath the mask.

"She was Ruby's age when she died?" His face was fashioned into a pantomime of empathy, but there was no hiding the hunger in his eyes. He smelled blood in the water.

"We're not talking about my daughter," Alice said, though the words wobbled on the edges far more than she would have preferred.

"If you cannot even protect your own daughter, Detective, how do you expect me to trust you to find my granddaughter's killer?"

Her pulse pounded in her ears, and she forced herself to concentrate on that. He was baiting her. He was running the table while she scrambled to grab hold of her fragile self-control. And they still didn't know where Trudy was.

She thought about her rib cage, thought about the air filling her lungs and the bones expanding to make space. Her mind traced over the idea of ivory nestled beneath flesh as she counted each rung. When she got to her collarbones, her pulse had returned to normal, and she was able to look up.

Maybe that was a mistake. The smugness in the set of his shoulders told her it was. The arrogance in the corners of his lips told her it was. His hands folded and relaxed over his knee told her it was.

But he wasn't the only one holding a sword.

"Do you know what I've found, Sterling?" she asked, surprised by the steadiness of her own voice. "When you have little girls, you realize just what kind of monsters are out there."

"It's Judge Burke, Detective. Or Your Honor, if you prefer," Sterling said, and it felt like a victory. It felt like she was getting to him. "And I'm well aware how dangerous the world is."

"The type of person it would take to prey upon someone so young . . ." Alice trailed off.

"Is out there right now, Detective," Sterling said. "While you're here wasting time talking to me."

"You think it's a waste of time? Talking to the victim's grandfather? The head of the family?"

Sterling had thought she would break down at the mere mention of Lila, she could tell. This was not what he'd planned. He pressed his lips together before relaxing his entire body again. "I've given you what

I can. Now it's time for you two to catch the bastard who did this." The hint of "or else" hung in the air, a vague threat that wasn't actually vague.

They stared at each other, neither of them victors despite both scoring points. Then he stood up in one graceful move. The interview was over. It was to be a draw, it seemed.

"We'll be in touch," Alice said, remaining seated. It was all she could say. She had no power here, not unless she wanted to arrest him, and it wasn't time for that yet.

He gave one nod before crossing the room.

"Oh, Sterling," Alice called out just as Nakamura was about to open the door for him. "Something you should know? I'm really good at recognizing monsters. Even when they're in disguise."

Sterling's cold eyes flicked over her face. "Funny. I am as well."

———

"Don't touch me." Alice shrugged Nakamura's hands off her shoulders. They were standing in the hallway, just outside the interrogation room. Everyone else had cleared out while they'd lingered behind. "Just—I need a minute."

You had a daughter, didn't you, Detective?

She scrubbed at her skin, wanting to rid herself of the memory of Sterling. It lingered anyway like bad perfume, thick and repulsive. Nauseating.

"Get some air," Nakamura said, and his voice came from a distance. The black was creeping in at the edges of her vision, and she started for the doors without acknowledging him again.

The night was warm against her too-cold skin.

You had a daughter, didn't you, Detective?

She leaned against the brick wall of the station, her fingers finding the cement grooves, tracing along them, over and over.

And she breathed. In. Out. In. Her lungs burned as they devoured the oxygen and called out for more. Her eyes stung where tears she never let fall pressed against the ducts. Her lips cracked from where her teeth sank into the soft flesh.

It had taken all of herself not to kill him in that room. Not to dig her thumb into his windpipe and watch the life fade from his evil eyes. Not to break every bone in his fingers, the ones he'd used to lay hands on a little girl. The ones he'd used to ruin Charlotte. To ruin Trudy.

You had a daughter, didn't you, Detective?

"Detective?" The woman's voice was kind, honeyed. She was from the South and liked to slur her words together until they became one. "You can go in now, hon."

Alice blinked, having trouble focusing her eyes. Everything was blurred and a bit sideways.

She followed the guard into the visitation room. It looked like every single one she'd ever been in. Sparse, gray, depressing.

There was only one man on the other side of the glass, sitting three seats from the wall. Her shoes slapped against the linoleum. The chair squeaked when she drew it back. The lights gleamed off the metal counter. She blinked again.

And he came into focus. The monster.

He didn't look like one. He had sandy-blond hair, thinning only a little at the sides and top. His face was classically handsome, with wide-spread blue eyes, a patrician nose, and a strong jawline. He had broad shoulders and muscle definition most often seen on those who spent their time behind bars.

He had taken her entire life.

She picked up the phone, and he mirrored the gesture. He didn't say anything, just waited for her. Monsters shouldn't be considerate.

"Why?" It was stupid and naive, as if she hadn't been a cop for years, and she asked it anyway. It was a weakness humans had, always having to know. Why?

He sucked on his lower lip, his eyes on her face. "I was bored."

Fierce pain bloomed in her chest, spread along her collarbones, along her arms, down through her pelvis. Her womb pulsed with it. She slammed the phone against the glass, wishing it would shatter, wishing she would shatter. Wishing the shards of her would slice him, a million tiny cuts that would bleed out onto the bleached speckled tile.

But it didn't break. The window separating them. He was safe from her. Protected.

He smiled.

And then he hung up the phone, stood, and walked over to the guard. He didn't look back as they led him from the room.

"Hey." There was something being pushed into her hand. Her fingers worked even though her mind was sluggish at understanding what was happening.

"Coffee," Nakamura said, leaning against the wall beside her.

She drank because it was something to do. The liquid was lukewarm and thicker than it was supposed to be, but it was caffeine injected into her bloodstream.

"You okay?" he asked, though clearly she wasn't. *You okay? I'm fine.*

The script. The one she would have to follow forever and always. *I'm fine.*

"No," she said instead.

"Okay."

CHAPTER THIRTY

CHARLOTTE

August 3, 2018
Five days after the kidnapping

Charlotte didn't turn around to watch as Alice left the diner. Instead, her gaze remained on the child in the photo Alice had left behind. She ran the tip of her finger over the smiling face. The girl had Detective Garner's eyes, but the similarities ended there.

It hurt to look at it, but she couldn't tear her gaze away even when the waitress came to check on her again.

"A grilled cheese," Charlotte ordered, because Alice had told her to get something.

The waitress walked away without any other acknowledgment.

Charlotte turned the picture over. On the back in sloppy handwriting was "Lila, Age 4."

She swiped at her eyes, angry and frustrated. At the world. At the detective. At herself. There were countless pictures of Ruby, just like the one on the table. Her own labeling was neater, but the sentiment was the same. A moment captured in time, a race to remember a little girl before she became older in the next split second.

Life softened those changes so that they weren't noticeable as you were living them. The day to day became routine. There were still milestones: a lost tooth, a first day of school. But most of the time, Ruby was just Ruby. Her bright, shining stardust girl.

Looking at those pictures, though, the ones that were just like Lila's, sharpened the moments. Stopped them when otherwise they would have rushed by without a thought.

Now all she had left were those ones that she had managed to capture. There seemed to be too few.

Warm toast and melted cheese slid in front of her, and the edge of the plate covered the picture. Panic raced through her at the thought of it being damaged. She smoothed the glossy paper down with a hand gone shaky.

What happened, Charlotte?

She couldn't remember. She couldn't. *What happened?*

There was a wisp of a memory there. Sand. Heat. A tiny sweaty palm in hers. But every time she chased it, it only dissolved further. Sky. Beach. Waves. The smell of strawberries.

Had it been Sterling? She searched for a glimpse of white hair, of that profile she knew too well. Of Ruby hearing her name called by a loved one.

It was blank.

What happened, Charlotte?

It had to be him. It had to be.

"I don't wanna go," Ruby shouted into the quiet of the house, her face red, her cheeks tearstained.

Frustration and desperation turned Charlotte's hands rough. She grabbed at the girl's soft arm, and Ruby cried out again when fingers dug into flesh.

Charlotte shook her head. No, she didn't remember that. All she remembered was beach. Waves. Sky. A tiny sweaty palm in hers. The smell of strawberry shampoo.

What happened, Charlotte?

"Get up." *Charlotte tugged on Ruby's arm. Her fingers would leave bruises, but she would feel sorry about it later. All that mattered now was getting Ruby out of the house.*

"No," *Ruby wailed at the top of her lungs. They would wake everyone if this continued much longer. It would ruin everything.*

Charlotte slapped her hand over her daughter's mouth, pressing hard.

Everything after the memory was blurry, but she could still feel Ruby's damp lips against her palm.

Before she realized it, she was up and moving. There were more people in the diner than there had been earlier, but they were all just blurred shapes and indistinguishable voices. She heard the waitress call after her as she slammed through the door and the bell hanging over it tinkled, wild and angry. Ignoring both, she ran down the stairs, stumbling a bit as she jammed the key in the car's lock.

It happened again. That gap. One minute she was in the parking lot by the diner, trying to control her pulse, her breathing. The next she was pulling to the side of the road. She didn't know where she was.

She turned the car off, and then her fingers found her eyebrows and plucked at the patchy hair there.

The small bite of pain helped her focus. She looked around, realizing it hadn't been mindless at all. The drive.

For thirty-six years, without fail, Sterling Burke had kept a long-standing appointment at the Old Tavern. It didn't matter who joined him; he would always sit on the patio and order Scotch neat and smoke a cigar.

He'd brought her there for the first time when she turned seven. The hostess had known who they were, had taken them right over to Sterling's table despite there being a line of people waiting. It had been her first taste of what their name meant in this town. It had been her first taste of knowing what it was like to be a Burke.

Sterling had let her try his Scotch and then ordered her a Shirley Temple. It had been too sweet, but she drank it all anyway. She'd felt classy, sophisticated. Good.

He'd always been able to do that for people, Sterling. He was skilled at reading them, at knowing what they desired most and giving it to them. More than his brains or his charm or his luck, it was that ability that he had used to drag himself out of poverty.

No one looking at him now in his $3,000 white linen suit would know he'd come from a modest family in the suburbs of Jacksonville, the son of a mechanic. At some point in his rise to prominence, someone tinted the scene to tell the story of a boy and his bootstraps, which appealed to the vast majority of Southern voters. But it had been more about a boy and his ability to lie and manipulate his way into positions of power and authority.

All of it became second nature to him. If he wanted something and he could get it, why not? Did it really matter if someone got hurt in the process?

She knew how dark the underbelly of the power was now, but back then, with her cherry-slicked lips and the stars in her eyes, it had seemed magical.

Tires squealed on asphalt to her left, and she jolted, only then realizing that she still had the photo from Detective Garner in her hand. It was crumpled against the steering wheel, a crease down the middle of the little girl's face. A tiny whimper escaped her lips as she tried to smooth it out, but she knew it was a lost cause. It wasn't fair that they damaged so easily.

She slipped the picture into the visor before her eyes found Sterling.

He was laughing, his head thrown back, one hand on his belly, the other clutching at his glass. The lazy fan above them was doing little to battle the humidity of the late-afternoon sun. But Sterling was unfazed. A Southern gentleman who could handle the heat.

Her fingertips rested on her knees, and then slowly, ever so slowly, inched down toward her calf and the underside of her seat. They crept along the fabric until they touched the cold, smooth metal of the gun. Ever since Enrique had given it to her, she'd kept it underneath the seat for easy access. She curled her palm around the grip and brought it up to her lap. It sat heavy against her thigh, and she stroked the length of the barrel, her eyes still on Sterling.

She hadn't slept at all the night before the beach. She hadn't slept for far too many nights.

Ruby had been warm in her arms on the porch. Ready for an adventure, any adventure. Charlotte had cataloged each second, each minute, of sitting there, rocking in the old, worn chair. She hadn't known when she'd see Ruby again.

The plan involved Trudy disappearing completely. No trail for Hollis to trace. No way for them to be found.

When Charlotte let herself dream, she pictured finding Trudy and Ruby. They'd buy a little house in South Carolina or California or Montana. Somewhere pretty. Somewhere they could breathe and stretch and see the sky. Somewhere they could forget they were broken. Somewhere they could try to actually live instead of survive.

It wouldn't have been like that, though. Charlotte had known even as she'd held her baby girl in her arms for probably the last time. She'd known.

What happened, Charlotte?

Why had Detective Garner asked her about Sterling? The tip of her thumb skated over the muzzle of the gun, and she thought of the bullets that were nestled in the magazine.

What if Sterling had found out?

There'd been passports, Social Security cards. Money. Wads of it, stashed under floorboards and in the bottoms of safes. What would he have done if he realized they were escaping?

Charlotte thought he might love her, in some dark and twisted way. It wasn't that he didn't pay attention to Ruby and Trudy, but she was the one he always wanted to control, to own, to break.

My favorite girl. It was a whisper, a promise, a vow. *Always my favorite girl.*

What if he thought she was leaving? What if he thought she was going with them?

Would he kill for that? Would he take away her incentive? Without Ruby she had no reason to escape.

Beach. Waves. Sky. A tiny sweaty palm in her own.

Had he been there? Why couldn't she remember?

Her finger found the trigger, but not to squeeze. Not yet. Just to test, to feel beneath her skin.

It felt like power.

For once in her life, she didn't feel weak, and all the noise and voices and sound just sort of . . . stopped. They all stopped.

Only when her lips started to tingle did she realize she'd been holding her breath, and when she sucked in air, everything else came rushing back with it. She slipped the gun under the seat once more and ducked low beneath the brim of her baseball cap when she thought she saw Sterling glance over.

Then Charlotte was driving again.

There was a moment on the beach she remembered. She'd been looking at the water, so dangerous and alluring to a five-year-old, and in that heartbeat realized Ruby wasn't there. She'd charged toward the waves, not stopping until she was thigh-deep in the ocean, her hands dragging through the water as if she could snatch a limb, a hand, a clump of hair. As if she could drag what would be Ruby's lifeless body into the oxygen.

Only when a man had gripped her arm had she realized it had been her own wailing that had caused the beach to go still.

The man had asked her questions with a mouth that moved but had no sound coming out of it.

Charlotte knew Ruby wasn't in the water. How had she known?

What happened, Charlotte?

When she didn't respond to the man, he'd pulled her to the beach and then flagged down a lifeguard.

Why had Ruby left? Why couldn't Charlotte answer? How had they gotten to the beach? Would Ruby have gone with someone she'd known?

Why had the detective mentioned Sterling?

She parked the Range Rover behind the house and sprinted across the back lawn. With luck, Hollis would still be at her ladies' luncheon.

Charlotte kicked off her shoes when she got to the kitchen and then took off running, her feet warm against the cool hardwood of the hallway. Her heart pounded with that one question.

The door to the study caught for only a second before it gave, and she tumbled over the threshold. Everything was in perfect order, as always, but there had to be something. Had to be.

She stared at the desk. The top of it was clear of any paper, so she pulled at the drawers. One by one they crashed to the floor, the edge of the bottom left one catching her toe.

Turning her face into her shoulder, she screamed so that her flesh muffled the pain. Once she'd caught her breath, she started digging. There were papers and notes and files. Her mother's drawer was obvious, and she pushed it aside after flipping through receipts from lunches and hair salons.

Her father's proved no more useful, though. When she was done, her fingernails scraped along the bottom, making sure there was no paper stuck in the crevices. Nothing.

She kicked at the wood with her uninjured foot and then went to work on the bookshelf, pulling the neatly aligned volumes to the floor. They plunged toward the thick carpet, their fall muffled by the expensive Oriental.

There had to be something.

When all the books were on the floor, she crouched and started shaking out the pages. Sharp pain radiated from her kneecaps from when she had dropped to them without regard for where the hardwood would be carpeted, but she ignored it. Her fingers caught along the edges of paper, tearing the guts from the books until she sat surrounded by her own destruction.

It was then that Hollis walked in.

The heels should have been warning enough, but there was a faint buzzing in Charlotte's ears that had shielded the sound.

Her mother stopped just inside the doorway, her eyes sliding over the desk and then to Charlotte, who was still wearing her T-shirt, jeans, and baseball cap. She was panting also, she realized, and there was snot running out of her nose, getting caught in the slight upturn of her lip.

Once again she was weak, so weak, beneath her mother's gaze. Cracked and poised to shatter, the girl made of glass.

"You'll need to clean this up" was all Hollis finally said. "The police will have a warrant by the morning."

Charlotte collapsed against the floor, the sobs finally taking over her body, as her mother walked out of the room.

CHAPTER
THIRTY-ONE

ALICE

August 4, 2018
Six days after the kidnapping

It was a Saturday night, so the bar was full. Mostly off-duty cops and the odd local here or there. A group of college students crowded around the jukebox in the back, giggling with each song selection.

Alice slid onto a stool at the very end of the long, smooth expanse of wood so she could avoid the mirror that ran the length of the wall behind it. This wasn't a day when she wanted to catch her own eyes in the reflection.

She ordered a whiskey sour and then let it sit at her elbow as she scanned the room. It had been years since she'd had alcohol. Her last drink had been two months after Lila was killed, the night she'd gone home with Ben Wilson and woke up the next morning with a hangover and no memory of the event at all.

It hadn't been the sex that had knocked her sober. It had been the fact that she'd forgotten, even for a minute, Lila's face. The smell of her hair. The way she giggled at knock-knock jokes and swore like a sailor. She'd been trying to numb the pain, not erase it.

So she'd stopped.

The whiskey sour was so pretty, though. It was a pale yellow, but in the dim light of the bar, it turned gold. She touched the pad of her finger to the cherry that swam among the ice cubes in the squat tumbler and sent it bobbing.

Then Alice brought the glass to her lips, her tongue darting out to taste the sweetness along the rim. The cool liquid burned on the way down her throat, only to settle in her stomach, an unwelcome presence. The alcohol would hit her bloodstream soon, but she wanted it to be sooner. She wanted to be drunk already; she wanted to be drunk yesterday or the day before or the day they found Ruby Burke's tiny body crumpled beneath peach sheets.

Forgetting Lila. It had never been worth it before, but now? Now, she chased oblivion. When the bartender made his way back to her end, she ordered a few shots of tequila. In the next minute there were three small glasses sitting in front of her.

"Cutting loose, huh?" Nakamura climbed onto the empty stool next to hers.

Of course he would find her here. It was the police bar, after all. If she'd wanted solitude, she could have gone farther afield.

She didn't answer him. Simply tossed back each of the shots, sinking into the pain as she would a too-hot bath.

"Turns out there's no Enrique Lopez," he said, and she could feel his eyes on her throat. She slammed the last glass down onto the bar that was now sticky from her sloppiness.

"Figured," she murmured as Nakamura signaled to the guy. He ordered a beer, and she got another whiskey sour. Both men tucked in their lips at the request, but neither said anything.

"So we have our first solid lead," he said, and nodded his thanks when his drink was set in front of him.

"If you can call it that."

He bumped her shoulder. "You've been more pessimistic than usual about this guy."

She shrugged. "Call me jaded."

"Oh, I have, and I will again," he said, laughter in his voice. He was letting go, unwinding. It was what she should be doing. Instead, she was seeking to obliterate every cell that remembered Ruby Burke's shoes against the sand. No. She wanted to obliterate every cell that remembered how Lila's dimples had popped out when she laughed. Not Ruby. Lila.

It was all starting to blur.

"Can we not?" She propped her forehead against her palm, her elbow sore against the wood. "Can we just not? For tonight?"

He took a long sip of beer. "Yup."

The silence lasted only seventy-six seconds. She counted.

"Are you doing okay?"

"Do I look like I'm doing okay?" She tipped her head so she could look at him from under heavy lashes.

"Honestly?" Nakamura asked. "Yeah."

She huffed out a surprised breath. "Really?"

"Can't ever really tell with you, Garner." He ran his thumbnail under the label on his bottle. "Most of the time? You're a mystery."

It was how she wanted it, how it needed to be. But she was still surprised. Sometimes she thought they could all—every single one of them—see the dirtiness of her soul, the blackness that lurked there now.

"Nah, I'm an open book," she said, and it was reckless. Lila's face kept blending into Ruby's, though, and she needed the adrenaline the taunt brought to keep her from tipping over some cliff.

He took the bait. "Oh yeah? Tell me something, then."

There was reckless and then there was dangerous. The line was a fine one, and the alcohol wasn't helping her define it. "Sometimes I don't care."

"About what?"

She shrugged, hoping it was all-encompassing. "This."

"Only sometimes?"

With a smirk, she gave him a cheers with her mostly empty glass. "Touché."

Their glasses were taken away and replaced with new ones, and she made a note to tip with a heavy hand.

"Tell me something, then," she said once they were left alone again.

"Sometimes I care too much." He shrugged.

She laughed at that. "Only sometimes?"

"Ah, you got me."

They sipped their drinks and watched the TVs and even swayed a bit on their stools when an old seventies rock ballad came on.

"Why do you care so much?" she asked when the notes faded into something faster, more modern.

He squinted and ran long fingers through his dark hair. "I'm selfish, I think? I like the feeling of saving people. Caring makes it easier to save people. Makes it easier to get up early and stay late, I guess. Make sacrifices you wouldn't have otherwise."

"Hero complex?"

It was tinged with self-deprecation, his laugh. "All my life. You know, they give you a badge and a gun, and suddenly that impulse to go looking for trouble just so you can be the good guy goes from pathetic to heroic."

"You've never been pathetic a day in your life, Nakamura." There was a lot she didn't know, but she knew that. Maybe White Hats existed only in old Westerns, but there had to be genuinely good people left in the world. Nakamura was one of them.

"You think too highly of me," he protested. "I wore a Superman cape up until the age of twelve."

She giggled, and they were both taken aback by the sound.

He recovered first. "So what about you? Why are you doing this if you don't care? Can't be for the money." They touched glasses in sad acknowledgment.

Alice considered the question.

There was a human need to be known by others. It drove criminals to confession; it withered the souls of those who had no one to be known by. She wasn't immune. That need was pulsing now, an infected wound, maybe, but there nonetheless.

"My dad was a cop," she started.

"No shit!" Nakamura's eyes lit up. "That's cool."

She rolled her eyes at his optimism. "He was shot on duty. Routine traffic stop gone bad, you know the story."

He dimmed as she expected. "Ah. I'm sorry."

Lifting one shoulder, she kept her eyes on the bar. "I was just a kid."

"Almost makes it worse, yeah?" he prodded.

"Maybe," she said. "The guy got off on a technicality. Something got messed up with his arrest, and he walked."

"Shit," Nakamura murmured.

"Never seemed fair, you know?" she said. "I've always been big on justice."

"You see that bullshit all the time, though." He glanced at her. "I'd think you'd get more frustrated than anything. Being in the same system."

It struck her as really funny, and the next thing she knew, she was doubled over. The laughter was tinged with mania and alcohol. "Oh man. Yeah. I know that now."

He was watching her with a cautious smile. "Sorry. Stating the obvious."

"Never underestimate wide-eyed optimism, buddy," she said. "There was a time in my life I thought I could be the change I wanted to see in the world. And all that bullshit."

Their silence then was companionable. He wasn't pushing, but she still had an itch at the base of her spine. She didn't yet feel known.

She nudged his shoulder. "Ask me more."

"Was it one thing? That shattered your rose-colored glasses?" The question tumbled out, and she knew it had been waiting there, that he'd been holding it back. He wanted to know if it was Lila.

"She wanted to be a police officer," Alice said with a smile. "In that way young kids do."

"I wanna be a police when I grow up." Lila snuggled into Alice's side. Her weight against Alice's ribs was familiar, so familiar. She'd felt it there when Lila had existed only within Alice's body. She'd been a constant pressure—her feet, her hands, her elbows, her knees. Always moving, always making her presence known. I am a being in this world, *Lila had screamed from the womb.*

*"A police*woman,*" Alice said with a smile. "Why do you want to be a policewoman?"*

It was what Lila knew, nothing more than that. Still, Alice asked.

"I wanna catch bad guys like you do," Lila said, tangling their fingers together.

Catching bad guys. Something twisted in her chest, a hand pulling all the tissue in her lungs tight.

"It wasn't Lila," Alice said, making it easy on him because she wanted to talk anyway. "Or, it wasn't *just* her. I thought the system made sense. I thought human error was the reason my father's killer was walking free. A cop had been distracted at the wrong time in the wrong place, and boom. A lifetime of resentment from my mother and yours truly."

Nakamura nodded, then signaled for refills.

"Maybe I had a little bit of that hero complex of yours," she said. It felt like a lifetime ago. A millennium. "But it wasn't an anomaly."

"The fuckup?"

She swallowed her mouthful of whiskey. "It was the norm."

"The good guys win sometimes," he said.

"Mostly they don't, though," she let slip. Or maybe he already knew she wouldn't use "we." Maybe he knew she wasn't a White Hat like him.

He slid her a glance, and she thought he probably hadn't known. Now he did. "So what do you do about it? Stop caring?" He paused. "You care about Ruby, though, don't you? Too much."

It was a testament to the hour and the number of times the bartender had been over already that he said it at all. Or it was a testament to how, once allowed, boundaries and other hesitancies blurred quickly.

"What makes you think I care about Ruby?"

He tipped his head, more reflective than judgmental of the harsh question. "Because of Lila."

She flinched, and for the first time she saw regret in the way the corners of his mouth tipped down.

"I'm sorry," he said, pushing his drink away. Then he reached in his back pocket for his wallet, pulling out a handful of twenties. It would more than cover their tab.

"Wait." She grabbed his wrist. His pulse spiked beneath her thumb, but his expression remained neutral and calm. "Ruby isn't Lila."

"I know that," he said slowly. "The cases are similar, though. It's expected that you would be affected by it."

"Do you know what people think?" she asked, not letting him go. If she did, he would walk away. And then would she ever be known? Did it even matter anymore? Everything was a bit hazy and sideways, and she didn't remember why she cared in the first place. "They think I'm trying to solve Lila's case."

"It was solved, though," he said. Stating the obvious again.

"They think I set the guy up," she said, and the words were like little weights lifted off her chest.

He reeled back, as far as he could go with his arm caught by her hand. "Has anyone said that to you?"

"No." She shrugged. "I see it in the way they look at me, though."

Her heart rate synced to his as they stood there, both knowing what he wanted to ask.

"I didn't," she finally said. "I would have. If I'd thought he'd done it and there wasn't evidence to prove it. I absolutely would have done it. But I didn't."

He relaxed, and only when the tendons in his arm softened beneath her fingers did she realize how tense he'd been. "So screw 'em, right?" he said.

"Yeah." She smiled and released him. He didn't run. "I don't care about Ruby. You should know that."

"Why?"

"Because I'm not solving my daughter's case," she said and wondered if she was even making sense. "And I think that's important for you to keep in mind."

"Just because she isn't your daughter doesn't mean you don't care about her," he said, but he was already watching her differently than he had been ten seconds earlier.

"That's where you're wrong," she said. "My daughter is the only thing I care about."

———

There was a missed call from Bridget on Alice's phone. She didn't see it until Nakamura bundled her into a taxi with cash for the driver.

It was from several hours ago, and it was too late to call the woman back. Alice did anyway.

Bridget picked up on the second ring.

"What do you have for me?" Alice asked, only a slight slur to the words.

"Have you been imbibing, Detective Garner?" Bridget's voice was amused.

The streetlamps created a soft golden-tinged kaleidoscope in the night, and her head lulled back against the taxi's leather seats. She was probably drunk.

"Shamelessly," Alice said. "What do you have for me?"

There was a pause. Bridget wasn't chewing gum. It was an odd thing to notice, but Alice did. The silence was heavier because of it. "I've got nothing," Bridget finally sighed.

"Why are you calling me, then?"

Another long beat. "I *should* have something."

Alice's pulse ticked up. "You keep saying that."

"'Cause it's true," Bridget said. "No one's this good."

"People are that good."

"Serial killers, maybe." There was a shrug in Bridget's voice. Then a pause. "Pros."

"Hired?" Alice watched the houses get shittier along the way. She was too tired for this conversation.

"Something like that," Bridget muttered. "Look. Let's talk in the morning, yeah? You coming in?"

"Hangover and everything." Alice smiled.

More silence.

Then: "You okay?" For once it didn't sound like a script.

"Do you ever want to be known?" Alice asked instead of answering. The answer was always no, anyway.

"Known? Sure, yeah," Bridget said, and there were spaces between the words where she would have snapped her gum.

The darkness wrapped around Alice, and she ignored the driver's eyes in the rearview mirror, watching her. "It's strange, isn't it? How we're always the good guy in our own story. The protagonist."

"You've lost me, kiddo," Bridget said, but she didn't sound lost.

"The good guy," Alice said again. "When you tell your story, you're the good guy, right?"

The taxi pulled into the parking lot of her building. Alice tossed some bills at the driver and climbed out into the still-warm air.

"Sure," Bridget said.

"But other people have stories, too," Alice said. It was gibberish at this point, but she was still talking. "The not-good guys."

The pause this time lasted three flights of stairs. Alice thought the woman might have hung up.

"They want to be known, too," Bridget said. Gone was the usual easiness in her voice.

"Do you think they deserve it?" Alice tripped over a discarded shoe but landed on her mattress. "To be known?"

"No," Bridget said, her voice sure, certain. "They don't."

Alice nodded, letting the phone drop to her side.

Tell me a story, she thought. *Make it a good one.*

CHAPTER THIRTY-TWO

TRUDY

August 4, 2018
Six days after the kidnapping

Trudy and Zeke didn't bother with the stale croissants and hard-boiled eggs their motel offered as a poor excuse for breakfast.

Instead, they picked up dollar hash browns and coffee at McDonald's and sat on a curb in the parking lot, letting the grease burn their fingertips.

"Where are we going to start?" Zeke asked the question she'd been trying not to think about, because she didn't really have an answer. When she'd left St. Petersburg, it had been emotion driving her, but she hadn't thought ahead. They were looking for a needle in a haystack when they didn't even know what a needle looked like.

She squinted at the sky. "Let's go to his old neighborhood."

"Your grandfather's?"

"Sterling's, yes." Trudy stood up, warming to the idea, which had been an offhand thought to begin with. People loved to gossip. "Maybe someone remembers him."

Her shadow fell along Zeke's face as he just sat looking up at her. "Trudy."

She had zero desire to engage in the conversation he wanted to have—where she might have to dodge questions she didn't know how to answer. Like, what were they doing here, chasing shadows and whims? So she pointed to the Honda parked a few spots away. "Driver, to the car."

He rolled his eyes but pushed to his feet. "Don't be an asshole," he said, but it lacked any bite.

Before he got behind the wheel, though, he looked over the roof of the car. "What do you really think you're going to find?"

Shrugging one shoulder, she avoided his eyes by opening her own door and sliding in. "Nothing, probably."

Zeke had an old GPS hookup, and Trudy put in Sterling's old address. She knew it well. There was a small painting of the house he'd grown up in that hung in his office at the mansion, and the inscription on it was those familiar numbers. Trudy thought he kept it there as a reminder of how far he'd come. Mellie thought it was a reminder of how far he could fall. Neither of them asked Sterling.

"What if you do find something?" Zeke asked after the GPS's calm British voice directed them out of the parking lot.

"I would be ecstatic."

He glanced over. "Would you?"

"If we find something that proves my grandfather was in any way connected to Ruby's murder, then I will personally put a bullet through his cold, black heart myself." It was a foolish thing to say. She was eighteen. What was she really going to do? But she said it anyway and believed it a little.

At the next stoplight, he pushed his shades up to meet her eyes. Whatever he saw there made him nod and turn back to the road.

They drove the rest of the way to the neighborhood with only the GPS breaking the silence.

The house was still there. Not much had changed, and it looked so similar to the one in the painting that it gave her chills. This was where evil had been born, had grown into what it was today.

Getting out of the car took a little pep talk to her legs, which didn't want to move. She slowly crossed the street, hesitant at the foot of the stairs. Zeke didn't push her. He seemed to get it.

Finally, her knuckles paused before she rapped on the door, almost afraid of what she would find. But she needn't have worried. A small, nervous man answered, tangling his fingers together over his mustard-yellow sweater-vest.

He was new to the area, had moved in not too long ago.

"I bought it from a nice young family about last year," he said, the air whistling just slightly out of his left nostril.

They nodded their thanks and were about to leave when Trudy remembered to ask, "Do you know any of your neighbors? Ones who have been here for a while?"

He shook his head and then paused. "Well, Mary Jo. Down the street and around the corner. It's a small yellow house with a wind chime on the porch. She might be able to help you."

Trudy smiled once more and then started down the steps behind Zeke.

"Let's check out a few more of the neighbors before heading over to Mary Jo's," she said when they hit the sidewalk.

Four more stops later—an older lady who smelled of cats, a no-answer, a young family with a baby, and a middle-aged couple who'd moved in ten years ago but still didn't know the Burkes—and Mary Jo was still looking like their best option.

"You don't have to say it," Trudy said to Zeke as they started toward the yellow house around the corner.

"Didn't say anything."

"You were thinking loudly." She jabbed her sunglasses into her hair.

"I'll try to keep it down in the future." There was a smile in his voice.

"You think this is a goose chase."

"I think it's a place to start," Zeke said. "When no one else seems to be doing anything productive."

And that took the fight out of her.

The front of Mary Jo's house was tidy but eclectic. The nervous man had been right about the wind chime, except there wasn't just one of them. They all hung along the rim of her porch, their jewels glittering in the sun. The mailbox was a basset hound with sad eyes and a gently wagging tail that came and went with the breeze.

She lifted her eyebrows at Zeke, amused. He smiled back.

A woman pushing eighty answered on the second knock. She was small, bent with age, and her wrinkled, papery skin hung on her bones. Her thick tortoiseshell Coke-bottle glasses sat at the edge of her nose, one wrong shift away from slipping off.

She looked Trudy and Zeke over, her eyes sweeping along their bodies. "No soliciting," she yelled, and then made to slam the door in their faces.

"Oh wait." Trudy managed to sneak a foot into the entryway as she slapped her hand against the wood, stopping it from closing.

Mary Jo glared down at Trudy's leg, and Trudy wondered if she was in real danger of losing it. "We're not selling anything," she rushed to say.

The woman's gaze snapped up to her face for a minute before she went back to imagining the ways she could chop off Trudy's foot. Probably.

"I'm Trudy and this is Zeke," Trudy said, the words tumbling out in a rush. "We're told you might be able to help us with some information we're looking for. About a family that used to live in the neighborhood."

That seemed to be the right thing to say, because Mary Jo relaxed her grip on the door, just a little bit. This time when she looked up, she really looked at them.

"Why didn't you say so?" she asked, as if she'd given them any chance. Trudy swallowed back a snarky response and smiled.

"So sorry," Trudy said. She could deal with a cranky old bitch if it meant getting answers. "Would you be able to answer a few questions for us?"

Mary Jo rubbed at the corner of her mouth, spreading the waxy red lipstick into the lines of her skin. "Who do you want to know about? Lots of families lived here."

"The Burkes." Trudy reached for her great-grandfather's name. "Beau Burke."

Mary Jo stilled, and then her eyes darted between them. "You blood, then?"

There was something in the way she asked the question that put Trudy on alert.

"No."

Mary Jo rubbed her thumb in that spot again, smearing the bloodred color farther onto her cheek. "You'll want to talk to Judith," she finally said.

Trudy's breath caught. "Judith?"

Holding up one finger, Mary Jo stepped back, digging into a massive tote bag on the table just inside the entryway.

"I'll ring her to let her know you're coming. It's two blocks over, that way." She waved in the general direction away from where they'd come.

Zeke nudged up against her shoulder, but she didn't take her eyes off the woman who was now bent over a piece of scrap paper, copying over an address.

"Here." Mary Jo slid it across to them when she was done. "Glad you're not family."

Trudy picked up the address, running the pad of her finger along the neat lines of ink. "Why's that?"

"Nasty people, those Burkes," Mary Jo muttered, her attention on her phone. "Judith will tell you all about them."

———

Judith's house was small and lovely and painted a robin's-egg blue.

"Are we really doing this?" Zeke asked, his eyes on the crisply white front door.

"She's probably an eighty-year-old woman," Trudy said, trying to convince herself as well. "What is she really going to do to us?"

"Feed us poisoned cookies," Zeke said, but he started toward the stairs. She followed. "And then bake us in her oven."

Judith, it turned out, was a petite woman with delicate bones and thinning silver hair that she had tucked back into a low chignon. She wore a pink cardigan despite the heat, and it matched the twin rose splotches on her cheeks.

"Mary Jo said you were asking about the Burkes," Judith said as they settled into the overstuffed couch across from her chair. She'd poured them tea and had store-bought cookies arranged on a fine china plate in front of them. This was a woman who was craving visitors. Trudy realized they could use that loneliness, that desperation, for human interaction.

"Yes," Trudy said, attempting a sip at the tea. It was too bitter, but she drank it anyway. "Did you know them?"

"Mmmm. Horrible family," Judith said with the same disgust Mary Jo had unleashed. "You said you weren't relations?"

Trudy shook her head and decided for a small bit of honesty. "I think the boy . . . Sterling, was it?"

Judith nodded.

"Him, yes. We think he was involved in something bad," Trudy said. "We're trying to find out more."

"That sounds like him," Judith said, drinking her own tea, her watery blue eyes curious.

The woman was younger than Mary Jo. Closer to her grandfather's age.

"Could you tell us about Sterling?" Trudy asked.

"Mean to the core, that boy was." Judith set the cup onto its saucer and crossed her legs. "My sister went to school with him. I was a few years behind them, but he was a piece of work even then."

"Oh yeah?" Trudy prompted. It sounded right.

"Even back then, no one wanted to say anything bad about the golden boy." There was a sneer in Judith's voice. "Didn't matter what he did."

Trudy shifted forward. "What did he do?"

"Drugs, sex." Judith shrugged. "Got in an accident once when he was younger. One of the passengers died. Sterling was drunk in the back seat, but rumor has it that he'd actually been driving. The child who he switched spots with got jail time. Now look at Sterling. No one even talks about it, do they?"

Bitterness. There was so much bitterness that it dripped off Judith's tongue. "Your sister was in the car?" Trudy guessed.

The woman's eyes widened. "Yes. She broke her leg. It took years of therapy to fix. Still walks with a limp."

"Did she testify? Your sister? That Sterling was driving?"

Judith's shoulders tightened. "Yes."

"They didn't believe her, though." It was Zeke who said it, and it wasn't a question.

"Even back then he got what he wanted," Judith said. "Have you met him?"

"Yes," Trudy whispered.

"Then you understand what it's like."

Trudy nodded. "Yes."

"I see him on the news still, sometimes," Judith said, her fingers twisting together. "Plays golf with the governor."

And the senators. And the mayor of St. Petersburg. Sterling owned the state. Anything they did to expose him would stretch far beyond a ruined reputation. Everyone connected to him would be tainted by his mess.

"He's in St. Petersburg now?" Trudy asked.

"Hmmm, yes." Judith's eyes sharpened. "Where did you say you all were from?"

"Miami." The lie came swift and easy.

Judith looked away, staring at a painting of water lilies that hung on the wall. Trudy wondered if they'd lost her.

"Is there anything else?" They hadn't found the right question yet. They needed to find the right question. The one that would lead them to an answer.

Judith was pleased to keep talking while she topped off their nearly full cups. *Desperate for company,* Trudy thought again.

Judith told them about all the other people in the car. She told them about her sister's lifelong recovery from the incident. She told them about Sterling's girlfriends, which leaned toward jealousy rather than the derision Judith was probably going for, and the guys he hung out with—"Hooligans, the lot of them."

But nothing struck Trudy as off. Zeke nudged her, and when she looked over, he tipped the screen of his phone in her direction. They'd been there for more than an hour and had nothing to show for it. Other than confirming Sterling was as big of an ass back then as he was now.

Judith was settled in, though. Neither Trudy nor Zeke had spoken in the past twenty minutes, but it didn't seem to matter. Stories tumbled from her lips like birds that had been caged.

Trudy shifted when the woman took a rare pause. "Judith, I'm so sorry, I think we have to be going. But thank you so much for your help. It was really informative."

Dismayed eyes flicked down to the mostly full plate of cookies and then back to their faces. "I have more snacks."

It was pathetic, and not in a way that Trudy could mock. She slid a look toward Zeke, who was frowning but also shifting back against the couch once more.

"Sure, we can stay a little longer," Trudy said, and Judith's face lit up.

"I'll just go . . . ," and she waved toward the kitchen before scuttling off.

Trudy turned toward Zeke and shrugged. "Sorry. I couldn't . . ."

"No." He shook his head. "That was just . . . sad. I don't mind staying."

She pressed her lips together. The unspoken thought that hung between them was that they had nowhere else to be. No more leads to follow. All the time in the world to listen to Judith blather on about Sterling's schoolmates. "She doesn't know anything."

Zeke didn't contradict her. "I know you were hoping she would."

Trudy nodded, not sure if there was anything else to say, really, but it didn't matter if there was. Judith bustled back in the room with a second plate of the same cookies.

Twenty minutes later, Trudy was regretting her moment of kindness and contemplating the best way to extract themselves from the situation without having to face Judith's hurt–puppy dog eyes again, when something snagged her attention.

". . . nasty family, too," Judith said with the same disgust she'd used for the Burkes. She hadn't seemed to realize her audience was no longer even engaged with what she was saying. "The Becketts. Not a good boy in that bunch."

Beckett. Beckett. That name sounded familiar, like a song she could hum while forgetting the lyrics.

"I'm sorry, who?" Trudy straightened from the bored slouch she'd fallen into. Her tone must have brought Zeke out of his daze as well.

Judith's eyes found hers, seemingly surprised she was getting a response after so much silence. "The Becketts."

Breathing in sharply through her nose, Trudy swallowed her knee-jerk, impatient response. "And who are they, again? Related to Sterling?"

"No, not family," Judith said, her thin eyebrows coming together. Perhaps she'd already explained this. Trudy shouldn't have tuned out.

"I mean, are they connected to the Burkes? Were they friends with Sterling?"

Why would Trudy know the name otherwise?

Judith shook her head. "No."

And after more than an hour of chattering at them, this was when Judith decided to clam up. Maybe because they were finally paying attention. There was something about an interested audience that lonely people craved and savored.

"But . . . ?" Trudy let the question trail off, not even knowing how else to prompt her to tell more. She didn't know the right question to ask.

"The boys were terrible," Judith said. "Don't know where they went wrong; their mama was a saint. She was friends with my girl."

"So not with Sterling," Trudy confirmed, her shoulders dropping. She would have gone back to tuning the woman out, except . . .

Beckett.

"No, Nathan—the oldest—was just out of high school, and Sterling was already in his robes. Sterling didn't even know Nathan. But that boy was following in his footsteps, nonetheless."

"Same trouble?" Trudy guessed. Nathan Beckett. One more note in the song slid into place, but the lyrics were still out of reach. Where had she heard the name before?

"Not quite the same." Judith tapped a nail against her teeth. "Sex, drugs, yes. But he wasn't as charming. Couldn't get away with things like Sterling could. Until he did."

"What did he get away with?" Trudy asked.

"Moved down to St. Petersburg, that one did," Judith said. And with that, everything in Trudy sharpened. St. Petersburg. That was too much of a coincidence.

"Isn't that where you said Sterling Burke is now?" Trudy asked as if she couldn't quite remember what the woman had said earlier.

"Yes," Judith said. "And come to think of it . . ."

She trailed off, and Trudy dug her fingers into the soft flesh of her thighs to keep from shaking those frail shoulders. This was all for show, the dramatics. Judith had a story she wanted to tell, and she was relishing the attention.

So Trudy played her part. "Did they cross paths down there?"

A spark of appreciation gleamed in Judith's eyes. "Nathan got into trouble. The kind he shouldn't have been able to talk himself out of."

The pieces were there; they just wouldn't fit.

It didn't matter, because now Judith was into it. She'd uncrossed her legs so she could lean forward. Waiting for Trudy to say her lines.

"What kind of trouble?" Trudy said.

Judith's eyebrows shot up, her lips pursed. "Killed a young woman," she said, her voice dropping as if someone was around to hear. The words were harsh in the quiet of her small sitting room. "It was nasty business. But it was only a blip in the news."

"Why's that?" Trudy's tongue was thick and heavy in her mouth, and she felt like she was just on the edge of something.

"The girl was just a maid," Judith said. "No one important."

It still should have mattered. People still should have cared. But Trudy knew better than to argue that point and derail Judith.

"It was in St. Petersburg?" she asked instead. Because that was one of the pieces. It had to be.

"Oh yes." Judith had all but slid out of her chair at this point, eyes locked on Trudy's face. Neither of them had looked toward Zeke since the conversation started. "Guess who his judge was?"

Trudy dragged in a deep breath. There it was. "Sterling Burke."

Everything around her shifted, and she tried to hold on to the pieces as they skittered away from her. Sterling Burke. St. Petersburg. Nathan Beckett. Where did she know that name?

Judith was nodding. "He let him off."

"How?" Zeke finally asked, and both she and Judith jumped at the reminder it wasn't just the two of them in the conversation.

The other woman recovered first. "Anything's possible with the right influence. A young handsome white boy from his hometown? And the woman was Latina and from a bad neighborhood, from what I heard. Sterling dismissed it on a technicality."

Trudy closed her eyes. It wasn't the first time she'd heard a rumor like that about her grandfather. He played with power, not justice, and he knew the rules of the game well. One rich boy wouldn't have mattered to him. But the optics of it would have. They would have mattered to the men he was trying to woo at the time.

She might have even written it off as unimportant. Just one more way her grandfather had proven himself as scum.

But—Nathan Beckett. Her whole world had narrowed down to that name.

Trust me.

Everything slowed, like time was three steps ahead of her. Zeke was talking, and then Judith. The words, though, were drawn out and coming from a distance. And that's when she realized she hadn't heard the name. She'd read it.

"Shit," she whispered. And the world snapped back into focus. The lights were too bright in the corners of her eyes, the smell of dying flowers in the vase by the windowsill too potent.

She pushed to her feet. "Bathroom," she managed to force out before she stumbled from the room. Bracing a hand against the hallway wall, she fumbled for her phone. Her fingers couldn't get it to work as she careened into the tiny kitchen in the back of the house.

Standing in the middle of the room, she focused until she could open the in-box.

She'd always thought of the person as N.

There were heavy footsteps behind her, and she knew without turning who it was.

"Zeke." Even *she* could hear the desperation, the fear in her voice. "Zeke."

He was in front of her, crouching a bit so he could see her face beyond the curtain of hair that fell over her shoulders.

"What is it?"

"Nathan Beckett," she breathed like it would mean anything to him. She stared at the message. One email. The sender: nbeckett. Nathan. Fucking. Beckett.

She flipped her wrist, then held the phone so he could see it, too.

"I was played," she whispered. She didn't want to actually say the words, but she forced them out through chapped lips. Her fault. This was all her fault.

"Who is it?" Zeke asked.

She thumbed in the name to the Google search bar. The page spun—the service was shit in Judith's house. "Come on. Come on."

Her fingers hurt from where she was clutching at the screen, but she couldn't relax her grip. She knew. She just knew this was it.

When the results loaded, she sank to her knees.

"What the hell?" Zeke hovered over her. She glanced up, and his eyes were wide, panicked. Hers had to be the same.

"Nathan Beckett," she whispered, clicking through to the first article that came up. "Sentenced to life in prison for the murder of Lila Garner."

"Lila Garner," Zeke repeated slowly.

She looked up at him once more. "Detective Alice Garner's daughter."

CHAPTER
THIRTY-THREE

ALICE

August 5, 2018
Seven days after the kidnapping

The phone woke Alice from a deep alcohol-induced sleep. She fumbled for the thing, flinching away from the flare of the screen in the darkness of her bedroom and the jangled notes playing on repeat.

She glanced at the digital clock on the floor next to her bed before she answered. Two thirty in the morning.

"What?" Her head was pounding, her lips were drying and cracked, her stomach rolled with its desire to be empty.

"Consider this your heads-up," the voice on the other end said. It took a few moments to place it, and during that time her hand had already come to curl around the gun she kept tucked beneath her pillow.

"The hell, Ben?" Her brain was still slow, still laden with the vapors of alcohol. This wasn't making sense yet.

"Look, I like you, I do," Ben continued, and she sat up while flipping the light on beside her. The glow sent her stomach clenching again.

She licked out, trying to wet her lips, but her tongue was equally dry. In just her underwear, she stumbled to her feet toward the bathroom.

"I don't like *you* very much right now," she said as she flipped on the water from the sink. It took a bit of angling to get her mouth under the tap, but it was worth it. She held the phone away, not needing to hear his laughter, while she gulped at the cool liquid.

"Yeah, and that's not going to get any better," he said, tinny and distant. She brought the phone back to her ear.

"That's right." Her brain seemed to finally be skipping along with a semblance of normalcy. "You're giving me a heads-up for something. It's not going to be that I won a pretty prize, is it? A million dollars? A different life than the shitty one I currently have?"

"See, this is why I like you," Ben said. "Finding humor in the darkest hours."

"Ben."

"I have credible sources and pictures that place you talking to Charlotte Burke in an unofficial capacity," he said, finally dropping the anvil. "We're going with it. It will be up at five in the morning."

She squeezed one eye closed. "It's almost three."

"Yeah."

"Ben?"

"Uh-huh?" There was a smirk in his voice, but she didn't have time for him.

"You suck at heads-ups," she said. And then hung up the phone to his laughter.

Shit.

She dunked her face into the stream of water, hoping the jolt of it would sort her out. Nothing was ready. Goddamn Ben Wilson could rot in hell.

The mirror reflected the panic that crept along her skin, but she couldn't let it grab hold. Her pupils were dilated, her hands were trembling, and the rise and fall of her chest was far from steady. She turned away, pushing her short hair back into a stubby ponytail.

Her closet was the first stop. There was a bag at the back with everything she needed. The rough fabric beneath her fingers was an anchor. A reminder.

She pulled it down, letting it bump against her hip, before dropping it to the floor. Then she slipped on a pair of jeans and a simple black T-shirt.

The pants were different from the ones she'd been wearing the other day when they'd interrogated Enrique. Those were slung over the chair in front of the simple desk she kept out of the way in the far corner of the room. She crossed over to it, her fingers digging into the fabric.

It took three tries before she got the right pocket, the one with the slip of paper that had the number written on it. The one they'd pretended was for his alibi but was actually his burner phone.

She fumbled in her blankets for where she'd tossed her cell after hanging up on Ben. Once she found it, she sat down on the edge of the mattress and smoothed out the paper on her thigh.

Despite the hour, the phone rang only once before the person on the other end picked up.

"Now," she said.

"All right."

There was a click, and she realized the call had ended. At least one thing seemed to be going right.

On impulse, she crossed back to the bathroom, sank to her knees in front of the sink's cabinets, and rummaged through the cleaning supplies and tampons until she found the small bottle of painkillers. She popped two, swallowed them dry, and then tossed the rest back into the dark recesses from where they'd come.

She propped her shoulder against the doorjamb, studying the bedroom, wasting precious seconds on being thorough. As much as she might want to, rushing right now could be disastrous. Meticulousness was the only thing that could combat panic, and she held tight to it.

At least everything in the apartment was ready for this. She'd kept it that way. Sparse and impersonal. There was nothing left to destroy.

Once Alice was satisfied that the room was set, she grabbed the duffel again, hauling it up onto her shoulder.

It was finally time.

CHAPTER THIRTY-FOUR

CHARLOTTE

August 4, 2018
Six days after the kidnapping

It was just before midnight, but there was no one else in the bar's parking lot. Most of the patrons were already where they wanted to be.

Sneaking out of the house unnoticed wasn't even a hardship anymore, either. Hollis had started taking sleeping pills she'd discreetly obtained from their family physician, and Mellie hadn't been sober since they'd found Ruby's body. It was deciding where she wanted to go once she was out that was the problem.

Nothing felt like the right decision anymore. Her skin itched with all the places she shouldn't go. Back to the beach. To a hotel. To the police station.

What happened, Charlotte?

With the windows cracked to let in the fresh air, she drove the not-quite-empty streets. The corner of her eye twitched, the exhausted, delicate muscle straining to focus on the road. Her exhausted, delicate soul trying not to shatter into so many pieces.

She hadn't left the mansion yesterday, after the police had completed their search. Instead, she'd straightened and tidied behind them. Something about the way their fingers had touched all the surfaces of the house had become a smudge against her own brain that she needed to wipe clean.

There was so much about her brain these days she wanted to wipe clean. She could barely live with herself long enough to function, to eat, to walk and breathe like everyone else. The cracks that had always been there were splintering into a thousand more thin lines so that everything within her was broken.

That moment in front of the restaurant still scared her. Because she'd wanted it so much, wanted to put a bullet through her father's head, watch the light blink out of his eyes, watch the evil that was Sterling Burke leave this world. She'd never wanted anything more in her life. Other than to have Ruby back.

She couldn't think about it. Couldn't think about anything. Instead, she let muscle memory take over, going through the simple motions of navigating the streets of St. Petersburg.

Charlotte had been driving for an hour by the time her headlights fell across a familiar car. Detective Nakamura's car. It was parked outside the police bar around the corner from the station, and for the second time in a handful of days, she wondered if she'd ended up someplace through a purpose she hadn't wanted to acknowledge.

She pulled up to the curb on the opposite side of the street from the bar and tugged the key out of the ignition. And then she waited.

It didn't take long for both Nakamura and Alice to spill out of the door. Alice seemed on the wrong side of tipsy, her narrow hips swaying just a bit too much, a reflection of the drunken cadence of her feet. Nakamura was grinning, amused by the spectacle, it seemed, and he waved down a passing cab.

After pushing Alice inside it with a wad of cash, Nakamura straightened, stretching his arms up high over his head. He was watching the disappearing taillights of the car and turned away only when the taxi took a sharp left onto First Street.

Charlotte glanced around to make sure the area was still empty, save for the two of them, and then slid out of the Range Rover.

"Detective," she called as soft as she could, not wanting to scare the man. He jumped anyway, his hand going to where his holster rested along his ribs. "I'm sorry."

He relaxed, immediately coming out of fight or flight with the ease of someone used to being startled. "Ms. Burke. No problem."

"Charlotte," she murmured out of habit.

Nakamura smiled at that but didn't correct himself. "What's wrong? Can I help you?"

Why had she stopped him? She didn't even know. "No, I . . ."

He stepped closer but kept his hands open and by his side. "You can talk to me, Charlotte."

What happened, Charlotte?

She shook her head. There was nothing to say. No confession.

She wondered if that's what he thought. That she was finally going to let the terrible things he guessed she'd done tumble from her lips, unable to hold them within herself any longer.

"I hate him." The words were out of her mouth before she even fully thought them. Maybe this was why she'd gotten out of the car. She wanted the detective to stop her before she became the monster they all thought she was.

He didn't falter at the conversational pivot. "Who, Charlotte? Who do you hate?"

What was she doing? He was all blurry at the edges, and she realized her eyes were damp with unshed tears.

Her phone vibrated in her back pocket, and she reached for it. He tensed at the sudden movement but sighed when she showed him what she pulled out.

She glanced at the name on the screen. *Trudy.*

"I'm sorry, I have to take this."

"Charlotte." His voice had taken on an edge. Perhaps he heard the fragility of her control just in those few seconds that she'd spoken. "Here, wait. Take my number. If you need me."

"I'm sorry," she said again, but she blindly reached for the card he was holding out. She shoved it in her pocket as she turned away from him. Her strides were long as she hurried to the car, and she climbed in without looking back. The Range Rover roared to life just as the call died. Panic clawed at her chest, and she pulled out, doing a quick U-turn on the deserted street. She could feel Nakamura's eyes on her as she called Trudy back.

CHAPTER THIRTY-FIVE

ALICE

August 5, 2018
Seven days after the kidnapping

"Would you like me to tell you a story?"

Alice whispered the words into Sterling Burke's ear, dragging the tip of the gun along his jaw as she did.

His eyes darted toward her, and she watched, satisfied, as he tried to work open his mouth, make his tongue form words. She let him struggle for a minute, coming around to perch on his desk.

Sterling's study was dark, with just the moonlight filtering in through the curtains.

It had been easy to slip the needle into his vein as the man slept, harder to carry him down the stairs as deadweight. But she'd brought Enrique along for just that purpose, and he'd barely grunted when he'd dropped Sterling in the study.

Now Sterling was bound, pinned to the chair. Helpless.

Alice tsk-tsked. "That's right. Silly me. You can't answer."

She pushed herself back until she was fully seated on the desk, her legs swinging lightly against one of the drawers. It was insolent. "Ricky here gave you a nice little cocktail of drugs to take care of that."

Ricky shifted against the wall, disturbing the shadows that had settled around his shoulders. But he made no other move to step toward them. This was her show.

"See, the thing is, dear Sterling, I don't want to hear a thing you have to say," she said, tapping the gun against his cheek. "You've said enough in your life. More words than you should ever have been allowed. You don't get to beg, or plead, or tell your sob story. You don't get to call me a cunt or spit on my face. Do you understand me?"

She pushed off the desk and leaned close so that their eyes were locked. "You're going to die without any last words to be remembered."

He didn't react, of course—he was paralyzed—and she almost, almost, wished he could. He didn't deserve a stage, though. He deserved silent screaming in his own head and a helpless knowledge that no one would hear it.

The desire to be known. It was so human. So painful.

"Ah, so my story." She grinned without humor, more a baring of teeth than anything else. Then she walked back around the desk to settle in the chair across from him. "Once upon a time." She paused. "That's how these always start, you know? Once upon a time, there was a boy. He was not a nice boy. He was a little shit of a boy, actually. His name was Nathan, and he grew into a little shit of a man. See, Nathan was never told no in his life. Kind of like you, I would guess."

She wagged the gun at him. "But the thing is, when you're an ass-hole, no matter how much luck you have, there are going to be women who don't want to worship at your altar.

"This is where our story takes a sad turn," she continued. "Because our antihero fresh off the bus in Tampa happened to be told no for the first time in his life. And guess what he decided to do about it?"

Sterling's eyes were locked on hers, and that's all she cared about. That he was conscious, that he could hear. Nothing else mattered.

"I'm thinking you can guess, dear Sterling," she said. "I imagine it's what happens when someone says no to you as well."

She got back to her feet, restless. "He raped her and dumped her body, didn't he?"

Moving behind him, she placed her hands on his thick shoulders. "But our blessed little antihero got lucky again. Come trial day, guess who his judge was? Yup, it was you. Sterling Burke, known far and wide for his leniency toward rich white boys who just 'made a mistake.'"

She pressed down hard and then let go. "You tossed the case, didn't you? On some flimsy excuse. And Nathan walked."

Ricky cleared his throat and glanced at his watch. She wished she had all night. But she didn't.

"Do you know one of the saddest parts of this story?" She leaned against the desk once more. "I bet you don't even remember who I'm talking about. Couldn't pick him—let alone the victim—out if your life depended on it." She paused. "Oh wait. It does."

Alice stroked a finger along the gun.

"It's a shame you didn't remember him," she said. "If you had, you would have been able to follow his truly illustrious career of escalating crimes. We don't have time for the details."

It was then that her breathing shifted; it was then that her heart rate kicked up. She dipped her fingers into the back pocket of her jeans and pulled out the well-loved four-by-six photo, just holding it between her thumb and finger.

"But it brings me to the second part of my story," she said, her voice hitching for the first time. She swallowed hard. "Once upon a time, there was a girl, and she was the best girl in the world."

Leaning in once more, she held Lila's picture up to his face. "Look at her." She dipped her head so she could make sure his eyes were open. "Look at her."

"Alice," Ricky murmured behind her, and there must have been something in her voice. A sob had been sitting deep in her chest that she'd thought she'd managed to tamp down. Maybe some of it had slipped into her words.

"Do you know what happened that day you let Nathan walk free? Just because he reminded you of yourself and all the evil things you wish were forgivable but never will be no matter how many of these guys you let go? Do you know what you let happen?"

She shoved the picture back in her pocket, no longer wanting his eyes on Lila. "He killed her. He stole her from me and kept her for two days. Do you know how many minutes, how many seconds, that is? I do. Because I counted every single one of them. Then he killed her. He wrapped her in a sheet and dumped her body. Just like she was trash. Like she was disposable."

At that, her hand lashed out, connecting with his cheek. The crack of skin on skin echoed in the room.

"It was because of you," she said, pressing her palm against her thigh to get herself back under control. "Gone. Because of you."

Ricky shifted again behind her, and she glanced over her shoulder at him, her eyebrows raised.

He shook his head, not interested in playing a role beyond the one he already had. She'd asked a lot of him. Keeping tabs on Charlotte and nudging her in certain directions when needed had been the hardest. Toward the end, Alice had cut off most contact with Ricky to be safe, but she'd seen it wear on him in the earlier months. There had been other requests, too. She'd sent him to Jacksonville to email Trudy. *Why?* He'd asked her. She hadn't answered, but some small part of her thought that she wanted someone to eventually tell this story. To know why it had happened. To know that this had all started in a quiet little house on the edge of a sleepy city in Florida.

After Ruby's death, she'd thought he would bow out. But, as with her, some grim determination to see it through drove him. Meeting his eyes now, though, she thought it might have broken him to continue on with the plan. For a split second, she wondered what would happen to him next, once Sterling was dead, once there was no longer a purpose there to hide the self-loathing, the shock, the disbelief.

In the next second, she realized it couldn't be her problem. She blinked, dismissing him from her mind, and turned back to Sterling.

Despite being bound and drugged, he didn't seem weak. He didn't seem defenseless. All she could see was a dirty soul the world would never miss.

"There was a debt to be paid," she said. "You'll pay it with your life."

Her voice was quiet now. Controlled.

"More than that, you'll pay with your reputation," she said. "Because people will know. They'll know what you did, they'll know who you are under that mask. They'll see the monster. And nothing, absolutely nothing, you can do can change that."

Alice breathed deeply.

"Her name was Lila Garner," she said. He needed to know her name. It needed to be the last thing he ever heard. "If you're wondering why you're about to die. Her name is Lila Garner."

She thought this was when he would scream, if he could. The moment she raised the gun to rest against his temple. He couldn't, though, and satisfaction tasted sweet on her tongue.

These were snapshots that she would remember. The terror in his eyes. The smell of leather and power. The weight of the gun against her palm. The steady click of the grandfather clock. They wouldn't erase the ones of Lila, but they would join them.

Everything was quiet. The house. Ricky. Even her heartbeat. She'd thought it would be loud in her ears, loud enough to drown out the reasons not to go through with this. But her pulse was a steady flutter beneath her wrist. Her breathing was even and deep.

There was no haze of rage blinding her vision. There were no tears.

Emotional. Erratic. They would call her that if they saw her now, a muzzle against the temple of a man who had played a part in Lila's death. But she wasn't. Nothing had felt more right, more true.

The gun was heavy and familiar. She filled her lungs to steady her hand, the pad of her finger pressing against metal.

She met his eyes one last time, and all she saw was an evil that had tainted too many lives and deserved to be extinguished.

Alice leaned in, her lips a breath away from his ear. "Everyone will know what you did," she whispered again.

Then she stepped to the side and pulled the trigger.

The shot was muffled, but the aftermath was not.

Both she and Ricky moved quickly and with precision. People saw what they wanted to see. Once they found the suicide letter, most wouldn't look further. But Nakamura might. The scene would have to look believable enough to hold up to at least his initial scrutiny.

Ricky worked on the special tape they'd used on Sterling's wrists. It bound to itself but didn't leave a residue on the skin. She slipped on a fresh pair of latex gloves and went to work arranging his body so that it slumped, like it would have if he'd pulled the trigger. It was a challenge, with his muscles still locked from the paralytic.

In the end, she was satisfied that for anyone who walked in the room and saw the gun dangling from the man's limp hand, it would look like suicide.

When they were done cleaning the scene for any signs of their presence, they stepped back, their shoulders bumping. She glanced at Ricky's sharp profile.

In the hours when the night slipped into day and she couldn't sleep, she wondered why he'd done it. Why he'd said yes. Most of the time it didn't matter; all that mattered was that he had. But in those moments, she wondered.

And she remembered his hand against her belly, the silence that followed. She remembered his eyes, deep shadows, when he saw the tiny body for the first time—ugly, bloody limbs, squished face, and rooting mouth. It hadn't been love but panic in the tightening of his jaw. She remembered the blank look when Lila curled a hand around his finger.

This wasn't revenge. This was penance. For never wanting something, for being relieved when it was gone.

"Let's go," she said.

Once they were outside, skirting along the back of the yard and into the alleyway, she pulled out the burner phone she'd picked up at Walmart weeks ago.

"Report it," she said after dialing the number to the station. The cops wouldn't be recording it, not if it didn't go through dispatch, but still, they couldn't be too careful.

He cleared his throat and then pitched his voice several tones lower. "Yeah . . . I think I heard a gunshot . . . the Burke residence . . . I was jogging by . . . yeah . . ."

There were a few seconds of silence, and then he nodded once, hung up, and pocketed the phone. He'd ditch it on the first opportunity.

"Are you good?" she asked.

He nodded. He'd be out of the state before the confusion even began to clear.

They weren't really ones for goodbye, she and him. For too long, they'd been two souls locked together, forced to move through the world bound by circumstances instead of choice. The ghost of that chain would linger far longer than she wanted to admit.

But just as he turned away, she laid a hand on his arm. "Hey. Thank you. I know it didn't . . . it didn't turn out like we wanted. But, thank you."

He glanced back at her, a sad smile on his lips, in his eyes. "She was mine, too." He shrugged.

She nodded, even though it was a pretty lie, and released him. Then he was gone.

Fading back into the shadows of the garage, she waited.

Minutes later, Nakamura's name popped up on her screen. The station would have called him once they connected the dots to their case.

"Garner," Nakamura said once she answered, his voice rough with sleep. It was still so early. "Someone called in a gunshot at the Burkes'. Uniforms are heading over, but we should probably check it out in case it's not bogus."

"Shit, okay," Alice said, going for surprised and slightly annoyed. "Yeah. I'll meet you over there."

CHAPTER THIRTY-SIX

TRUDY

August 4, 2018
Six days after the kidnapping

Trudy hadn't moved from where she'd crouched on the cold tile of Judith's kitchen floor.

"What do we do?" she finally whispered. The muscles in her legs trembled underneath her fingers, and it was only then that she realized how still she'd been holding herself. Everything ached. Everything.

Zeke just shook his head and stared down at her phone screen like it would tell them a different story. Different from the one where a man connected to Sterling had murdered Alice Garner's daughter.

"Did she kill . . . ?" Trudy trailed off, not even able to finish the question.

There were times she fancied herself old. Old beyond her years. It was a phrase she'd heard on the TV shows that ran after midnight to compete with infomercials. She'd liked the idea of it and repeated the words to herself in her mirror while lining her eyes in black. Old beyond her years.

It was rare she felt young anymore. The last time had been her running across the grass with Ruby at their summer party, sparklers and lightning bugs and the promise of summer and everything that meant.

But now she felt young. So young. She wanted someone to hold her. She wanted the lies, that it would all be okay, that *she* would be okay.

Trudy breathed in, the dust in the air sticking to the roof of her mouth. "Did she kill Ruby?"

"We have to tell someone," Zeke said, his voice just as hushed as hers, as if they were keeping confidences. "Call Charlotte."

"No, what if we're wrong?" There was panic at the thought of calling her aunt with the information, panic at what the woman would do. "We have to go back. We need to be there."

He ran his hand over his mouth and nodded. "Yeah, okay."

But they stayed where they were, frozen. Eventually she began to read the articles her phone had pulled up on Nathan Beckett, because there was nothing else to do.

"Come on." Zeke finally snagged her beneath her armpits and hauled her to her feet.

She swayed, drunk off the rush of fear and panic and adrenaline. Zeke laid a palm against her spine and gave her a gentle push to get her moving. Her limbs followed his unspoken order, but her brain was still foggy.

They murmured excuses to Judith, who watched them with eyes that saw too much. Trudy thought the woman must have noticed the mascara tracks on her cheeks.

"Did you get what you needed?" she asked as they turned toward the door.

Trudy paused, but neither of them answered. And then they were outside, putting space between them and those watery blue eyes, the store-bought cookies, the bitter tea, the answers they'd been looking for.

Zeke had been right. She hadn't actually wanted to find them.

They drove the first twenty minutes in silence, the miles beneath the wheels bringing them closer to a decision that would have to be made.

"Nathan Beckett took Lila from the mall," Trudy finally said. Her breathing had turned ragged, each breath shallow and nearly useless. The mall. Something flickered at the edge of her memory. The mall, a week before Ruby's disappearance. How had they found her? "A nice lady" had helped her, Ruby had said. Trudy closed her eyes and was back there crouched on the linoleum, her feet sticky from melted ice cream. She remembered the soft fall of brown hair against a sharp jaw as the woman turned to look back at the scene before she rounded the corner out of sight. Had that been the detective? Trudy's stomach heaved at the thought. Had that been a test run? "God. She's sick."

Zeke might have said something; she didn't know.

"Her murder was five years ago," Trudy said, her thumb finding the edge of her teeth and pressing down. "Has she been planning this the whole time?"

They flew past three semis, and Trudy glanced at the speedometer. It held steady around ninety miles per hour.

"It was the choice she could live with," Zeke said, his slow, steady words salt against an open wound.

"Fuck you," Trudy said, and it was a whisper at first, startling in its intensity as if it were pulled from the deepest part of her belly. It didn't stay a whisper. "Don't you dare throw those words back in my face."

He kept his eyes on the road, his teeth clenched.

She undid her seat belt, shifting toward him, not really knowing what she intended to do. "This isn't us bullshitting out of our asses, Zeke. This isn't a game."

"My mom isn't a game, either," Zeke said quietly, as if he couldn't keep the words in his mouth.

She lashed out then. Her fingernails slashed at his face, leaving angry marks against his cheeks. Pain. It ached in her body, a live thing that pulsed and twisted and bruised, and she wanted it to ache in his.

He winced, but she didn't back off.

She pressed her fingers into the hollow of his throat and felt the skittering of his pulse beneath her palm as she cut off his air.

There was no logic for it, but she didn't know logic in that moment. In that heady, dangerous, desperate moment. All she wanted was to make him take back those words.

The choices you could live with.

Only after he realized she wasn't relenting did he lift his hand to slap at her arm. It was a quick downward slash, hard bone against hard bone. It broke her grip on his neck, but it deterred her for only a second.

When his attention was back on the road, she launched herself at him.

He snagged her wrist in one large hand, then twisted so that a sharp bolt of pain shot along her forearm. She whimpered.

"Stop," he said, and she was reminded of that hulking giant in the park who scared everyone including her, even though she pretended he didn't.

Maybe there was a monster in everyone, lying dormant. There was one in her. It roared and frothed at the lips and prowled, a caged beast now that Zeke had her pinned against the car seat. Zeke's monster looked back, its eyes quiet and steady. "Stop," he said again.

He felt the fight go out of her; he must have. But she didn't relent, because that would be a weakness she wasn't ready to lay bare. He tugged her wrist just a little farther in the wrong direction, a warning that sent fire up to her shoulder, and then he released her.

When she was free again, she curled her body into the corner of the car, tucking her legs up against her chest, her body begging her to protect her vulnerable organs.

"I didn't mean it like that," Zeke said, back to the gruff man who didn't have a monster to keep tamed. "She couldn't get to Beckett, right?"

She didn't answer.

"I'm guessing she would have killed him otherwise," Zeke said.

"He was arrested before she could, though," Trudy said.

He nodded. "She couldn't get to him."

"So she decided to kill a child?" Her voice was wobbly again, on the edge of screaming, but not quite there.

"I'm not saying it's okay," Zeke said, in that same measured tone he'd been using since they'd got in the car.

"But?"

"No 'but,'" he said. "It's not okay, it's not justified."

"Everything can be justified. Isn't that what you've said?"

He had. He'd said that.

He lifted a shoulder and pressed on the gas. "Life's about choices."

She sat on her hands so that she didn't gouge his eyes out with her fingernails.

They didn't say anything else, and it took a long time for her muscles to stop shivering from some indistinguishable mix of fury and despair.

It was an hour later when the pop of the blown tire jolted her.

"Shit," Zeke muttered as he pulled off onto the shoulder. The car came to a shaky stop, and she blinked hard, trying to make the situation make sense.

Slamming his palm into the middle of the steering wheel, he swore. "I don't have a spare."

And just like that, she was young again. Not sure what to do, what path to take. She wanted to be told the right choice to make.

It was late. The sun had long ago set, and the sky was that deep velvet blue that spoke of midnight or close to it.

At best, this would set them back hours. At worst, days.

She'd have to call someone. There was no longer the option not to.

Trudy got out without saying anything and paced in the narrow strip of dirt and pebbles that hugged the highway. A pickup passed them but didn't slow.

She yelled at the lights as they faded into the distance. She yelled because she had to do something with this rage and desperation and frustration that beat so painfully against her rib cage. She yelled because she was tired of people being shit, and life being shittier. She yelled because little girls shouldn't have to die.

It took her a while to realize she was in Zeke's arms and they were on the ground. Her throat was sore, like she'd swallowed glass, and she thought she might have been yelling a long time. He held her in his lap, rocking her like she was a child, whispering nonsense. Not even to calm her down. It seemed more like he just wanted her to realize she wasn't alone.

"We have to call someone," Zeke said when her sobs turned into hiccups muffled against his shoulder.

They did. She knew it. Trudy closed her eyes, trying to focus on anything other than the pain. Whom? Whom could they trust? Mellie was useless. Sterling was never, and would never be, an option. Not in Trudy's world. Hollis was a last resort, at best.

"Nakamura?" she finally offered.

He lifted one shoulder. "Up to you. He seemed like an okay guy, but so did Alice."

"And cops close ranks," she said. She also had not earned any trustworthy points in their books over the course of the investigation. Whom would the man believe? His partner or the little shit of a teenager with an attitude problem? No. He was out.

That left Charlotte, with her haunted eyes and the fragile way she held her shoulders straight, as if she relaxed at all she would fall apart.

It was the choice she was going to have to live with, though.

Trudy slid out of Zeke's lap onto the hard ground and unlocked her phone. She thumbed to the contacts and gave herself to the count of five to change her mind. Then she hit "Call."

The line rang and rang and rang. It was late, maybe past midnight at this point, but Charlotte was a light sleeper, and if she saw who was calling, she'd answer immediately.

When it kicked over to voice mail, Trudy swore and then tried to breathe evenly. If she gave in to the fear and desperation that clawed at the back of her throat, she would be useless. So she bit her lip and watched the little numbers on the clock switch over to the next. She would give Charlotte five minutes and then call her back.

Just when she decided to cut that short to three minutes, her phone lit up.

"Charlotte," she said on a sob that surprised even her.

"Trudy. Where are you? Are you hurt?"

She could tell from Charlotte's voice that the woman was on the edge of control herself. "I'm fine, I'm fine."

"What happened? What's wrong?"

Trudy froze, unable to put a voice to everything she'd learned. It was too big for her, too big for her small body, too big for her tongue, too big for her thoughts. The power of it, how it would change the world once it was told, scared her. But being scared was her natural state; she understood it.

If she were actually young, she would have handed the phone to Zeke, had him explain. Or she would have started crying great, heaving gasps that would have left her aunt terrified and helpless.

Beyond her years. She saw her red-slicked mouth curve over the words in her own mirror. Over and over again until they didn't make sense.

She wasn't young.

"It was Detective Garner," Trudy said finally. "Alice Garner. She did it."

Silence greeted the revelation. But the line was still open.

Finally, there was a shaky breath. "Are you sure?"

Trudy nodded before remembering she was on the phone. "I think so. Sterling apparently had some kind of connection to the man who killed her daughter."

Something slammed, like a palm against a hard surface, and Charlotte cursed, low and harsh and unnatural. She sounded like someone Trudy didn't know.

Trudy pulled her legs to her chest and bit into her kneecaps in an attempt to control her breathing.

"All right," Charlotte finally said. "Trudy, listen to me. Are you listening?"

And just like that, her aunt was back, her voice steady and even.

"Yes, I'm listening."

"I want you to go to the closest ATM," Charlotte said the second the agreement left Trudy's lips. "Take out as much money as you can. Drive until you're in a different state. It doesn't matter which. In the morning, when the banks open, find one. Clean out your emergency account. You brought that passport with you?"

"Yes."

"Disappear," Charlotte said. "Do you understand what I'm telling you?"

"Yes," Trudy whispered again. There were already plans in place. Ones laid down to save Ruby. What she didn't want to think about was why Charlotte was so insistent she go. What was her aunt going to do that she didn't want Trudy involved with? She didn't ask the question.

"Lose the phone immediately," Charlotte said. "Are you with anyone right now?"

Her eyes found Zeke. "Yeah. My friend Zeke."

"Do you trust him?"

"Yes."

Charlotte paused. "Have him drop you at the closest bus station when you cross the state line. But then you're going to have to cut ties with him."

"Okay," Trudy said around the small pang. It wasn't like they were that close. But they'd been in this together. She'd long forgotten what it had felt like to have someone at her back. Just because.

"Trudy," Charlotte started. And then stopped.

There was so much to say in the silence that followed. Everything between them had always been so complicated. But in this moment, this moment when Trudy realized she probably wouldn't see her aunt again, she wanted nothing more than to apologize.

Apologize for the resentment and the pain and for every time Trudy had lashed out. Apologize for the world being unfair even though it wasn't Trudy's place to do that. Apologize because there had been a time when she'd stopped saying "I love you" and never started again.

But mostly she wanted to apologize for the fact that she wasn't the type of person to apologize.

So she didn't say anything, and her aunt didn't, either, and Trudy wished it were different but knew it never would be.

"Goodbye," she finally whispered, soft and final. Then she hung up on the quiet breathing that filled the other side of the line.

"She wants you to run," Zeke said, his eyes on her face.

Trudy nodded.

He tilted his head. "What do you want?"

What she wanted was for Alice Garner to pay for what she'd done. An eye for an eye. That's how the woman lived—that's what shaped her. Why not let it destroy her?

But it would ruin Trudy, returning to St. Petersburg. There was nothing left there for her other than vengeance. She could let it turn her soul black, but then she would be no better than Alice, blind to anything other than a warped sense of justice.

Or, she could run.

She thought of nights spent shaking and bruised and terrified under blankets. She thought of the lifetime of barbed words that followed. She thought of perfect lipstick that hid cruel truths. She thought of her feet, buried deep in the city's cement.

She thought of Charlotte and knew she would mourn that loss. She thought of Mellie and knew she wouldn't. She thought of Ruby's grave.

She thought about choices she could live with.

The night had gone still as if it were waiting for her answer. Trudy looked at Zeke, met his eyes, let him see the clarity in hers. "How far to Georgia?"

CHAPTER THIRTY-SEVEN
CHARLOTTE

August 5, 2018
Seven days after the kidnapping

The "goodbye" was soft and fragile and so unlike Trudy that it was jarring to Charlotte.

Her lips moved to form words, to say something, anything, but even as she tried to give voice to them, she realized it was too late. Trudy had already hung up.

If this was to be their goodbye, at least it fit them, full of silence and sadness and an unspoken recognition that they had been through too much to speak platitudes now.

Her brain was too fuzzy anyway. She couldn't think about Trudy; there was no space for her anymore. There was no space for anything beyond what needed her attention.

Alice Garner.

There were flashes of the woman—at the mall, at the beach, at the diner. There had always been something harsh about her face: the slashes of her cheekbones and the thinness of her lips. But her eyes had seemed kind.

"You helped us," Charlotte said.

Alice's face didn't soften. "That doesn't mean I'm helping you now."

What had come next? What had the woman said?

She pulled back onto the road. It was midnight, and she had a gun. But she didn't have a plan. Not yet. So she drove. Mindless.

It was only when she pulled the keys from the ignition that she realized where she'd ended up. The small turquoise house was dark, and there were no other cars in the driveway.

Her knuckles were white against the steering wheel. Was this where Alice had kept Ruby? Was this where she'd died?

Charlotte was out of the car on her knees, heaving, before her mind caught up with her body. The night air was cool against her sweat-slicked skin, and the sour taste of bile lingered in the crevices of her mouth. She pushed back onto her calves and swiped at the tears that were falling, unchecked, along her cheeks, slipping down her neck, pooling in the dip of her collarbones.

Ruby.

Her head throbbed, a punishment for her weakness, for the way her body had seized and rebelled at the sight of the house. Charlotte rocked up to her feet, digging her fingers into her temple as if that would help alleviate the pain.

She kept her eyes away from the house as she made her way along the private boardwalk over the dunes.

When she crested the little hill, eternity stretched out before her, an endless ocean.

The waves, which had turned an inky silver beneath the moon, lapped at the sand, and she thought maybe she could just keep walking until the water swallowed her, until the throbbing agony in her chest burned away along with the oxygen.

Instead, her knees buckled, and she collapsed on the beach. She was so tired that her very bones felt fragile, brittle, like they could shatter.

Always falling apart, just like they said she would.

It wouldn't take much to find sweet relief from this life, from this pain that felt more real and more constant than anything else she'd ever known. She had a gun.

But what would everyone think when they found her sprawled in the same location where Ruby had been only days earlier? A headline would flash across a screen; lines would be drawn between facts even if there was no truth to the connection; a man slouched over milky corn-flakes would grunt at his spouse, *"Didn't I tell you?"* Then they would move on, life would interfere, and forever and always they would think Charlotte Burke had killed her own daughter.

Did it matter? The answer came easy, like she'd already decided on something.

Perhaps she had.

There was the gun. There was Alice Garner. There was a tight heat beneath her breastbone that demanded action. And there was a quiet voice in her head that whispered what needed to be done.

For once in her life, she was going to be strong.

What had she said to Alice in the diner? When her thoughts had been loose and unguarded around a woman she'd had no reason to trust.

"I used to think I had ethics or some sort of moral compass, at least."

Alice watched her, unblinking. "And then Ruby . . ."

"Now I have none."

CHAPTER
THIRTY-EIGHT

ALICE

August 5, 2018
Seven days after the kidnapping

Alice couldn't take her eyes off the speck of blood. It was rusty brown and sat at the very edge of her nail bed, innocuous as an errant dab of polish. She wanted to rub the splotch into her skin until it disappeared, until it became a part of her.

She and Nakamura were leaning against the back wall of the study that still reeked of copper while EMTs and techs and officers hovered and tried to pretend they were being helpful. Two young officers stood in the corner, their elbows pointy things as they held themselves rigid and scribbled in notebooks. She couldn't imagine what they were writing.

Everyone was so loud even though it was the time of morning that called for hushed voices.

Nakamura nudged her.

It took longer than it should have to turn her head, and when she did, she saw concern in the downward tug of his mouth. Had he asked her something?

"Hmm?" There shouldn't have been blood. They'd worn gloves, been careful, been safe. She curled her hand into a fist and shoved it into the pocket of her jeans.

"Are you okay?" Nakamura asked, and Alice couldn't tell if the delay had been because he was studying her face or because her mind was slow to process the question. She could tell, though, that it hadn't been what he'd asked moments earlier when his words had been nothing but white noise to her.

Now they were back to the script. *Are you okay?*

"I guess you were right, huh?" Nakamura said when he realized she wasn't going to respond.

"About?"

There was another pause, more worry writing itself into the lines of his face. He was thrown by the emptiness of her voice, by her confusion. She was as well.

"Sterling being our guy."

You were right. The letter had been found just as she'd planned.

It wouldn't hold up to anyone who examined it too carefully. Most wouldn't, though. Most would take the neat admission of murder and graver sins at face value, their minds recoiling from the latter and latching on to the former. It was a good story, one that was satisfying and easy to follow, one that soothed concerns over random predators and kept fears of serial killers at bay. But best of all, it was one that gave them a good bad guy to hate.

Tell a story. Create a villain.

It would be a thorn that snagged at Nakamura's skin, though. For all that he teased Alice about her need for a solid narrative to sell to the jury, he was a veteran cop and a damn good one. It didn't make sense how the letter laid it out, not with all that he knew about the timeline, the players, the motives. But she'd been planting seeds the whole time. The pictures, the connections, the patterns.

"Who do you think did it, Alice?" Nakamura asked just like she'd wanted him to.

"What do you want me to say?"

"I want you to say what's in your gut."

A beat, a pause. Let the tension build. "Sterling Burke."

Nakamura smiled. *"And that's why you're on the case."*

All she could hope is that the letter would distract him long enough.

Long enough for what? It was a dark question that circled and paced and crawled along the inside of her skull, one that she didn't want to answer.

Her womb pulsed, and her throat ached from the scream that she held tethered inside her body. This wasn't how she was supposed to feel, not after months of planning, not after years of waiting.

She pressed her thumbnail against the rough fabric of her jeans pocket. Sterling Burke's DNA was on her—on her hand, on her skin, on her clothes.

The muscles in her throat fluttered as if they were going to snap shut; her fingers shook, her jaw ached. The numbness in her bones, it was still there, but beneath it was a panic that pressed greedy hands against the thick fog.

"I need some air," she gasped, pushing off the wall. A few gazes flicked her way, but there was no suspicion behind shuttered eyes, no curiosity. She could just leave, walk out of the house, get in the car, and drive away, and not a single person would stop or question her.

The idea was terrifying.

On a better day she wouldn't have been surprised by Bridget. But as it was, she didn't notice the woman until she'd reached out, long fingers wrapping around the delicate bones of Alice's wrists.

"Can I borrow you for a sec, then, kiddo?" Bridget asked, her voice light and easy. There was an undercurrent to it, though, which finally snapped Alice out of her haze. Here. Here was the suspicion that was so lacking in the other room.

Bridget let go of her once Alice nodded. They both turned, silently making their way along the corridor, through the kitchen, down the back steps of the porch. By some unspoken agreement, they didn't stop until they reached the shadows by the side of the garage.

They squared off then, like two boxers who knew well the way their opponent dipped and jabbed and attacked, and the space between them felt like a chasm that would never be bridged again.

Bridget rubbed at her arm, just over the ink of her tic-tac-toe tattoo, her thumb dragging over the *x*'s and then the *o*'s.

"I don't know why you did it," Bridget finally said. "And I don't want to hear whatever fucked-up justification you've come up with."

Alice had been expecting it. Ever since the woman had pulled her away from a crime scene when she never pulled Alice away from a crime scene. Ever since the press of a calloused thumb against the delicate bones of Alice's hand in the hallway. Ever since that call last night. *No, they don't deserve to have their stories told.*

"Do you know what you did wrong?" Bridget asked.

Everything.

"It was too perfect," Alice said instead.

"The sand was genius," Bridget said. "The enemy of evidence."

Alice just waited. She knew this.

Bridget laughed without humor. "Fuck you."

There must have been sound—the scuffle of feet against loose stone, the chatter of a busy crime scene, the sirens even though the emergency was long over. But the silence stretched and twisted and bent between them so that it pulled tight the fibers of Alice's muscles.

Bridget finally ran a hand through her shorn bleached-blonde hair. "Why, Alice?"

The question was so inherently human. *Why?* Everyone always wanted to know.

"I thought you didn't want 'why,'" Alice reminded her.

Bridget sighed. "You're right. I liked ya, Garner."

She'd liked Bridget. As much as she could like someone. That wasn't much these days, though. "What gave it away?"

"You wanted to be known."

Alice smiled at that, just a little bit. "Thought that was my arena. Did your science fail you, then?"

Bridget shook her head. "It told me a cop did it. You told me you did it."

"A cop or a pro, you mean?" Alice clarified, thinking back to their conversation the night before.

"No," Bridget said. "Or maybe. There should have been something. All that blood."

It was a poke, a finger pressing against the tender rim of an open wound. Bridget was watching her face, perhaps for a reaction. But Alice couldn't give her one. She was hollow. Her chest, her heart, her belly— everything was hollow.

There *had* been blood, and she'd cleaned it up.

"It could have been a pro, I guess," Bridget continued when Alice didn't react. "But I saw you in her room, Alice."

In Ruby's room with the porcelain elephant that had reminded Alice of Lila. It had been only a second that she'd let herself feel what she'd been keeping so tightly locked up, let herself think of Ruby as a little girl who liked the circus and elephants and hadn't deserved to die. So different from Lila, but still the same.

Bridget wrinkled up her nose. "I didn't think much of it. Or if I did, I chalked it up to your daughter. But every time I worked on the evidence, it was there. That memory of you. I started wondering, you know?"

Of course she knew. That's how the best cops worked. A small moment stuck, niggled at the brain until you finally gave in to it.

"So I dug a little bit," Bridget said. "I told myself it was to rule you out."

It was easy to tell yourself things you wanted to hear.

"You know what struck me?" Bridget said. "The sheets."

Alice blinked slowly. "My area again."

"Rubbed off on me, haven't you?" Bridget smiled without humor. "Why was she wrapped in sheets? Your lot says it's because the guy feels remorse and guilt. Which usually rules out a serial killer."

A seed planted, a distraction.

"But your daughter was wrapped in sheets, wasn't she?" Bridget asked. "Found that out last night. It was an anomaly in the case. Made the cops investigating look at you. Probably for too long."

"They wasted so much time," Alice murmured. What had been a source of deep frustration then had become inspiration.

"Weird coincidence, huh?" Bridget ignored Alice's interruption. "Then you called back last night."

If the woman had already suspected her, Alice might as well have confessed during that conversation. A part of her wondered if she'd wanted this.

The sheets. The email name. Sending Ricky to Jacksonville to leave breadcrumbs that could so easily be followed. There was that need to be known, one that wooed and entrapped even the savviest killer. But it was more than that. All she'd wanted was justice. And something in her knew that she wasn't exempt from that.

Alice scratched at the fleck of blood that was no longer really there. "What now?"

The woman's eyes traced down to Alice's holster, then back to her face. "You still have your gun."

"Why didn't you turn me in first? Why give me a warning?" Alice realized that's what this was. A warning. A head start. Bridget knew she wasn't going to run. She also knew Alice wasn't going to let herself be arrested. The woman was letting her end it on her terms. It was a kindness Alice hadn't been expecting.

Long enough for what?

"I liked ya, Garner," Bridget said once more, and it was goodbye. It was *Leave*. It was *You have five minutes before I tell Nakamura everything*.

Alice nodded once and stood up. She was at the door before she stopped and looked back. "You're one of the good ones."

Bridget shook her head. "Clearly not."

And that was it. Alice was in the alley in the next heartbeat, leaving the chaos of the crime scene behind her.

CHAPTER THIRTY-NINE

CHARLOTTE

August 5, 2018
Seven days after the kidnapping

There was a lightness to the sky, a suggestion that the night was breaking and giving way to the day. Goose bumps covered Charlotte's skin, and her body protested when she shifted. There were other hints that she hadn't moved in hours—the ache in her fingers where they wrapped around her arms, the stiffness in her neck as if the vertebrae had locked together, the dryness in her mouth as her tongue dragged along her palate.

She ignored the trivial discomforts and pushed up until she was standing. The sand tugged at her feet as she made her way back to the stairs, as if begging her to stay and sink into oblivion. But she'd made her decision.

So she walked on.

The car door was still ajar, just as she'd left it, and the battery had to be dead. That didn't matter, though, as she had no plans to drive out of there herself. Her fingers crawled along the driver's side floor, the fabric scratchy against the tips of them. She stopped when she felt the cool metal, then slid her hand farther underneath the seat until her palm closed around the grip.

An hour ago, a day ago, a month ago, she would never have believed herself strong enough to do what needed to be done. But she was no longer that girl.

She pulled the gun from its hiding place.

Just before she shut the door, she ducked back into the car to grab her sweater and the little white card she'd dropped into the cup holder earlier in the night. It had Detective Nakamura's number scrawled across the back in broken and fading black ink.

Then she started toward the quiet side of the house, keeping to the shadows once she hit the stairs leading up to the porch that overlooked the ocean.

The door was locked, but she'd expected it. She wrapped her hand into the softness of the sweater and then drew her arm back.

The glass shattered beneath her fist.

CHAPTER FORTY

ALICE

August 5, 2018
Seven days after the kidnapping

Alice had a gun but no plan. She stopped at the end of the alley and looked left, looked right. The animal in her, the one whose sole focus was survival, howled at her that it wasn't too late to escape. Here was her chance.

But escape to what? What kind of life would that be?

She'd always known it was going to end this way. Back, back, back when she was just a broken figure curled on the rug of her living room, watching as Lila's killer escaped the death he'd so deserved. Back when she'd gone a week without food, hunched over a computer, beady eyes devouring every website and article that filled in the blanks to a story that she should never have known. Back when Sterling Burke had just been random letters arranged in a certain way on the page.

She had known there was no surviving this.

It was relief instead of surprise that crept into the soft spaces of her body when her phone buzzed and she saw who it was.

Charlotte.

The text was just an address, one Alice knew well.

Here. Here was her plan.

———

"My father took me to the bank one time when I was younger."

Charlotte stood at the windows overlooking the ocean. She must have heard Alice come in, but she hadn't turned around.

Her slim frame was a dark silhouette against the brightness from the windows. Her arms were wrapped around her thin waist, long hair tumbled over narrow shoulders, and Alice thought back to the day on the beach. A painting, this woman was. All soft strokes and pastel colors.

But something about the straightness of her spine told Alice she was no longer made up of just gossamer and clouds.

"I was about nine at the time," Charlotte continued. "He'd always liked the treatment he got when he went. The cashiers all dropped what they were doing and rushed over. The manager brought him coffee. I think he wanted me to see it, to be impressed, even though I was so young. He liked those small things that made him feel big. I liked the lemon candy Mr. Josten kept on his desk."

It was then that Alice noticed the blood dripping on the white carpet beneath Charlotte's feet. She couldn't take her eyes off the small copper spots.

"The thing was? When he stepped out of the room and everyone relaxed? It was all gone. The respect, the admiration. It was just a front," Charlotte said. "I could tell, even then. They all hated him. Because everyone hates Sterling Burke."

They were both quiet, still, except for that slow trickle of blood running down Charlotte's hand.

"He knew it, too," the woman continued. "That's what he wanted me to see. Not the fawning. He wanted me to see that they did it even though they couldn't stand him."

Charlotte finally turned toward her. There was a deep gash on her forearm, and Alice realized she must have broken a window to get into the house. That jagged wound had been made from glass.

"Do you know why I remember that day?" Charlotte asked, cradling her injured arm. "Because I had never realized before that anyone was allowed to hate my father. It was a foreign concept to me. I thought the only reality was loving him. That day I knew, though. And he did, too. He was showing me that hating him was a possibility. But not playing his game wasn't one."

"Did you hate him?" Alice asked. But once it was out, she realized the question had been silly, childish. Hate was simple and easy to understand. Whatever Charlotte felt wasn't that straightforward.

"No," Charlotte said.

"He's dead now." It was cold and unkind and without any softness to cushion the blow. Alice didn't recognize who she was anymore. Had she lost so much of the person she'd once been? The person who would never say *He's dead now* to a daughter whose hand was bleeding onto the carpet, who should hate her father but still didn't.

But Charlotte just blinked at her. "Good."

The moment passed without any flash of grief. Maybe Charlotte was just as numb as Alice.

"You hated him," Charlotte said.

Alice nodded. "Yes." For her, it was just that simple.

Charlotte's eyes were gaping holes in the shadows that caressed her face. Alice waited for the inevitable, that question that no one could resist.

It came with a shuddered breath and a half step forward and a flutter of eyelashes against cheeks. But it was not the *why* Alice had been expecting.

333

"You didn't mean to kill her."

The words were surprising enough that the confirmation slipped past Alice's lips before she could swallow it.

"No."

She wished she could pull it back, but it hung there between them anyway. There was no justification for Ruby's death; Alice deserved no redemption arc in this story. And she was once again reminded of why she hadn't let Sterling talk. Because nothing came from it except frayed lifelines thrown to someone who was drowning in grief, who could barely keep their head above water. It was a false sense of hope, though, because the explanations would do nothing to bring them to safety. At most, they'd provide the briefest moment of air before the waves took them under again.

"Tell me."

Tell me a story. Make me understand. This was Charlotte's *why.*

"I didn't know about you," Alice said, because she had to start somewhere. "I didn't realize . . . not at first."

"What?"

"I didn't realize you were a victim," Alice said, and Charlotte flinched. "I was just . . . I was learning Sterling. His flaws, his family, his successes. What could hurt him. What could bring him down."

"But . . . didn't . . . You were the one who helped Trudy, right?" Charlotte asked slowly.

"That came later," Alice said, and she wanted to duck her chin, hide her face. She forced herself to meet Charlotte's eyes instead. "I first heard about Sterling two years ago, and it took a while to get past the superficial mentions in society columns. I knew that he had two daughters, two granddaughters. I knew that you all lived with him. But that was just touching the surface."

Charlotte watched her but didn't prompt her to go on.

She did anyway. "About a year ago I stumbled on Trudy's blog," Alice said. A turning point.

"Her blog?"

Alice tipped her head. She'd guessed no one else had known about it. "She runs a site to help sexual abuse victims. She's not as anonymous as she thinks she is."

Charlotte paled a little at that, pressed her lips together, and then nodded.

"It was my first in. The first chink in the shining armor that Sterling presented to the world," Alice said. "I thought, if it had happened to Trudy . . ."

"It could be happening again," Charlotte said quietly.

Alice didn't need to confirm it. "I'd put in for a transfer as soon as I realized how Sterling was connected to Beckett. It took about a year to go through. But being down here helped. I was able to get information from people who wouldn't put such things down on paper. It didn't take much. Everyone likes to talk about the Burkes in St. Petersburg."

Charlotte's nostrils flared at that. "I'm sure."

"Killing Sterling would have been easy. A simple bullet to the brain. But I didn't just want to kill him," Alice said.

"You wanted to ruin him."

She nodded. "If he died like that, they'd erect statues to him in every plaza in the city."

"But you didn't just ruin him," Charlotte's voice cracked. Her arms came up to wrap around her stomach. "You ruined us."

"I didn't . . ." *I didn't mean to.* The words were so empty, so meaningless. That hadn't been the plan. "I wasn't getting anywhere. Not really. I wanted him exposed, stripped naked for the world to see. I wanted his name to be tainted, his reputation to be shredded. And I wanted him to know why it was happening."

Charlotte's barely controlled composure broke at that. "Ruby had nothing to do with any of that," she said, her fingers balling into fists. Alice knew she wanted to land a punch, knew she wanted to do far worse.

"I know," Alice whispered. She licked dry lips. "I needed access. I knew if it was a kidnapping, we'd be assigned the case. So I nudged Trudy. It was supposed to be a win-win. I get security codes, the family's schedule, the lay of the house. Trudy gets Ruby out of a bad situation. But you left too early."

A plan altered.

"What?" The word was said on an exhale.

"You were supposed to take her to the end-of-the-summer school fair Wednesday night," Alice said. "Trudy had emailed me one last time to say thank you, to say goodbye. I'd pieced together enough to figure out her plan."

"But then we found out that Sterling and Hollis were going to be out all day Sunday," Charlotte said.

Alice nodded. "I know. If you had waited to report it on Sunday evening, I would have been off shift. Someone else would have gotten the case. It was supposed to be Wednesday. So I needed you to think she was really gone so you'd report it right away. In the afternoon. It couldn't wait until the night."

"That's bullshit," Charlotte said, anger swiftly replacing confusion. "You must have known. You were prepared to walk off with her. To keep her for days."

"It was plan B the whole time," Alice said. They had been ready for the possibility. There had been too many variables not to plan for something to go wrong. When the original plan had fallen apart, they'd adjusted; they'd had to. But a small part of her had hoped she'd still be able to get Ruby and Trudy out, that keeping Ruby for a few days was just a hiccup, one that would be resolved after she killed Sterling. "Taking her . . . That's not how I wanted it to happen."

And Charlotte looked at her then as Alice had looked at Charlotte before—with a mixture of disbelief and pity. *You thought you could dress in grown-ups' clothes and do something as dramatic as seek revenge?*

Shame flushed Alice's cheeks hot, and with it came every other emotion she'd locked in a tiny space in a dark corner of her brain. Guilt, remorse, grief, fear, relief—they flooded her veins, turning her blood heavy and sticky with the weight of them.

"So then what?" Charlotte's voice sandpaper and steel, rough but strong. "You claim you never even wanted to kidnap her, but my daughter is dead. Because of you."

One wrong step, that's all it had been.

This house had a garage, unlike most of the others in the neighborhood, which was one of the reasons Alice had picked it. There was also an inside set of stairs—bare, steep ones made of concrete—leading up to the kitchen to provide Alice cover if she'd needed to bring Ruby in.

Ruby had been going stir-crazy, as little girls tended to do. That day, Alice had brought french fries as a treat, but it had backfired. Ruby had started screaming, sobbing, her face pinched red as fat tears streamed down into the collar of her shirt. She'd started for the stairs, but Alice had managed to wrap an arm around her heaving chest and pull her back. It could have ended there; it should have ended there.

But Ruby's heel had connected with Alice's kneecap, and she'd loosened her grip enough for the girl to wiggle free. Ruby had sprinted toward the steps with the perverse disobedience of someone very young. Her feet had tangled beneath her, though. Her arms pinwheeled while she desperately fought gravity, fought the downward pull of her small body. The air had turned to molasses, and Alice had been unable to push her limbs through it to get to the girl before the inevitable smack of skull against concrete.

She'd gone limp in an instant.

One wrong step, that's all it had been. One flawed plan. One bad decision by an evil man. One moment of distraction when Lila had been able to dart away from her at the mall that day. One flutter in her womb that promised life. One breath, one heartbeat. One wrong step. It had all led them here.

Charlotte was watching Alice now, and Alice didn't want to tell her what had happened because she knew it would just hurt more. But the woman had asked for those frayed lifelines, the ones that would snap under the force of desperate hands tugging at them. Even if Charlotte didn't realize that they wouldn't help, Alice at least owed her an answer.

"Ruby tripped."

Out of everything Alice had said, that was what took Charlotte to her knees. She brought the heels of her hands to her eyes, pressing hard, but the tears streamed down her face anyway.

"Fuck you," she whispered, and then she screamed it again—a raw, guttural cry that came from deep in her belly and echoed off the walls—the very walls that had held the story Alice hadn't wanted to tell. "Fuck you."

The hatred in the words was a hand pressing against Alice until her own legs gave out and she was on the floor. This had to end. It had to. Why wouldn't this end?

She stared across the distance to Charlotte, this mother who was no longer a mother. And she saw herself so clearly in the curve of the woman's back, in the arm that was still bleeding, in the shallow breathing that was so loud in the quiet room, in the sobs that trembled through delicate muscles. She saw herself so clearly that she thought perhaps they were one person, one overwhelming grief that was slowly suffocating both of them.

"You piece of shit," Charlotte gasped out. "You think you can just . . . look me in the face and make excuses? You killed my daughter."

It hurt, it hurt, it hurt, but Alice didn't protest even as she curled over her organs as if to protect them from the blow. She hadn't pulled a trigger, hadn't wrapped fingers around the girl's throat, hadn't pushed her. But she'd killed her just the same. "Yes," she whispered, her voice hoarse.

Charlotte swallowed once, and they locked eyes. Alice thought that just for a moment Charlotte saw herself in Alice as well. Saw herself in the arch of her neck and the sorrow in her shoulders and the acceptance in the tilt of her head. Mothers who were no longer mothers.

Then Charlotte blinked and pushed herself to her feet, the connection broken.

"Everyone's going to know what you did," the woman said, so similar to what Alice had told Sterling earlier that the words jumbled and lost their meaning. "They're going to know what kind of monster you are."

Charlotte crossed over to the small coffee table, and that's when Alice heard the sirens. They weren't close, but they would be soon. The woman held up the phone, and Alice could see now what she'd missed earlier. There had been someone listening in the whole time.

"Please," Alice begged. She just wanted this to end, wanted relief from the enormity of all that she had done as it crashed to pieces around her. "Please."

There was tinny screaming now through the speaker, and Alice realized it was Nakamura. He was telling Charlotte to wait, to not do anything rash.

The helplessness he had to feel at that moment would be immense, and Alice felt sorry for him. But more than anything, she needed Charlotte to not listen to his pleas.

The sirens blared. Had this been Charlotte's plan? To get Alice to confess and then see her arrested? If it was, then Alice would need to move. Now. She'd been given a chance to end it on her terms, and she thought that's what Charlotte wanted as well.

But instead of reassuring Nakamura, Charlotte hung up the phone. Then she stepped closer.

"I care nothing about what you want," Charlotte said, reaching over to the gun that had been only a few feet away from Alice the whole time. "I'm not doing this for you."

Alice breathed out once, relief turning her hands shaky. She sat back on her heels so that she was kneeling at the feet of this woman, this woman who'd had her whole life torn from her because of Alice.

This woman whom people thought of as weak, who was told she was made of glass, who believed it for far too long.

Alice tipped her face up so that she could meet Charlotte's eyes. "I always knew."

"Knew what?" Charlotte asked slowly, like she thought it was a delay tactic.

"That you were stronger than anyone thought you were," Alice said, her palms relaxed against her thighs. For the first time in days, months, years, she felt at peace.

Something flickered in Charlotte's eyes. Surprise. A protest. Acceptance. But she didn't say anything as she brought the gun to Alice's head.

Alice finally closed her eyes.

———

The snapshots came. Of Ruby. Dimples in baby-fat cheeks. Red curls tangled by sea-salt air. An upturned nose that would have forever doomed her to cuteness. Strawberry shampoo and sticky hands. Of Lila. Chubby legs racing toward the waves. Cupid-bow lips that were just as quick to pout or laugh. Skinned knees and stuffed animals clutched in tiny hands.

She thought of elephants and favorite shoes.

She thought of crocodile tears and tantrums and voices turned scratchy from screaming.

She thought of pigtails and a quick smile and the solid weight of a little girl against her hip as they raced against butterflies.

They came in snapshots, those moments. And they told a story.

ACKNOWLEDGMENTS

A deep and sincere thank-you to Charlotte Herscher, my amazingly talented editor. Not only was your voice in my head while writing this, but you also helped shift me in the exact direction the story needed to go. You keep me grounded in the best ways, even when I am panicking and considering moving to the Himalayas to never write again. This would be a lesser book without your constructive insights and spot-on questions. Thank you for always making me a stronger writer.

To Megha Parckh, your tireless support and enthusiasm mean the world to me. I am so lucky to have you on my team and forever grateful for all that you've done to get my books from idea to finished product. I could not ask for a better editor.

I'd also like to thank the entire team of people it takes to put out a book: from the eagle-eyed copyeditors who deserve armfuls of awards for the mistakes they catch, to the proofers who see things literally everyone else has missed, to the incredibly talented designers who create a cover to perfectly capture thousands and thousands of words, to the marketing team who makes sure the book gets into readers' hands, to the dozens of people whose hard work goes into making this a reality. Thank you.

And none of this would have been possible without my agent extraordinaire, Abby Saul. Apart from your sharp editing skills, your professionalism, your kindness, and your humor, I am eternally thankful that you always have my back. I cannot overstate how grateful I am to have you in my corner.

Finally, to my family and friends, thank you forever and always.

To Katie Smith and Abby McIntyre, I am thankful beyond belief to have such trustworthy first readers as you.

To Dana Underwood, who is my biggest cheerleader, always—your encouragement gives me the courage to even do any of this. You don't realize how grateful I am for that.

And to Deb and Bernie Labuskes, a thank-you will never be enough.

ABOUT THE AUTHOR

Brianna Labuskes is also the author of the psychological thriller *It Ends With Her*. Born in Harrisburg, Pennsylvania, she graduated from Penn State University with a degree in journalism and has worked as an editor at both small-town papers and national media organizations such as *Politico* and *Kaiser Health News*, covering politics and policy. She lives in Washington, DC. Visit her at www.briannalabuskes.com.